Danube

Black Sea

THRACE

Byzantium

MACEDONIA

BITHYNIA

rundisium

EPIRUS

ASIA

CAPPADOCIA

ARMENIA

•Antioch

SYRIA

MESOPOTAMIA

Crete

Cyprus

SEA

JUDAEA

•Petra

ARABIA

EGYPT

Red Sea

BY ROBERT HARRIS

FICTION

The Ghost

Imperium

Pompeii

Archangel

Enigma

Fatherland

NONFICTION

Selling Hitler: The Story of the Hitler Diaries

CONSPIRATA

A NOVEL OF ANCIENT ROME

ROBERT HARRIS

SIMON & SCHUSTER
NEW YORK   LONDON   TORONTO   SYDNEY

Simon & Schuster
1230 Avenue of the Americas
New York, NY 10020

First Simon & Schuster hardcover edition February 2010

Published in the United Kingdom by Hutchinson as *Lustrum*

For information about special discounts for bulk purchases, please contact Simon & Schuster Special Sales at 1-866-506-1949 or business@simonandschuster.com.

The Simon & Schuster Speakers Bureau can bring authors to your live event. For more information or to book an event contact the Simon & Schuster Speakers Bureau at 1-866-248-3049 or visit our website at www.simonspeakers.com.

Designed by Kyoko Watanabe

Manufactured in the United States of America

1   3   5   7   9   10   8   6   4   2

Library of Congress Cataloging-in-Publication Data
Harris, Robert.
Conspirata / Robert Harris.—1st Simon & Schuster hardcover ed.
p.   cm.
1. Tiro, M. Tullius (Marcus Tullius), b. 103 or 4 B.C.—Fiction.
2. Cicero, Marcus Tullius—Fiction.   3. Rome—History—Republic,
265–30 B.C.—Fiction.   I. Title.
PR6058.A69147C66 2010
823'.914—dc22   2009034374

ISBN 978-0-7432-6610-9

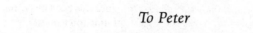

To Peter

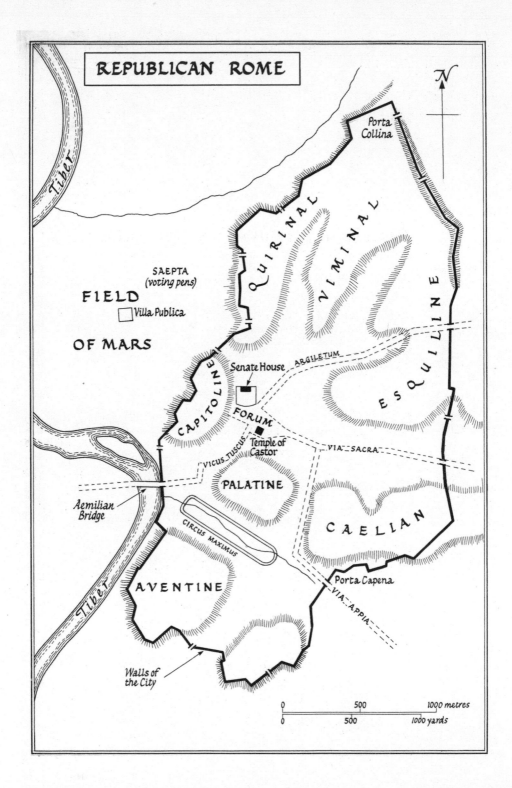

We look on past ages with condescension, as a mere preparation for *us* . . . but what if we're only an after-glow of *them*?

J. G. Farrell, *The Siege of Krishnapur*

AUTHOR'S NOTE

A few years before the birth of Christ, a biography of the Roman orator and statesman Cicero was produced by his former secretary, Tiro.

That there was such a man as Tiro, and that he wrote such a work, is well attested. "Your services to me are beyond count," Cicero once wrote to him, "in my home and out of it, in Rome and abroad, in my studies and literary work . . ." He was three years younger than his master, born a slave, but long outlived him, surviving—according to Saint Jerome—until he reached his hundredth year. Tiro was the first man to record a speech in the Senate verbatim, and his shorthand system, known as *Notae Tironianae*, was still in use in the church in the sixth century; indeed, some traces of it (the symbol "&," the abbreviations "etc.," "n.b.," "i.e.," "e.g.") survive to this day. He also wrote several treatises on the development of Latin. His multivolume life of Cicero is referred to as a source by the first-century historian Asconius Pedianus in his commentary on Cicero's speeches; Plutarch cites it twice. But, like the rest of Tiro's literary output, the book disappeared amid the collapse of the Roman Empire.

What kind of work it might have been still occasionally intrigues scholars. In 1985, Elizabeth Rawson, fellow of Corpus Christi College, Oxford, speculated that it would probably have been in the Hellenistic tradition of biography—a literary form "written in an unpretentious, unrhetorical style; it might quote documents, but it liked apophthegms by its subject, and it could be gossipy and irresponsible . . . It delighted in a subject's idiosyncrasies . . . Such biography was written not for statesmen and generals, but for what the Romans called *curiosi*."*

That is the spirit in which I have approached the re-creation of Tiro's vanished work. Although an earlier volume, *Imperium*, described Cicero's rise to power, it is not necessary, I hope, to read one in order to follow the other. This is a novel, not a work of history: wherever the demands of the

---

*Elizabeth Rawson, *Intellectual Life in the Late Roman Republic* (London: Duckworth, 1985), pp. 229–30.

two have clashed, I have unhesitatingly plumped for the former. Still, I have tried as far as possible to make the fiction accord with the facts, and to use Cicero's actual words—of which, thanks in large part to Tiro, we have so many. Readers wishing to clarify the political terminology of the Roman republic, or who would like to refer to a list of characters mentioned in the text, will find a glossary and dramatis personae at the end of the book.

R.H.

PART ONE

CONSUL

63 B.C.

*O condicionem miseram non modo administrandae
verum etiam conservandae rei publicae!*

The preservation of the republic no less than
governing it—what a thankless task it is!

CICERO, SPEECH, 9 NOVEMBER 63 B.C.

I

TWO DAYS BEFORE the inauguration of Marcus Tullius Cicero as consul of Rome, the body of a child was pulled from the River Tiber, close to the boat sheds of the republican war fleet.

Such a discovery, though tragic, would not normally have warranted the attention of a consul-elect. But there was something so grotesque about this particular corpse, and so threatening to civic peace, that the magistrate responsible for keeping order in the city, Gaius Octavius, sent word to Cicero asking him to come at once.

Cicero at first was reluctant to go, pleading pressure of work. As the consular candidate who had topped the poll, it fell to him, rather than his colleague, to preside over the opening session of the Senate, and he was writing his inaugural address. But I knew there was more to it than that. He had an unusual squeamishness about death. Even the killing of animals in the games disturbed him, and this weakness—for, alas, in politics a soft heart is always perceived as a weakness—had started to be noticed. His immediate instinct was to send me in his place.

"Of course I shall go," I replied carefully. "But—" I let my sentence trail away.

"But?" he said sharply. "But what? You think it will look bad?"

I held my tongue and continued transcribing his speech. The silence lengthened.

"Oh, very well," he groaned at last. He heaved himself to his feet. "Octavius is a dull dog, but steady enough. He wouldn't summon me unless it was important. In any case I need to clear my head."

It was late December, and from a dark gray sky blew a wind that was quick enough and sharp enough to steal your breath. Outside in the street a dozen petitioners were huddled, hoping for a word, and as soon as they saw the consul-elect stepping through his front door they ran across the road toward him. "Not now," I said, pushing them back. "Not today." Cicero threw the edge of his cloak over his shoulder and tucked his chin down onto his chest, and we set off briskly down the hill.

We must have walked about a mile, I suppose, crossing the Forum at
an angle and leaving the city by the river gate. The waters of the Tiber
were fast and high, flexed by yellowish-brown whirlpools and writhing
currents. Up ahead, opposite Tiber Island, amid the wharfs and cranes of
the Navalia, we could see a large crowd milling around. (You will get a
sense of how long ago all this happened, by the way—more than half a
century—when I tell you that the island was not yet linked by its bridges
to either bank.) As we drew closer many of the onlookers recognized Cicero and there was a stir of curiosity as they parted to let us through. A
cordon of legionnaires from the marine barracks was protecting the scene.
Octavius was waiting.

"My apologies for disturbing you," said Octavius, shaking my master's
hand. "I know how busy you must be, so close to your inauguration."

"My dear Octavius, it is a pleasure to see you at any time. You know
my secretary, Tiro?"

Octavius glanced at me without interest. Although he is remembered
today only as the father of Augustus, he was at this time aedile of the plebs
and very much the coming man. He would probably have made consul
himself had he not died prematurely of a fever some four years after this
encounter. He led us out of the wind and into one of the great military
boathouses, where the skeleton of a liburnian, stripped for repair, sat on
huge wooden rollers. Next to it on the earth floor an object lay shrouded
in sailcloth. Without pausing for ceremony, Octavius threw aside the material to show us the naked body of a boy.

He was about twelve, as I remember. His face was beautiful and serene, quite feminine in its delicacy, with traces of gold paint glinting on
the nose and cheeks, and with a bit of red ribbon tied in his damp brown
curls. His throat had been cut. His body had been slashed open all the
way down to the groin and emptied of its organs. There was no blood,
only that dark, elongated cavity, like a gutted fish, filled with river mud.
How Cicero managed to contemplate the sight and maintain his compo-
sure I do not know, but he swallowed hard and kept on looking. Eventually he said hoarsely, "This is an outrage."

"And that's not all," said Octavius. He squatted on his haunches, took
hold of the lad's skull between his hands, and turned it to the left. As the
head moved, the gaping wound in the neck opened and closed obscenely,
as if it were a second mouth trying to whisper a warning to us. Octavius
seemed entirely indifferent to this, but then of course he was a military

man and no doubt used to such sights. He pulled back the hair to reveal a deep indentation just above the boy's right ear, and pressed his thumb into it. "Do you see? It looks as if he was felled from behind. I'd say by a hammer."

"His face painted. His hair beribboned. Felled from behind by a hammer," repeated Cicero, his words slowing as he realized where his logic was leading him. "And then his throat cut. And finally his body . . . eviscerated."

"Exactly," said Octavius. "His killers must have wanted to inspect his entrails. He was a sacrifice—a human sacrifice."

At those words, in that cold dim place, the hairs on the nape of my neck stirred and spiked, and I knew myself to be in the presence of Evil— Evil as a palpable force, as potent as lightning.

Cicero said, "Are there any cults in the city you have heard of that might practice such an abomination?"

"None. There are always the Gauls, of course—they are said to do such things. But there aren't many of them in town at the moment, and those that are here are well behaved."

"And who is the victim? Has anyone claimed him?"

"That's another reason I wanted you to come and see for yourself." Octavius rolled the body over onto its stomach. "There's a small owner's tattoo just above his backside, do you see? Those who dumped the body may have missed it. 'C.Ant.M.f.C.n.' 'Caius Antonius, son of Marcus, grandson of Caius.' There's a famous family for you! He was a slave of your consular colleague, Antonius Hybrida." He stood and wiped his hands on the sailcloth, then casually threw the cover back over the body. "What do you want to do?"

Cicero was staring at the pathetic bundle on the floor as if mesmerized. "Who knows about this?"

"Nobody."

"Hybrida?"

"No."

"What about the crowd outside?"

"There's a rumor going around there's been some kind of ritual killing. You above all know what crowds are like. They're saying it's a bad omen on the eve of your consulship."

"They may be right."

"It's been a hard winter. They could do with calming down. I thought we might send word to the College of Priests and ask them to perform some kind of ceremony of purification—"

"No, no," said Cicero quickly, pulling his gaze away from the body. "No priests. Priests will only make it worse."

"So what shall we do?"

"Tell no one else. Burn the remains as quickly as possible. Don't let anyone see them. Forbid anyone who has seen them from disclosing the details, on pain of imprisonment, or worse."

"And the crowd?"

"You deal with the body. I'll deal with the crowd."

Octavius shrugged. "As you wish." He sounded unconcerned. He had only one day left in office—I should imagine he was glad to be rid of the problem.

Cicero went over to the door and inhaled a few deep breaths, bringing some color back to his cheeks. Then I saw him, as I had so often, square his shoulders and clamp a confident expression on his face. He stepped outside and clambered up onto a stack of timber to address the crowd.

"People of Rome, I have satisfied myself that the dark rumors running through the city are false!" He had to bellow into that biting wind to make himself heard. "Go home to your families and enjoy the rest of the festival!"

"But I saw the body!" shouted a man. "It was a human sacrifice, to call down a curse on the republic!"

The cry was taken up by others: "The city is cursed!" "Your consulship is cursed!" "Fetch the priests!"

Cicero raised his hands. "Yes, the corpse was in a dreadful state. But what do you expect? The poor lad had been in the water a long time. The fish are hungry. They take their food where they can. You really want me to bring a priest? To do what? To curse the fish? To *bless* the fish?" A few people began to laugh. "Since when did Romans become frightened of *fish*? Go home. Enjoy yourselves. The day after tomorrow there will be a new year, with a new consul—one who you can be sure will always guard your welfare!"

It was no great oration by his standards but it did what was required. There were even a few cheers. He jumped down. The legionnaires cleared a path for us through the mob and we retreated quickly toward the city. As we neared the gate I glanced back. At the fringes of the crowd people were already beginning to wander away in search of fresh diversions. I turned to Cicero to congratulate him on the effectiveness of his remarks, but he was leaning over the roadside ditch, vomiting.

Such was the state of the city on the eve of Cicero's consulship—a vortex of hunger, rumor, and anxiety; of crippled veterans and bankrupt farmers begging at every corner; of roistering bands of drunken young men terrorizing shopkeepers; of women from good families openly prostituting themselves outside the taverns; of sudden conflagrations, violent tempests, moonless nights, and scavenging dogs; of fanatics, soothsayers, beggars, fights. Pompey was still away commanding the legions in the East, and in his absence an uneasy, shifting mood swirled around the streets like river fog, giving everyone the jitters. There was a sense that some huge event was impending but no clear idea what it might be. The new tribunes were said to be working with Caesar and Crassus on a vast and secret scheme for giving away public land to the urban poor. Cicero had tried to find out more about it but had been rebuffed. The patricians were certain to resist it, whatever it was. Goods were scarce, food hoarded, shops empty. Even the moneylenders had stopped making loans.

As for Cicero's colleague as consul, Antonius Hybrida—Antonius the Half-Breed: half man, half beast—he was both wild and stupid, as befitted a candidate who had run for office on a joint ticket with Cicero's sworn enemy Sergius Catilina. Nevertheless, knowing the perils they would face, and feeling the need for allies, Cicero had made strenuous efforts to get on good terms with him. Unfortunately, his approaches had come to nothing, and I shall say why. It was the custom for the two consuls-elect to draw lots in October to decide which province each would govern after his year in office. Hybrida, who was steeped in debt, had set his heart on the rebellious but lucrative lands of Macedonia, where a vast fortune was waiting to be made. However, to his dismay he drew instead the peaceful pastures of Nearer Gaul, where not even a fieldmouse was stirring. It was Cicero who drew Macedonia, and when the result was announced in the Senate Hybrida's face had assumed such a picture of childish resentment and surprise that the entire chamber had been convulsed by laughter. He and Cicero had not spoken since.

Little wonder, then, that Cicero was finding it so hard to compose his inaugural address and that when we returned to his house from the river and he tried to resume his dictation his voice kept trailing off. He would

stare into the distance with a look of abstraction on his face and repeatedly wonder aloud why the boy had been killed in such a manner, and of
what significance it was that he belonged to Hybrida. He agreed with
Octavius: the likeliest culprits were the Gauls. Human sacrifice was certainly one of their cults. He sent a message to a friend of his, Quintus
Fabius Sanga, who was the Gauls' principal patron in the Senate, asking
in confidence if he thought such an outrage was possible. But Sanga sent
a rather huffy letter back within the hour, saying of course not, and that
the Gauls would be gravely offended if the consul-elect persisted in such
damaging speculation. Cicero sighed, threw the letter aside, and attempted to pick up the threads of his thoughts. But he could not weave
them together into anything coherent, and shortly before sunset he called
again for his cloak and boots.

I had assumed his intention was to take a turn in the public gardens
not far from the house, where he often went when he was composing a
speech. But as we reached the brow of the hill, instead of turning right he
pressed on toward the Esquiline Gate, and I realized to my amazement he
intended to go outside the sacred boundary to the place where the corpses
were burned—a spot he usually avoided at all costs. We passed the porters
with their handcarts waiting for work just beyond the gate, and the squat
official residence of the carnifex, who, as public executioner, was forbidden to live within the precincts of the city. Finally we entered the sacred
grove of Libitina, filled with cawing crows, and approached the temple.
In those days this was the headquarters of the undertakers' guild: the
place where one could buy all that was needed for a funeral, from the
utensils with which to anoint a body to the bed on which the corpse was
cremated. Cicero asked me for some money and went ahead and spoke to
a priest. He handed him the purse, and a couple of official mourners appeared. Cicero beckoned me over. "We are just in time," he said.

What a curious party we must have made as we crossed the Esquiline Field in single file, the mourners first, carrying jars of incense, then
the consul-elect, then me. All around us in the dusk were the dancing
flames of funeral pyres, the cries of the bereaved, and the sickly smell of
incense—strong, yet not quite strong enough to disguise the stink of
burning death. The mourners led us to the public ustrina, where a pile
of corpses on a handcart were waiting to be thrown onto the flames. Devoid
of clothes and shoes, these unclaimed bodies were as destitute in death as
they had been in life. Only the murdered boy's was covered: I recognized

it by the sailcloth shroud into which it had now been tightly sewn. As a couple of attendants tossed it easily onto the metal grille, Cicero bowed his head and the hired mourners set up a particularly noisy lamentation, no doubt in the hope of a good tip. The flames roared and flattened in the wind, and very quickly that was it: he had gone to whatever fate awaits us all.

It was a scene I have never forgotten.

Surely the greatest mercy granted us by Providence is our ignorance of the future. Imagine if we knew the outcome of our hopes and plans, or could see the manner in which we are doomed to die—how ruined our lives would be! Instead we live on dumbly from day to day as happily as animals. But all things must come to dust eventually. No human being, no system, no age is impervious to this law; everything beneath the stars will perish; the hardest rock will be worn away. Nothing endures but words.

And with this in mind, and in the renewed hope that I may live long enough to see the task through, I shall now relate the extraordinary story of Cicero's year in office as consul of the Roman republic and what befell him in the four years afterward—a span of time we mortals call a lustrum, but which to the gods is no more than the blinking of an eye.

II

THE FOLLOWING DAY, inaugural eve, it snowed—a heavy fall, of the sort one normally sees only in the mountains. It clad the temples of the Capitol in soft white marble and laid a shroud as thick as a man's hand across the whole of the city. I had never witnessed such a phenomenon before; nor, despite my great age, have I heard of the like again. Snow in Rome? This surely had to be an omen. But of what?

Cicero stayed firmly in his study, beside a small coal fire, and continued to work on his speech. He placed no faith in portents. When I burst in and told him of the snow, he merely shrugged. "What of it?" And when tentatively I began to advance the argument of the Stoics in defense of augury—that if there are gods, they must care for men, and that if they care for men, they must send us signs of their will—he cut me off with a laugh: "Surely the gods, given their immortal powers, should be able to find more articulate means of communication than snowflakes. Why not send us a letter?" He turned back to his desk, shaking his head and chuckling at my credulity. "Really, go and attend to your duties, Tiro, and make sure no one else bothers me."

Chastened, I went away and checked the arrangements for the inaugural procession and then made a start on his correspondence. I had been his secretary for sixteen years by this time, and there was no aspect of his life, public or private, with which I was not familiar. My habit in those days was to work at a folding table just outside his study, fending off unwanted visitors and keeping an ear open for his summons. It was from this position that I could hear the noises of the household that morning: Terentia marching in and out of the dining room, snapping at the maids that the winter flowers were not good enough for her husband's new status, and berating the cook about the quality of that night's menu; little Marcus, now well into his second year, toddling unsteadily after her and shouting in delight at the snow; and darling Tullia, thirteen and due to be married in the summer, practicing her Greek hexameters with her tutor.

Such was the extent of my work that it was not until after noon that I was able to put my head out of doors again. Despite the hour the street for once was empty. The city felt muffled, ominous; as still as midnight. The sky was pale, the snowfall had stopped, and frost had formed a glittering white crust over the surface. Even now—for such are the peculiarities of memory in the very old—I can recall the sensation of breaking it with the tip of my shoe. I took a last breath of that freezing air and was just turning to go back into the warmth when I heard, very faint in the hush, the crack of a whip and the sound of men crying and groaning. A few moments later a litter borne by four liveried slaves came swaying around the corner. An overseer trotting alongside waved his whip in my direction.

"Hey, you!" he shouted. "Is that Cicero's house?"

When I replied that it was, he called over his shoulder—"This is the street!"—and lashed out at the slave nearest him with such force the poor fellow nearly stumbled. To get through the snow he had to pull his knees up high to his waist and in this way he floundered on toward me. Behind him a second litter appeared, then a third, and a fourth. They drew up outside the house, and the instant they had set down their burdens the porters all sank down in the snow, collapsing over the shafts like exhausted rowers at their oars. I did not care for the look of this at all.

"It may be Cicero's house," I protested, "but he is not receiving visitors."

"He will receive us!" came a familiar voice from inside the first litter, and a bony hand clawed back the curtain to reveal the leader of the patrician faction in the Senate, Quintus Lutatius Catulus. He was wrapped in animal skins right up to his pointed chin, giving him the appearance of a large and malevolent weasel.

"Senator," I said, bowing, "I shall tell him you're here."

"And not just I," said Catulus.

I looked along the street. Clambering stiffly out of the next litter and cursing his old soldier's bones was the conqueror of Olympus and father of the Senate, Vatia Isauricus, while nearby stood Cicero's great rival in the law courts, the patricians' favorite advocate, Quintus Hortensius. He in turn was holding out his hand to a fourth senator whose shriveled, nut-brown, toothless face I could not place. He looked very decrepit. I guessed he must have stopped attending debates a long while ago.

"Distinguished gentlemen," I said, in my most unctuous manner, "please follow me and I shall inform the consul-elect."

I whispered to the porter to show them into the tablinum and hurried toward Cicero's study. As I drew close, I could hear his voice in full declamatory flow—"To the Roman people I say, enough!"—and when I opened the door I found him standing with his back to me, addressing my two junior secretaries, Sositheus and Laurea, his hand outstretched, his thumb and middle finger formed into a circle. "And to you, Tiro," he continued, without turning around, "I say: not another damned interruption! What sign have the gods sent us now? A shower of frogs?"

The secretaries sniggered. On the brink of achieving his life's ambition, he had put the perturbations of the previous day out of his mind and was in a great good humor.

"There's a delegation from the Senate to see you."

"Now that's what I call an ominous portent. Who's in it?"

"Catulus, Isauricus, Hortensius, and another I don't recognize."

"The cream of the aristocracy? Here?" He gave me a sharp look over his shoulder. "And in this weather? It must be the smallest house they've ever set foot in! What do they want?"

"I don't know."

"Well, be sure you make a thorough note." He gathered his toga around him and stuck out his chin. "How do I look?"

"Consular," I assured him.

He stepped over the discarded drafts of his speech and made his way into the tablinum. The porter had fetched chairs for our visitors but only one was seated—the trembling old senator I did not recognize. The others stood together, each with his own attendant close at hand, clearly uncomfortable at finding themselves on the premises of this lowborn "new man" they had so reluctantly backed for consul. Hortensius actually had a handkerchief pressed to his nose, as if Cicero's lack of breeding might be catching.

"Catulus," said Cicero affably, as he came into the room. "Isauricus. Hortensius. I'm honored." He nodded to each of the former consuls, but when he reached the fourth senator I could see even his prodigious memory temporarily fail him. "Rabirius," he concluded after a brief struggle. "Gaius Rabirius, isn't it?" He held out his hand but the old man did not react, and Cicero smoothly turned the gesture into a sweeping indication of the room. "Welcome to my home. This is a pleasure."

"There's no pleasure in it," said Catulus.

"It's an outrage," said Hortensius.

"It's war," asserted Isauricus, "that's what it is."

"Well, I'm very sorry to hear it," replied Cicero pleasantly. He did not always take them seriously. Like many rich old men they tended to regard the slightest personal inconvenience as proof of the end of the world.

Hortensius clicked his fingers, and his attendant handed Cicero a legal document with a heavy seal. "Yesterday the Board of Tribunes served this writ on Rabirius."

At the mention of his name Rabirius looked up. "Can I go home?" he asked plaintively.

"Later," said Hortensius in a stern voice, and the old man bowed his head.

"A writ on Rabirius?" repeated Cicero, looking at him with bemusement. "And what conceivable crime is he capable of?" He read the writ aloud so I could make a note of it. " 'The accused is herein charged with the murder of the tribune Lucius Saturninus and the violation of the sacred precincts of the Senate House.' " He looked up in puzzlement. "Saturninus? It must be—what?—forty years since he was killed."

"Thirty-six," corrected Catulus.

"And Catulus should know," said Isauricus, "because he was there. As was I."

Catulus spat out his name as if it were poison. "Saturninus! What a rogue! Killing him wasn't a crime—it was a public service." He gazed into the distance as if surveying some grand historical mural on the wall of a temple: *The Murder of Saturninus in the Senate House.* "I see him as plainly as I see you, Cicero. A rabble-rousing tribune of the very worst kind. He murdered our candidate for consul and the Senate declared him a public enemy. After that even the plebs deserted him. But before we could lay our hands on him, he and some of his gang barricaded themselves up on the Capitol. So we blocked the water pipes! That was your idea, Vatia."

"It was." The old general's eyes gleamed at the memory. "I knew how to conduct a siege, even then."

"Of course they surrendered after a couple of days, and were lodged in the Senate House till their trial. But we didn't trust them not to escape again, so we got up on the roof and tore off the tiles and pelted them. There was no hiding place. They ran to and fro squealing like rats in a ditch. By the time Saturninus stopped twitching, you could barely tell who he was."

"And Rabirius was with you both on the roof?" asked Cicero. Glancing up from my notes at the old man—his expression vacant, his head trembling slightly—it was impossible to imagine him involved in such an action.

"Oh yes, he was there," confirmed Isauricus. "There must have been about thirty of us. Those were the days," he added, bunching his fingers into a gnarled fist, "when we still had some juice in us!"

"The crucial point," said Hortensius wearily—he was younger than his companions and obviously bored of hearing the same old story—"is not whether Rabirius was there or not. It's the crime with which he is being charged."

"Which is what? Murder?"

"Perduellio."

I must confess I had never even heard of it, and Cicero had to spell it out for me. "Perduellio," he explained, "is what the ancients called treason." He turned to Hortensius. "Why use such an obsolete law? Why not just prosecute him with treason, pure and simple, and have done with it?"

"Because the sentence for treason is exile, whereas for perduellio it's death—and not by hanging, either." Hortensius leaned forward to emphasize his words. "If they find him guilty, Rabirius will be crucified."

"What is this place?" demanded Rabirius, getting to his feet. "Where am I?"

Catulus gently pressed him down into his seat. "Calm yourself, Gaius. We're your friends."

"But no jury is going to find *him* guilty," objected Cicero quietly. "The poor fellow's clearly lost his brains."

"Perduellio isn't heard before a jury. That's what's so cunning. It's heard before two judges, specially appointed for the purpose."

"Appointed by whom?"

"Our new urban praetor, Lentulus Sura."

Cicero grimaced at the name. Sura was a former consul, a man of great ambition and boundless stupidity, two qualities which in politics often go together.

"And whom has Old Sleepy-Head chosen as judges? Do we know?"

"Caesar is one. And Caesar is the other."

"*What?*"

"Gaius Julius Caesar and his cousin Lucius are to be selected to hear the case."

"*Caesar* is behind this?"

"Naturally the verdict is a foregone conclusion."

"But there must be a right of appeal," insisted Cicero, now thoroughly alarmed. "A Roman citizen cannot be executed without a proper trial."

"Oh yes," said Hortensius bitterly, "if Rabirius is found guilty, of course he has the right of appeal. But here's the catch. Not to a court—only to the entire people, drawn up in full assembly, on the Field of Mars."

"And what a spectacle that will be!" broke in Catulus. "Can you imagine it? A Roman senator on trial for his life in front of the mob? They'll never vote to acquit him—it would rob them of their entertainment."

"It will mean civil war," said Isauricus flatly, "because we won't stand for it, Cicero. D'you hear us?"

"I hear you," he replied, his eyes rapidly scanning the writ. "Which of the tribunes has laid the charge?" He found the name at the foot of the document. "Labienus? He's one of Pompey's men. He's not normally a troublemaker. What's he playing at?"

"Apparently his uncle was killed alongside Saturninus," said Hortensius with great contempt, "and his family honor demands vengeance. It's nonsense. The whole thing is just a pretext for Caesar and his gang to attack the Senate."

"So what do you propose to do?" said Catulus. "We voted for you, remember? Against the better judgment of some of us."

"What do you want me to do?"

"What do you think? Fight for Rabirius's life! Denounce this wickedness in public, then join Hortensius as his defense counsel when the case comes before the people."

"Well, that would be a novelty," said Cicero, eyeing his great rival, "the two of us appearing together."

"The prospect is no more appealing to me than it is to you," rejoined Hortensius coldly.

"Now, now, Hortensius, don't take offense. I'd be honored to act as your colleague in court. But let's not rush into their trap. Let's try to see if we can settle this matter without a trial."

"How can it be avoided?"

"I'll go and talk to Caesar. Discover what he wants. See if we can reach a compromise." At the mere mention of the word "compromise" the three ex-consuls all started to object at once. Cicero held up his hands. "He must want something. It will do us no harm at least to hear his terms. We owe it to the republic. We owe it to Rabirius."

"I want to go home," said Rabirius plaintively. "Please can I go home now?"

Cicero and I left the house less than an hour later, the unfamiliar snow crunching and squeaking beneath our boots as we descended the empty street toward the city. Once again we went alone, which I now find remarkable to contemplate—this must have been one of the last occasions when Cicero was able to venture out in Rome without a bodyguard. He did, however, pull up the hood of his cloak to avoid being recognized. Even the busiest thoroughfares in daylight could not be counted safe that winter.

"They will have to compromise," he said. "They may not like it, but they have no choice." He suddenly swore and kicked at the snow in his frustration. "Is this what my consulship is going to consist of, Tiro? A year spent running back and forth between the patricians and the populists, trying to stop them tearing one another to pieces?" I could think of no hopeful reply, so we trudged on in silence.

Caesar's home at this time stood some way beneath Cicero's, in Subura. The building had been in his family for at least a century and had no doubt been fine enough in its day. But by the time Caesar had come to inherit it, the neighborhood was impoverished. Even the virginal snow, smudged with the soot of burned-out fires and dotted with human shit thrown from the tenement windows, somehow served only to emphasize the squalor of the narrow streets. Beggars held out trembling hands for money, but I had brought none with me. I recall urchins pelting an elderly, shrieking whore with snowballs, and twice we saw fingers and feet poking out from beneath the icy mounds that marked where some poor wretch had frozen to death in the night.

And it was down here in Subura, like some great shark attended by shoals of minnows hoping for his scraps, that Caesar lurked and awaited his chance. His house was at the end of a street of shoemakers, flanked by two tottering apartment blocks, seven or eight stories high. The frozen washing strung between them made it seem as though a pair of drunks with torn sleeves were embracing above his roof. Outside the entrance a dozen rough-looking fellows stamped their feet around an iron brazier. I felt their hungry, crafty eyes stripping the clothes from my back even as we waited to be admitted.

"Those are the citizens who will be judging Rabirius," muttered Cicero. "The old fool doesn't stand a chance."

The steward took our cloaks and showed us into the atrium, then went to tell his master of Cicero's arrival, leaving us to inspect the death masks of Caesar's ancestors. Strangely, there were only three consuls in Caesar's direct line, a thin tally for a family that claimed to go back to the foundation of Rome and to have its origins in the womb of Venus. The goddess herself was represented by a small bronze. The statue was exquisite but scratched and shabby, as were the carpets, the frescoes, the faded tapestries, and the furniture: all told a story of a proud family fallen on hard days. We had plenty of leisure to appreciate these heirlooms as time passed and still Caesar did not appear.

"You can't help but admire the fellow," said Cicero, after he had paced around the room three or four times. "Here am I, about to become the preeminent man in Rome, while he hasn't even made it to praetor yet. But I am the one who must dance attendance on him!"

After a while I became aware that we were being watched from behind a door by a solemn-faced girl of about ten who must have been Caesar's daughter, Julia. I smiled at her and she darted away. A little while later Caesar's mother, Aurelia, emerged from the same room. Her narrow, dark-eyed, watchful face, like Caesar's, had something of the bird of prey about it, and she exuded a similar air of chilly cordiality. Cicero had been acquainted with her for many years. All three of her brothers, the Cottas, had been consul, and if Aurelia had been born a man she would certainly have achieved the rank herself, for she was shrewder and braver than any of them. As it was she had to content herself with furthering the career of her son, and when her eldest brother died she fixed it so that Caesar would take his place as one of the fifteen members of the College of Priests—a brilliant move, as I shall soon describe.

"Forgive him, Cicero, for his rudeness," she said. "I've reminded him you're here, but you know how he is." There was a footstep, and we glanced behind us to see a woman in the passage leading to the door. No doubt she had hoped to slip past unnoticed, but one of her shoes must have come undone. Leaning against the wall to refasten it, her auburn hair awry, she glanced guiltily in our direction, and I do not know who was the more embarrassed: Postumia—which was the woman's name—or Cicero, for he knew her very well as the wife of his great friend the jurist and senator Servius Sulpicius. Indeed, she was due to have dinner with Cicero that very evening.

He quickly turned his attention back to the bronze of Venus and pretended to be in the middle of a conversation—"This is very fine; is it a Myron?"—and did not look up until she had gone.

"That was tactfully done," said Aurelia approvingly, then her expression darkened and she shook her head. "I don't reproach my son for his liaisons—men will be men—but some of these modern women are shameless beyond belief."

"What are you two gossiping about?"

It was a trick of Caesar's, both in war and in peace, to appear unexpectedly from the rear, and at the sound of that flint-dry voice we all three turned. I can see him now, his large head looming skull-like in the dimming afternoon light. People ask me about him all the time: "You met Caesar? What was he like? Tell us what he was like—the great god Caesar!" Well, I remember him most as a curious combination of hard and soft—the muscles of a soldier within the loosely belted tunic of an effete dandy; the sharp sweat of the exercise yard laid over by the sweet scent of crocus oil; pitiless ambition sheathed in honeyed charm. "Be wary of her, Cicero," he continued, emerging from the shadows. "She's twice the politician we are, aren't you, Mama?" He caught her by the waist from behind and kissed her beneath her ear.

"Now stop that," she said, freeing herself and pretending to be annoyed. "I've played the hostess long enough. Where's your wife? It's not seemly for her to be out unaccompanied all the time. Send her to me the moment she returns." She inclined her head graciously toward Cicero. "My best wishes to you for tomorrow. It's a remarkable achievement to be the first in one's family to achieve the consulship."

Caesar watched her go admiringly. "Seriously, Cicero," he said, "the women in this city are far more formidable than the men, your own wife being a fine example."

Was Caesar hinting by this remark that he desired to seduce Terentia? I doubt it. The most hostile tribe of Gaul would have been a less grueling conquest. But I could see Cicero bridling. "I'm not here to discuss the women of Rome," he said, "expert though you may be."

"Then why have you come?"

Cicero nodded to me. I opened my document case and handed Caesar the writ.

"Are you trying to corrupt me?" responded Caesar with a smile, handing it straight back to me. "I can't discuss this. I'm to be a judge."

"I want you to acquit Rabirius of these charges."

Caesar chuckled in that mirthless way of his, and tucked a thin strand of hair behind his ear. "No doubt you do."

"Now, Caesar," said Cicero with an edge of impatience in his voice, "let's speak plainly. Everyone knows that you and Crassus give the tribunes their orders. I doubt whether Labienus even knew the name of this wretched uncle of his until you put it into his head. As for Sura—he would have thought perduellio was a fish unless someone told him otherwise. This is yet another of your designs."

"Really, I cannot speak about a case I have to judge."

"Admit it: the true purpose of this prosecution is to intimidate the Senate."

"You must direct your questions to Labienus."

"I'm directing them to you."

"Very well, since you press me, I'd rather call it a reminder to the Senate that if they trample on the dignity of the people by killing their representatives, the people will have their vengeance, however long it takes."

"And you really think you'll enhance the dignity of the people by terrorizing a helpless old man? I've just come from Rabirius. His wits have been entirely withered by age. He has no idea what's going on."

"If he's no idea what's going on, how can he be terrorized?"

There was quite a long pause, then Cicero said, in a different tone, "Listen, my dear Gaius, we've been good friends for many years." (This was putting it a bit strongly, I thought.) "May I give you some friendly advice, in the manner of an older brother to his junior? A glittering career lies ahead of you. You're young—"

"Not that young! I'm already three years older than Alexander the Great was when he died."

Cicero laughed politely; he thought he was joking. "You're young," he repeated. "You have a powerful reputation. Why jeopardize it by provoking such a confrontation? Killing Rabirius will not only set the people against the Senate, it will be a stain on your honor. It might play well with the mob today, but it will count against you tomorrow with all the sensible men."

"I'll take the risk."

"You do realize that as consul I'll be obliged to defend him?"

"Well, that would be a grave error, Marcus—if I may respond with equal friendliness? Consider the balance of forces which will be ranged against you. We have the support of the people, the tribunes, half the praetors—why, even Antonius Hybrida, your own consular colleague, is on our side! Who does that leave you with? The patricians? But they despise you. They'll throw you over the moment you're of no use to them. As I see it, you have only one choice."

"Which is?"

"To join us."

"Ah." Cicero had a habit when he was weighing someone up of resting his chin in the palm of his hand. He contemplated Caesar in this way for a while. "And what would that entail?"

"Support for our bill."

"And in return?"

"I daresay my cousin and I can find it in our hearts to show some compassion to poor Rabirius, on the grounds of his impaired mind." Caesar's thin lips smiled but his dark eyes stayed fixed on Cicero. "What do you say?"

Before Cicero could respond we were interrupted by the arrival home of Caesar's wife. Some say Caesar married this woman, whose name was Pompeia, purely at the urging of his mother, for the girl had useful family connections in the Senate. But on the basis of what I saw that afternoon I should say her attractions belonged to a more obvious sphere. She was much younger than he, barely twenty, and the cold had imparted a pretty blush to her creamy throat and cheeks, and a sparkle to her large gray eyes. She embraced her husband, arching against him like a cat, and then made an almost equal fuss of Cicero, flattering him for his speeches and even a volume of his poetry which she claimed to have read. It occurred to me she was drunk. Caesar regarded her with amusement.

"Mama wants to see you," he said, at which she pouted like a girl. "Well, go on," he commanded, "don't make a sour face. You know what she's like," and he gave her a pat on her rear to send her on her way.

"So many women, Caesar," observed Cicero drily. "Where will they emerge from next?"

Caesar laughed. "I fear you'll take away a bad impression of me."

"My impression is quite unchanged, I assure you."

"So, then: Do we have a bargain?"

"It depends on what your bill contains. All we have so far are election slogans. 'Land for the landless.' 'Food for the hungry.' I'll need a few more details than that. And also perhaps some concessions." But Caesar did not respond. His expression was blank. After a while the silence became embarrassing, and it was Cicero who ended it by grunting and turning aside. "Well, it's getting dark," he said to me. "We should go."

"So soon? You'll take no refreshment? Then let me show you out." Caesar was entirely affable: his manners were always impeccable, even when he was condemning a man to death. "Think of it," he continued as he led us down the shabby passage. "If you join us, how easy your term of office will be. This time next year your consulship will be over. You'll leave Rome. Live in a governor's palace. Make enough money in Macedonia to set you up for life. Come home. Buy a house on the Bay of Naples. Study philosophy. Write your memoirs. Whereas—"

The doorkeeper stepped forward to help Cicero on with his cloak, but Cicero waved him away and turned on Caesar. "Whereas? Whereas what? If I don't join you? What then?"

Caesar put on an expression of pained surprise. "None of this is aimed at you personally. I hope you understand that. We mean you no harm. In fact I want you to know that if ever you find yourself in personal danger you can always rely on my protection."

"*I* can always rely on *your* protection?" Seldom did I see Cicero at a loss for words. But on that freezing day, in that cramped and faded house, in that scruffy neighborhood, I watched him struggle to find the language that would adequately convey his feelings. In the end he couldn't manage it. Draping his cloak over his shoulders, he stepped out into the snow and, under the sullen gaze of the band of ruffians still lingering in the street, he bade Caesar a curt farewell.

"*I* can always rely on *his* protection?" repeated Cicero as we trudged back up the hill. "Who is he to talk to me in such a way?"

"He's very confident," I ventured.

"Confident? He treats me as if I were his client!"

The day was ending, and with it the year, fading swiftly in that way of winter afternoons. In the windows of the tenements lamps were being lit. People were shouting to one another above our heads. There was a lot of smoke from the fires and I could smell food cooking. At the street corners the pious had put out little dishes of honey cakes as new year offerings to the neighborhood gods, for we worshipped the spirits of the crossroads in those days rather than the great god Augustus, and the hungry birds were pecking at them, rising and fluttering and settling again as we hurried past.

"Do you want me to send a message to Catulus and the others?" I asked.

"And tell them what? That Caesar has undertaken to spare Rabirius if I betray them behind their backs and that I'm going away to consider his proposal?" He was striding ahead, his irritation lending strength to his legs. I was sweating to keep up. "I noticed you weren't making a note of what he said."

"It didn't seem appropriate."

"You must always make a note. From now on everything is to be written down."

"Yes, Senator."

"We're heading into dangerous waters, Tiro. Every reef and current must be charted."

"Yes, Senator."

"Can you remember the conversation?"

"I think so. Most of it."

"Good. Write it all down as soon as we get back. I want to keep a record by me. But don't say a word to anyone—especially not in front of Postumia."

"Do you think she'll still come to dinner?"

"Oh yes, she'll come—if only to report back to her lover. She's quite without shame. Poor Servius. He's so proud of her."

As soon as we reached the house Cicero went upstairs to change while I retired to my little room to write down everything I could remember. I have that roll here now as I compose my memoir: Cicero preserved it among his secret papers. Like me, it has become yellowish and brittle and faded with age. But again like me, it is still comprehensible, just about, and when I hold it up close to my eyes I hear again Caesar's rasping voice in my ear: *"You can always rely on my protection . . ."*

It took me an hour or more to finish my account, by which time Cicero's guests had arrived and gone in for dinner. After I had done I lay down on my narrow cot and thought of all I had witnessed. I do not mind admitting I was uneasy, for Nature had not equipped me with the nerves for public life. I would have been happy to have stayed on the family estate: my dream was always to have a small farm of my own, to which I could retire and write. I had some money saved up and secretly I had been hoping Cicero might give me my freedom when he won the consulship. But the months had gone by and he had never mentioned it, and now I was past forty and beginning to worry I might die in servitude. The last night of the year is often a melancholy time. Janus looks backward as well as forward and sometimes each prospect seems equally unappealing. But that evening I felt particularly sorry for myself.

Anyway, I kept out of Cicero's way until very late, when I reasoned the meal must be close to finishing, then went to the dining room and stood beside the door where Cicero could see me. It was a small but pretty room, freshly decorated with frescoes designed to give the diners the impression they were in Cicero's garden at Tusculum. There were nine around the table, three to a couch—the perfect number. Postumia had turned up, exactly as Cicero had predicted. She was in a loose-necked gown and looked serene, as if the embarrassment of the afternoon had never occurred. Next to her reclined her husband, Servius, one of Cicero's oldest friends and the most eminent jurist in Rome: no mean achievement in that city full of lawyers. But immersing oneself in the law is a little like bathing in freezing water—bracing in moderation, shriveling in excess—and Servius over the years had become ever more hunched and cautious, whereas Postumia remained a beauty. Still, he had a following in the Senate, and his ambition—and hers—burned strong. He planned to stand for consul himself in the summer, and Cicero had promised to support him.

The only friend of Cicero's of longer standing than Servius was Atticus. He was lying beside his sister, Pomponia, who was married—unhappily, alas—to Cicero's younger brother, Quintus. Poor Quintus: he looked as if he had taken refuge from her shrewish taunts in the wine as usual. The final guest was young Marcus Caelius Rufus, who had been Cicero's pupil, and who kept up a stream of jokes and stories. As for Cicero, he reclined between Terentia and his beloved Tullia and was putting on a show of such nonchalance, laughing at Rufus's gossip, you would never have guessed he had a care. But it is one of the tricks of the successful politician to be able to hold many things in mind at once and to switch between them as the need arises; otherwise life would be insupportable. After a while he glanced toward me and nodded. "Friends," he said, loudly enough to cut through the general chatter, "it is getting late, and Tiro has come to remind me I have an inaugural address to make in the morning. Sometimes I think he should be the consul and I the secretary." There was laughter and I felt the gaze of everyone turn on me. "Ladies," he continued, "if you would forgive me, I wonder if the gentlemen might join me in my study for a moment."

He dabbed the corners of his mouth with his napkin and threw it onto the table, then stood and offered his hand to Terentia. She took it with a smile all the more striking because it was so rare. She was like some twiggy winter plant that had suddenly put forth a bloom, warmed by the sun of Cicero's success—so much so that she had actually set aside her lifelong parsimony and dressed herself in a manner befitting the wife of a consul and future governor of Macedonia. Her brand-new gown was sewn with pearls, and other newly purchased jewels glinted all about her: at her narrow throat and thin bosom, at her wrists and on her fingers, even woven into her short dark curls.

The guests filed out, the women turning toward the tablinum, the men moving into the study. Cicero told me to close the door. Immediately the pleasure drained from his face.

"What's all this about, Brother?" asked Quintus, who was still holding his wineglass. "You look as if you've eaten a bad oyster."

"I hate to spoil a pleasant evening, but a problem has arisen." Grimly Cicero produced the writ that had been served on Rabirius, then described the afternoon's delegation from the Senate and his subsequent visit to Caesar. "Read out what the rascal said, Tiro," he ordered.

I did as he asked, and when I came to the final part—Caesar's offer of protection—all four exchanged glances.

"Well," said Atticus, "if you turn your back on Catulus and his friends after all the promises you made to them before the election, you may have need of his protection. They'll never forgive you."

"Yet if I keep my word to them, and oppose the populists' bill, then Caesar will find Rabirius guilty, and I'll be obliged to defend him on the Field of Mars."

"And that you simply must not do," said Quintus. "Caesar's quite right. Defeat is certain. At all costs, leave his defense to Hortensius."

"But that's impossible! I can hardly stay neutral as the president of the Senate while a senator is crucified. What kind of consul would that make me?"

"A live one, rather than a dead one," replied Quintus, "because if you throw in your lot with the patricians, believe me, you'll be in real danger. Almost everyone will be against you. Even the Senate won't be united—Hybrida will see to that. There are plenty on those benches just waiting for an opportunity to bring you down, Catilina first among them."

"I've an idea," said young Rufus. "Why don't we smuggle Rabirius out of the city and hide him in the country somewhere till this blows over?"

"Could we?" Cicero pondered the suggestion, then shook his head. "No. I admire your spirit, Rufus, but it wouldn't work. If we deny Caesar Rabirius, he's perfectly capable of trumping up a similar charge against Catulus or Isauricus—and can you imagine the consequences of *that*?"

Servius, meanwhile, had picked up the writ and was studying it intently. His eyesight was weak and he had to hold the document so close to the candelabrum I feared it might catch fire. "Perduellio," he muttered. "That's a strange coincidence. I was planning to propose in the Senate this very month that the statute of perduellio be repealed. I'd even looked up all the precedents. I have them laid out on my desk at home."

"Perhaps that's where Caesar got the idea," said Quintus. "Did you mention it to him?"

Servius's face was still pressed to the writ. "Of course not. I never speak to him. The fellow's an utter scoundrel." He glanced up to discover Cicero staring at him. "What is it?"

"I think I know how Caesar might have heard of perduellio."

"How?"

Cicero hesitated. "Your wife was at Caesar's house when we arrived this afternoon."

"Don't be absurd. Why would Postumia visit Caesar? She barely knows him. She was with her sister all day."

"I saw her. So did Tiro."

"Well then, maybe you did, but I'm sure there's some innocent explanation." Servius pretended to carry on reading. After a while he said, in a low and resentful voice, "I was puzzled why you'd waited till after dinner to discuss Caesar's proposal. Now I understand. You felt unable to speak openly in front of my wife, in case she ran to his bed and repeated what you said."

It was a horribly embarrassing moment. Quintus and Atticus both stared at the floor; even Rufus held his tongue for a change.

"Servius, Servius, old friend," said Cicero, taking him by the shoulders. "You're the one man in Rome I most wish to see succeed me as consul. My trust in you is absolute. Never doubt it."

"But you have insulted the honor of my wife, which is also an insult to me, so how can I accept your trust?" He pushed Cicero's hands away and walked with dignity out of the room.

"Servius!" called Atticus, who could not bear any kind of unpleasantness. But the poor cuckold had already gone, and when Atticus moved to follow him, Cicero said quietly, "Leave him, Atticus. It's his wife he needs to speak to, not us."

There was a long silence, during which I strained my ears for the sound of raised voices in the tablinum, but the only noise was of dishes being cleared from the dining room. Eventually, Rufus gave a roar of laughter. "So that's why Caesar is always one step ahead of his enemies! He has spies in all your beds!"

"Shut up, Rufus," said Quintus.

"Damn Caesar!" cried Cicero suddenly. "There's nothing dishonorable about ambition. I'm ambitious myself. But his lust for power is not of this world. You look into those eyes of his, and it's like staring into some dark sea at the height of a storm!" He flung himself into his chair and sat drumming his fingertips against the arms. "I don't see what choice I have. At least if I agree to his terms I can gain myself some time. They've already been working on this damned bill of theirs for months."

"What's so wrong with giving free farms to the poor anyway?" asked Rufus, who, like many of the young, had populist sympathies. "You've been out on the streets. You've seen what it's like this winter. People are starving."

"I agree," said Cicero. "But it's food they need, not farms. Farming demands years of skill, and backbreaking labor. I'd like to see those layabouts I met outside Caesar's house today working the fields from dawn till dusk! If we're forced to rely on them for food, we'll all be starving in a year."

"At least Caesar is concerned about them—"

"*Concerned* about them? Caesar is concerned about no man except himself! Do you really think Crassus, the richest man in Rome, is *concerned* about the poor? They want to dole out the public land—at no expense to themselves, by the way—to create an army of supporters so huge it will keep them in power forever. Crassus has his eyes on Egypt. The gods alone know what Caesar wants—the entire planet, probably. '*Concerned!*' Really, Rufus, you do talk like a young fool sometimes. Have you learned nothing since you came to Rome except how to gamble and whore?"

I do not think Cicero meant his words to sound as harsh as they did, but I could tell they struck Rufus like a slap, and when he turned away his eyes were shining with suppressed tears—and not merely of humiliation, either, but of anger, for he was no longer the charming adolescent idler Cicero had taken in as a pupil, but a young man of growing ambition: a change Cicero had failed to notice. Even though the discussion went on for a while longer, Rufus took no further part in it.

"Tiro," said Atticus, "you were there at Caesar's house. What do you think your master should do?"

I had been waiting for this moment, for I was invariably the last to be asked his opinion in these inner councils, and I always tried to prepare something to say. "I think that by agreeing to Caesar's proposal, it may be possible to gain some concessions in the bill. These can then be presented to the patricians as a victory."

"And then," mused Cicero, "if they refuse to accept them, the blame will clearly be theirs, and I shall be released from my obligation. It's not a bad idea."

"Well said, Tiro!" declared Quintus. "Always the wisest man in the room." He yawned excessively. "Now, come on, Brother." He reached down and pulled Cicero to his feet. "It's getting late and you have a speech to make tomorrow. You must get some sleep."

By the time we made our way through the house to the vestibule, the place was silent. Terentia and Tullia had retired to bed. Servius and his wife had gone home. Pomponia, who hated politics, had refused to wait for her husband and had departed with them, according to the porter. Outside, Atticus's carriage was waiting. The snow gleamed in the moonlight. From somewhere down in the city rose the familiar cry of the night watchman, calling the midnight hour.

"A new year," said Quintus.

"And a new consul," added Atticus. "Well done, my dear Cicero. I am proud to be your friend."

They shook his hand and slapped his back, and eventually—but only grudgingly, I could not help noticing—Rufus did the same. Their words of warm congratulation flickered briefly in the icy air and vanished. Afterward, Cicero stood in the street, waving to their carriage until it rounded the corner. As he turned to go back indoors he stumbled slightly and plunged his foot into the snowdrift piled against the doorstep. He pulled out his wet shoe, shook it crossly, and swore, and it was on the tip of my tongue to say it was an omen; but wisely, I think, I held my peace.

III

I DO NOT KNOW how the ceremony goes these days, when even the most senior magistrates are merely errand boys, but in Cicero's time the first visitor to call upon the new consul on the day of his swearing-in was always a member of the College of Augurs. Accordingly, just before dawn, Cicero stationed himself in the atrium alongside Terentia and his children to await the augur's arrival. I knew he had not slept well, for I had heard him moving about upstairs, pacing up and down, which is what he always did when he was thinking. But his powers of recuperation were miraculous, and he looked fit and keen enough as he stood with his family, like an Olympian who has been training his whole life for one particular race and at last is about to run it.

When all was ready I signaled to the porter and he opened the heavy wooden door to admit the keepers of the sacred chickens, the pularii—half a dozen skinny little fellows, looking a bit like chickens themselves. Behind this escort loomed the augur himself, tapping the floor with his curved staff: a veritable giant in his full rig of tall conical cap and abundant purple robe. When he saw him coming down the passageway Little Marcus shrieked and hid behind Terentia's skirts. The augur that day was Quintus Caecilius Metellus Celer, and I should say something of him, for he was to be an important figure in Cicero's story. He was just back from fighting in the East—a real soldier, something of a war hero, in fact, after beating off an enemy attack on his winter quarters while greatly outnumbered. He had served under the command of Pompey the Great, who also happened to be married to his sister, which had not exactly hindered his promotion. Not that it mattered. He was a Metellus, and therefore more or less predestined to be consul himself in a couple of years; that day he was due to be sworn in as praetor. His wife was the notorious beauty Clodia, a member of the Claudian family: all in all you could not have been much better connected than Metellus Celer, who was by no means as stupid as he looked.

"Consul-elect, good morning!" he barked, as if addressing his legionnaires at reveille. "So the great day has come at last. What will it hold, I wonder?"

"You're the augur, Celer. You tell me."

Celer threw back his head and laughed. I found out later he had no more faith in divination than Cicero had, and was a member of the College of Augurs only out of political expediency. "Well, I can predict one thing, and that is that there will be trouble. There was a crowd outside the Temple of Saturn when I passed just now. It looks as though Caesar and his friends may have posted their great bill overnight. What an amazing rogue he is!"

I was standing directly behind Cicero, so I couldn't see his face, but I could tell by the way his shoulders stiffened that this news immediately set him on his guard.

"Right," continued Celer, ducking to avoid a low beam, "which way is your roof?"

Cicero ushered the augur toward the stairs, and as he passed me he whispered urgently, "Go and find out what's going on, as quickly as you can. Take the boys. I need to know every clause."

I beckoned to Sositheus and Laurea to join me, and led by a couple of slaves with torches we set off down the hill. It was hard to find our way in the darkness and the ground was treacherous with snow. But as we came out into the Forum I saw a few lights glinting ahead, and we headed for those. Celer was right. A bill had been nailed up in its traditional place outside the Temple of Saturn. Despite the hour and the cold, such was the public excitement that a couple of dozen citizens had already gathered to read the text. It was very long, several thousand words, arranged on six large boards, and was proposed in the name of the tribune Rullus, although everyone knew that the authors were really Caesar and Crassus. I set Sositheus on the beginning part, Laurea on the end, while I took the middle.

We worked quickly, ignoring the people behind us complaining we were blocking their view, and by the time we had it all down the night was nearly over and the first day of the new year had arrived. Even without studying all the details I could tell it would cause Cicero great trouble. The republic's state land in Campania was to be compulsorily seized and divided into five thousand farms, which would be given away free. An elected commission of ten men would decide who got what, and would have sweeping powers to raise taxes abroad and buy and sell more land in

Italy as they saw fit, without reference to the Senate. The patricians would be incensed, and the timing of the promulgation—just hours before Cicero had to give his inaugural address—was obviously meant to put the maximum amount of pressure on the incoming consul.

When we got back to the house Cicero was still on the roof, seated for the first time on his ivory curule chair. It was bitterly cold up there, with snow still on the tiles and parapet. He was swaddled in a rug, almost up to his chin, and wore a curious hat made of rabbit fur, with flaps that covered his ears. Celer stood nearby with the pularii clustered around him. He was sectioning the sky with his wand, wearily checking the heavens for birds and lightning. But the air was very still and clear and he was obviously having no success. The instant Cicero saw me he seized the tablets with his mittened hands and began flicking through them rapidly. The hinged wooden frames clattered over, *click click click,* as he absorbed each page.

"Is it the populists' bill?" asked Celer, alerted by the noise and turning around.

"It is," replied Cicero, his eyes scanning the writing with great rapidity, "and they could not have designed a piece of legislation more likely to tear the republic apart."

"Will you have to respond to it in your inaugural address?" I asked.

"Of course. Why else do you think they've published it now?"

"They've certainly picked their moment well," said Celer. "A new consul. His first day in office. No military experience. No great family behind him. They're testing your mettle, Cicero." A shout came from down in the street. I looked over the parapet. A crowd was forming to escort Cicero to his inaugural. Across the valley, the temples of the Capitol were beginning to stand out sharply against the morning sky. "Was that lightning?" said Celer to the nearest sacred chicken keeper. "I hope to Jupiter it was. My balls are freezing off."

"If you saw lightning, augur," replied the chicken keeper, "lightning there must have been."

"Right, then, lightning it was, and on the left side, too. Write it down, boy. Congratulations, Cicero—a propitious omen. We'll be on our way." But Cicero seemed not to have heard. He was sitting motionless in his chair, staring straight ahead. Celer put his hand on his shoulder as he passed. "My cousin, Quintus Metellus, sends his regards, by the way, along with a gentle reminder that he's still outside the city waiting for that triumph you promised him in return for his vote. So is Licinius Lucullus, come to that. Don't forget they've hundreds of veterans they can call on. If this thing comes to civil war—as it may well—they're the ones who can come in and restore order."

"Thank you, Celer. Bringing soldiers into Rome—that's certainly the way to avoid civil war."

The remark was meant to be sarcastic, but sarcasm bounces off the Celers of this world like a child's arrow off armor. He left Cicero's roof with his self-importance quite undented. I asked Cicero if there was anything I could get him. "Yes," he said gloomily, "a new speech. Leave me alone for a while." I did as he asked and went downstairs, trying not to think about the task that now confronted him: speaking extempore to six hundred senators on a complicated bill he had only just seen, with the certainty that whatever he said was bound to infuriate one faction or the other. It was enough to turn my stomach liquid.

The house was filling quickly, not just with clients of Cicero's but with well-wishers walking in off the street. Cicero had ordered that no expense be spared on his inauguration, and whenever Terentia raised her concerns about the cost, he would always answer with a smile, "Macedonia will pay." So everyone who turned up was presented on arrival with a gift of figs and honey. Atticus, who was a leader of the Order of Knights, had brought a large detachment of Cicero's equestrian supporters; these, together with Cicero's closest colleagues in the Senate, marshaled by Quintus, were all being given mulled wine in the tablinum. Servius was not among them. I managed to tell both Atticus and Quintus that the populists' bill had been posted and that it was bad.

Meanwhile, the hired flautists were also enjoying the household's food and drink, as were the percussionists and dancers, the agents from the precincts and the tribal headquarters, and of course the officials who came with the consulship: the scribes, summoners, copyists, and criers from the Treasury, along with the twelve lictors provided by the Senate to ensure the consul's protection. All that was missing from the show was its leading actor, and as time went on it became harder and harder for me to explain his absence, for everyone by this time had heard of the bill and wanted to know what Cicero was planning to say about it. I could only reply that he was still taking the auspices and would be down directly. Terentia, decked out in her new jewels, hissed at me that I had better take control of the situation before the house was entirely stripped bare, and so I hit on the ruse of sending two slaves up to the roof to fetch the curule chair, with instructions to tell Cicero that the symbol of his authority was required to lead the procession—an excuse which also had the merit of being true.

This did the trick, and shortly afterward Cicero descended—divested, I was glad to see, of his rabbit fur hat. His appearance provoked a raucous cheer from the packed crowd, many of whom were now very merry on his mulled wine. Cicero handed me back the wax tablets on which the bill was written. "Bring them with you," he whispered. Then he climbed onto a chair, gave the company a cordial wave, and asked all those present who were on the staff of the Treasury to raise their hands. About two dozen did so; astonishing as it now seems, this was the total number of men who at that time administered the Roman Empire from its center.

"Gentlemen," he said, resting his hand on my shoulder, "this is Tiro, who has been my chief private secretary since before I was a senator. You are to regard an order from him as an order from me, and all business that is to be discussed with me may also be raised with him. I prefer written to oral reports. I rise early and work late. I won't tolerate bribes, or corruption in any form, or gossip. If you make a mistake, don't be afraid to tell me, but do it quickly. Remember that, and we shall get along well enough. And now: to business!"

After this little speech, which left me blushing, the lictors were handed their new rods along with a purse of money for each man, and finally Cicero's curule chair was brought down from the roof and displayed to the crowd. It drew gasps and a round of applause all to itself, as well it might, for it was carved from Numidian ivory, and had cost over a hundred thousand sesterces ("Macedonia will pay!"). Then everyone drank more wine—even little Marcus took some from an ivory beaker—the flute players started up, and we went out into the street to begin the long walk across the city.

It was still icy cold but the sun was coming up, breaking over the rooftops in lines of gold, and the effect of the light on the snow was to give Rome a celestial radiance such as I had never seen before. The lictors led the parade; four of them carried aloft the curule chair on an open litter. Cicero walked beside Terentia. Tullia was behind him, accompanied by her fiancé, Frugi. Quintus carried Marcus on his shoulders while on either side of the consular family marched the knights and the senators in gleaming white. The flutes piped, the drums beat, the dancers leaped. Citizens lined the streets and hung out of their windows to watch. There was much cheering and clapping, but also—to be honest—some booing, especially in the poorer parts of Subura, as we paraded along the Argiletum toward the Forum. Cicero nodded from side to side and occasionally raised his right hand in salute, but his expression was very grave, and I knew he must be turning over in his mind what lay ahead. In the period before a big speech a part of him was always unreachable. Occasionally I saw both Atticus and Quintus try to speak to him, but he shook his head, wishing to be left alone with his thoughts. When we reached the Forum it was packed with crowds. We passed the rostra and the empty Senate House and finally began our ascent of the Capitol. The smoke from the altar fires was curling above the temples. I could smell the saffron burning and hear the lowing of the bulls awaiting sacrifice. As we neared the Arch of Scipio I looked back and there was Rome—her hills and valleys, towers and temples, porticoes and houses all veiled white and sparkling with snow, like a bride in her gown awaiting her groom.

We entered the Area Capitolina to find the remainder of the Senate waiting for us, arrayed before the Temple of Jupiter. I was ushered along with Cicero's family and the rest of the household to the wooden stand that had been erected for spectators. A trumpet blast echoed off the walls, and the senators turned as one to watch as Cicero passed through their ranks—all those crafty faces, reddened by the cold, their covetous eyes studying the consul-elect: the men who had never won the consulship and knew they never would, the men who desired it and feared they might fail, and those who had held it once and still believed it was rightly theirs. Hybrida, Cicero's fellow consul, was already in position at the foot of the temple steps. Above the scene the great bronze roof looked molten in the brilliant winter sunshine. Without acknowledging each other, the two consuls-elect slowly mounted to the altar, where the chief priest, Metellus Pius, lay on a litter, too sick to get to his feet. Surrounding Pius were the six vestal virgins and the other fourteen pontiffs of the state religion. I could clearly make out Catulus, who had rebuilt the temple on behalf of the Senate and whose name appeared above the door ("greater than Jove," some wags called him in consequence). Next to him was Isauricus. I recognized also Scipio Nasica, Pius's adopted son; Junius Silanus, who was the husband of Servilia, the cleverest woman in Rome; and finally, standing slightly apart from the rest, incongruous in his priestly garments, I spotted the thin and broad-shouldered figure of Julius Caesar, but unfortunately I was too far away to read his expression.

There was a long silence. The trumpet sounded again. A huge creamy bull with red ribbons tied to its horns was led toward the altar. Cicero pulled up the folds of his toga to shroud his head, and then in a loud voice recited from memory the state prayer. The instant he had finished, the attendant stationed behind the bull felled it with such a hammer blow that the crack echoed around the portico. The creature crashed onto its side, and as the attendants sawed open its stomach the vision of the dead boy rose disconcertingly before my eyes. They had its entrails on the altar for inspection even before the wretched animal had died. There was a groan from the congregation, who interpreted the bull's thrashings as ill luck, but when the haruspices presented the liver to Cicero for his inspection they declared it unusually propitious. Pius—who was quite blind in any case—nodded weakly in agreement, the innards were flung on the fire, and the ceremony was over. The trumpet wailed into the cold clear air for a final time, a gust of applause carried across the enclosed space, and Cicero was consul.

The Senate's first session of the new year was always held in the Temple of Jupiter, with the consul's chair placed on a dais directly beneath the great bronze statue of the Father of the Gods. No citizen, however eminent, was permitted entry to the Senate unless he was a member. But because I had been charged by Cicero with making a shorthand record of proceedings—the first time this had ever been done—I was allowed to sit near him during debates. You may well imagine my feelings as I followed him up the wide aisle between the wooden benches. The white-robed senators poured in behind us, their animated speculation like the roar of an incoming tide. Who had read the populists' bill? Had anyone spoken to Caesar? What would Cicero say?

As the new consul reached the dais I turned to watch those figures I knew so well coming in to take their seats. To the right of the consular chair flowed the patrician faction—Catulus, Isauricus, Hortensius, and the rest—while to the left headed those who supported the populists' cause, notably Caesar and Crassus. I searched for Rullus, in whose name the bill had been laid, and spotted him with the other tribunes. Until very recently he had been just another rich young dandy, but now he had taken to wearing the clothes of a poor man and had grown a beard to show his populist sympathies. Farther along I saw Catilina fling himself

down on one of the front benches reserved for praetorians, his powerful
arms spread wide, his long legs outstretched. His expression was heavy
with thought; no doubt he was reflecting that but for Cicero it would
have been he in the consul's chair that day. His acolytes took their places
behind him—men like the bankrupt gambler Curius and the immensely
fat Cassius Longinus, whose flab occupied the space of two normal
senators.

I was so interested in noting who was present and how they were behaving that I briefly took my eyes off Cicero, and when I looked around
he had disappeared. I wondered if he might have gone outside to throw
up, which he often did when he was nervous before a difficult speech. But
when I went behind the dais I found him, hidden from view, standing at
the back of the statue of Jupiter, engaged in an intense discussion with
Hybrida. He was staring deep into Hybrida's bloodshot blue eyes, his
right hand gripping his colleague's shoulder, his left making forceful gestures. Hybrida was nodding slowly in response, as if dimly understanding
something. Finally a slow smile spread across his face. Cicero released him
and the two men shook hands, then they both stepped out from behind
the statue. Hybrida went off to take his place, while Cicero brusquely
asked if I had remembered the transcription of the bill. I replied that I
had. "Good," he said. "Then let us begin."

I found my place on a stool at the bottom of the dais, opened my
tablet, pulled out my stylus, and prepared to take down what would be
the first official shorthand record of a Senate session. Two other clerks,
trained by myself, were in position on either side of the chamber to tran-
scribe their own versions: afterward we would compare notes so as to
produce a complete summary. I still had no idea how Cicero was planning to handle the occasion. I knew he had been trying for days to craft a
speech appealing for consensus, but that it had proved so hopelessly bland
he had thrown away draft after draft in disgust. Nobody could be sure
how he was going to react. The anticipation in the chamber was intense.
When he mounted the dais the chatter dropped away at once, and one
could sense the entire Senate leaning forward to hear what he had to say.

"Gentlemen," he began, in his usual quiet manner of opening a speech,
"it is the custom that magistrates elected to this great office should start
with some expression of humility, recalling those ancestors of theirs who
have also held the rank, and expressing the hope that they may prove
worthy of their example. In my case such humility, I am pleased to say, is

not possible." That drew some laughter. "I am a new man," he proclaimed. "I owe my elevation not to family, or to name, or to wealth, or to military renown, but to the people of Rome, and as long as I hold this office I will be the people's consul."

It was a wonderful instrument, that voice of Cicero's, with its rich tone and its hint of a stutter—an impediment that somehow made each word seem fought for and more precious—and his words resonated in the hush like a message from Jove. Tradition demanded that he should talk first about the army, and as the great carved eagles looked down from the roof, he lauded the exploits of Pompey and the Eastern legions in the most extravagant terms, knowing his words would be relayed by the fastest means possible to the great general, who would study them with keen interest. The senators stamped their feet and roared in prolonged approval, for every man present knew that Pompey was the most powerful man in the world and no one, not even his jealous enemies among the patricians, wanted to seem reluctant in his praise.

"As Pompey upholds our republic abroad, so we must play our part here at home," continued Cicero, "resolute to protect its honor, wise in charting its course, just in pursuit of domestic harmony." He paused. "Now, you all know that this morning, before the sun had even risen, the bill of the tribune Servilius Rullus, for which we have been waiting so long, was finally posted in the Forum. And the moment I heard of this, by my instructions, a number of copyists came running up all together to bring an exact transcript of it to me." He stretched down his arm and I passed him the three wax tablets. My hand was shaking, but his never wavered as he held them aloft. "Here is the bill, and I earnestly assure you that I have examined it as carefully as is possible in the circumstances of today and in the time allowed me, and that I have reached a firm opinion."

He waited, and looked across the chamber—to Caesar in his place on the second bench, staring impassively at the consul, and to Catulus and the other patrician ex-consuls on the front bench opposite.

"It is nothing less," he said, "than a dagger, pointed toward the body politic, that we are being invited to plunge into our own heart!"

His words produced an immediate eruption—of shouted anger and dismissive gestures from the populists' benches and a low, masculine rumble of approval from the patricians'.

"A dagger," he repeated, "with a long blade." He licked his thumb and flicked open the first notebook. "Clause one, page one, line one. The election of the ten commissioners . . ."

In this way he cut straight through the posturing and sentiment to the nub of the issue, which was, as it always is: power. "Who proposes the commission?" he asked. "Rullus. Who determines who is to elect the commissioners? Rullus. Who summons the assembly to elect the commissioners? Rullus . . ." The patrician senators began joining in, chanting the unfortunate tribune's name after every question. "Who declares the results?"

"Rullus!" boomed the Senate.

"Who alone is guaranteed a place as a commissioner?"

"Rullus!"

"Who wrote the bill?"

"*Rullus!*" And the house collapsed in tears of laughter at its own wit, while poor Rullus flushed pink and looked this way and that as if seeking somewhere to hide. Cicero must have gone on for half an hour in this fashion, clause by clause, quoting the bill and mocking it and shredding it, in such savage terms that the senators around Caesar and on the tribunes' bench began to look distinctly grim. To think that he had had only an hour or so to collect his thoughts was marvelous. He denounced it as an attack on Pompey—who could not stand for election to the commission in absentia—and as an attempt to reestablish the kings in the guise of commissioners. He quoted freely from the bill—*"the ten commissioners shall settle any colonists they like in whatever towns and districts they choose, and assign them lands wherever they please"*—and made its bland language sound like a call for tyranny.

"What then? What kind of settlement will be made in those lands? What will be the method and arrangement of the whole affair? 'Colonies will be settled there,' Rullus says. Where? Of what kind of men? In what places? Did you, Rullus, think that we should hand over to you, and to the real architects of your schemes"—and here he pointed directly at Caesar and Crassus—"the whole of Italy unarmed, that you might strengthen it with garrisons, occupy it with colonies, and hold it bound and fettered by every kind of chain?"

There were shouts of "No!" and "Never!" from the patrician benches. Cicero extended his hand and averted his gaze from it, in the classic gesture of rejection. "Such things as these I will resist passionately and vigorously. Nor will I, while I am consul, allow men to set forth those plans against the state which they have long had in mind. I have decided to carry on my consulship in the only manner in which it can be conducted with dignity and freedom. I will never seek to obtain a province, any honors, any distinctions or advantage, nor anything that a tribune of the people can prevent me from obtaining."

He paused to emphasize his meaning. I had my head down, writing, but at that I looked up sharply. *"I will never seek to obtain a province."* Had he really just said that? I could not believe it. As the implications of his words sank in, the senators began to murmur.

"Yes," said Cicero, over the swelling notes of disbelief, "your consul, on this first of January, in a crowded Senate, declares that, if the republic continues in its present state, and unless some danger arises which he cannot honorably avoid meeting, he will not accept the government of a province."

I glanced across the aisle to where Quintus was sitting. He looked as if he had just swallowed a wasp. Macedonia—that shimmering prospect of wealth and luxury, of independence from a lifetime of drudgery in the law courts—was gone!

"Our republic has many hidden wounds," declared Cicero, in the somber tone he always used in peroration. "Many wicked designs of evil citizens are being formed. Yet there is no external danger. No king, no people, no nation is to be feared. The evil is confined entirely within our gates. It is internal and domestic. It is the duty of each of us to remedy it to the best of our power. If you promise me your zeal in upholding the common dignity, I will certainly fulfil the most ardent wish of the republic—that the authority of this order, which existed in the time of our ancestors, may now, after a long interval, be seen to be restored to the state." And with that he sat down.

Well, it certainly was a memorable address, and accorded with Cicero's first law of rhetoric, that a speech must always contain at least one surprise. But the shocks were not over yet. It was the custom when the presiding consul had finished his opening remarks for him to call next upon his colleague to give his opinion. The loud applause of the majority, and the catcalls from the benches around Catilina and Caesar, had barely died away, when Cicero shouted out, "The house recognizes Antonius Hybrida!"

Hybrida, who was sitting on the front bench nearest Cicero, glanced sheepishly across at Caesar, then got to his feet. "This bill that's been

proposed by Rullus—from what I've seen of it—I have to say—in my
opinion—given the state of the republic—it's really not such a good idea."
He opened and closed his mouth a couple of times. "So I'm against it," he
said, and sat down abruptly. After a moment's silence a great noise poured
out from the Senate, made up of all kinds of emotions—derision, anger,
pleasure, shock. It was clear that Cicero had just pulled off a remarkable
political coup, for everyone had taken it as certain that Hybrida would
support his allies the populists. Now he had reversed himself entirely, and
his motivation could not be more obvious—with Cicero ruling himself
out of the running for a province, Macedonia would be his after all! The
patrician senators on the benches behind Hybrida were leaning forward
and clapping him on the back in sarcastic congratulations, and he was
squirming at their taunts and looking nervously across the aisle at his
erstwhile friends. Catilina seemed stupefied, like a man turned to stone.
As for Caesar, he simply leaned back and folded his arms and studied the
ceiling of the temple, shaking his head and smiling slightly, while the
pandemonium continued.

The rest of the session was an anticlimax. Cicero worked his way down
the list of praetors and then began calling the former consuls, asking each
his opinion of Rullus's bill. They split exactly along factional lines. Cicero did not even call Caesar: he was still too junior, having not yet held
imperium. The only really menacing note was struck by Catilina. "You
have called yourself the people's consul," he sneered at Cicero, when at
long last his turn came to speak. "Well, we shall see what the people have
to say about that!" But the day belonged to the new consul, and when the
light began to fade and he declared the session adjourned until after the
Latin Festival, the patricians escorted him out of the temple and across
the city to his home as if he were one of their own, rather than a despised
"new man."

Cicero was in a great good humor as he stepped across the threshold,
for nothing is more pleasing in politics than to catch your opponents off
guard, and the defection of Hybrida was all that anyone could talk about.
Quintus, however, was furious, and the moment the house was at last
emptied of well-wishers, he turned on his brother with an anger I had
never before witnessed. It was all the more embarrassing because Atticus
and Terentia were also present.

"Why did you not consult any of us before giving away your province?" he demanded.

"What does it matter? The effect is what counts. You were sitting opposite them. Who did you think looked sicker—Caesar or Crassus?"

But Quintus was not to be deflected. "When was this decided?"

"To be honest, I've had it in mind ever since I drew the lot for Macedonia."

At this, Quintus threw up his hands in exasperation. "Do you mean to say that when we were talking to you last night, you'd already made up your mind?"

"More or less."

"But why didn't you tell us?"

"First, because I knew you'd disagree. Second, because I thought there was still just a chance Caesar might produce a bill I could support. And third, because what I choose to do with my province is my business."

"No, it's not just *your* business, Marcus, it's *our* business. How are we to pay off our debts without the income from Macedonia?"

"You mean, how are *you* to finance *your* campaign for the praetorship this summer?"

"That's unfair!"

Cicero seized Quintus's hand. "Brother, listen to me, you will have your praetorship. And you won't acquire it through bribery, but through the good name of the Cicero family, which will make the triumph all the sweeter. You must see I had to separate Hybrida from Caesar and the tribunes? My only hope of piloting the republic through this storm is to keep the Senate united. I can't have my colleague plotting behind my back. Macedonia had to go." He appealed to Atticus and Terentia. "Who wants to govern a province, in any case? You know I couldn't bear to leave you all behind in Rome."

"And what's to stop Hybrida simply taking Macedonia off you and supporting the prosecution of Rabirius?" persisted Quintus.

"Why would he bother? His only reason for joining their schemes was money. Now he can pay off his debts without them. Besides, nothing's signed and sealed—I can always change my mind. And meanwhile by this noble gesture I show the people I'm a man of principle who puts the welfare of the republic ahead of his own personal gain."

Quintus looked at Atticus. Atticus shrugged. "The logic is sound," he said.

"And what do you think, Terentia?" asked Quintus.

Cicero's wife had kept very quiet, which was unlike her. Even now she did not say anything but continued to stare at her husband, who stared back at her impassively. Slowly, she reached up to her hair, and from those tight, dark curls, she plucked the diadem that was fastened there. Still without taking her eyes from Cicero's face, she removed the necklace from her throat, unclipped the emerald brooch from her breast, and slid the gold bracelets from each of her wrists. Finally, grimacing with the effort, she pulled the rings off her fingers. When she had finished, she cupped all this newly purchased jewelry in her two hands and let it fall. The glittering gems and precious metal scattered noisily across the mosaic floor. Then she turned and walked out of the room.

IV

WE HAD TO leave Rome at first light the next morning, part of that great exodus of magistrates, their families, and retainers required to attend the Latin Festival on the Alban Mount. Terentia accompanied her husband, and the atmosphere between them inside their carriage was as chilly as the January mountain air outside. The consul kept me busy, dictating first a long dispatch to Pompey, describing political affairs in Rome, and then a series of shorter letters to each of the provincial governors, while Terentia kept her eyes averted from him and pretended to sleep. The children traveled with their nurse in another carriage. Behind us stretched a great convoy of vehicles conveying the elected rulers of Rome—first Hybrida and then the praetors: Celer, Cosconius, Pompeius Rufus, Pomptinus, Roscius, Sulpicius, Valerius Flaccus. Only Lentulus Sura, as urban praetor, stayed behind in the city to guard its welfare. "The place will burn to the ground," observed Cicero, "with that idiot in charge."

We reached Cicero's house at Tusculum early in the afternoon, but there was little time to rest, as he had to leave almost at once to judge the local athletes. The highlight of the Latin Games was traditionally the swinging competition, with so many points awarded for height, so many for style, and so many for strength. Cicero had not a clue which competitor was the best, and so ended up announcing that all were equally worthy victors and that he would award a prize to everyone, paid for out of his own pocket. This gesture won warm applause from the assembled country folk. As he rejoined Terentia in the carriage I heard her remark to him, "Presumably Macedonia will pay?" He laughed, and that was the beginning of a thaw between them.

The main ceremony took place at sunset on the summit of the mountain, which was accessible only by a steep and twisting road. As the sun sank it grew brutally cold. Snow lay ankle-deep on the rocky ground. Cicero walked at the head of the procession, surrounded by his lictors. Slaves carried torches. From all the branches of the trees and in the bushes the

locals had hung small figures or faces made of wood or wool, a reminder
of a time when human sacrifice had been practiced and a young boy
would be strung up to speed the end of winter. There was something in-
describably melancholy about the whole scene—the bitter chill, the gathering twilight, and those sinister emblems rustling and turning in the
wind. On the highest piece of ground the altar fire spat out orange sparks
against the stars. An ox was sacrificed to Jupiter, and libations of milk
from the nearby farms were also offered. "Let the people refrain from
strife and quarreling," proclaimed Cicero, and the traditional words
seemed weighted with an extra meaning that evening.

By the time the ceremony was over an immense full moon had risen
like a blue sun and was casting an unhealthy light across the scene. It did
at least have the merit of illuminating our path very clearly as we turned
to descend, but then occurred two events which were to be talked about
for weeks afterward. First, the moon was suddenly and inexplicably blot-
ted out, exactly as if it had been plunged into a black pool, and the procession, which had been relying on its light, was obliged to come to an
abrupt and undignified halt while more torches were lit. The interruption
did not last long, but it is strange how being stranded on a mountain path
in darkness can work on one's imagination, especially if the vegetation
around one is sewn with hanging effigies. Quite a few voices were raised
in panic, not least when it was realized that all the other stars and constel-
lations were still shimmering brightly. I raised my eyes to the heavens
with the rest, and that was when we saw a shooting star—pointed at the
tip like a flaming spear—spurt across the night sky to the west, exactly in
the direction of Rome, where it faded and vanished. Loud exclamations
of wonder were followed by more mutterings in the dark as to what all
this portended.

Cicero said nothing but waited patiently for the procession to resume.
Later that night, after we had safely reached Tusculum, I asked him what
he made of it all. "Nothing," he replied, warming his chilled bones at the
fire. "Why should I? The moon went behind a cloud and a star crossed
the sky. What else is there to be said?"

The following morning a message arrived from Quintus, who was
looking after Cicero's interests back in Rome. Cicero read the letter and
then showed it to me. It reported that a great wooden cross had been
erected on the Field of Mars, rising up starkly over the snowy plain, and
that the plebs were flocking out of the city to look at it. "Labienus is go-

ing around openly saying that the cross is for Rabirius, and that the old man will be hanging from it by the end of the month. You should return as soon as possible."

"I will say one thing for Caesar," said Cicero. "He doesn't waste much time. His court hasn't even heard any evidence yet, but he wants to keep up the pressure on me." He stared into the fire. "Is the messenger still here?"

"He is."

"Send a note ahead to Quintus and tell him we'll be back by nightfall, and another to Hortensius. Say I appreciated his visit the other day. Tell him I have thought the matter over and I shall be delighted to appear beside him in defense of Gaius Rabirius." He nodded to himself. "If it's a fight Caesar wants, he shall have one." When I reached the door he called me back. "Also, send one of the slaves to find Hybrida, and ask him if he would care to travel back with me in my carriage to Rome, to settle our arrangement. I need to have something in writing before Caesar gets to him and persuades him to change his mind."

Thus I found myself later that day seated opposite one consul and next to the other, trying to write down the terms of their agreement as we bounced along the Via Latina. An escort of lictors rode ahead of us. Hybrida brought out a small flask of wine from which he took regular nips, occasionally offering it with a shaky hand to Cicero, who declined politely. I had never seen him for an extended period at such close quarters before. His once noble nose was red and squashed—broken in battle, he always claimed, but everyone knew he had gotten it in a tavern brawl— his cheeks were purple, and his breath smelled so strongly of drink I felt I should go dizzy from the fumes. *Poor Macedonia,* I thought, *to have such a creature as its governor.* Cicero proposed that they should simply swap provinces, which would save having to put the matter to a vote in the Senate. ("As you want," said Hybrida. "You're the lawyer.") In return for receiving Macedonia, Hybrida undertook to oppose the populists' bill and to support the defense of Rabirius. He also agreed to pay Cicero one-quarter of the revenue he derived as governor. Cicero, for his part, promised to do his best to ensure that Hybrida's term was extended to two or three years, and to act as his defense counsel in the event that he was afterward prosecuted for corruption. He hesitated over this last condition, as the chances of Hybrida being put on trial, given his character, were plainly high, but in the end he gave an undertaking and I wrote it down.

When the haggling was concluded, Hybrida produced his flask again, and this time Cicero consented to take a sip. I could tell by his expression that the wine was undiluted and not to his taste, but he pretended to find it pleasant, and then the two consuls settled back in their seats, seemingly satisfied at a job well done.

"I always thought," said Hybrida, suppressing a burp, "that you rigged that ballot for our provinces."

"How could I have done that?"

"Oh, there are plenty of ways, as long as the consul's in on it. You can have the winning token hidden in your palm and substitute it for the one you draw. Or the consul can do it for you when he announces what you've got. So you really didn't do that?"

"No," said Cicero, slightly affronted. "Macedonia was mine by right."

"Is that a fact?" Hybrida grunted and raised his flask. "Well, we've fixed it now. Let's drink to fate."

We had reached the plain, and the fields beyond the road stretched flat and bare. Hybrida started humming to himself.

"Tell me, Hybrida," said Cicero after a while, "did you lose a boy a few days ago?"

"A what?"

"A boy. About twelve years old."

"Oh, him," replied Hybrida, in an offhand way, as if he were in the regular habit of losing boys. "You heard about that?"

"I didn't just hear about it, I saw what was done to him." Cicero was suddenly staring at Hybrida with great intensity. "As a mark of our new friendship will you tell me what happened?"

"I'm not sure I should do that." Hybrida gave Cicero a crafty look. Drunkard he might have been, but he was not without cunning, even in his cups. "You've said some hard things about me in the past. I've got to get used to trusting you."

"If you mean by that remark, will anything you say privately go beyond the two of us, let me put your mind at ease. We are now bound together, Hybrida, whatever may have happened between us earlier. I shan't do anything to jeopardize our alliance, which is at least as precious to me as it is to you, even if you tell me you killed the boy yourself. But I feel I need to know."

"Very prettily put." Hybrida burped again and nodded to me. "And the slave?"

"He is utterly trustworthy."

"Then have another drink," said Hybrida, once more holding out the flask, and when Cicero hesitated he shook it in his face. "Go on. I can't abide a man who stays sober while others drink." So Cicero swallowed his distaste and took another gulp of wine while Hybrida described what had happened to the boy as cheerfully as if he were relating a tale from a hunting trip. "He was a Smyrnan. Very musical. I forget his name. He used to sing to my guests at dinner. I lent him to Catilina for a party just after Saturnalia." He took another swig. "Catilina really hates you, doesn't he?"

"I expect so."

"Me, I'm easier by nature. But Catilina? Oh no! He's a Sergius through and through. Can't bear the thought that he was beaten to the consulship by a common man, and a provincial to boot." He pursed his lips and shook his head. "After you won the election, I swear he lost his mind. Anyway, at this party he was pretty wild and, to cut a long tale short, he suggested we should swear an oath, a sacred oath, which required a sacrifice appropriate to the undertaking. He had my boy summoned, and told him to start singing. And then he got behind him, and"—Hybrida made a sweeping gesture with his fist—"bang. That was it. Quick at least. The rest I didn't stay for."

"Are you telling me Catilina killed the boy?"

"He split his skull."

"Dear gods! A Roman senator! Who else was present?"

"Oh, you know—Longinus, Cethegus, Curius. The usual gang."

"So four members of the Senate—five, including you?"

"You can leave me out of it. I was sickened, I can tell you. That lad cost me thousands."

"And what kind of oath 'appropriate' to such an abomination did he have you all swear?"

"Actually, it was to kill you," said Hybrida cheerfully and raised his flask. "Your health." And he burst out laughing. He laughed so much, he spluttered the wine. It leaked from his battered nose and trickled down his stubbled chin and stained the front of his toga. He brushed at it ineffectively, and then very gradually the motions ceased. His hand dropped, he slowly nodded forward, and very soon after that he fell asleep.

• • •

This was the first occasion on which Cicero heard of any conspiracy against him, and to begin with he was unsure how to respond. Was it just some piece of drunken, bestial debauchery, or was it to be taken as a serious threat? As Hybrida started snoring he gave me a look of infinite revulsion and passed the remainder of the journey in silence with his arms folded, a brooding expression on his face. As for Hybrida, he slept all the way to Rome, so deeply that when we reached his house he had to be lifted out of the carriage by the lictors and laid out in the vestibule. His slaves seemed entirely used to receiving their master in this fashion, and as we left, one was tipping a jug of water over the consul's head.

Quintus and Atticus were waiting when we arrived home, and Cicero quickly told them what he had heard from Hybrida. Quintus was all for making the story public at once, but Cicero was not convinced. "And then what?" he asked.

"The law should be allowed to take its course. The perpetrators must be publicly accused, prosecuted, disgraced, and exiled."

"No," said Cicero. "A prosecution would stand no chance of success. First, who would be mad enough to bring one? And if, by a miracle, some brave and foolhardy soul were willing to take on Catilina, where would he find the evidence for a conviction? Hybrida will refuse to be a witness, even with a promise of immunity—you may be sure of that. He'll simply deny the whole thing ever happened, and break off his alliance with me. And the corpse has gone, remember? Indeed there are witnesses to the fact I've already made a speech assuring the people there has been no ritual killing!"

"So we do nothing?"

"No, we watch, and we wait. We need to get a spy in Catilina's camp. He won't trust Hybrida anymore."

"We should also take extra precautions," said Atticus. "How long do you have the lictors?"

"Until the end of January, when Hybrida starts his term as president of the Senate. They come back to me again in March."

"I suggest we ask for volunteers from the Order of Knights to protect you in public while they're not around."

"A private bodyguard? People will say I'm putting on airs. It will have to be done discreetly."

"It will be, don't worry. I'll arrange it."

So it was agreed, and in the meantime Cicero set about trying to find an agent who might gain the confidence of Catilina, and who could then report back in secret on what he was up to. He first broached the matter a couple of days later with young Rufus. He summoned him to the house and began by apologizing for his rudeness after dinner. "You must understand, my dear Rufus," he explained, walking him around the atrium with his arm across his shoulders, "that it is one of the failings of the old always to see the young for what they were rather than for what they have become. I treated you as that tearaway who came into my household as a boy three years ago, whereas I now realize you are a man of nearly twenty, making his way in the world and deserving of greater respect. I am truly sorry for any offense and hope none has been taken."

"The fault was mine," responded Rufus. "I won't pretend I agree with your policies. But my love and respect for you is unshaken, and I won't allow myself to think ill of you again."

"Good lad." Cicero pinched his cheek. "Did you hear that, Tiro? He loves me! So you wouldn't want to kill me?"

"Kill you? Of course not! Whatever made you think I would?"

"Others who share your views have talked of killing me—Catilina to name but one," and he described to Rufus the killing of Hybrida's slave and the terrible oath Catilina had made his confederates swear.

"Are you certain?" asked Rufus. "I've never heard him mention such a thing."

"Well, he has undoubtedly spoken of his desire to murder me—Hybrida assures me of it—and if ever he does again, I'd like to think you'd give me warning."

"Oh, I see," said Rufus, looking at Cicero's hand on his shoulder. "That's why you've brought me up here—to ask me to be your spy."

"Not a spy, a loyal citizen. Or has our republic sunk to such a level that killing a consul comes second to friendship?"

"I'd neither kill a consul nor betray a friend," replied Rufus, detaching himself from Cicero's embrace, "which is why I'm glad that the shadow over our friendship has been lifted."

"An excellent lawyer's answer. I taught you better than I realized."

After he had gone, Cicero said thoughtfully, "That young man is on his way to repeat every word I've just said to Catilina"—an observation which may well have been true, for certainly from that day onward Rufus kept clear of Cicero but was often to be seen in Catilina's company. It was an ill-assorted gang he had joined: high-spirited youngbloods like Corne-

lius Cethegus, out for a fight; aging and dissolute noblemen like Marcus
Laeca and Autronius Paetus, whose public careers had been frustrated by
their private vices; mutinous ex-soldiers led by rabble-rousers like Gaius
Manlius, who had been a centurion under Sulla. What bound them together was loyalty to Catilina—who could be quite charming when he
was not trying to kill you—and a desire to see the existing state of affairs
in Rome smashed to pieces. Twice when Cicero had to address public assemblies, as part of his opposition to Rullus's bill, they set up a constant
racket of jeers and whistles, and I was glad that Atticus had made arrangements to protect him, especially as the Rabirius affair was now catching
fire.

Rullus's bill, Rabirius's prosecution, Catilina's death threat—you must
remember that Cicero was having to contend with all these three at once,
as well as coping with the general business of running the Senate. Histo-
rians in my opinion often overlook this aspect of politics. Problems do
not queue up outside a statesman's door, waiting to be solved in an or-
derly fashion, chapter by chapter, as the books would have us believe;
instead they crowd in en masse, demanding attention. Hortensius, for
example, arrived to discuss tactics for the defense of Rabirius only a few
hours after Cicero had been howled down at the public assembly on
Rullus's bill. And there was a further consequence of this overwork. Because Cicero was so preoccupied, Hortensius, who had little else to do,
had effectively taken control of the case. Settling himself in Cicero's study
and looking very pleased with himself, he announced that the matter was
solved.

"Solved?" repeated Cicero. "How?"

Hortensius smiled. He had employed a team of scribes, he said, to
gather evidence, and they had turned up the intriguing fact that a ruffian
named Scaeva, the slave of a senator, Quintus Croton, had been given his
freedom immediately after Saturninus's murder. The scribes had inquired
further in the state archives. According to Scaeva's papers of manumission, he was the one who had "struck the fatal blow" that killed Saturninus, and for this "patriotic act" he had been rewarded with his liberty by
the Senate. Both Scaeva and Croton were long since dead, but Catulus,
once his memory had been jogged, claimed to remember the incident
well enough and had sworn an affidavit that after Saturninus had been
stoned unconscious, he had seen Scaeva climb down to the floor of the
Senate House and finish him off with a knife.

"And that," said Hortensius in conclusion, passing Catulus's affidavit to Cicero, "I think you will agree, destroys Labienus's case against our client and, with a bit of luck, will bring this wretched business to a swift conclusion." He sat back in his chair and looked about him with an air of great satisfaction. "Don't tell me you disagree?" he added, noticing Cicero's frown.

"In principle of course you are right. But I wonder in practice whether this will help us much."

"Of course it will! Labienus has no case left. Even Caesar will have to concede that. Really, Cicero," he said with a smile and the tiniest wag of a manicured finger, "I could almost believe you're jealous."

Cicero remained unconvinced. "Well, we shall see," he remarked to me after this conference. "But I fear Hortensius has no idea of the forces ranged against us. He still imagines Caesar to be just another ambitious young senator on the make. He has not yet glimpsed his depths."

Sure enough, on the very day Hortensius submitted his evidence to Caesar's special court, Caesar and his fellow judge—his elder cousin—without even hearing any witnesses pronounced Rabirius guilty and sentenced him to death by crucifixion. The news spread through Rome's cramped streets like a firestorm, and it was a very different Hortensius who appeared in Cicero's study the following morning.

"The man is a monster! A complete and utter swine!"

"And how has our unfortunate client reacted?"

"He doesn't yet know what's happened. It seemed kinder not to tell him."

"So now what do we do?"

"We have no alternative. We appeal."

Hortensius duly lodged an immediate appeal with the urban praetor, Lentulus Sura, who in turn referred the question to an assembly of the people, summoned for the following week on the Field of Mars. This was ideal terrain from the prosecution's point of view: not a court with a respectable jury, but a great swirling multitude of citizens. To enable them all to vote on Rabirius's fate, the entire proceedings would have to be crammed into one short winter's day. And as if that wasn't enough, Labienus was also able to use his powers as tribune to stipulate that no defense speech should last for longer than half an hour. On hearing of this restriction, Cicero observed, "Hortensius needs half an hour merely to clear his throat!" and as the date of the hearing drew closer, he and his fellow counsel bickered more frequently. Hortensius saw the matter in purely legal terms. The main thrust of his speech, he declared, would be to establish that the real killer of Saturninus was Scaeva. Cicero disagreed, seeing the trial as wholly political. "This isn't a court," he reminded Hortensius. "This is the mob. Do you seriously imagine, in all the noise and excitement, with thousands of people milling about, that anybody is going to care a fig that the actual fatal blow was struck by some wretched slave who's been dead for years?"

"What line would you take, then?"

"I think we must concede at the outset that Rabirius was the killer, and claim that the action was legally sanctioned."

Hortensius threw up his hands. "Really, Cicero, I know you've a reputation as a tricky fellow and all that, but now you're simply being perverse."

"And I'm afraid you spend too much time on the Bay of Naples talking to your fish. You no longer know this city as I do."

Unable to reach an agreement, they decided that Hortensius would speak first and Cicero last, and each would argue as he pleased. I was glad that Rabirius was too feebleminded to grasp what was going on, because otherwise he would have been in despair, especially as Rome was anticipating his trial as if it were a circus. The cross on the Field of Mars had become a regular meeting place and was festooned with placards demanding justice, land, and bread. Labienus also got hold of a bust of Saturninus and set it up on the rostra, garlanded with laurel. It did not help that Rabirius had a reputation as a vicious old skinflint; even his adopted son was a moneylender. Cicero was in no doubt that the verdict would go against Rabirius, and decided at least to try to save his life. He therefore laid an emergency resolution before the Senate reducing the penalty for perduellio from crucifixion to exile. Thanks to Hybrida's support, this was narrowly passed, despite angry opposition from Caesar and the tribunes. Metellus Celer went out of the city late that night with a party of slaves and tore down the cross, smashed it up, and burned it.

This, then, was how matters stood on the morning of the trial. Even as Cicero was checking his speech and dressing to go down to the Field of Mars, Quintus turned up in his chamber and urged his brother to withdraw as defense counsel. He had done all he could, argued Quintus, and would only suffer an unnecessary loss of prestige when Rabirius was found guilty. It might also be physically dangerous for him to confront the populists outside the city walls. I could see that Cicero was tempted by these arguments. But not the least of the reasons why I loved him, despite his faults, was that he possessed that most attractive form of courage: the bravery of a nervous man. After all, any rash fool can be a hero if he sets no value on his life or hasn't the wit to appreciate danger. But to understand the risks, perhaps even to flinch at first, but then to summon the strength to face them down—that in my opinion is the most commendable form of valor, and that was what Cicero displayed that day.

Labienus was already in place on the platform when we reached the Field of Mars, alongside his precious stage prop, the bust of Saturninus. He was an ambitious soldier, one of Pompey's fellow countrymen from Picenum, and he affected to copy the great general in all things—his girth, his swaggering gait, even his hair, which he wore swept back in a Pompeian wave. When he saw Cicero and his lictors approaching, he put his fingers in his mouth and let out a derisive whistle, and this was taken up by the crowd, which must have numbered about ten thousand. It was an intimidating noise, and it intensified as Hortensius appeared leading Rabirius by the hand. The old fellow did not look frightened so much as bewildered by the racket and the numbers pressing forward to get a glimpse of him. I was pushed and shoved as I struggled to stay close to Cicero. I noticed a line of legionnaires, their helmets and breastplates glinting in the bright January light, and behind them, sitting in a stand on a row of seats reserved for distinguished spectators, the military commanders Quintus Metellus, conqueror of Crete, and Licinius Lucullus, Pompey's predecessor in the East. Cicero made a face at me when he saw them, for he had promised both aristocratic generals triumphs in return for their support at election time and had so far done nothing about it.

"It must be a crisis," Cicero whispered to me, "if Lucullus has left his palace on the Bay of Naples to mingle with the common herd!"

He clambered up the ladder onto the platform, along with Hortensius and finally Rabirius, who had such difficulty mounting the rungs his advocates finally had to reach down and haul him up. All three glistened with the spittle that had been showered on them. Hortensius looked especially appalled, for obviously he had not realized how unpopular the Senate had become in that hard winter. The orators sat down on their bench with Rabirius between them. A trumpet sounded, and across the river the red flag was hoisted over the hill of Janiculum to signal that the city was in no peril of assault and the assembly could begin.

As the presiding magistrate, Labienus both controlled proceedings and acted as prosecutor, and this gave him a tremendous advantage. A bully by nature, he elected to speak first and was soon shouting abuse at Rabirius, who sank lower and lower in his seat. He did not bother to summon witnesses. He did not need to: he had the votes already. He finished with a stern peroration about the arrogance of the Senate and the greed of the small clique that controlled it, and the necessity to make a harsh example of Rabirius, so that never in the future would any consul dare to imagine he could sanction the murder of a fellow citizen and hope to escape unpunished. The crowd roared in agreement. "I realized then," Cicero confided in me afterward, "with the force of a revelation, that the true target of this lynch mob of Caesar's was not Rabirius at all but me, as consul, and that somehow I had to regain control of the situation before my authority to deal with the likes of Catilina was destroyed entirely."

Hortensius went next and did his best, but those great orotund purple passages for which he was so famous belonged to another setting—and, in truth, another era. He was past fifty, had more or less retired, was out of practice—and it showed. Some in the audience near the platform actually began to talk over him, and I was close enough to see the panic in his face as Hortensius gradually realized that he—the great Hortensius, the Dancing Master, the King of the Law Courts—was actually losing his audience! The more frantically he flung out his arms and patrolled the platform and swiveled his noble head, the more risible he seemed. Nobody was interested in his arguments. I could not hear all of what he said, as the din was tremendous, with thousands of citizens milling around and chatting to one another while they waited to vote. He broke off, sweating despite the cold, and wiped his face with his handkerchief, then called his witnesses, first Catulus and next Isauricus. Each came up to the platform and was heard respectfully. But the moment Hortensius resumed his speech the racket of conversation started up again. By then he could have combined the tongue of Demosthenes with the wit of Plautus—it would not have made a difference. Cicero stared straight ahead into the din, white-faced, immobile, as if chiseled out of marble.

At length Hortensius sat down and it was Cicero's turn to speak. Labienus called on him to address the assembly, but such was the volume of noise he did not rise at first. Instead he examined his toga carefully and brushed away a few invisible specks. The hubbub continued. He checked his fingernails. He folded his arms. He looked around him. He waited. It went on a long time. And amazingly, a kind of sullen, respectful silence did eventually fall over the Field of Mars. Only then did Cicero nod, as if in approval, and slowly get to his feet.

"Although it is not my habit, fellow citizens," he said, "to begin a speech by explaining why I am appearing on behalf of a particular individual, nonetheless, in defending the life, the honor, and the fortunes of Gaius Rabirius I consider it my duty to lay before you an explanation. For this trial is not really about Rabirius—old, infirm, and friendless as he is. This trial, gentlemen, is nothing less than an attempt to ensure that from now on there should be no central authority in the state, no concerted action of good citizens against the frenzy and audacity of wicked men, no refuge for the republic in emergencies, and no security for its welfare. Since this is so," he continued, his voice becoming louder, his hands and his gaze rising slowly to the heavens, "I beg of most high and mighty Jupiter and all the other immortal gods and goddesses to grant me their grace and favor, and I pray that by their will this day that has dawned may see the salvation of my client and the rescue of the constitution!"

Cicero used to say that the bigger a crowd the more stupid it is, and that a useful trick with an immense multitude is always to call on the supernatural. His words carried like a rolling drum across the hushed plain. There was still some chatter at the periphery, but it was too far away to drown him out.

"Labienus, you summon this assembly as a great populist. But of the two of us, which is really the people's friend? You, who think it right to threaten Roman citizens even in the midst of their assembly with the executioner; who, on the Field of Mars, gives orders for the erection of a cross for the punishment of citizens? Or I, who refuse to allow this assembly to be defiled by the presence of the executioner? What a friend of the people our tribune is, what a guardian and defender of its rights and liberties!"

Labienus waved his hand at Cicero, as if he were a horsefly to be swiped away, but there was petulance in the gesture: like all bullies, he was better at handing out injuries than absorbing them.

"You maintain," continued Cicero, "that Gaius Rabirius killed Lucius Saturninus, a charge which Quintus Hortensius, in the course of his most ample defense, has proved to be false. But if it were up to me, I would brave this charge. In fact I would admit it. I would plead guilty to it!" A rumble of anger began to spread among the crowd, but Cicero shouted over their jeers. "Yes, yes, I would admit it! I only wish I could proclaim that my client's *was* the hand that struck down that public enemy Saturninus!" He pointed dramatically at the bust, and it was some while before he could carry on, such was the volume of the hostility directed at him. "You say your uncle was there, Labienus. Well, suppose he was. And suppose he was there not because his ruined fortunes left him no choice, but because his intimacy with Saturninus led him to put his friend before his country. Was that a reason why Gaius Rabirius should desert the republic and disobey the command and authority of the consul? What should I do, gentlemen, if Labienus, like Saturninus, caused a massacre of the citizens, broke from prison, and seized the Capitol with an armed force? I tell you what I should do. I should do as the consul did then. I should bring a motion before the Senate, exhort you to defend the republic, and take arms myself to oppose, with your help, an armed enemy. And what would Labienus do? *He would have me crucified!*"

Yes, it was a brave performance, and I hope I have given here some flavor of the scene: the orators on the platform with their querulous client, the lictors lined up around the base to protect the consul, the teeming citizenry of Rome—plebs and knights and senators all pressed together—the legionnaires in their plumed helmets and the generals in their scarlet cloaks, the sheep pens set out and made ready for the vote; the noise of it, the temples gleaming on the distant Capitol, and the bitter January cold. I kept a lookout for Caesar, and occasionally I thought I glimpsed his lean face peering from the crowd. Catilina was certainly there with his claque, including Rufus, who was yelling his share of insults at his former patron. Cicero finished, as he always did, by standing with his hand on the shoulder of his client and appealing for the mercy of the court—"he does not ask you to grant him a happy life but only an honorable death"—and then it was all over and Labienus gave orders for the voting to begin.

Cicero commiserated with the dejected Hortensius, then jumped down from the platform and came over to where I was standing. He was still full of fire as always after a big speech, breathing deeply, his eyes shining, his nostrils flared, like a horse at the end of a grueling race. It had been a stirring performance. I remember one phrase in particular: "Narrow indeed are the bounds within which Nature has confined our lives, but those of our glory are infinite." Unfortunately, fine words are no substitute for votes, and when Quintus joined us he announced grimly that all was lost. He had just come from observing the first ballots cast—the centuries were voting unanimously to condemn Rabirius, which meant that the old man would be obliged to leave Italy immediately, his house would be pulled down, and all his property confiscated.

"This is a tragedy," swore Cicero.

"You did your best, Brother. At least he is an old man and has lived his life."

"I'm not thinking of Rabirius, you idiot, but of my consulship!"

Just as he was speaking, we heard a shout and a scream. A scuffle had started nearby, and when we turned we could clearly see the tall figure of Catilina in the thick of it, laying about him with his fists. Some of the legionnaires ran to separate the combatants. Beyond them, Metellus and Lucullus had risen to their feet to watch. The augur, Celer, who was standing beside his cousin Metellus, had his hands cupped to his mouth and was urging the soldiers on. "Just look at Celer there," said Cicero, with a hint of admiration, "simply itching to join in. He loves a fight!" He became thoughtful and then said suddenly, "I'm going to talk to him."

He set off so abruptly that his lictors had to scramble to get ahead of him to clear a path. When the two generals saw the consul approaching they glowered at him. Both had been stuck outside the city for a long while waiting for the Senate to vote them their triumphs—years, in the case of Lucullus, who had whiled away his time building a vast retreat at Misenum on the Bay of Naples as well as his mansion north of Rome. But the Senate was reluctant to accede to their demands, chiefly because both had quarreled with Pompey. So they were trapped. Only holders of imperium could have a triumph, but entering Rome to argue for a triumph would automatically end their imperium. One could sympathize with their frustration.

"Imperator," said Cicero, raising his hand in salute to each man in turn. "Imperator."

"We have matters we need to discuss with you," began Metellus in a menacing tone.

"I know exactly what you are about to say and I assure you I shall keep my promise and argue your case in the Senate to the full extent of my powers. But that's for another day. Do you see how hard-pressed I am at the moment? I need some assistance, not for my sake but for the nation's. Celer, will you help me save the republic?"

Celer exchanged glances with his cousin. "I don't know. That depends on what you want me to do."

"It's dangerous work," warned Cicero, knowing full well this would make the challenge irresistible to a man such as Celer.

"I've never been called a coward. Tell me."

"I want you to take a detachment of your cousin's excellent legionnaires, cross the river, climb the Janiculum, and haul down the flag."

Even Celer swayed back on his heels at that, for the lowering of the flag—signaling the approach of an enemy army—would automatically suspend the assembly, and the Janiculum was always heavily protected by guards. Both he and his cousin turned to Lucullus, the senior of the trio, and I watched as that elegant patrician calculated the odds. "It's a fairly desperate trick, Consul," he said.

"It is. But if we lose this vote, it will be a disaster for Rome. No consul will ever again be sure he has the authority to suppress an armed rebellion. I don't know why Caesar wishes to set such a precedent, but I do know we can't afford to let him."

In the end, it was Metellus who said, "He's right, Lucius. Let's give him the men. Quintus," he said to Celer, "are you willing?"

"Of course."

"Good," said Cicero. "The guards should obey you as praetor, but in case they make trouble, I'll send my secretary with you," and to my dismay he pulled his ring from his finger and pressed it into my hand. "You're to tell the commander the consul says an enemy threatens Rome," he said to me, "and the flag must be lowered. My ring is the proof you are my emissary. Do you think you can do that?"

I nodded. What else could I do? Metellus meanwhile was beckoning to the centurion who had weighed in against Catilina, and very soon afterward I found myself panting along behind a contingent of thirty legionnaires, their swords drawn, moving at the double, with Celer and the centurion at their head. Our mission—let us be frank about this—was to disrupt the Roman people in a lawful assembly, and I remember thinking, *Never mind Rabirius,* this *is treason.* We left the Field of Mars and trotted across the Sublician Bridge, over the swollen brown waters of the Tiber, then traversed the flat plain of the Vaticanum, which was filled with the squalid tents and small makeshift huts of the homeless. At the foot of the Janiculum the crows of Juno watched from the bare branches of their sacred grove—such a mass of gnarled black shapes that when we passed and sent them crying into the air it was as if the very wood itself had taken flight. We toiled on up the road to the summit, and never did a hill seem so steep. Even as I write, I can feel again the thump of my heart and the searing of my lungs as I sobbed for breath. The pain in my side was as sharp as a spear tip being pressed into my flesh.

On the ridge of the hill, at the highest point, stood a shrine to Janus, with one face turned to Rome and the other to the open country, and above this, atop a high pole, flew a huge red flag, flapping and cracking in the stiff wind. About twenty legionnaires were huddled around two large braziers, and before they could do anything to stop us we had them surrounded.

"Some of you men know me!" shouted Celer. "I am Quintus Caecilius Metellus Celer—praetor, augur, lately returned from the army of my brother-in-law, Pompey the Great. And this fellow," he said, gesturing to me, "comes with the ring of our consul, Cicero. His orders are to lower the flag. Who's in command here?"

"I am," said a centurion, stepping forward. He was an experienced man of about forty. "And I don't care whose brother-in-law you are, or what authority you have, that flag stays flying unless an enemy threatens Rome."

"But an enemy does threaten Rome," said Celer. "See!" And he pointed to the countryside west of the city, which was all spread out beneath us. The centurion turned to look, and in a flash Celer had seized him from behind by his hair and had the edge of his sword at the soldier's throat. "When I tell you there's an enemy coming," he hissed, "there's an enemy coming, understand? And do you know how I know there's an enemy coming, even though you can't see anything?" He gave the man's hair a vicious tug, which made him grunt. "Because I'm a fucking *augur,* that's why. Now take down that flag, and sound the alarm."

Nobody argued after that. One of the sentries unfastened the rope and hauled down the flag while another picked up his trumpet and blew several piercing blasts. I looked across the river to the Field of Mars and the thousands all standing around there, but the distance was too great to judge what was happening at first. Only gradually did it become apparent that the crowd was draining away and that the clouds of dust rising at the edge of the field were being raised by people fleeing to their homes. Cicero described to me afterward the effect of the trumpet and the realization that the flag was coming down. Labienus had tried to calm the crowd and assure them it was a trick, but people in a mass are as stupid and easily frightened as a school of fish or a herd of beasts. In no time word spread that the city was about to be attacked. Despite the pleas of Labienus and his fellow tribunes, voting had to be abandoned. Many of the fences of the sheep pens were smashed by the stampeding citizens. The stand where Lucullus and Metellus had been sitting was knocked over and trampled to pieces. There was a fight. A pickpocket was stabbed to death. The pontifex maximus, Metellus Pius, suffered some kind of seizure and had to be rushed back to the city, unconscious. According to Cicero, only one man remained calm and that was Gaius Rabirius, rocking back and forth on his bench, alone on the deserted platform amid the chaos, his eyes closed, humming to himself some strange and discordant tune.

For a few weeks after the uproar on the Field of Mars it seemed that Cicero had won. Caesar in particular went very quiet and made no attempt to renew the case against Rabirius. On the contrary: the old man retired to his house in Rome, where he lived on in a world of his own, entirely unmolested, until a year or so later, when he died. It was the same story with the populists' bill. Cicero's coup in buying off Hybrida had the effect of encouraging other defections, including one of the tribunes, who was bribed by the patricians to switch sides. Blocked in the Senate by Cicero's coalition and threatened with a veto in the popular assembly, Rullus's immense bill, the product of so much labor, was never heard of again.

Quintus was in a great good humor. "If this were a wrestling match between you and Caesar," he declared, "it would all be over. Two falls decide the winner, and you have now laid him out flat twice."

"Unfortunately," replied Cicero, "politics is neither as clean as a wrestling match, nor played according to fixed rules."

He was absolutely certain that Caesar was up to something, otherwise his inactivity made no sense. But what was it? That was the mystery.

At the end of January, Cicero's first month as president of the Senate was completed. Hybrida took over the curule chair and Cicero busied himself with his legal work. His lictors gone, he went down to the Forum escorted by a couple of stout fellows from the Order of Knights. Atticus was as good as his word: they stayed close, but not so conspicuously that anyone suspected they were other than the consul's friends. Catilina made no move. Whenever he and Cicero encountered each other, which was inevitable in the cramped conditions of the Senate House, he would ostentatiously turn his back. Once I thought I saw him draw his finger across his throat as Cicero passed by, but nobody else seemed to notice. Caesar, needless to say, was all affability, and indeed congratulated Cicero on the power of the speeches and the skill of his tactics. That was a lesson to me. The really successful politician detaches his private self from the insults and reverses of public life, so that it is almost as if they happen to someone else; Caesar had that quality more than any man I ever met.

Then one day came the news that Metellus Pius, the pontifex maximus, had died. It was not entirely a surprise. The old soldier was nearer seventy than sixty and had been ailing for several years. He never regained consciousness after the stroke he suffered on the Field of Mars. His body lay in state in his official residence, the old palace of the kings, and Cicero, as a senior magistrate, took his turn as one of the guard of honor standing watch over the corpse. The funeral was the most elaborate I had ever seen. Propped on his side, as though at a dinner, and dressed in his priestly robes, Pius was carried on a flower-decked litter by eight fellow members of the College of Priests, among them Caesar, Silanus, Catulus, and Isauricus. His hair had been combed and pomaded and his leathery skin massaged with oil; his eyes were wide open. He seemed much more alive now that he was dead. His adopted son, Scipio, and his widow, Licinia Minor, walked behind the bier, followed by the vestal virgins and the chief priests of the official deities. Then came the chariots bearing the leaders of the Metelli clan, Celer at the front. To see the family all together—and to see as well the actors parading behind them in the death masks of Pius's ancestors—was to be reminded that this was still the most powerful political clan in Rome. The immense cortege passed along the Via Sacra, through the Fabian Arch (which was draped in black for the occasion), and across the Forum to the rostra, where the litter was raised upright so that the mourners could gaze on the body for a final time. The center of Rome was packed. The entire Senate wore togas dyed black. Spectators clustered on the temple steps, on balconies and roofs and the bases of the statues, and they stayed all the way through the eulogies, even though they lasted for hours. It was as if we all knew that in bidding farewell to Pius—stern, stubborn, haughty, brave, and perhaps a little stupid—we were bidding farewell to the old republic, and that something else was struggling to be born.

Once the bronze coin had been placed in Pius's mouth and he had been borne off to lie with his ancestors, the question naturally arose: Who should be his successor? By universal consent the choice lay between the two most senior members of the Senate: Catulus, who had rebuilt the Temple of Jupiter, and Isauricus, who had triumphed twice and was even older than Pius. Both coveted the office; neither would yield to the other. Their rivalry was comradely but intense. Cicero, who had no preference, at first took little interest in the contest. The electorate was in any case confined to the fourteen surviving members of the College of Priests. But then, about a week after Pius's funeral, while he was waiting outside the Senate House with the others for the session to begin, he chanced upon Catulus and casually asked if any decision on filling the post had yet been reached.

"No," said Catulus. "And it won't be soon, either."

"Really? Why is that?"

"We met yesterday and agreed that in view of the fact that there are two candidates of equal merit, we should go back to the old method, and let the people choose."

"Is that wise?"

"I certainly think so," said Catulus, tapping the side of his beaky nose and giving one of his thin smiles, "because I believe that in a tribal assembly I shall win."

"And Isauricus?"

"He also believes that *he* will win."

"Well, good luck to you both. Rome will be the winner whoever is the victor." Cicero began to move away but then checked himself, and a slight frown crossed his face. He returned to Catulus. "One more thing, if I may? Who proposed this widening of the franchise?"

"Caesar."

Although Latin is a language rich in subtlety and metaphor, I cannot command the words, either in that tongue or even in Greek, to describe Cicero's expression at that moment. "Dear gods," he said in a tone of utter shock. "Is it possible he means to stand himself?"

"Of course not. That would be ridiculous. He's far too young. He's thirty-six. He's not yet even been elected praetor."

"Yes, but even so, in my opinion, you would be well advised to reconvene your college as quickly as possible and go back to the existing method of selection."

"That is impossible."

"Why?"

"The bill to change the franchise was laid before the people this morning."

"By whom?"

"Labienus."

"Ah!" Cicero clapped his hand to his forehead.

"You're alarming yourself unnecessarily, Consul. I don't believe for an instant Caesar would be so foolish as to stand, and if he did he would be *crushed.* The Roman people are not entirely mad. This is a contest to be head of the state religion. It demands the utmost moral rectitude. Can you imagine Caesar responsible for the vestal virgins? He has to live among them. It would be like entrusting your hen coop to a fox!"

Catulus swept on, but I could see that the tiniest flicker of doubt had entered his eyes, and soon the gossip started that Caesar was indeed intending to stand. All the sensible citizens were appalled at the notion, or made ribald jokes and laughed out loud. Still, there was something about it—something breathtaking about the sheer cheek of it, I suppose—that even his enemies could not help but admire. "That fellow is the most phenomenal gambler I have ever encountered," remarked Cicero. "Each time he loses, he simply doubles his stake and rolls the dice again. Now I understand why he gave up on Rullus's bill and the prosecution of Rabirius. He saw that the chief priest was unlikely to recover, calculated the odds, and decided the pontificate was a much better bet than either." He shook his head in wonder and set about doing what he could to make sure this third gamble also failed. And it would have, but for two things.

The first was the incredible stupidity of Catulus and Isauricus. For several weeks, Cicero went back and forth between them, trying vainly to make them see that they could not both stand, that if they did they would split the anti-Caesar vote. But they were proud and irritable old men. They would not yield, or draw lots, or agree on a compromise candidate, and in the end both their names went forward.

The other decisive factor was money. It was said at the time that Caesar bribed the tribes with so much cash the coin had to be transported in wheelbarrows. Where had he found it all? Everyone said the source must be Crassus. But even Crassus would surely have balked at the twenty million—*twenty million!*—Caesar was rumored to have laid out to the bribery agents. Whatever the truth, by the time the vote was held on the Ides of March, Caesar must have known that defeat would mean his ruin. He could never have repaid such a sum if his career had been checked. All that would have been left to him were humiliation, disgrace, exile, possibly even suicide. That is why I am inclined to believe the famous story that on the morning of the poll, as he left his little house in Subura to walk to the Field of Mars, he kissed his mother goodbye and announced he would either return as pontifex maximus or not return at all.

The voting lasted most of the day, and by one of those ironies which abound in politics, it fell to Cicero, who was once again in March the senior presiding magistrate, to announce the result. The early-spring sun had fallen behind the Janiculum, and the sky was streaked in horizontal lines of purple, red, and crimson, like blood seeping through a sodden bandage. Cicero read out the returns in a monotone. Of the seventeen tribes polled, Isauricus had won four, Catulus six, and Caesar had been backed by seven. It could scarcely have been closer. As Cicero climbed down from the platform, obviously sick to his stomach, the victor flung back his head and raised his arms to the heavens. He looked almost demented with delight—as well he might, for he knew that come what may he would now be pontifex maximus for life, with a huge state house on the Via Sacra and a voice in the innermost counsels of the state. In my opinion, everything that happened subsequently to Caesar stemmed from this amazing victory. That crazy outlay of twenty million was actually the greatest bargain in history: it would buy him the world.

V

FROM THIS TIME on men began to look upon Caesar differently. Although Isauricus accepted his defeat with the stoicism of an old soldier, Catulus—who had set his heart on the chief pontificate as the crown of his career—never entirely recovered from the blow. The following day he denounced his rival in the Senate. "You are no longer working underground, Caesar!" he shouted in such a rage his lips were flecked with spittle. "Your artillery is planted in the open and it is there for the capture of the state!" Caesar's only response was a smile. As for Cicero, he was of two minds. He agreed with Catulus that Caesar's ambition was so reckless and gargantuan it might one day become a menace to the republic. "And yet," he mused to me, "when I notice how carefully arranged his hair is, and when I watch him adjusting his parting with one finger, I can't imagine that he could conceive of such a wicked thing as to destroy the Roman constitution."

Reasoning that Caesar now had most of what he wanted, and that everything else—a praetorship, the consulship, command of an army—would come in due course, Cicero decided the time had come to try to absorb him into the leadership of the Senate. For example, he felt it was unseemly to have the head of the state religion bobbing up and down during debates, alongside senators of the second rank, trying to catch the consul's eye. Therefore he resolved to call upon Caesar early, straight after the praetorians. But this conciliatory approach immediately landed him with a fresh political embarrassment—and one which showed the extent of Caesar's cunning. It happened in the following way.

Very soon after Caesar was elected—it must have been within three or four days at most—the Senate was in session with Cicero in the chair when suddenly there was a shout at the far end of the chamber. Pushing his way through the crowd of spectators gathered at the door was a bizarre apparition. His hair was wild and disordered and powdery with dust. He had hastily thrown on a purple-edged toga, but it did not entirely conceal the military uniform he was wearing underneath. In place of red shoes his feet were clad in a soldier's boots. He advanced down the central aisle, and whoever was speaking halted in mid-sentence as all eyes turned on the intruder. The lictors, standing near me just behind Cicero's chair, stepped forward in alarm to protect the consul, but then Metellus Celer shouted out from the praetorian benches: "Stop! Don't you see? It's my brother!" and sprang up to embrace him.

A great murmur of wonder and then alarm went around the chamber, for everyone knew that Celer's younger brother, Quintus Caecilius Metellus Nepos, was one of Pompey's legates in the war against King Mithridates, and his dramatic and disheveled appearance, obviously fresh from the scene of war, might well mean that some terrible calamity had befallen the legions.

"Nepos!" cried Cicero. "What is the meaning of this? Speak!"

Nepos disentangled himself from his brother. He was a haughty man, very proud of his handsome features and fine physique. (They say he preferred to lie with men rather than women, and certainly he never married or left issue; but that is just gossip, and I should not repeat it.) He threw back his magnificent shoulders and turned to face the chamber. "I come directly from the camp of Pompey the Great in Arabia!" he declared. "I have traveled by the swiftest boats and the fastest horses to bring you great and joyful tidings. The tyrant and foremost enemy of the Roman people Mithridates Eupator, in the sixty-eighth year of his life, is dead. The war in the East is won!"

There followed that peculiar instant of startled silence that always succeeds dramatic news, and then the whole of the chamber rose in thunderous acclamation. For a quarter of a century Rome had been fighting Mithridates. Some say he massacred eighty thousand Roman citizens in Asia; others allege one hundred fifty thousand. Whichever is true, he was a figure of terror. For as long as most could remember, the name of Mithridates had been used by Roman mothers to frighten their children into good behavior. And now he was gone! And the glory was Pompey's! It did not matter that Mithridates had actually committed suicide rather than been killed by Roman arms. (The old tyrant had taken poison, but because of all the precautionary antidotes he had swallowed over the years, it had had no effect and he had been obliged to call in a soldier to finish him off.) It did not matter either that most knowledgeable observers credited Lucius Lucullus, still waiting outside the gates for his triumph, as the strategist who had really brought Mithridates to his knees. What mat-

tered was that Pompey was the hero of the hour, and Cicero knew what
he had to do. The moment the clamor died down, he rose and proposed
that in honor of Pompey's genius, there should be five days of national
thanksgiving. This was warmly applauded. Then he called on Hybrida to
utter a few inarticulate words of praise, and next he allowed Celer to laud
his brother for traveling a thousand miles to bring the glad tidings. That
was when Caesar got up; Cicero gave him the floor in honor of his status
as chief priest, assuming he was going to offer ritual thanks to the gods.

"With all due respect to our consul, surely we are being niggardly with
our gratitude?" said Caesar silkily. "I move an amendment to Cicero's
motion. I propose the period of thanksgiving be doubled to ten full days,
and that for the rest of his life Gnaeus Pompey be permitted to wear his
triumphal robes at the Games, so that the Roman people even in their
leisure will ever be reminded of the debt they owe him."

I could almost hear Cicero's teeth grinding behind his fixed smile as he
accepted the amendment and put it to the vote. He knew that Pompey
would mark well that Caesar had been twice as generous as he. The motion passed with only one dissenting voice: that of young Marcus Cato,
who declared in a furious voice that the Senate was treating Pompey as if
he were a king, crawling to him and flattering him in a way that would
have sickened the founders of the republic. He was jeered, and a couple
of senators sitting near to him tried to pull him down. But looking at the
faces of Catulus and the other patricians, I could tell how uncomfortable
his words had made them.

Of all these great figures from the past who roost like bats in my memory
and flutter from their caves at night to disturb my dreams, Cato is the
strangest. What a bizarre creature he was! He was not much more than
thirty at this time, but his face was already that of an old man. He was
very angular. His hair was unkempt. He never smiled and rarely bathed:
he gave off a ripe smell, I can tell you. Contrariness was his religion. Even
though he was immensely rich, he never rode in a litter or a carriage but
went everywhere on foot, and frequently refused to wear shoes, or sometimes even a tunic—he desired, he said, to train himself to care nothing
for the opinion of the world on any matter, trivial or great. The clerks at
the Treasury were terrified of him. He had served there as a junior magistrate for a year, and they often told me how he had made them justify

every item of expenditure, down to the tiniest sum. Even after he had left the department he always came into the Senate chamber carrying a full set of Treasury accounts, and there he would sit, in his regular place on the farthest backbench, hunched forward over the figures, gently rocking back and forth, oblivious to the laughter and talk of the men around him.

The day after the news about the defeat of Mithridates, he came to see Cicero. The consul groaned when I told him Cato was waiting. He knew him of old, having acted briefly as his advocate when Cato—in another of his otherworldly impulses—had resolved to sue his cousin Lepida in order to force her to marry him. Nevertheless he ordered me to show him in.

"Pompey must be stripped of his command immediately," announced Cato the moment he entered the study, "and summoned home at once."

"Good morning, Cato. That seems a little harsh, don't you think, given his recent victory?"

"The victory is precisely the trouble. Pompey is supposed to be the servant of the republic, but we are treating him as our master. He will return and take over the entire state if we're not careful. You must propose his dismissal tomorrow."

"I most certainly will not! Pompey is the most successful general Rome has produced since Scipio. He deserves all the honors we can grant him. You're falling into the same error as your great-grandfather, who hounded Scipio out of office."

"Well, if you won't stop him, I shall."

"You?"

"I intend to put myself forward for election as tribune. I want your support."

"Do you, indeed!"

"As tribune I shall veto any bill that may be introduced by one of Pompey's lackeys to further his designs. It is my intention to be a politician entirely different from any who has gone before."

"I am sure you will be," replied Cicero, glancing over the young man's shoulder at me, and giving me the very slightest wink.

"I propose to bring to public affairs for the first time the full rigor of a coherent philosophy, subjecting each issue as it arises to the maxims and precepts of Stoicism. You know that I have living in my household none other than Athenodorus Cordylion—who I think you will agree is the leading scholar of the Stoics. He will be my permanent advisor. The re-

public is drifting, Cicero, that is how I see it—drifting toward disaster on
the winds and currents of easy compromise. We should never have given
Pompey these special commands."

"I supported those commands."

"I know, and shame on you! I saw him in Ephesus on my way back to
Rome a year or two ago, all puffed up like some Eastern emperor. Where's
his authorization for all these cities he's founded and provinces he's occupied? Has the Senate discussed it? Have the people voted?"

"He's the commander on the spot. He must be allowed a degree of
autonomy. And having defeated the pirates, he needed to set up bases to
secure our trade. Otherwise the brigands would simply have come back
again when he left."

"But we are meddling in places we know nothing about! Now we have
occupied Syria. Syria! What business do we have in Syria? Next it will be
Egypt. This is going to require permanent legions, stationed overseas.
And whoever commands the legions needed to control this empire, be it
Pompey or someone else, will ultimately control Rome, and whoever
raises a voice against it will be condemned for his lack of patriotism. The
republic will be finished. The consuls will simply manage the civilian side
of things, on behalf of some dictator overseas."

"No one doubts that there are dangers, Cato. But this is the business
of politics—to surmount each challenge as it appears and be ready to deal
with the next. The best analogy for statesmanship, in my opinion, is
navigation—now you use the oars and now you sail, now you run before
a wind and now you tack into it, now you catch a tide and now you ride
it out. All this takes years of skill and study, not some manual written by
Zeno."

"And where does it take you, this voyage of yours?"

"A very pleasant destination called survival."

"Ha!" Cato's laugh was as disconcerting as it was rare: a kind of harsh,
humorless bark. "Some of us hope to arrive at a more inspiring land than
that! But it will require a different kind of seamanship from yours. These
will be my precepts," he said, and he proceeded to count them off on his
long and bony fingers: "Never be moved by favor. Never appease. Never
forgive a wrong. Never differentiate between things that are wrong—
what is wrong is wrong, whatever the size of the misdemeanor, and that
is the end of the matter. And finally, never compromise on any of these
principles. 'The man who has the strength to follow them—' "

" '—is always handsome however misshapen, always rich however needy, always a king however much a slave.' I am familiar with the quotation, thank you, and if you want to go and live a quiet life in an academy somewhere, and apply your philosophy to your chickens and your fellow pupils, it might possibly even work. But if you want to run this republic, you will need more books in your library than a single volume."

"This is a waste of time. It is obvious you will never support me."

"On the contrary, I shall certainly vote for you. Watching you as a tribune promises to be one of the most entertaining spectacles Rome will ever have seen."

After he had gone, Cicero said to me, "That man is at least half mad, and yet there is something to him."

"Will he win?"

"Of course. A man with the name of Marcus Porcius Cato will always rise in Rome. And he has a point about Pompey. How do we contain him?" He thought for a while. "Send a message to Nepos inquiring if he has recovered from his journey, and inviting him to attend a military council at the end of tomorrow's session of the Senate."

I did as commanded, and the message duly came back that Nepos was at the consul's disposal. So after the house was adjourned the following afternoon, Cicero asked a few senior ex-consuls with military experience to remain behind, in order to receive a more detailed report from Nepos of Pompey's plans. Crassus, who had tasted the delights both of the consulship and of the power that flows from great wealth, was increasingly obsessed with the one thing he had never had—military glory—and he was anxious to be included in this council of war. He even lingered around the consul's chair in the hope of an invitation. But Cicero despised him more than anyone except Catilina and delighted in this opportunity to snub his old adversary. He ignored him so pointedly that eventually Crassus stamped off in a rage, leaving a dozen or so gray-headed senators gathered around Nepos. I stood discreetly to one side, taking notes.

It was shrewd of Cicero to include in this conclave men like Gaius Curio, who had won a triumph a decade earlier, and Marcus Lucullus, Lucius's younger brother, for my master's gravest weakness as a statesman was his inexperience of military affairs. In his youth, in delicate health, he had hated everything about military life—the raw discomfort, the bone-headed discipline, the dull camaraderie of the camp—and had retreated as soon as possible to his studies. Now he felt his inexperience keenly, and he had to leave it to the likes of Curio and Lucullus, Catulus and Isauricus, to question Nepos. They soon established that Pompey had a force of eight well-equipped legions, with his personal headquarters encamped— at any rate the last time Nepos had seen him—south of Judea, a few hundred miles from the city of Petra. Cicero invited opinions.

"As I see it, there are two options for the remainder of the year," said Curio, who had fought in the East under Sulla. "One is to march north to the Cimmerian Bosphorus, aim for the port of Pantikapaion, and bring the Caucasus into the empire. The other, which personally I would favor, is to strike east and settle affairs with Parthia once and for all."

"There is a third choice, don't forget," added Isauricus. "Egypt. It's ours for the taking, after Ptolemy left it to us in his will. I say he should go west."

"Or south," suggested M. Lucullus. "What's wrong with pressing on to Petra? There's very fertile land beyond the city, down on that coast."

"North, east, west, or south," summed up Cicero. "It seems Pompey is spoiled for choice. Do you know which he favors, Nepos? I am sure the Senate will ratify his decision, whatever it may be."

"Actually, I understand he favors withdrawing," said Nepos.

The deep silence that followed was broken by Isauricus. *"Withdrawing?"* he repeated in astonishment. "What do you mean, *withdrawing*? He has forty thousand seasoned men at his disposal, with nothing to stop them in any direction."

" 'Seasoned' is your word for them. 'Exhausted' would be more accurate. Some of them have been fighting and marching out there for more than a decade."

There was another pause as the implications of this settled over the gathering.

Cicero said, "Do you mean to tell us he wants to bring them all back to Italy?"

"Why not? It is their home, after all. And Pompey has signed some extremely effective treaties with the local rulers. His personal prestige is worth a dozen legions. Do you know what they now call him in the East?"

"Please tell us."

" 'The Warden of Land and Sea.' "

Cicero glanced around at the faces of the former consuls. Most wore expressions of incredulity. "I think I speak for all of us, Nepos, when I tell you that the Senate would not be happy with a complete withdrawal."

"Absolutely not," said Catulus, and all the gray heads nodded in agreement.

"In which case, what I propose is this," continued Cicero. "That we send a message back with you to Pompey, conveying—obviously—our pride and delight and gratitude for his mighty feats of arms, but also our desire that he should leave the army in place for a fresh campaign. Of course, if he wants to lay down the burden of command after so many years of service, the whole of Rome would understand and warmly welcome home her most distinguished son—"

"You can suggest whatever you like," interrupted Nepos rudely, "but I shan't be carrying the message. I'm staying in Rome. Pompey has discharged me from military service, and it is my intention to canvass for election as tribune. And now, if you'll excuse me, I have other business to attend to."

Isuaricus swore as he watched the young officer swagger out of the chamber. "He wouldn't have dared talk like that if his father had still been alive. What kind of generation have we bred?"

"And if that's how a puppy like Nepos speaks to us," said Curio, "imagine what his master will be like, with forty thousand legionnaires behind him."

" 'The Warden of Land and Sea,' " murmured Cicero. "I suppose we should be grateful he's left us the air." That drew some laughter. "I wonder what pressing matter Nepos has to attend to that's more important than talking to us." He beckoned me over and whispered in my ear, "Run after him, Tiro. See where he goes."

I hurried down the aisle and reached the door in time to glimpse Nepos and his retinue of attendants heading across the Forum in the direction of the rostra. It was around the eighth hour of the day, still busy, and amid the bustle of the city I had no trouble hiding myself—not that Nepos was the type of man much given to looking over his shoulder. His little entourage passed the Temple of Castor, and it was lucky I had moved up close behind it, because a little way up the Via Sacra they abruptly vanished and I realized they had stepped into the official residence of the pontifex maximus.

My first impulse was to head back to Cicero and tell him, but then a shrewder instinct checked me. There was a row of shops opposite the

great mansion, and I pretended to browse for jewelry, all the time keeping
an eye on Caesar's door. I saw his mother arrive in a litter, and then his
wife leave by the same means, looking very young and beautiful. Various
people went in and out, but no one I recognized. After about an hour the
impatient shopkeeper announced he wished to close, and he ushered me
out onto the street just as the unmistakable bald head of Crassus emerged
from a small carriage and darted through the doorway into Caesar's home.
I lingered for a while but no one else appeared, and not wishing to push
my luck any further I slipped away to give Cicero the news.

   He had left the Senate House by this time, and I found him at home
working on his correspondence. "Well, at least that clears up one mystery," he said when I described what I had seen. "We now know where
Caesar got the twenty million to buy his office. It didn't all come from
Crassus. A lot of it must have come from the Warden of Land and Sea."
He tilted back in his chair and became very pensive, for, as he later observed, "When the chief general in the state, the chief moneylender, and
the chief priest all start meeting together, the time has come for everyone
else to be on their guard."

It was around this time that Terentia began to play an important role in
Cicero's consulship. People often wondered why Cicero was still married
to her after fifteen years, for she was excessively pious and had little beauty
and even less charm. But she had something rarer. She had character. She
commanded respect, and increasingly as the years went on he sought her
advice. She had no interest in philosophy or literature, no knowledge of
history; not much learning of any sort, in fact. However, unburdened by
education or natural delicacy, she did possess a rare gift for seeing straight
through to the heart of a thing, be it a problem or a person, and saying
exactly what she thought.

   To begin with, not wishing to alarm her, Cicero did not mention Catilina's oath to murder him. But it was typical of Terentia's shrewdness
that she soon discovered it for herself. As a consul's wife she had supervi-
sion of the cult of the Good Goddess. I cannot tell you what this entailed,
as everything to do with the Goddess and her serpent-infested temple on
the Aventine is closed to men. All I know is that one of her fellow priestesses, a patriotic woman of noble family, came to Terentia one day in a
tearful state and warned her that Cicero's life was in danger, and that he

should be on his guard. She refused to say more. But naturally Terentia would not leave it at that, and by a combination of flattery, cajolery, and threats that must have been worthy of her husband, she slowly extracted the truth. Having done so, she then forced the unfortunate woman to come back to the house and repeat her story to the consul.

I was working with Cicero in his study when Terentia threw open the door. She did not knock; she never did. Being both richer than Cicero and more nobly born, she tended not to show the customary deference of wife to husband. Instead, she simply announced: "There is someone here you must see."

"Not now," he said, without looking up. "Tell them to go away."

But Terentia stood her ground. "It's ———," she said, and here she named the lady, whose identity I shall conceal, not for her sake (she is long dead) but for the honor of her descendants.

"And why should I see *her*?" grumbled Cicero, and for the first time he glanced up irritably at his wife. But then he noticed the grimness of her expression and his tone changed. "What is it, woman? What's wrong?"

"You need to listen for yourself." She stood aside to reveal a matron of rare if fading beauty whose eyes were red and puffy from weeping. I made as if to leave, but Terentia ordered me very firmly to stay where I was. "The slave is a highly skilled note-taker," she explained to the visitor, "and entirely discreet. If he so much as breathes a word to anyone, I can assure you I shall have him skinned alive." And she gave me a look which left me in no doubt that she would do precisely that.

The subsequent meeting was almost as embarrassing for Cicero, who had a prudish streak, as it was for the lady, who was obliged, under prompting from Terentia, to confess that for several years she had been the mistress of Quintus Curius. He was a dissolute senator and friend of Catilina. Already expelled once from the Senate for immorality and bankruptcy, he seemed certain to be thrown out again at the next census and was in desperate straits.

"Curius has been in debt as long as I've known him," explained the lady, "but never as badly as now. His estate is mortgaged three times over. One moment he threatens to kill us both rather than endure the disgrace of bankruptcy, the next he boasts of all the fine things he's going to buy for me. Last night I laughed at him. I said, 'How could *you* afford to buy *me* anything? It's *I* who has to give money to *you*!' I provoked him. We argued. Eventually he said, 'By the end of the summer we shall have all the money we need.' That was when he told me of Catilina's plans."

"Which are?"

She glanced down at her lap for a moment, then straightened herself and gazed steadily at Cicero. "To murder you, and then to seize control of Rome. To cancel all debts, confiscate the property of the rich, and divide the magistracies and priesthoods among his followers."

"Do you believe they mean it?"

"I do."

Terentia interrupted. "But she's left out the worst part! To bind them to him more closely, Catilina made them swear a blood oath on the body of a child. They slaughtered him like a lamb."

"Yes," confessed Cicero, "I know," and he held up his hand to forestall her protest. "I'm sorry. I didn't know how seriously to take it. There seemed no point in upsetting you over nothing." To the lady he said: "You must give up the names of all those involved in this conspiracy."

"No, I can't—"

"What's said can't be unsaid. I must have their names."

She wept for a while. She must have known she was trapped. "At least will you give me your word you'll protect Curius?"

"I can't promise that. I'll see what I can do. Come, madam: the names."

It took her some time to speak, and when she did I could hardly hear her. "Cornelius Cethegus," she whispered. "Cassius Longinus. Quintus Annius Chilo. Lentulus Sura and his freedman Umbrenus—" The names suddenly started to tumble out, as if by reciting them quickly she could shorten her ordeal. "Autronius Paetus, Marcus Laeca, Lucius Bestia, Lucius Vargunteius—"

"Wait!" Cicero was gazing at her in astonishment. "Did you just say Lentulus Sura—the urban praetor—and his freedman Umbrenus?"

"—Publius Sulla, and his brother, Servius." She stopped abruptly.

"And that is all?"

"Those are all the senators I've heard him mention. There are others outside the Senate."

Cicero turned to me. "How many is that?"

"Ten," I counted. "Eleven, if you add Curius. Twelve, if you include Catilina."

"*Twelve senators?*" I seldom saw Cicero more flabbergasted. He blew out his cheeks and sat back in his chair as if he had been struck. He let out a long breath. "But men like the Sulla brothers and Sura don't even have the excuse of bankruptcy! This is just treason, plain and simple!" Suddenly he was too agitated to sit still. He jumped to his feet and started pacing the narrow floor. "Dear gods! What's going on?"

"You should have them arrested," said Terentia.

"No doubt I should. But once I started down that path, even if I could do it—which I can't—where would it end? There are these twelve, and who knows how many more dozens besides? I can certainly think of plenty of others who might be involved. There's Caesar for a start—where does he stand in all this? He backed Catilina for the consulship last year and we know he's close to Sura—it was Sura, remember, who allowed the prosecution of Rabirius. And Crassus—what about him? I wouldn't put anything past him! And Labienus—he's Pompey's tribune—is Pompey involved?"

Back and forth, back and forth he went.

"They can't *all* be plotting to kill you, Cicero," Terentia pointed out, "otherwise you'd have been dead long ago."

"They may not plot together, but they all see an opportunity in chaos. Some are willing to kill to bring chaos about, and others just desire to stand back and watch chaos take hold. They are like boys with fire, and Caesar is the worst of the lot. It's a kind of madness—there's madness in the state." He went on in this style for some time, his eyes, as it were, turned inward, his imagination aflame with prophetic visions of Rome in ruins, the Tiber red with blood, the Forum strewn with hacked-off heads, visions he laid out for us in graphic detail. "I must prevent it. I have to stop it. There must be a means of stopping it—"

Throughout all this, the lady who had brought him the information sat watching him in wonder. At length he halted in front of her, bent low, and clasped her hands. "Madam, it can't have been an easy thing for you to come to my wife with this tale, but thank Providence you did! It's not just I, it is Rome herself who stands forever in your debt."

"But what am I to do now?" she wept. Terentia gave her a handkerchief and she dabbed at her eyes. "I can't go back to Curius after this."

"You have to," said Cicero. "You're the only source I have."

"If Catilina discovers I've betrayed his plans to you he'll kill me."

"He'll never know."

"And my husband? My children? What do I say to them? To have consorted with another man is bad enough—but with a traitor—?"

"If they knew your motives, they'd understand. Look upon this as your atonement. It's vital you act as if nothing had happened. Find out all you can from Curius. Draw him out. Encourage him, if necessary. But you mustn't risk coming here again—that's far too dangerous. Pass on what you learn to Terentia. You two can easily meet and talk together privately in the precincts of the temple without arousing suspicion."

She was naturally reluctant to enmesh herself in such a net of betrayal. But Cicero could persuade anyone to do anything if he set his mind to it. And when, without promising actual immunity to Curius, he made it clear he would do all he could to show leniency to her lover, she surrendered. Thus the lady went away to act as his spy, and Cicero began to lay his plans.

VI

AT THE BEGINNING of April the Senate rose for the spring recess. The lictors once again returned to Hybrida, and Cicero decided it would be safer if he took his family out of Rome to stay by the sea. We slipped away at first light, while most of the other magistrates were preparing to attend the theater, and set off south along the Via Appia accompanied by a bodyguard of knights. I suppose there must have been thirty of us in all. Cicero reclined on cushions in his open carriage, alternately being read to by Sositheus and dictating letters to me. Little Marcus rode on a mule with a slave walking beside him. Terentia and Tullia each had a litter to herself, carried by porters armed with concealed knives. Each time a group of men passed us on the road I feared it might be a gang of assassins, and by the time we reached the edge of the Pontine Marshes at twilight, after a hard day's traveling, my nerves were fairly well shredded. We put up for the night at Tres Tabernae, and the croaking of the marsh frogs and the stench of stagnant water and the incessant whine of the mosquitoes robbed me of all rest.

The next morning we resumed our journey by barge. Cicero sat enthroned in the prow, his eyes closed, his face tilted toward the warm spring sun. After the noise of the busy highway the silence of the canal was profound, the only sound the steady clop of the horse's hooves on the towpath. It was most unlike Cicero not to work. At the next stop a pouch of official dispatches awaited us, but when I tried to give it to him he waved me away. It was the same story when we reached his villa at Formiae. He had bought this place a couple of years earlier—a handsome house on the coastline, facing out to the Mediterranean Sea, with a wide terrace where he usually wrote or practiced his speeches. But for the whole of our first week in residence he did little except play with the children, taking them fishing for mackerel and jumping the waves on the little beach beneath the low stone wall. Given the gravity of his problems, I was puzzled at the time by his behavior. Now I realize, of course, that he *was* working, only in the way that a poet works: he was clearing his mind and hoping for inspiration.

At the beginning of the second week, Servius Sulpicius came to dine, accompanied by Postumia. He had a villa just around the bay, at Caieta. He had barely spoken to Cicero since the revelation of his wife's dalliance with Caesar, but he turned up looking cheerful for once, whereas she seemed unusually morose. The reason for their contrasting humors became clear just before dinner, when Servius drew Cicero aside for a private word. Fresh from Rome, he had a most delicious morsel of gossip to impart. He could hardly contain his glee. "Caesar has taken a new mistress: Servilia, the wife of Junius Silanus!"

"So Caesar has a new mistress? You might as well tell me there are fresh leaves on the trees."

"But don't you see? Not only does it put paid to all those groundless rumors about Postumia and Caesar, it also makes it much harder for Silanus to beat me in the consular election this summer."

"And why do you think that?"

"Caesar wields a great block of populist votes. He's hardly going to throw them behind his mistress's husband, is he? Some of them might actually come to me. So with the approval of the patricians and with your support as well, I really do believe I'm home and dry."

"Well then, I congratulate you, and I shall be proud to pronounce you the winner in three months' time. Do we know yet how many candidates there are likely to be?"

"Four are certain."

"You and Silanus, and who else?"

"Catilina."

"Catilina's definitely standing then?"

"Oh yes. No question of it. Caesar's already let it be known he'll be backing him again."

"And the fourth?"

"Lucius Murena," said Servius, naming a former legate of Lucullus who was presently the governor of Further Gaul. "But he's too much of a soldier to have a following in the city."

They dined that night under the stars. From my quarters I could hear the sighing of the sea against the rocks, and occasionally the voices of the quartet carried to me on the warm salty air, along with the pungent smell of their grilled fish. In the morning, very early, Cicero came himself to wake me. I was startled to find him sitting at the end of my narrow mattress, still wearing his clothes from the previous evening. It was barely light. He did not appear to have slept. "Get dressed, Tiro. It's time we were moving."

As I pulled on my shoes he told me what had happened. At the end of dinner, Postumia had found an excuse to speak with him alone. "She took my arm and asked me to walk a turn with her along the terrace, and I thought for a moment I was about to be invited to replace Caesar in her bed, for she was a little drunk and that dress of hers was practically open to her knees. But no: it seems her feelings for Caesar have curdled from lust to the bitterest hatred and all she wanted to do was betray him. She says Caesar and Servilia are made for one another: 'Two colder-hearted creatures there never were created.' She says—and here I quote her ladyship verbatim—'Servilia wants to be a consul's wife, and Caesar likes to fuck consuls' wives, so what union could be more perfect? Don't take any notice of what my husband tells you. Caesar is going to do everything he can to make sure Silanus wins.' "

"Is that such a bad thing?" I asked stupidly, for I was still half asleep. "I thought you always said Silanus was dull but respectable, and so perfect for high office."

"I do want him to win, you dunderhead! And so do the patricians, and so it now seems does Caesar. Silanus is therefore unstoppable. The real fight is going to be for the second consulship—and that, unless we are very careful, is going to be won by Catilina."

"But Servius is so confident—"

"Not confident—complacent, which is exactly what Caesar wants him to be."

I splashed some cold water on my face. I was at last beginning to wake up. Cicero was already halfway out of the door.

"May I ask where we are going?" I called.

"South," he replied over his shoulder, "to the Bay of Naples, to see Lucullus."

He left a note of explanation for Terentia, and we were gone before she woke. We traveled fast in a closed carriage to avoid being recognized—a necessary precaution since it seemed that half the Senate, weary of Rome's unusually long winter, was en route to the warm spas of Campania. We reduced the escort to make better speed and only two men guarded the consul: a great ox of a knight called Titus Sextus and his equally hefty brother, Quintus; they rode on horseback fore and aft of us.

As the sun rose higher, the air became warmer and the sea bluer, and the aromas of mimosa blossom and of sun-dried herbs and fragrant pines gradually infiltrated the carriage. From time to time I would part the curtain and gaze out at the landscape, and I vowed to myself that if ever I did get that little farm I so desired, it would be down here in the south. Cicero meanwhile saw nothing. He slept throughout the entire journey and woke only toward the end of the afternoon as we jolted down the narrow lane to Misenum, where Lucullus had his—well, I was going to call it a house, but the word hardly fits that veritable palace of pleasure, the Villa Cornelia, which he had bought and extended on the coast. It stood on the promontory where the herald of the Trojans lies buried and commanded perhaps the most exquisite view in Italy, from the island of Prochyta all the way across the wondrous blueness of the Bay of Naples to the mountains of Capreae. A gentle breeze rustled the tops of an avenue of cypresses and we descended from our dusty carriage as if into Paradise.

On hearing who was in his courtyard, Lucullus himself wafted out to greet us. He was in his middle-fifties, very languid and affected, and just beginning to run to fat: seeing him in his silken slippers and Greek tunic you would never have believed he was a great general, the greatest for over a century; he looked more like a retired dancing master. But the detachment of legionnaires guarding his house and the lictors sprawled in the shade of the plane trees served as a reminder that he had been hailed by his victorious army as imperator in the field and still commanded military imperium. He insisted Cicero must dine with him and stay the night, but that first he must bathe and rest. Such was either his chilliness or his exquisite manners that he expressed not the slightest curiosity as to why Cicero had turned up on his doorstep uninvited.

The consul and his escort were led away by flunkies and I assumed I would be consigned to the slaves' quarters. But not at all: as the consul's private secretary I too was conducted to a guest room, fresh clothes were fetched for me, and then a most remarkable thing occurred, which I blush to remember but must set down if this is to be an honest account. A female slave appeared. She was Greek, I discovered, so I was able to converse with her in her own tongue. She was in her twenties, and very charming, in a short-sleeved dress—slender, olive-skinned, with a mass of long black hair all pinned up and waiting to fall, in a soft cascade. Her name was Agathe. With much giggling and insistent gesturing she persuaded me to undress and step into a small windowless cubicle, which was entirely covered in mosaics of sea creatures. I stood there for a moment, feeling somewhat foolish, until all at once the ceiling seemed to dissolve and begin pouring forth warm fresh water. This was my first experience of one of Sergius Orata's famous shower baths, and I luxuriated in it for a long while before Agathe returned and led me into the next-door room to be cleansed and massaged—and oh, what sweet delight was that! Her smile revealed teeth as white as ivory and a mischievous pink tongue. When I met up with Cicero on the terrace an hour or so later I asked if he had tried out one of these extraordinary showers.

"Certainly not! Mine came equipped with a young whore. I never heard of such degeneracy," and then he peered at me and said in disbelief, "Don't tell me you did!" I turned scarlet, at which he started laughing very loudly, and for many months thereafter whenever he wished to tease me he would bring up the episode of Lucullus's shower bath.

Before we dined, our host took us on a tour of his palace. The main part of the house was a century old and had been built by Cornelia, the mother of the Gracchi brothers, but Lucullus had tripled it in size, adding wings and terraces and a swimming pool—all of it hewn out of the solid rock. The views on every side were astounding, the rooms sumptuous. We were led into a tunnel lined with torches that cast their light on glistening mosaics of Theseus in the labyrinth. Steps took us down to the sea and out onto a platform positioned just above the lapping waves. Here was Lucullus's particular pride—a great expanse of man-made pools filled with every species of fish you could name, including huge eels decorated with jewelry which came at the sound of his call. He knelt and a slave handed him a silver bucket full of food which he gently tipped into the water. Immediately the surface roiled with smooth and powerful bodies. "They all have names," he said, and pointed to a particularly fat and repulsive creature with gold rings in its fins. "I call that one Pompey."

Cicero laughed politely. "And whose place is that?" he asked, nodding across the water to another huge villa with a fish farm.

"That belongs to Hortensius. He thinks he can breed better fish than I, but he will never manage it. Good night, Pompey," he said to the eel in a caressing voice. "Sleep well."

I thought we must have seen everything, but Lucullus had saved the climax till last. We ascended by a different route, a wide staircase tunneled into the bowels of the dripping rock beneath the house. We passed through several heavy iron gates manned by sentries, until we came at last to a series of chambers, each of which was crammed with the treasure Lucullus had carted back from the Mithridatic War. Attendants passed their torches over glittering heaps of jewel-encrusted armor, shields, dinner plates, beakers, ladles, basins, gold chairs, and gold couches. There were heavy silver ingots and chests full of millions of tiny silver coins, and a golden statue of Mithridates more than six feet high. After a while our exclamations of wonder dwindled to silence. The riches were stupefying. Then, as we went back into the tunnel, there came a very faint scuffling noise from somewhere close at hand, which at first I thought was rats, but which Lucullus explained was the noise of the sixty prisoners—friends of Mithridates, and some of his generals—whom he had been keeping down there for the past five years in readiness for his triumphal parade, at the end of which they would be strangled.

Cicero put his hand to his mouth and cleared his throat. "Actually, Imperator, it's about your triumph that I've come to see you."

"I thought it might be," said Lucullus, and in the torchlight I saw the briefest of smiles pass over his fleshy face. "Shall we eat?"

Naturally we dined on fish—oysters and sea bass, crab and eel, gray and red mullet. It was all too rich for me: I was accustomed to plainer fare and took little. Nor did I utter a word during dinner, but kept a subtle distance between myself and the other guests, to signify my awareness that my presence was a special favor. The Sextus brothers ate greedily, and from time to time one or the other would rise from the table and go into the garden to vomit noisily to clear space for the next course. Cicero as usual was sparing in his consumption, while Lucullus chewed and swallowed steadily but without any apparent pleasure.

I found myself secretly observing him, for he fascinated me, and still does. In truth I believe he was the most melancholy man I ever met. The blight of his life was Pompey, who had replaced him as supreme commander in the East and who had then, through his allies in the Senate, blocked Lucullus's hopes of a triumph. Many men would have accepted this, but not Lucullus. He had everything in the world he wanted except the one thing he most desired. So he flatly refused to enter Rome or sur-render his command, and instead diverted his talents and ambition into creating ever more elaborate fish ponds. He became bored and listless, his domestic life unhappy. He was married twice, the first time to one of the sisters of Clodius, from whom he separated in scandalous circumstances, alleging she had committed incest with her brother, who had then en-couraged a mutiny against him in the East. The second marriage, which still endured, was to a sister of Cato, but she was also said to be flighty and unfaithful: I never set eyes on her, so I cannot judge. I did, however, meet her child, Lucullus's young son, then two years old, who was brought out by his nurse to kiss his father good night. Seeing the way Lucullus treated him, I could tell he loved the lad deeply. But the moment he had gone away to bed, the veils came down once more over Lucullus's large blue eyes and he resumed his joyless chomping.

"So," he said eventually, between mouthfuls, "my triumph?" There was a fragment of fish stuck on his cheek which he didn't know about. It was peculiarly distracting.

"Yes," repeated Cicero, "your triumph. I was thinking of laying a mo-tion before the Senate straight after the recess."

"And will it pass?"

"I don't believe in calling votes that I can't win."

The *chomp, chomp* continued for a while longer.

"Pompey won't be pleased."

"Pompey will have to accept that others are allowed to triumph in this republic as well as he."

"And what's in it for you?"

"The honor of proposing your eternal glory."

"Balls." Lucullus finally wiped his mouth and the particle of fish dis-appeared. "You've really traveled fifty miles in a day just to tell me this? You can't expect me to believe it."

"Oh dear, you're too shrewd for me, Imperator! Very well, I confess I also wanted to have a political talk with you."

"Go on."

"I believe we are drifting toward calamity." Cicero pushed away his plate and, summoning all his eloquence, he proceeded to describe the state of the republic in the starkest terms, dwelling especially on Caesar's support for Catilina and on Catilina's revolutionary program of canceling debts and seizing the property of the rich. He did not have to point out what a threat this posed to Lucullus, reclining in his palace amid all his silk and gold: it was perfectly obvious. Our host's face became grimmer and grimmer, and when Cicero had finished he took his time before replying.

"So it is your firm opinion that Catilina could win the consulship?"

"It is. Silanus will take the first place and he the second."

"Well then, we have to stop him."

"I agree."

"So what do you propose?"

"Well, that is why I've come. I'd like you to stage your triumph just before the consular elections."

"Why?"

"For the purpose of your procession, I assume you plan to bring into Rome several thousand of your veterans from all across Italy?"

"Naturally."

"Whom you will entertain lavishly and reward generously out of the spoils of your victory?"

"Of course."

"And who will therefore listen to your advice about whom to support in the consular elections?"

"I would like to think so."

"In which case I know just the candidate they should vote for."

"I thought you might," said Lucullus with a cynical smile. "You have in mind your great ally Servius."

"Oh no. Not him. The poor fool doesn't stand a chance. No, I'm thinking of your old legate—and their former comrade-in-arms—Lucius Murena."

Accustomed as I was to the twists and turns of Cicero's stratagems, it had never crossed my mind that he might abandon Servius so readily. For a moment I could not believe what I had just heard. Lucullus looked equally surprised. "I thought Servius was one of your closest friends."

"This is the Roman republic, not a coterie of friends. My heart certainly urges me to vote for Servius. But my head tells me he can't beat Catilina. Whereas Murena, with your backing, might just be able to manage it."

Lucullus frowned. "I have a problem with Murena. His closest lieu-

tenant in Gaul is that depraved monster my former brother-in-law—
a man whose name is so disgusting to me I refuse to pollute my mouth by
even uttering it."

"Well then, let me utter it for you. Clodius is not a man I have any
great liking for myself. But in politics one cannot always pick and choose
one's enemies, let alone one's friends. To save the republic, I must abandon an old and dear companion. To save the republic, you must embrace
the ally of your bitterest foe." He leaned across the table and added softly,
"Such is politics, Imperator, and if ever the day comes when we lack the
stomach for such work, we should get out of public life *and stick to breeding fish!*"

For a moment I feared he had gone too far. Lucullus threw down his
napkin and swore that he would not be blackmailed into betraying his
principles. But as usual Cicero had judged his man well. He let Lucullus
rant on for a while, and then when he had finished he made no response
but simply gazed across the bay and sipped his wine. The silence seemed
to go on for a very long time. The moon above the water cast a path of
shimmering silver. Finally, in a voice leaden with suppressed anger, Lucullus said that he supposed Murena might make a decent enough consul if
he was willing to take advice, whereupon Cicero promised to lay the issue
of his triumph before the Senate as soon as the recess ended.

Neither man having much appetite left for further conversation, we
all retired early to our rooms. I had not long been in mine when I heard
a gentle knocking at the door. I opened it and there stood Agathe. She
came in without a word. I assumed she had been sent by Lucullus's steward, and told her it was not necessary, but as she climbed into my bed she
assured me it was of her own volition, and so I joined her. We talked between caresses, and she told me something of herself—of how her par-
ents, now dead, had been led back as slaves from the East as part of
Lucullus's war booty, and how she could just vaguely remember the village in Greece where they had lived. She had worked in the kitchens, and
now she looked after the imperator's guests, and in due course, as her
looks faded, she would return to the kitchens, if she was lucky; if not, it
would be the fields, and an early death. She talked about all this without
any self-pity, as one might describe the life of a horse or a dog. Cato called
himself a Stoic, I thought, but this girl really was one, smiling at her fate
and armored against despair by her dignity. I said as much to her, and she
laughed.

"Come, Tiro," she said, holding up her arms and beckoning me to her, "no more solemn words. Here is my philosophy: enjoy such brief ecstasy as the gods permit us, for it is only in these moments that men and women are truly not alone."

When I woke with the dawn she had gone.

Do I surprise you, reader? I remember I surprised myself. After so many years of chastity I had ceased even to imagine such things and was content to leave them to the poets: "What life is there, what delight, without golden Aphrodite?" Knowing the words was one thing; I never expected to know their meaning.

I had hoped we might stay for one more night at least, but the next morning Cicero announced that we were leaving. Secrecy was absolutely vital to his plans, and the longer he lingered in Misenum the more he feared his presence would become known. So after a final brief conference with Lucullus we set off back in the closed carriage. As we descended toward the coastal road I stared back at the house over my shoulder. There were many slaves to be seen, working in the gardens and moving beneath the different parts of the great villa, preparing it for another perfect spring day. Cicero was also looking back.

"They flaunt their wealth," he murmured, "and then they wonder why they are so hated. And if that is how stupendously rich Lucullus has become, who never actually defeated Mithridates, can you imagine the colossal wealth that Pompey must now possess?"

I could not imagine it, and nor did I wish to. It sickened me. Never before had the pointlessness of piling up treasure for its own sake been more apparent to me than it was on that warm blue morning as the house receded behind me.

Now that he had settled on his strategy, Cicero was eager to pursue it, and for that we needed to return to Rome. As far as he was concerned the holiday was over. Reaching the seaside villa at Formiae at dusk, we rested overnight, and then set off again at first light. If Terentia was irritated by this neglect of her and the children she did not show it. She knew he would travel quicker without them. We were back in Rome by the Ides of April, and Cicero at once set about making discreet contact with Murena. The governor was still in his province of Further Gaul, but it turned out he had sent back his lieutenant Clodius to start planning his election campaign. Cicero hemmed and hawed about what to do, for he did not trust Clodius; nor did he want to tip off his plans to Caesar and Catilina by going openly to the young man's house. Eventually he decided to approach him via his brother-in-law, the augur Metellus Celer, and this led to a memorable encounter.

Celer lived up on the Palatine Hill, on Victory Rise, close to the house of Catulus, in a street of fine residences overlooking the Forum. Cicero reasoned that nobody would find it surprising to see a consul dropping by to visit a praetor. But when we entered the mansion we discovered its master was away for the day on a hunting trip. Only his wife was at home, and it was she who came out to greet us, accompanied by several maids. As far as I am aware, this was the first occasion on which Cicero met Clodia, and she made a striking impression on him of beauty and of cleverness. She was thirty or thereabouts, famous for her large brown eyes with long lashes—"Lady Ox-Eyes," Cicero used to call her—which she employed to great effect, giving men flirtatious sidelong glances, or fixing them with beguiling and intimate stares. She had an expressive mouth and a caressing voice, pitched perfectly for gossip. Like her brother, she affected a fashionable "urban" accent. But woe betide the man who tried to be too familiar with her—she was capable of turning in an instant into a true Claudian: haughty, ruthless, cruel. A rake named Vettius, who had tried to seduce her and failed, circulated quite a good pun about her: *In triclinio Coa, in cubiculo nola* ("A silky island in the dining room, a rocky fortress in bed"), with the result that two of her other admirers, Marcus Camurtius and Marcus Caesernius, took revenge on her behalf: they beat him up, and then, to make the punishment fit the crime, they buggered him half to death.

One would have thought this a world utterly alien to Cicero, and yet there was a part of his character—a quarter of him, let us say—that was irresistibly drawn to the rakish and the outrageous, even while the other three-quarters thundered in the Senate against loose morals. Perhaps it was the streak of the actor in him; he always loved the company of theater people. He also liked men and women who were not boring, and no one could ever say that Clodia was that. At any rate, each expressed great pleasure at meeting the other, and when Clodia, with one of her wide-eyed sideways looks, asked in her breathy voice if there was anything—anything at all—she could do for Cicero in her husband's absence, he replied that actually there was: he would like to have a private word with her brother.

"Appius or Gaius?" she asked, assuming he must mean one of the older two, each of whom was as stern and humorless and ambitious as the other.

"Neither. I wanted to talk to Publius."

"Publius! The wicked boy! You have picked my favorite." She sent a slave at once to fetch him, no doubt from whichever gambling den or brothel was his current haunt, and while they awaited his arrival she and Cicero strolled around the atrium, studying the death masks of Celer's consular ancestors. I withdrew quietly into the shadows and therefore I could not hear what they were saying, but I heard their laughter, and I realized the source of their amusement was the frozen, waxy faces of generation after generation of Metelli—who were, it must be admitted, famed for their stupidity. At length Publius Clodius swept into the house, gave a low and (I thought) sarcastic bow to the consul, kissed his sister lovingly on the mouth, and then stood with his arm around her waist. He had been in Gaul for more than a year, but had not changed much. He was still as pretty as a woman, with thick golden curls, loose clothes, and a drooping way of looking at the world which was full of condescension. To this day I cannot decide whether he and Clodia really were lovers, or whether they simply enjoyed outraging respectable society. But I learned afterward that Clodius behaved this way with all three of his sisters in public, and certainly Lucullus had believed the rumors of incest.

Anyway, if Cicero was shocked he did not show it. Smiling his apologies to Clodia, he asked if he might be allowed a word with her younger brother in private. "Well, all right," she replied with mock reluctance, "but I am very jealous," and after a final lingering, flirtatious handshake with the consul she disappeared into the interior of the great house, leaving the three of us alone. Cicero and Clodius exchanged a few pleasantries about Further Gaul and the arduousness of the journey across the Alps, and then Cicero said, "Now tell me, Clodius, is it true that your chief, Murena, is going to seek the consulship?"

"It is."

"That's what I'd heard. It surprised me, I must confess. How do you think he can possibly win?"

"Easily. There are any number of ways."

"Really? Give me one."

"Obligation: the people still remember the generous games he staged before he was elected praetor."

"Before he was elected praetor? My dear fellow, that was three years ago! In politics, three years is ancient history! Believe me, Murena is entirely forgotten here. Out of sight is out of mind as far as Rome is concerned. I ask again: Where do you propose to find the votes?"

Clodius maintained his smile. "I believe many of the centuries will support him."

"Why? The patricians will vote for Silanus and Servius. The populists will vote for Silanus and Catilina. Who will be left to vote for Murena?"

"Give us time, Consul. The new campaign hasn't even started yet."

"The new campaign started the moment the old one ended. You should have been going around all year. And who will run this miraculous canvass?"

"I shall."

"You?"

Cicero uttered the word with such derision I winced, and even Clodius's arrogance seemed briefly dented. "I have some experience."

"What experience? You're not even a member of the Senate."

"Well then, damn you! Why did you bother even coming to see me if you're so certain we're going to lose?"

His expression was one of such outrage, Cicero burst out laughing. "Who said anything about losing? Did I? Young fellow," he continued, putting his arm around Clodius's shoulders, "I know a thing or two about winning elections, and I can tell you this: you have every chance of winning—just as long as you do exactly as I tell you. But you need to wake up before it's too late. *That* is why I wanted to see you."

And so saying, he walked Clodius round and round the atrium and explained his plan, while I followed with my notebook open and took down his directions.

VII

CICERO INFORMED ONLY the most trusted senators of his intention to propose a triumph for Lucullus—men like his brother, Quintus; the former consul, Gaius Piso; the praetors, Pomptinus and Flaccus; friends such as Gallus, Marcellinius, and the elder Frugi; and the patrician leaders Hortensius, Catulus, and Isauricus. They in turn initiated others into the scheme. All were sworn to secrecy, told on which day to attend the chamber and requested above everything to keep together, whatever happened, until the house adjourned. Cicero did not tell Hybrida.

On the appointed date the Senate House was unusually crowded. Elderly nobles who had not attended for many years were present, and I could see that Caesar scented danger of some kind, for he had a habit at such moments of almost literally sniffing the air, tilting his head back slightly and peering around him suspiciously (he did exactly that, I remember, moments before he was murdered). But Cicero had arranged the whole thing masterfully. A very tedious bill was at that time making its way onto the statute book, restricting the right of senators to claim expenses for unofficial trips to the provinces. This is precisely the sort of self-interested legislation which excites every elected bore in politics, and Cicero had lined up an entire bench of them and promised each he could speak for as long as he liked. The moment he read out the order of business some senators groaned and rose to leave, and after about an hour of listening to Quintus Cornificius—a very dreary speaker at the best of times—attendance was thinning fast. Some of our side pretended to go, but actually lingered in the streets close to the Senate House. Eventually even Caesar could stand it no longer and departed, together with Catilina.

Cicero waited a little longer, then stood and announced he had received a new motion which he would like to place before the house. He called on Lucullus's brother, Marcus, to speak, who thereupon read out a letter from the great general requesting that the Senate grant him a triumph before the consular elections. Cicero declared that Lucullus had

waited long enough for his just reward and he would now put the matter to a vote. By this time the patrician benches had filled up again with
those who had been lurking nearby, while on the populists' side there
was hardly anyone to be seen. Messengers ran off to fetch Caesar. Meanwhile, all who favored a triumph for Lucullus moved to stand around
his brother, and after heads had been counted Cicero duly declared that
the motion had been passed 120 to 16 and that the house should stand
adjourned. He hurried down the aisle, preceded by his lictors, just as
Caesar and Catilina arrived at the door. They obviously realized that
they had just been ambushed and had lost something significant, but
it would take them an hour or two to work out exactly what. For now
they could only stand aside and let the consul's procession pass. It was a
delicious moment, and Cicero relived it again and again over dinner that
night.

The trouble really started the following day in the Senate. Belatedly,
the populists' benches were packed, and it was a rowdy house. Crassus,
Catilina, and Caesar had by this time worked out what Cicero was up to,
and one after the other they rose to demand that the vote be taken again.
But Cicero would not be intimidated. He ruled that there had been a
proper quorum, Lucullus deserved his triumph, and the people were in
need of a spectacle to cheer them up: as far as he was concerned the issue
was closed. Catilina, however, refused to sit down and continued to demand a revote. Calmly Cicero tried to move on to the bill about travel
expenses. As the uproar continued I thought the session might have to be
suspended. But Catilina still had not entirely given up hope of winning
power by the ballot box rather than the sword, and he recognized that the
consul was right in one respect at least: the urban masses always enjoyed
a triumph, and would not understand why they had been promised the
pleasure one day only to be deprived of it the next. At the last moment he
threw himself heavily back onto the front bench, sweeping his arm dis-
missively at the chair in a gesture of anger and disgust. Thus it was settled:
Lucullus would have his day of glory in Rome.

That night Servius came to see Cicero. He brusquely rejected the offer
of a drink and demanded to know if the rumors were true.

"What rumors?"

"The rumors that you've abandoned me and are supporting Murena."

"Of course they're not true. I'll vote for you, and shall say as much to
anyone who asks me."

"Then why have you arranged to ruin my chances by filling the city with Murena's old legionnaires in the week of the poll?"

"The question of when Lucullus holds his triumph is entirely a matter for him"—an answer which, while true in a strictly legal sense, was grossly misleading in every other. "Are you sure you won't have a drink?"

"Do you really think I'm such a fool as that?" Servius's stooped frame was quivering with emotion. "It's bribery, plain and simple. And I give you fair warning, Consul: I intend to lay a bill before the Senate making it illegal for candidates, or their surrogates, to hold either banquets or games just before an election."

"Listen, Servius, may I give you some advice? Money, feasting, entertainment—these have always been a part of an election campaign, and always will be. You can't just sit around waiting for the voters to come to you. You need to put on a show. Make sure you go everywhere in a big crowd of supporters. Spread a little money around. You can afford it."

"That's bribing the voters."

"No, it's *enthusing* them. Remember, these are poor citizens for the most part. They need to feel their vote has value, and that great men have to pay them some attention, if only once a year. It's all they have."

"Cicero, you completely amaze me. Never did I think to hear a Roman consul say such a thing. Power has entirely corrupted you. I shall introduce my bill tomorrow. Cato will second the motion and I expect you to support it—otherwise the country will draw its own conclusions."

"Typical Servius—always the lawyer, never the politician! Don't you understand? If people see you going around not to canvass but to collect evidence for a prosecution, they'll think you've given up hope. And there's nothing more fatal during an election campaign than to appear unconfident."

"Let them think what they like. The courts will decide. That is what they're there for."

The two men parted badly. Nevertheless, Servius was right in one respect: Cicero, as consul, could hardly let himself be seen to condone bribery. He was obliged to support the campaign finance reform bill when Servius and Cato laid it before the Senate the next day.

Election canvasses normally lasted four weeks; this one went on for eight. The amount of money expended was amazing. The patricians set up a war chest to fund Silanus, into which they all paid. Catilina received financial support from Crassus. Murena was given one million sesterces by Lucullus. Only Servius made a point of spending nothing at all, but went around with a long face, accompanied by Cato and a team of secretaries recording every example of illegal expenditure. Throughout this time Rome slowly filled with Lucullus's veterans, who camped out on the Field of Mars by day and came into the city at night to drink and gamble and whore. Catilina retaliated by bringing in supporters of his own, mostly from the northwest, in particular Etruria. Ragged and desperate, they materialized out of the primeval forests and swamps of that benighted region: ex-legionnaires, brigands, herdsmen. Publius Cornelius Sulla, nephew of the former dictator, who supported Catilina, paid for a troop of gladiators, ostensibly to entertain but really to intimidate. At the head of this sinister assembly of professional and amateur fighters was the former centurion Gaius Manlius, who drilled them in the meadows across the river from the Field of Mars. There were terrible running battles between the two sides. Men were clubbed to death; men drowned. When Cato, in the Senate, accused Catilina of organizing this violence, Catilina slowly got to his feet.

"If a fire is raised to consume my fortunes," he said very deliberately, turning to look at Cicero, "then I will put it out—not with water but by demolition."

There was a silence, and then, as the meaning of his words sank in, a shocked chorus of "Oh!" rang around the chamber—"Oh!"—for this was the first time Catilina had hinted publicly that he might be willing to use force. I was taking a shorthand record of the debate, sitting in my usual place, below and to the left of Cicero, who was in his curule chair. He immediately spotted his opportunity. He stood and held up his hand for silence.

"Gentlemen, this is very serious. There should be no mistake as to what we have just heard. Clerk, read back to the chamber the words of Sergius Catilina."

I had no time to feel nervous as for the first and only time in my life I addressed the Senate of the Roman republic: " 'If a fire is raised to consume my fortunes,' " I read from my notes, " 'then I will put it out—not with water but by demolition.' "

I spoke as loudly as I could and sat down quickly, my heart pounding with such violence it seemed to shake my entire body. Catilina, still on his feet, his head on one side, was looking at Cicero with an expression I find it hard to describe—a sneer of insolence was part of it, and contempt, and blazing hatred obviously, and even perhaps a hint of fear: that twitch of alarm that can drive a desperate man to desperate acts. Cicero, his point made, gestured to Cato to resume his speech, and only I was close enough to see that his hand was shaking. "Marcus Cato still has the floor," he said.

That night Cicero asked Terentia to speak to her highly placed informant, the mistress of Curius, to try to find out exactly what Catilina meant. "Obviously, he's realized he's going to lose, which makes this a dangerous moment. He might be planning to disrupt the poll. 'Demolition?' See if she knows why he used that particular phrase."

Lucullus's triumph was to take place the following day, and in this atmosphere Quintus naturally worried about the arrangements for Cicero's security. But nothing could be done. There was no chance of varying the route, which was fixed by solemn tradition. The crowds would be immense. It was only too easy to imagine a determined assassin darting forward, thrusting a long blade into the consul, and disappearing into the throng. "But there it is," said Cicero. "If a man is set on killing you, it's hard to stop him, especially if he's willing to die in the attempt. We shall just have to trust to Providence."

"And the Sextus brothers," added Quintus.

Early the next morning Cicero led the entire Senate out to the Field of Mars, to the Villa Publica, where Lucullus was lodging prior to entering the city, surrounded by the pitched tents of his veterans. With characteristic arrogance, Lucullus kept the delegation waiting for a while, and when he appeared, he presented a gaudy apparition, robed in gold, his face painted in red lead. Cicero recited the official proclamation of the Senate, then handed him a laurel wreath, which Lucullus held aloft and showed to his veterans, slowly turning full circle to roars of approval before delicately placing it on his head. Because I was now on the staff of the Treasury, I was given a place in the parade, behind the magistrates and senators but ahead of the war booty and the prisoners, who included a few of Mithridates's relatives, a couple of minor princes, and half a dozen generals. We passed into Rome through the Triumphal Gate, and my chief recollections are of the oppressive heat of that summer day, and the contorted faces of the crowds lining the streets, and the rank smell of the beasts—the oxen and mules, dragging and carrying all that bullion and those works of art—their animal grunts and bellows mingling with the shouts of the spectators, and far behind us, like distant rolling thunder, the tramp of the legionnaires' boots. It was quite disgusting, I have to

say—the whole city stinking and shrieking like a vivarium—and no more
so than after we had passed through the Circus Maximus and had come
back along the Via Sacra to the Forum, where we had to wait until the rest
of the procession caught up with us. Standing outside the Carcer was the
public executioner, surrounded by his assistants. He was a butcher by
training and looked it, squat and broad in his leather apron. This was
where the crowd was thickest, drawn as always by the shivering thrill of
close proximity to death. The miserable prisoners, yoked at the neck,
their faces burned red by this sudden exposure to the sun after years of
darkness, were led up one by one to the carnifex, who took them down
into the Carcer and strangled them—thankfully out of sight, but still I
could see that Cicero was keeping his face averted and talking fixedly to
Hybrida. A few rows back Catilina watched Cicero with almost lascivious
interest.

Such are my principal memories of the triumph, although I must recount one other, which is that when Lucullus drove across the Forum in
his chariot, he was followed on horseback by Murena, who had finally
arrived in Rome for the election, having left his province to the care of his
brother. He received a great ovation from the multitudes. The consular
candidate looked the very picture of a war hero, in his gleaming breastplate and gorgeous scarlet-plumed helmet, even though he had not fought
in the army for years and had grown rather plump in Further Gaul. Both
men dismounted and started climbing the steps to the Capitol, where
Caesar waited with the College of Priests. Lucullus was ahead, of course,
but his legate was only a few paces behind, and I appreciated then Cicero's
genius in laying on what was, in effect, an immense election rally for
Murena. Each of the veterans received a bounty of nine hundred and fifty
drachmas, which in those days was about four years' pay, and then the
entire city and the surrounding neighborhoods were treated to a lavish
banquet. "If Murena can't win after this," Cicero observed to me as he set
off for the official dinner, "he doesn't deserve to live."

The next day, the public assembly voted the bill of Servius and Cato
into law, and when Cicero returned home, he was met by Terentia. Her
face was white and trembling but her voice was calm. She had just come
from the Temple of the Good Goddess, she said. She had some terrible
news. Cicero must brace himself for the blow. Her friend, that noble lady
who had come to her to warn her of the plot against his life, had that
morning been discovered dead in the alley beside her house. Her head

had been smashed in from behind by a hammer blow, her throat cut, and her organs removed.

As soon as he had recovered from the shock Cicero summoned Quintus and Atticus. They came at once and listened, appalled. Their first concern was for the consul's safety. It was agreed that a couple of men would stay in the house overnight and patrol the downstairs rooms. Others would escort him in public during the day. He would vary his route to and from the Senate. A fierce dog would be acquired to guard the door.

"And how long must I go on living like a prisoner? Until the end of my life?"

"No," responded Terentia, displaying her rare gift for getting to the heart of the matter, "until the end of Catilina's life, because as long as he's in Rome you'll never be safe."

He saw the wisdom of this, reluctantly grunted his assent, and Atticus went off to send a message to the Order of Knights. "But why did he have to *kill* her?" he wondered aloud. "If he suspected she was my informant, why couldn't he simply have warned Curius not to speak openly in front of her?"

"Because," said Quintus, "he likes killing people."

Cicero thought for a while, then turned to me. "Send one of the lictors to find Curius, and tell him I want to see him straightaway."

"You mean to invite into your house someone who is part of a plot to murder you?" exclaimed Quintus. "You must be mad!"

"I won't be alone. You'll be here. He probably won't come. But if he does, at least we may find out something." He glanced around at our worried expressions. "Well? Does anyone have a better idea?"

Nobody did, so I went out to the lictors who were playing bones in a corner of the atrium and ordered the most junior to find Curius and bring him back to the house.

It was one of those endless hot summer days when the sun seems reluctant to sink, and I remember how still it was, the motes of dust motionless in the shafts of fading light. On such evenings, when the only sounds even in the city are the drone of insects and the soft trilling of the birds, Rome seems older than anywhere in the world; as old as the earth itself; entirely beyond time. How impossible it was to believe that forces were at work in its very heart, in the order of the Senate, that might destroy it! We sat around quietly, too tense to eat the meal that had been set upon the table. The additional bodyguards ordered by Atticus arrived and stationed themselves in the vestibule. When, after an hour or two, the lengthening shadows made the house gloomy, and the slaves went around lighting the candles, I assumed Curius either had not been found or had refused to come. But then at last we heard the front door open and slam shut, and the lictor came in with the senator, who looked around him suspiciously—first at Cicero, then at Atticus, Quintus, Terentia, and me, and then back at Cicero again. He certainly was a handsome figure: one had to give him that. Gambling was his vice, not drink, and I suppose throwing dice leaves less of a mark upon a man.

"Well, Curius," said Cicero quietly, "this is a terrible business."

"I'll talk to you alone, not in front of others."

"Not talk in front of others? By the gods, you'll talk in front of the entire Roman people if I say so! Did you kill her?"

"Damn you, Cicero!" Curius swore and lunged toward the consul, but Quintus was on his feet in a moment and blocked his way.

"Steady, Senator," he warned.

"Did you kill her?" repeated Cicero.

"No!"

"But you know who did?"

"Yes! You!" Once more he tried to push his way past Quintus, but Cicero's brother was an old soldier and stopped him easily. "You killed her, you bastard!" he shouted again, struggling against Quintus's restraining arms, "by making her your spy!"

"I'm prepared to bear my share of guilt," replied Cicero, gazing at him coolly. "Will you?"

Curius muttered something inaudible, pulled himself free of Quintus, and turned away.

"Does Catilina know you're here?"

Curius shook his head.

"Well, that at least is something. Now listen to me. I'm offering you a chance, if you've brains enough to take it. You've hitched your fate to a madman. If you didn't know it before, you must realize it now. How did Catilina know she'd been to see me?"

Again Curius mumbled something no one could hear. Cicero cupped his hand to his ear. "What? What are you saying?"

"Because I told him!" Curius glared at Cicero with tearful eyes. He struck his breast with his fist. "She told me, and I told him!" And he struck himself again—hard, hard, hard blows—in the manner of some Eastern holy man lamenting the dead.

"I need to know everything. Do you understand me? I need names, places, plans, times. I need to know who exactly will strike at me, and in what location. It's treason if you don't tell me."

"And treachery if I do!"

"Treachery against evil is a virtue." Cicero got to his feet. He put his hands on Curius's shoulders and stared hard into his face. "When your lady came to see me, it was your safety as much as mine that was her concern. She made me promise, on the lives of my children, that I would grant you immunity if this plot was ever exposed. Think of her, Curius, lying there—beautiful, brave, broken—be worthy of her love and her memory, and act now as you know she would have wanted."

Curius wept; indeed, I could hardly restrain my own tears, such was the pitiful vision Cicero conjured up: that and the promise of immunity did the trick. When Curius had pulled himself together sufficiently, he promised to get word to Cicero the moment he heard any definite news of Catilina's plans. Thus Cicero's thin line of information from the enemy's camp remained intact.

He did not have long to wait.

The following day was election eve, and Cicero was due to preside over the Senate. But because of the fear of an ambush, he had to follow a circuitous route, along the Esquiline and down to the Via Sacra. The journey took twice as long as usual and it was mid-afternoon by the time we arrived. His curule chair was placed on the doorstep and he sat there in the shade, reading through some letters, surrounded by his lictors, waiting for the auguries to be taken. Several senators wandered over to ask if he had heard what Catilina was supposed to have said that morning. Apparently, he had addressed a meeting in his house in the most inflammatory terms. Cicero replied that he had not, and sent me off to see if I could discover anything. I walked around the senaculum and approached one or two senators with whom I was on friendly terms. The place was certainly buzzing with rumors. Some said that Catilina had called for the richest men in Rome to be murdered, others that he had urged an uprising. I jotted a few sentences down and was just returning to Cicero when

Curius brushed past me and slipped into my hand a note. He was sickly white with terror. "Give this to the consul," he whispered, and before I could reply he was gone. I looked around. A hundred or more senators were talking in small groups. As far as I could tell no one had seen the encounter. I hurried over to Cicero and handed him the message.

I bent to his ear and whispered, "It's from Curius."

He opened it and studied it for a moment, and his face tensed. He passed it up to me. It said, *You will be murdered tomorrow during the elections.* At just that moment the augurs came up and declared that the auspices were propitious. "Are you certain about that?" asked Cicero in a grim voice. Solemnly they assured him that they were. I could see him weighing in his mind what best to do. Finally he stood and indicated to his lictors that they should pick up his chair, and he followed them into the cool shadows of the Senate chamber. The senators filed in behind us. "Do we know what Catilina actually said this morning?"

"Not in any detail."

As we walked up the aisle he said to me quietly, "I fear this warning may have some substance to it. If you think about it, it's the one time when they can be sure precisely where I'll be—on the Field of Mars, presiding over the ballot. And with all those thousands of people milling around, how easy it would be for ten or twenty armed men to hack their way through to me and take me down." By this time we had reached the dais and the benches were filling. He glanced back, searching the white-robed figures. "Is Quintus here?"

"No, he's canvassing." Indeed, a great many senators were absent. All the candidates for consul, and most of those for tribune and praetor—including Quintus and Caesar—had chosen to spend the afternoon meeting voters rather than attending to the business of the state. Only Cato was in his place, reading his Treasury accounts. Cicero grimaced and tightened his fist, crushing Curius's message. He stood that way for quite some time until he became conscious that the house was watching him. He mounted the steps to his chair.

"Gentlemen," he announced, "I have just been informed of a grave and credible conspiracy against the republic, involving the murder of your leading consul." There was a gasp. "In order that the evidence may be examined and debated, I propose that the start of the elections tomorrow be postponed, until the nature of this threat has been properly assessed. Are there any objections?" In the excited murmur that followed no clear voice could be heard. "In that case, the Senate will stand adjourned until first light tomorrow." With these words he swept down the aisle followed by his lictors.

Rome was now plunged into a state of great confusion. Cicero went straight back to his house and immediately set about trying to find out precisely what Catilina had said, dispatching clerks and messengers to potential informants across the city. I was ordered to fetch Curius from his house on the Aventine. At first his doorkeeper refused to admit me—the senator was seeing no one, he said—but I sent a message to him on behalf of Cicero and eventually was allowed in. Curius was in a state of nervous collapse, torn between his fear of Catilina and his anxiety not to be implicated in the murder of a consul. He flatly refused to go with me and meet Cicero face-to-face, saying it was too dangerous. It was only with great difficulty that I persuaded him to describe the meeting at Catilina's house.

All Catilina's henchmen were there, he said: some eleven senators, in total, including himself. There were also half a dozen members of the Order of Knights—he named Nobilior, Statilius, Capito, and Cornelius—as well as the ex-centurion Manlius and scores of malcontents from Rome and all across Italy. The scene was dramatic. The house was stripped entirely bare of possessions—Catilina was bankrupt and the place mortgaged—apart from a silver eagle that had once been the consul Marius's personal standard when he fought against the patricians. As for what Catilina had actually said, according to Curius it went something like this (I took it down as he dictated it):

"Friends, ever since Rome rid itself of kings it has been ruled by a powerful oligarchy that has had control of everything—all the offices of state, the land, the army, the money raked in by taxes, our provinces overseas. The rest of us, however hard we try, are just a crowd of nobodies. Even those of us who are highborn have to bow and scrape to men who in a properly run state would stand in awe of us. You know who I mean. All influence, power, office, and wealth are in their hands; all they leave for us is danger, defeat, prosecutions, and poverty.

"How long, brave comrades, will we endure it? Is it not better to die courageously and have done with it than to drag out lives of misery and dishonor as the playthings of other men's insolence? But it need not be like this. We have the strength of youth and stout hearts, while our enemies are enfeebled by age and soft living. They have two, three, or four houses joined together, when we have not a home to call our own. They have pictures and statues and fish ponds, while all we have are destitution and debts. Misery is all we have to look forward to.

"Awake, then! Before you glimmers the chance for liberty—for honor and glory and the prizes of victory! Use me in whatever way you like, as a commander or as a soldier in your ranks, and remember the rich spoils that can be won in war! This is what I shall do for you if I am consul. Refuse to be slaves! Be masters! And let us show the world at last that we are men!"

That, or something very like it, was the burden of Catilina's speech, and after he had delivered it he withdrew to an inner room for a more private discussion with his closest comrades, including Curius. Here, with the door firmly closed, he reminded them of their solemn blood oath, declared that the hour had come to strike, and proposed that they should kill Cicero on the Field of Mars during the confusion of the elections the following day. Curius claimed to have stayed only for part of this discussion before slipping away to pass on the warning to Cicero. He refused to swear an affidavit confirming this story. He absolutely insisted he would not be a witness. His name had to be kept out of it at all costs. "You must tell the consul that if he calls on me, I shall deny everything."

By the time I got back to Cicero's house the door was barred and only those visitors who were known and trusted were being admitted. A crowd had gathered in the street. When I went into his study, Quintus and Atticus were already there. I relayed Curius's message and showed him his description of what Catilina had said. "Now I have him!" he said. "He's gone too far this time!" And he sent for the leaders of the Senate. At least a dozen came during the course of that afternoon and evening, among them Hortensius and Catulus. Cicero showed them what Catilina was supposed to have said, along with the unsigned death threat. But when he refused to divulge his source ("I have given my word"), I could see that several—particularly Catulus, who had at one time been a great friend of Catilina—became skeptical. Indeed, knowing Cicero's cleverness, they obviously wondered if he might be making the whole thing up in order to discredit his enemy. Unnerved by their reaction, Cicero began to lose confidence.

There are times in politics, as in life generally, when whatever one does is wrong; this was just such an occasion. To have gone ahead with the elections and said nothing would have been a mad gamble. On the other hand, postponing them without adequate evidence now looked jittery. Cicero passed a sleepless night worrying about what he should say in the Senate, and for once in the morning it showed. He looked like a man under appalling strain.

The next day when the Senate reassembled there was not an inch of space on the benches. Senators lined the walls and crammed the gangways. The auspices had been read and the doors opened soon after daybreak. It was the earliest session that anyone could remember. Yet already the summer heat was building. The question was: Would the consular election go ahead or not? Outside, the Forum was packed with citizens, mostly Catilina's supporters, and their angry chants, demanding to be allowed to vote, could be heard in the chamber. Beyond the city walls on the Field of Mars the sheep pens and ballot urns were set up and waiting. Inside the Senate House it felt as if two gladiators were about to fight. As Cicero stood, I could see Catilina in his place on the front bench, his cronies around him, as coolly insolent as ever, with Caesar close by, his arms folded.

"Gentlemen," Cicero began, "no consul lightly intervenes in the sacred business of an election—especially not a consul such as I, who owes everything he has to election by the Roman people. But yesterday I was given warning of a plot to desecrate this most holy ritual—a plot, an intrigue, a conspiracy of desperate men, to take advantage of the tumult of polling day to murder your consul, foment chaos in the city, and so enable them to take control of the state. This despicable scheme was hatched not in some foreign land, or low criminal's hovel, but in the heart of the city, in the house of Sergius Catilina."

The senators listened in absolute stillness as Cicero read out the anonymous note from Curius (*"You will be murdered tomorrow during the elections"*), followed by Catilina's words (*"How long, brave comrades, will we endure it . . . ?"*), and when he had finished there was not a pair of eyes directed anywhere other than at Catilina. "At the end of this seditious rant," concluded Cicero, "Catilina retired with others to consider, not for the first time, how best I might be killed. Such is the extent of my knowledge, gentlemen, which I felt it my duty to lay before you, so that you might decide how best to proceed."

He sat down, and after a pause someone called out, "Answer!" and then others took up the cry, angrily hurling the word like a javelin at Catilina: "Answer! Answer!" Catilina gave a shrug, and a kind of half smile, and heaved himself to his feet. He was a huge man. His physical presence alone was sufficient to intimidate the chamber into silence.

"Back in the days when Cicero's ancestors were still fucking goats, or however it is they amuse themselves in the mountains he comes from—" He was interrupted by laughter; some of it, I have to say, from the patrician benches around Catulus and Hortensius. "Back in those days," he continued, once the racket had died down, "when my ancestors were consuls and this republic was younger and more virile, we were led by fighters, not lawyers. Our learned consul here accuses me of sedition. If that is what he chooses to call it, sedition it is. For my part, I call it the truth. When I look at this republic, gentlemen, I see two bodies. One," he said, gesturing to the patricians and from them up to Cicero, sitting dead still in his chair, "is frail, with a weak head. The other"—he pointed to the door and the Forum beyond it—"is strong, but has no head at all. I know which body I prefer, and it won't go short of a head as long as I'm alive!"

Looking at those words written down now, it seems amazing to me that Catilina wasn't seized and accused of treason on the spot. But he had powerful backers, and no sooner had he resumed his seat than Crassus was on his feet. Ah, yes, Marcus Licinius Crassus—I have not devoted nearly enough space to him so far in this portion of my narrative! But let me rectify that. This hunter of old ladies' legacies; this lender of money at usurious rates; this slum landlord; this speculator and hoarder; this former consul, as bald as an egg and as hard as a piece of flint—this Crassus was a most formidable speaker when he put his cunning mind to it, which he did on that July morning.

"Forgive my obtuseness, colleagues," he said. "Perhaps it's just me, but I've been listening intently and I've yet to hear a solitary piece of evidence that justifies postponing the elections by a single instant. What does this so-called conspiracy actually amount to? An anonymous note? Well, the consul himself could have written it, and there are plenty who wouldn't put it past him! The report of a speech? It didn't sound particularly remarkable to me. Indeed, it reminded me of nothing so much as the sort of speech that that radical new man Marcus Tullius Cicero used to make before he threw in his lot with my patrician friends on the benches opposite!"

It was an effective point. Crassus grasped the front of his toga between his thumbs and forefingers and spread his elbows, in the manner of a country gentleman delivering his opinion of sheep at market.

"The gods know, and you all know—and I thank Providence for it—I am not a poor man. I have nothing to gain from the cancellation of all debts; very much the reverse. But I do not think that Catilina can be barred from being a candidate, or these elections delayed an hour longer, purely on the basis of the feeble evidence we've just heard. I therefore propose a motion, *that the elections begin immediately, and that this house do adjourn and repair to the Field of Mars.*"

"And I second the motion!" said Caesar, springing to his feet. "And I ask that it be put to the vote at once, so that no more of the day may be wasted by these delaying tactics, and the election of the new consuls and praetors may be concluded by sunset, in accordance with our ancient laws."

Just as a pair of scales that are finely balanced may suddenly be plunged one way or another by the addition of a few grains of wheat, so the whole atmosphere of the Senate that morning abruptly tilted. Those who had been howling down Catilina only a short while earlier now began clamoring for the elections to start, and Cicero wisely decided not even to put the matter to a vote. "The mood of the house is clear," he said in a stony voice. "Polling will begin at once." And he added, quietly: "May the gods protect our republic." I don't think many people heard him, certainly not Catilina and his gang, who didn't even observe the normal courtesy of letting the consul leave the chamber first. Fists in the air, roaring in triumph, they pushed their way down the crowded aisle and out into the Forum.

Cicero was now in a fix. He could hardly go home like a coward. He had to follow Catilina, for nothing could happen until he, as the presiding magistrate, arrived on the Field of Mars to take control of the proceedings. Quintus, whose concern for his brother's safety was always paramount, and who had foreseen exactly this outcome, had brought along his old army breastplate, and he insisted that Cicero wear it beneath his toga. I could tell that Cicero was reluctant, but in the drama of the moment he allowed himself to be persuaded, and while a group of senators stood around to shield him, I helped him out of his toga, assisted Quintus in strapping on the bronze armor, and then readjusted his toga. Naturally, the rigid shape of the metal was clearly visible beneath the white wool, but Quintus reassured him that, far from being a problem, this was all to the good: it would act as a deterrent to any assassin. Thus protected, and with a tight escort of lictors and senators surrounding him, Cicero walked, head erect, from the Senate House and into the glare and noise of election day.

The population was streaming westward toward the Field of Mars, and we were carried with the flow. More and more supporters emerged and adhered around Cicero, until I should say that a protective layer of at least four or five men stood between him and the general throng. A huge crowd can be a terrifying sight—a monster, unconscious of its own strength, with subterranean impulses to stampede this way or that, to panic and to crush. The crowd on the election field that day was immense, and we drove into it like a wedge into a block of wood. I was next to Cicero, and we were jostled and pushed along by our escort until at last we reached the area set aside for the consul. This consisted of a long platform with a ladder up to it, and a tent behind it where he could rest. To one side, behind sheep fencing, was the enclosure for the candidates, of whom there were perhaps twenty (both the consulships and the eight praetorships all had to be decided that day). Catilina was talking to Caesar and when they saw Cicero arrive, red-faced from the heat and wearing armor, they both laughed heartily and began gesturing to the others to look. "I should never have worn this damn thing," Cicero muttered. "I'm sweating like a pig, and it doesn't even protect my head and neck."

Nevertheless, as the elections were already running late, he had no time to take it off, but immediately had to go into a conclave with the augurs. They declared that the auspices were good, so Cicero gave the order for proceedings to begin. He mounted the platform, followed by the candidates, and recited all the prayers in a firm voice and without a hitch. The trumpets sounded, the red flag was hoisted up its staff above the Janiculum, and the first century trooped over the bridge to cast its ballots. Thereafter it was a matter of keeping the lines of voters moving, hour after hour, as the sun burned its fiery arc across the sky and Cicero boiled like a lobster in his breastplate.

For what it is worth, I believe that he would have been assassinated that day if he had not taken the course he did. Conspiracies thrive in darkness, and by shining such a strong light on the plotters he had temporarily frightened them off. Too many people were watching: if Cicero had been struck down, it would have been obvious who was responsible.

And, in any case, because he had raised the alarm, he was now surrounded by such a number of friends and allies it would have taken scores of determined men to get to him.

So the business of the day went on as usual, with no hand raised against him. He had one small satisfaction at least, which was to declare his brother elected praetor. But Quintus's vote was smaller than expected, whereas Caesar topped the poll by a mile. The results for the consulship were as expected: Junius Silanus came in first and Murena second, with Servius and Catilina tied in last place. Catilina gave a mocking bow to Cicero and left the field with his supporters: he had not expected a different outcome. Servius, on the other hand, took his defeat badly, and came to see Cicero in his tent after the declaration to pour out a tirade against him for permitting the most corrupt campaign in history. "I shall challenge it in the courts. My case is overwhelming. This battle is not over yet, by any means!" He stamped off, followed by his attendants carrying their document cases full of evidence. Cicero, slumped with exhaustion on his curule chair, swore as he watched him leave. I tried to make some consoling remarks, but he told me roughly to be quiet and to do something useful for a change by helping him take off that damned breastplate. His skin had been chafed raw by the metal edges, and the moment he was free of it he seized it in both hands and hurled it in a fury to the other side of the tent, where it landed with a clatter.

VIII

A TERRIBLE MELANCHOLY NOW overcame Cicero, of a depth I had never seen before. Terentia went off with the children to spend the rest of the summer in the higher altitudes and cooler glades of Tusculum, but the consul stayed in Rome, working. The heat was more than usually oppressive; the stink of the great drain beneath the Forum rose to envelop the hills, and many hundreds of citizens were carried off by the sweating fever, the stench of their corpses adding to the noisome atmosphere. I have often wondered what history would have found to say about Cicero if he had also succumbed to a fatal illness at that time—and the answer is "very little." At the age of forty-three he had won no military victories. He had written no great books. True, he had achieved the consulship, but then so had many nonentities, Hybrida being the most obvious example. The only significant law he had carried onto the statute book was Servius's campaign finance reform act, which he heartily disliked. In the meantime Catilina was still at liberty and Cicero had lost a great deal of prestige by what was seen as his panicky behavior on the eve of the poll. As the summer turned to autumn his consulship was almost three-quarters done and dribbling away to nothing—a fact he realized more keenly than anybody.

One day in September I left him alone with a pile of legal papers to read. It was almost two months after the elections. Servius had made good his threat to prosecute Murena and was seeking to have his victory declared null and void. Cicero felt he had little choice except to defend the man whom he had done so much to make consul. Once again he would appear alongside Hortensius, and the amount of evidence to be mastered was immense. But when I returned some hours later the documents were still untouched. He had not moved from his couch. He was clutching a cushion to his stomach. I asked if he was ill. "I have a dryness of the heart," he said. "What's the point of going on with all this work and striving? No one will ever remember my name—not even in a year's time, let alone in a thousand. I'm finished—a complete failure." He sighed and stared at the ceiling, the back of his hand resting on his forehead. "Such dreams I had, Tiro—such hopes of glory and renown. I meant to be as famous as Alexander. But it's all gone awry somehow. And do you know what most torments me as I lie awake at night? It's that I cannot see what I could have done differently."

He continued to keep in touch with Curius, whose grief at the death of his mistress had not abated; in fact he had become ever more obsessed. From him Cicero learned that Catilina was continuing to plot against the state, and now much more seriously. There were disturbing reports of covered wagons full of weapons being moved under cover of darkness along the roads outside Rome. Fresh lists of possibly sympathetic senators had been drawn up, and according to Curius these now included two young patrician senators, Marcus Claudius Marcellus and Quintus Scipio Nasica. Another ominous sign was that Gaius Manlius, Catilina's wild-eyed military lieutenant, had disappeared from his usual haunts in the back streets of Rome and was rumored to be touring Etruria, recruiting armed bands of supporters. Curius could produce no written evidence for any of this—Catilina was much too cunning for that—and eventually, after asking a few too many questions, he came under suspicion from his fellow conspirators and began to be excluded from their inner circle. Thus Cicero's only firsthand source of information gradually went dry.

At the end of the month he decided to risk his credibility once again by raising the matter in the Senate. It was a disaster. "I have been informed—" he began, but could proceed no further because of the gusts of merriment that blew around the chamber. "I have been informed" was exactly the formulation he had used twice before when raising the specter of Catilina, and it had become a kind of satirical catchphrase. Wags in the street would shout it after him as he went by: "Oh, look! There goes Cicero! Has he been informed?" His enemies in the Senate yelled it out while he was speaking: "Have you informed yourself yet, Cicero?" And now inadvertently he had said it again. He smiled weakly and affected not to care, but of course he did. Once a leader starts to be laughed at as a matter of routine he loses authority, and then he is finished. "Don't go out without your armor!" someone called as he processed from the chamber, and the house was convulsed with mirth. He locked himself away in his study soon after that, and I did not see much of him for several days. He spent more time with my junior Sositheus than he did with me; I felt oddly jealous.

There was another reason for his gloom, although few would have guessed it, and he would have been embarrassed if they had. In October his daughter was to be married—an occasion he confided to me that he was dreading. It was not that he disliked her husband, young Gaius Frugi, of the Piso clan: on the contrary, it was Cicero, after all, who had arranged the betrothal, years earlier, to bring in the votes of the Pisos. It was simply that he loved his little Tulliola so much that he could not bear the thought of their being parted. When, on the eve of the wedding, he saw her packing her childhood toys away as tradition demanded, tears came into his eyes and he had to leave the room. She was just fourteen. The following morning the ceremony took place in Cicero's house, and I was honored to be asked to attend, along with Atticus and Quintus and a whole crowd of Pisos (by heavens, what an ugly and lugubrious crowd they were!). I must confess that when Tullia was led down the stairs by her mother, all veiled and dressed in white, with her hair tied up, and the sacred belt knotted around her waist, I cried myself; I cry now, remembering her girlishly solemn face as she recited that simple vow, so weighted with meaning: "Where you are Gaius, I am Gaia." Frugi placed the ring on her finger and kissed her very tenderly. We ate the wedding cake and offered a portion to Jupiter, and then at the wedding breakfast, while little Marcus sat on his sister's knee and tried to steal her fragrant wreath, Cicero proposed the health of the bride and groom.

"I give to you, Frugi, the best that I have to give: no nature kinder, no temper sweeter, no loyalty fiercer, no courage stronger, no—"

He could not go on, and under cover of the loud and sympathetic applause he sat down.

Afterward, hemmed in as usual by his bodyguards, he joined the procession to Frugi's family home on the Palatine. It was a cold day. Not many people were about; few joined us. When we reached the mansion Frugi was waiting. He hoisted his bride into his arms and, ignoring Terentia's mock entreaties, carried her over the threshold. I had one last glimpse of Tullia's wide fearful eyes staring out at us from the interior, and then the door closed. She was gone, and Cicero and Terentia were left to walk slowly home in silence, hand in hand.

That night, sitting at his desk before he went to bed, he remarked for the twentieth time on how empty the place seemed without her. "Only one small member of the household gone, and yet how diminished it is! Do you remember how she used to play at my feet, Tiro, when I was working? Just here." He gently tapped his foot against the floor beneath his table. "How often did she serve as the first audience for my speeches— poor uncomprehending creature! Well, there it is. The years sweep us on like leaves before a gale, and it cannot be helped."

Those were his last words to me that evening. He went off to his bed and I, after I had blown out the candles in the study, retired to mine. I said good night to the guards in the atrium and carried my lamp to my tiny room. I placed it on the nightstand beside my cot, undressed, and lay awake as usual thinking over the events of the day, until slowly I felt my mind beginning to dissolve into sleep.

It was midnight—very quiet.

I was woken by fists pounding on the front door. I sat up with a start. I could only have been asleep for a few moments. The distant hammering came again followed by ferocious barking, shouts, and running feet. I seized my tunic and pulled it on as I hurried into the atrium. Cicero, fully dressed, was already descending the stairs from his bedroom, preceded by two guards with drawn swords. Behind him wrapped in a shawl was Terentia, with her hair in curlers. The banging resumed again, sharper now—sticks or shoes beating against the heavy wood. Little Marcus started howling in the nursery. "Go and ask who it is," Cicero told me, "but don't open the door," and then, to one of the knights: "Go with him."

Cautiously I advanced along the passage. We had a guard dog by this time—a massive black and brown mountain dog named Sargon, after the Assyrian kings. He was snarling and barking and yanking on his chain with such ferocity I thought he would tear it from the wall. I called out, "Who's there?"

The reply was faint but audible: "Marcus Licinius Crassus!"

Above the noise of the dog I called to Cicero: "He says it's Crassus!"

"And is it?"

"It sounds like him."

Cicero thought about it for a moment. I guessed he was calculating that Crassus would cheerfully see him dead, but also that it was hardly likely a man of Crassus's eminence would try to murder a serving consul.

He drew back his shoulders and smoothed down his hair. "Well then, if he says it's Crassus, and it sounds like Crassus, you'd better let him in."

I opened the door a crack to see a group of a dozen men holding torches. The bald head of Crassus shone in the yellow light like a harvest moon. I opened the door wider. Crassus eyed the snarling dog with distaste, then edged past it into the house. He was carrying a scruffy leather document case. Behind him came his usual shadow, the former praetor Quintus Arrius, and two young patricians, friends of Crassus who had only lately taken their seats in the Senate—Claudius Marcellus and Scipio Nasica, whose names had been featured on the most recent list of Catilina's potential sympathizers. Their escort tried to follow them in, but I told them to wait outside: four enemies at one time was quite enough, I decided. I relocked the door.

"So what's all this about, Crassus?" asked Cicero as his old foe stepped into the atrium. "It's too late for a social call and too early for business."

"Good evening, Consul." Crassus nodded coldly. "And good evening to you, madam," he said to Terentia. "Our apologies for disturbing you. Don't let us keep you from your bed." He turned his back on her and said to Cicero, "Is there somewhere private we can talk?"

"I'm afraid my friends get nervous if I leave their sight."

"Are you suggesting we're assassins?"

"No, but you keep company with assassins."

"Not any longer," said Crassus with a thin smile, and patted his document case. "That's why we're here."

Cicero hesitated. "All right, in private, then." Terentia started to protest. "Don't alarm yourself, my dear. My guards will be right outside the door and the strong arm of Tiro will be there to protect me." (This was a joke.)

He ordered some chairs to be taken to his study, and the six of us just about managed to squeeze into it. I could see that Cicero was nervous. There was something about Crassus that always made his flesh crawl. Still, he was polite enough. He asked his visitors if they would like some wine, but they declined. "Very well," he said. "Sober is better than drunk. Out with it."

"There's trouble brewing in Etruria," began Crassus.

"I know the reports. But as you saw when I tried to raise the matter, the Senate won't take it seriously."

"Well, they need to wake up quickly."

"You've certainly changed your tune!"

"That's because I've come into possession of certain facts. Tell him, Arrius."

"Well," said Arrius, looking shifty. He was a clever fellow, an old soldier, lowborn, and Crassus's creature in all matters. He was much mocked behind his back for his silly way of speaking, adding an *h* to some of his vowels, presumably because he thought it made him sound educated. "I was in Hetruria up till yesterday. There are bands of fighters gathering right across the region. I hunderstand they're planning to hadvance on Rome."

"How do you know that?"

"I served with several of the ringleaders in the legions. They tried to persuade me to join them, and I let them think I might—purely to gather hintelligence, you hunderstand," he added quickly.

"How many of these fighters are there?"

"I should say five thousand, maybe ten."

"As many as that?"

"If there aren't that many now, there will be soon enough."

"Are they armed?"

"Some. Not all. They have a plan, though."

"And what is this plan?"

"To surprise the garrison at Praeneste, seize the town, fortify it, and use it as a base to rally their forces."

"Praeneste is almost impregnable," put in Crassus, "and less than a day's march away from Rome."

"Manlius has also sent supporters the length and breadth of Hitaly to stir up hunrest."

"My, my," said Cicero, looking from one to the other, "how well informed *you* are!"

"You and I have had our disagreements, Consul," said Crassus coldly, "but I'm a loyal citizen, first and last. I don't want to see a civil war. That's why we're here." He placed the document case on his lap, opened it, and pulled out a bundle of letters. "These messages were delivered to my house earlier this evening. One was addressed to me; two others were for my friends here, Marcellus and young Scipio, who happened to be dining with me. The rest are addressed to various other members of the Senate. As you can see, the seals on those are still unbroken. Here you are. I want there to be no secrets between us. Read the one that came for me."

Cicero gave him a suspicious look, glanced through the letter quickly, and then handed it to me. It was very short: *"The time for talking is over. The moment for action has arrived. Catilina has drawn up his plans. He wishes to warn you there will be bloodshed in Rome. Spare yourself and leave the city secretly. When it is safe to return, you will be contacted."* There was no signature. The handwriting was neat and entirely without character: a child could have done it.

"You see why I felt we had to come straightaway," said Crassus. "I've always been a supporter of Catilina. But we want no part of this."

Cicero put his chin in his hand and said nothing for a while. He looked from Marcellus to Scipio. "And the warnings to you both? Are they exactly the same?" The two young senators nodded. "Anonymous?" More nods. "And you've no idea who they're from?" They shook their heads. For two such arrogant young Roman noblemen, they were as docile as lambs.

"The identity of the sender is a mystery," declared Crassus. "My doorkeeper brought the letters in to us when we'd finished dinner. He didn't see who delivered them—they were left on the step and whoever was the courier ran away. Naturally Marcellus and Scipio read theirs at the same time as I read mine."

"Naturally. May I see the other messages?"

Crassus reached into his document case and gave him the unopened letters one at a time. Cicero examined each address in turn and showed it to me. I remember a Claudius, an Aemilius, a Valerius, and others of that ilk, including Hybrida: about eight or nine in total; all patricians.

"He seems to be warning his hunting companions," said Cicero, "for old times' sake. It's strange, is it not, that they should all be sent to you? Why is that, do you think?"

"I have no idea."

"It's certainly an odd conspiracy that approaches a man who says he doesn't even belong to it and asks him to act as its messenger."

"I can't pretend to explain it."

"Perhaps it's a hoax."

"Perhaps. But when one considers the alarming developments in Etruria, and then remembers how close Catilina is to Manlius . . . No, I think one has to take it seriously. I fear I owe you an apology, Consul. It seems Catilina may be a menace to the republic after all."

"He's a menace to everyone."

"Anything I can do to help—you have only to ask."

"Well, for a start, I'll need those letters, all of them."

Crassus exchanged looks with his companions, but then he stuffed the letters into the document case and gave it to Cicero. "You'll be producing them in the Senate, I assume?"

"I think I must, don't you? I'll also need Arrius to make a statement of what he's discovered in Etruria. Will you do that, Arrius?"

Arrius looked to Crassus for guidance. Crassus gave a slight nod. "Habsolutely," he confirmed.

Crassus said, "And you'll be seeking the Senate's authority to raise an army?"

"Rome must be protected."

"May I just say that if you require a commander for such a force, you need look no further? Don't forget I was the one who put down the revolt of Spartacus. I can put down the revolt of Manlius just as well."

As Cicero afterward observed, the brazenness of the man was astonishing. Having helped create the danger in the first place by supporting Catilina, he now hoped to claim the credit for destroying it! Cicero made a noncommittal reply, to the effect that it was rather late at night to be imagining armies into being and appointing generals, and that he would like to sleep on matters before deciding how to respond.

"But when you make your statement you'll give me credit for my patriotism in coming forward, I hope?"

"You may rely on it," said Cicero, ushering him out of the study and into the atrium, where the guards were waiting.

"If there's anything more I can do—" said Crassus.

"Actually, there is one matter I'd appreciate your help on," said Cicero, who never missed an opportunity to press home an advantage. "This prosecution of Murena, if it succeeds, would rob us of a consul at a very dangerous moment. Will you join Hortensius and me in defending him?"

Of course this was the last thing Crassus wanted to do, but he made the best of it. "It would be an honor."

The two men shook hands. "I cannot tell you," said Cicero, "how pleased I am that any misunderstandings that may have existed between us in the past are now cleared up."

"I feel exactly the same, my dear Cicero. This has been a good night for both of us—and an even better night for Rome."

And with many mutual protestations of friendship, trust, and regard,

Cicero conducted Crassus and his companions to the door, bowed to him, wished him a sound night's sleep, and promised to talk to him in the morning.

"What a complete and utter lying shit that bastard is!" he exclaimed the moment the door had closed.

"You don't believe him?"

"What? That Arrius just happened to be in Etruria and by chance fell into idle conversation with men who are taking up arms against the state and who then on a whim urged him to join them? No I don't. Do you?"

"Those letters are very odd. Do you think he wrote them himself?"

"Why would he do that?"

"I suppose so that he could come to you in the middle of the night and play the part of the loyal citizen. They do give him the perfect excuse to withdraw his support from Catilina." Suddenly I became excited, for I thought I saw the truth. "That's it! He must have sent Arrius out to take a look at what was happening in Etruria, and then when Arrius came back and told him what was going on, he took fright. He's decided Catilina's certain to lose, and wants publicly to distance himself."

Cicero nodded approvingly. "That's clever." He wandered back along the passage and into the atrium, his hands clasped behind his back, his head hunched forward, thinking. Suddenly he stopped. "I wonder—" he began.

"What?"

"Well, look at it the other way around. Imagine that Catilina's plan works: that Manlius's ragamuffin army does indeed capture Praeneste and then advances on Rome, gathering support in every town and village through which it passes. There's panic and slaughter in the capital. The Senate House is stormed. I am killed. Catilina effectively takes control of the republic. It's not impossible—the gods know, we have few enough here to defend us, while Catilina has many supporters living within our walls. Then what would happen?"

"I don't know. It's a nightmare."

"I can tell you precisely what would happen. The surviving magistrates would have no option except to summon home the one man who could save the nation: Pompey the Great, at the head of his Eastern legions. With his military genius, and with forty thousand trained men under his command, he'd finish off Catilina in no time, and once he'd done that, nothing would stand between him and the dictatorship of the entire world. And which of his rivals does Crassus fear and hate more than any other?"

"Pompey?"

"Pompey. Exactly. That's it. The situation must be much more perilous even than I thought. Crassus came to see me tonight to betray Catilina not because he's worried he might fail but because he's frightened he'll succeed."

The next morning at first light we left the house accompanied by four knights, including the Sextus brothers, who henceforth would seldom leave the consul's side. Cicero kept the hood of his cloak well up and his head well down, while I carried the case of letters. Every few paces I had to take an extra step to keep up with his long stride. When I asked him where we were going, he replied: "We need to find ourselves a general."

It seems odd to relate, but overnight all Cicero's recent misery and despair had left him. Faced with this immense crisis he seemed—not happy; that would be absurd to say—but invigorated. He almost bounded up the steps to the Palatine, and when we turned into Victory Rise I realized our destination must be the house of Metellus Celer. We passed the portico of Catulus and drew into the doorway of the next house, which stood vacant, its windows and entrance boarded up. Determined not to be seen, Cicero said that he would wait here while I went next door and announced that the consul wished to see the praetor alone and in the strictest confidence. I did as he asked and Celer's steward quickly reported back that his master would join us as soon as he could get away from his morning levee. When I returned to fetch Cicero, I found him talking to the watchman of the empty house. "This place belongs to Crassus," he told me as we walked away. "Can you believe it? It's worth a fortune but he's leaving it empty so that he can get a better price next year. No wonder he doesn't want a civil war—it's bad for business!"

Cicero was conducted by a servant down an alleyway between the two houses, through the rear door, and directly into the family apartments. There, Celer's wife, Clodia, alluring in a silken robe over her nightdress, and with the musky smell of the bedchamber still upon her, waited to greet him. "When I heard you were coming clandestinely through the back door I hoped it was to see *me*," she said reproachfully, fixing him with her sleepy eyes, "but now I hear it's my husband you want, which really is too boring of you."

"I fear everyone is a bore," said Cicero, bowing to kiss her hand, "compared to she who reduces us all, however eloquent, to stammering wrecks."

It was a measure of Cicero's revived spirits that he had the energy to flirt, and the contact between his lips and her skin seemed to last far longer than was necessary. What a scene: the great and prudish orator bent over the hand of the most titled trollop in Rome! It actually flashed into my mind—a wild, fantastical notion—that Cicero might one day leave Terentia for this woman, and I was glad when Celer came bustling into the room in his usual hearty military manner and the intimate atmosphere was instantly dissolved.

"Consul! Good morning! What can I do for you?"

"You can raise an army and save your country."

"An army? That's a good one!" But then he saw that Cicero was serious. "What are you talking about?"

"The crisis I have for so long predicted is upon us at last. Tiro, show the praetor the letter addressed to Crassus." I did so, and watched Celer's face grow rigid as he read the words.

"This was sent to Crassus?"

"So he says. And these others were also delivered to him last night for distribution across the city." Cicero gestured to me, and I handed Celer the bundle of letters. He read a couple and compared them. When he had finished, Clodia lifted them from his hands and studied them herself. He made no effort to stop her, and I made a note in my mind to remember that she was privy to all his secrets. "And that's only the half of it," continued Cicero. "According to Quintus Arrius, Etruria is swarming with Catilina's men. Manlius is raising a rebel army equivalent to two legions. They plan to seize Praeneste, and Rome will be next. I want you to take command of our defenses. You'll need to move swiftly if we're to stop them."

"What do you mean by swiftly?"

"You'll leave the city today."

"But I have no authority—"

"I'll get you the authority."

"Hold on, Consul. There are things I need to think about before I go off raising troops and rampaging through the countryside."

"Such as?"

"Well, first I must certainly consult my brother Nepos. And then I have my other brother—my brother by marriage—Pompey the Great, to think about—"

"We haven't the time for all that! If every man starts considering his family's interests ahead of his nation's we'll never get anywhere. Listen, Celer," he said, softening his tone in that way I'd heard him do so often, "your courage and firm action have already saved the republic once when Rabirius was in peril. Ever since then I've known that history has cast you to play the hero's part. There's glory as well as peril in this crisis. Remember Hector: 'No sluggard's fate, ingloriously to die / But daring that which men to be shall learn.' Besides, if you don't do it, Crassus will."

"Crassus? He's no general! All he knows about is money."

"Maybe, but he's already sniffing around the chance for military glory. Give him a day or two and he'll have bought himself a majority in the Senate."

"If there's military glory to be had, Pompey will want it, and my brother has come back to Rome expressly to ensure he gets it." Celer gave me back the letters. "No, Consul—I appreciate your faith in me, but I can't accept without their approval."

"I'll give you Nearer Gaul."

"What?"

"Nearer Gaul—I'll give it to you."

"But Nearer Gaul isn't yours to give."

"Yes it is. It's presently my allotted province, swapped with Hybrida for Macedonia, if you recall. It was always my intention to renounce it. You can have it."

"But it's not a basket of eggs! There'll have to be a fresh ballot among the praetors."

"Yes, which you will win."

"You'll rig the ballot?"

"*I* shan't rig the ballot. That would be most improper. No, no, I'll leave that side of things to Hybrida. He may not have many talents, but rigging ballots I believe is one of them."

"What if he refuses?"

"He won't. We have an understanding. Besides," said Cicero, flourishing the anonymous letter addressed to Hybrida, "I'm sure he'd prefer it if this wasn't made public."

"Nearer Gaul," said Celer, rubbing his broad chin. "It's better than Further Gaul."

"Darling," said Clodia, putting her hand on her husband's arm, "it really is a very good offer, and I'm sure Nepos and Pompey will understand."

Celer grunted, and rocked back and forth on his heels a few times. I could see the greed in his face. Eventually he said, "How soon do you think I could be given this province?"

"Today," said Cicero. "This is a national emergency. I shall argue that there must be no uncertainty about commands anywhere in the empire, and that my place is in Rome, just as yours is in the field, putting down the rebel forces. We'll be partners in defense of the republic. What do you say?"

Celer glanced at Clodia. "It will put you ahead of all your contemporaries," she said. "Your consulship will be guaranteed."

He grunted again, and turned back to Cicero. "Very well," he replied, and extended his massive, muscled arm toward the consul. "For the sake of my country, I say yes."

From Celer's house Cicero walked the few hundred paces to Hybrida's, roused the presiding consul from his habitual drunken stupor, sobered him up, told him about the rebel army gathering in Etruria, and gave him his lines for the day. Hybrida balked at first when told he would have to rig the ballot for Nearer Gaul, but then Cicero showed him the letter from the conspirators with his name written on it. His glassy red-veined eyes almost popped out of his head and he began to sweat and shake in alarm.

"I swear to you, Cicero, I knew nothing about it!"

"Yes, but unfortunately, my dear Hybrida, as you well know, this city is full of jealous and suspicious minds which might easily be persuaded to believe otherwise. If you really want to prove your loyalty beyond question, I suggest you oblige me in this matter of Nearer Gaul, and you may rely on my absolute support."

So that took care of Hybrida, and then it was simply a matter of squaring the right senators, which Cicero proceeded to do before the afternoon session while the auspices were being taken. By now the city was awash with rumors about a rebel assault and a plot to murder the leading magistrates. Catulus, Isauricus, Hortensius, the Lucullus brothers, Silanus, Murena, even Cato, who was now a tribune-elect alongside Nepos—each was drawn aside and given a whispered briefing. Cicero at these moments looked like nothing so much as a crafty carpet salesman in a crowded bazaar, glancing furtively over his customer's shoulder and then backward over his own, his voice low, his hands moving expressively as he sought to close a deal. Caesar watched him from a distance, and I in turn watched Caesar. His expression was unreadable. There was no sign of Catilina.

When the senators all trooped in for the start of the session, Cicero took his place at the end of the front bench nearest to the consular dais, which was where he always sat in the months when he was not presiding; Catulus was on his other side. From this vantage point, by a series of nods and eye gestures at Hybrida and occasional audible whispers, Cicero was normally able to control proceedings even in those months when he did not have the chair. To be fair to him, Hybrida was almost credible when he had a script to read out, as he had that day. With his broad shoulders squared and his noble head thrown back, and in a voice that had been pickled rich in wine, he declared that public events had taken a grave turn overnight, and called upon Quintus Arrius to make a statement.

Arrius was one of those senators who did not speak often but when he did was listened to with respect. I don't know why. Perhaps the absurdity of his voice seemed to lend it a peculiar sincerity. He rose now and delivered a very full report of what he had seen happening in the countryside: that armed bands were congregating in Etruria, recruited by Manlius; that their numbers might soon swell to ten thousand; that he understood their intention was to attack Praeneste; that the security of Rome itself was threatened; and that similar uprisings were planned in Apulia and Capua. By the time he resumed his seat there was an audible and growing swell of panic. Hybrida thanked him and next called on Crassus, Marcellus, and Scipio to read aloud the messages they had received the previous evening. He gave the letters to the clerks, who passed them to their original recipients. Crassus was first on his feet. He described the mysterious arrival of the warnings and how he had gone at once with the others to see Cicero. Then he read his out in a firm, clear voice: *"The time for talking is over. The moment for action has arrived. Catilina has drawn up his plans. He wishes to warn you there will be bloodshed in Rome. Spare yourself and leave the city secretly. When it is safe to return, you will be contacted."*

Can you imagine the cumulative effect of those words, gravely intoned by Crassus and then repeated, more nervously, by Scipio and Marcellus? The shock was all the greater as Crassus was known to have supported Catilina for the consulship not once but twice. There was a profound hush, and then someone shouted, "Where is he?" The cry was taken up by others. "Where is he? Where is he?" In the pandemonium Cicero briefly whispered something to Catulus, and the old patrician took the floor.

"In view of the appalling news this house has just received," declared Catulus, "and in accordance with the ancient prerogatives of this order, I propose that the consuls should be empowered to take all necessary measures for the defense of the realm, under the provisions of the Final Act. These powers shall include, but not be limited to, the authority to levy troops and conduct war, to apply unlimited force to allies and citizens alike, and to exercise supreme command and jurisdiction both at home and abroad."

"Quintus Lutatius Catulus has proposed that we adopt the Final Act," said Hybrida. "Does anyone wish to oppose it?"

All heads now turned to Caesar, not least because the legitimacy of the Final Act was the central issue at the heart of the prosecution of Rabirius. But Caesar, for the first time in my experience, looked utterly overwhelmed by events. He noticeably did not exchange a word with his neighbor, Crassus, or even glance at him—a rare occurrence, as normally they were very thick together—and I deduced from this that Crassus's betrayal of Catilina had taken him entirely by surprise. He made no gesture of any sort, but stared straight ahead into the middle distance, thus giving some of us an early preview of those marble busts of him which gaze impassively with sightless eyes across every public building in Italy.

"Then if no one opposes it," said Hybrida, "the motion passes, and the chair recognizes Marcus Tullius Cicero."

Only now did Cicero rise, to a deep rumble of acclaim from those selfsame senators who just a few weeks earlier had been mocking him for his alarmism. "Gentlemen," he said, "I wish to congratulate Antonius Hybrida for the very firm manner in which he has handled this crisis today." The senators murmured in approval; Hybrida beamed. "For my own part, trusting in the shield provided by my friends and allies, I shall remain in Rome and continue to defy this murderous madman, Catilina, as I always have. Because no one can say how long this threat will continue, I hereby ask formally to be relieved of my allotted province, in accordance with the promise I made at the start of my consulship—a promise all the more urgent in this hour of trial for our republic."

Cicero's patriotic self-sacrifice was warmly approved, and Hybrida at once produced the sacred urn and put into it one marked token representing Nearer Gaul and seven blanks—or so it appeared. In fact, I learned later, he had put in only blanks. The eight praetors then came forward, and the first to try his luck was the haughty figure of Lentulus Sura, whom Cicero knew to be deeply involved in Catilina's schemes. Sura, one of the most inbred boobs in the Senate, was closely related to Hybrida in all sorts of ways: for one thing, he had married the widow of Hybrida's brother and was bringing up the son of that union, Mark Antony, as his own; and this same Mark Antony was engaged to Hybrida's daughter, Antonia. So I watched Hybrida closely to see if he would be able to go through with the deception he had promised. But politics has loyalties all of its own, and they greatly supersede those to in-laws. Sura thrust his arm deep into the urn and handed his token to Hybrida, who announced it blank and showed it to the chamber. Sura shrugged and turned away; it wasn't a province he was after in any case, but Rome itself.

Pomptinus went next, and then Flaccus, with the same result. Celer was fourth to draw a lot. He looked very cool as he made his way to the dais and picked his token. Hybrida took it from him and seemed to turn away, toward the light, to read it carefully, and that is when he must have made the switch, for when he held it up for inspection everyone nearby could clearly see the cross that was marked upon it.

"Celer draws Nearer Gaul!" he announced. "May the gods favor his appointment."

There was applause. Cicero was on his feet at once.

"I propose that Quintus Caecilius Metellus Celer be now invested with full military imperium, and be given the authority to raise an army to defend his province."

"Does anyone object?" asked Hybrida.

For a moment I thought Crassus was going to get to his feet. He seemed to half lean forward, hesitate, and then think better of it.

"The motion is passed unanimously."

After the Senate adjourned Cicero and Hybrida convened a council of war with all the praetors to issue the necessary edicts for the defense of the

city. A message was dispatched at once to the commander of the garrison
at Praeneste ordering him to strengthen the guard. A long-standing offer
from the prefect of Reate to send a hundred men was accepted. In Rome
the gates were to be closed an hour earlier than usual. There would be a
curfew at the twelfth hour and street patrols throughout the night. The
ancient prohibition on carrying arms within the precincts of the city
would be suspended in the case of soldiers loyal to the Senate. Wagons
would be searched at random. Access to the Palatine would be blocked at
sunset. All the gladiator schools in and around the capital would be closed
and the fighters dispersed to distant towns and colonies. Huge rewards, of
up to one hundred thousand sesterces, were to be offered to anyone—
slaves as well as freemen—with information about potential traitors.
Celer would leave at first light to begin mustering fresh levies of troops.
Finally, it was agreed that various reliable men should be approached and
asked to bring a prosecution against Catilina for violence against the
state, in return for guarantees of their personal protection.

Throughout all this Lentulus Sura sat calmly, with his freedman Publius Umbrenus seated beside him taking notes, and afterward Cicero
complained bitterly to me of this absurdity: that two of the chief plotters
should be able to attend the innermost security council of the state and
report back on its decisions to their fellow criminals! But what could he
do? It was the same old story: he had no evidence.

Cicero's guards were anxious to get him home before darkness fell,
and so once the business was concluded we went out cautiously into the
thickening twilight and then hurried across the Forum, through Subura
and up the Esquiline Hill. About an hour later Cicero was in his study
composing dispatches notifying the provincial governors of the Senate's
decisions when the guard dog set up its infernal barking again. Moments
later the porter came in to tell us that Metellus Celer had arrived to see
the consul and was waiting in the atrium.

It was obvious straightaway that Celer was agitated. He was pacing
around the room and cracking his knuckles while Quintus and Titus Sextus kept a careful watch on him from the passageway.

"Well, Governor," said Cicero, seeing at once that his visitor needed
calming down, "the afternoon went smoothly enough, I thought."

"From your point of view perhaps, but my brother isn't happy. I told
you there'd be trouble. Nepos says that if the rebels in Etruria are as seri-

ous as we make out, Pompey himself should be brought home to deal with them."

"But we haven't the time to wait for Pompey and his army to travel a thousand miles back to Rome. We'll all be slaughtered in our beds long before he gets here."

"So *you* say, but Catilina swears he means no threat to the state, and insists those letters have nothing to do with him."

"You've spoken to him?"

"He came to see me just after you left the Senate. To prove his peaceful intentions he's offered to surrender himself into my personal custody for as long as I wish."

"Ha! What a rogue! You sent him away with a flea in his ear, I trust?"

"No, I've brought him here to see you."

"*Here*? He's in my *house*?"

"No, he's waiting in the street. I think you should talk to him. He's alone and unarmed—I'll vouch for him."

"Even if he is, what possible good can come of talking to him?"

"He's a Sergius, Consul," said Celer icily, "descended from the Trojans. He deserves some respect for his blood, if nothing else."

Cicero glanced at the Sextus brothers. Titus shrugged. "If he's on his own, Consul, we can handle him."

"Fetch him in then, Celer," said Cicero, "and I'll hear what he has to say. But I promise you, we're wasting our time."

I was horrified that Cicero would take such a risk, and while Celer went off to get Catilina I actually dared to remonstrate with him. But he cut me off. "It will show good faith on my part if I can announce in the Senate that at least I was willing to receive the villain. Who knows anyway? Perhaps he's come to apologize."

He forced a smile, but I could tell that this unexpected development had strained his nerves. As for me, I felt like one of the condemned men in the Games when the tiger is let into the arena, for that was how Catilina came prowling into that room—wild and wary, full of barely suppressed fury: I half expected him to spring at Cicero's throat. The Sextus brothers stepped in close behind him as he came to a halt a couple of paces in front of Cicero. He raised his hand in mock salute. "Consul."

"Say your piece, Senator, and then get out."

"I hear you've been spreading lies about me again."

"You see?" said Cicero, turning to Celer. "What did I tell you? This is pointless."

"Just hear him out," said Celer.

"Lies," repeated Catilina. "I don't know a damned thing about these letters people are saying I sent last night. I'd have to be a rare fool to dispatch such messages all across the city."

"I'm willing to believe you personally didn't send them," replied Cicero, "but there are plenty of men around you stupid enough to do such a thing."

"Balls! They're blatant forgeries. Do you know what I think? I think you wrote them yourself."

"You'd do better to direct your suspicions toward Crassus—he's the one who's used them as an excuse to turn his back on you."

"Old Baldhead is playing his own game, the same as he always does."

"And the rebels in Etruria? Are they nothing to do with you, either?"

"They're poor and starving wretches, driven to desperate lengths by the moneylenders—they have my sympathy, but I'm not their leader. I'll make the same offer to you I've made to Celer. I'll surrender myself into your custody and live in this house, where you and your guards can keep an eye on me, and then you can see how innocent I am."

"That is not an offer but a joke! If I don't feel safe living in the same city as you, I'll hardly feel safe under the same roof."

"So there's nothing I can do that will satisfy you?"

"Yes. Remove yourself from Rome and Italy entirely. Go into exile. Never return."

Catilina's eyes glittered and his large hands contracted into fists. "My first ancestor was Sergestus, companion of Aeneas, the founder of our city—and *you* dare to tell *me* to leave?"

"Oh, spare us the family folklore! Mine at least is a serious offer. If you go into exile I'll see to it no harm befalls your wife and children. Your sons won't suffer the shame of having a father who is condemned—because you will be condemned, Catilina, be in no doubt about that. You'll also escape your creditors, which I'd have thought was another consideration."

"And what about my friends? How long will they be subjected to your dictatorship?"

"My dictatorship, as you call it, is only in force to protect us all against *you*. Once you're gone it won't be needed, and I for one would be pleased to start afresh and offer a clean slate to all men. Voluntary exile would be a noble course, Catilina—one worthy of those ancestors you're always talking about."

"So now the grandson of a chickpea farmer presumes to lecture a Sergius on what is noble? He'll be telling you next, Celer!" Celer stared stiffly ahead, like a soldier on parade. "Look at him," sneered Catilina. "Typical Metelli—they always prosper whatever happens. But you realize, Cicero, that secretly he despises you? They all do. I at least have the guts to say to your face what they only whisper behind your back. They may use you to protect their precious property. But once you've done their dirty work they'll want nothing more to do with you. Destroy me if you will; in the end you'll only destroy yourself."

He turned on his heel, pushed past the Sextus brothers, and strode out of the house. Cicero said, "Why is it he always seems to leave a smell of sulphur behind him?"

"Do you think he'll go into exile?" asked Celer.

"He might. I don't think he knows from one moment to the next what he's going to do. He's like an animal: he'll follow whatever impulse seizes him. The main thing is to maintain our guard and vigilance—I in the city, you in the countryside."

"I'll leave at first light." He made a move toward the door, then stopped and turned. "By the way, all that stuff about us despising you—there's not a word of truth in it, you know?"

"I know that, Celer, thank you." Cicero smiled at him, and maintained the smile until he heard the door close, at which point it slowly faded from his face. He sank back onto the nearest chair and held out his hands, palms upward, contemplating them in wonder, as if their violent trembling was the strangest thing he had ever seen.

IX

THE FOLLOWING DAY Quintus came to see Cicero in great excitement, bearing a copy of a letter that had been posted outside the offices of the tribunes. It was addressed to a number of prominent senators, among them Catulus, Caesar, and Lepidus, and was signed by Catilina:

> *Unable to withstand that group of enemies who have persecuted me with false charges, I have departed for exile in Massilia. I leave not because I am guilty of the heinous crimes of which I am accused but to preserve the peace of the state and to spare the republic the bloodshed that would ensue if I struggled against my fate. I commend my wife and family to your care and my honor to your memories. Farewell!*

"Congratulations, Brother," said Quintus, clapping him on the back. "You've seen him off."

"But is this certain?"

"As certain as can be. He was seen early this morning riding out of the city with a few companions. His house is locked and deserted."

Cicero winced and tugged at his earlobe. "Even so, something about it smells wrong to me."

Quintus, who had hurried up the hill specially to convey the good news, was irritated by his caution. "Catilina's been obliged to flee. It's tantamount to a confession. You've beaten him."

And slowly, as the days passed and nothing was heard of Catilina, it did begin to seem that Quintus was right. Nevertheless, Cicero refused to relax the security restrictions in Rome; indeed, he went around with even more protection than before. Accompanied by a dozen men he ventured outside the city to see Quintus Metellus, who still possessed military imperium, and asked him to go to the heel of Italy and take charge of the region of Apulia. The old man grumbled, but Cicero swore that after this last mission his triumph was assured, and Metellus—secretly glad to have something to occupy him, I suspect—set off at once. Another former consul also hoping for a triumph, Marcius Rex, went north to Faesulae. The praetor, Quintos Pompeius Rufus, whom Cicero trusted, was ordered to go to Capua to raise troops. Meanwhile, Metellus Celer continued recruiting an army in Picenum.

At some point during this time the rebel leader Manlius sent a message to the Senate:

> *We call on gods and men to witness that our object in taking up*
> *arms was not to attack our country or endanger others, but to protect*
> *ourselves from wrong. We are poor needy wretches; the cruel harshness*
> *of moneylenders has robbed most of us of our homes, and all of us have*
> *lost reputation and fortune.*

He demanded that every debt contracted in silver (as most debts were) be repaid in copper: an effective relief of three-quarters. Cicero proposed sending a stern reply that there could be no negotiations until the rebels laid down their arms. The motion carried in the Senate, but many outside whispered that the rebels' cause was just.

October gave way to November. The days began to be dark and cold; the people of Rome grew weary and depressed. The curfew had put a stop to many of those entertainments with which they normally warded off the encroaching gloom of winter. The taverns and the baths closed early; the shops were bare. Informers, eager for the huge rewards for denouncing traitors, took the opportunity to pay back scores against their neighbors. Everyone suspected everyone else. Matters became so serious that eventually Atticus bravely took it upon himself to talk to Cicero.

"Some citizens are saying you've deliberately exaggerated the threat," he warned his friend.

"And why would I do that? Do they think it gives me pleasure to turn Rome into a jail in which I'm the most closely guarded prisoner?"

"No, but they think you're obsessed with Catilina and have lost all sense of proportion; that your fears for your own personal safety are making their lives intolerable."

"Is that all?"

"They believe you're acting like a dictator."

"Do they really?"

"They also say you're a coward."

"Well then, damn the people!" exclaimed Cicero, and for the first time I saw him treat Atticus coldly, refusing to respond to his further attempts at conversation with anything more than monosyllables. Eventually his friend wearied of this frosty atmosphere, rolled his eyes at me, and went away.

Late on the evening of the sixth day of November, long after the lictors had gone off for the night, Cicero was reclining in the dining room with Terentia and Quintus. He had been reading dispatches from magistrates all over Italy, and I was just handing him some letters for his signature when Sargon started barking furiously. The noise made us all jump; everyone's nerves were shredded by then. Cicero's three guards all got to their feet. We heard the front door open and the sound of an urgent male voice, and suddenly into the room strode Cicero's former pupil Caelius Rufus. It was his first appearance on the premises for months, all the more startling because he had gone over to Catilina at the start of the year. Quintus jumped up, ready for a fight.

"Rufus," said Cicero calmly, "I thought you were a stranger to us these days."

"I'll never be a stranger to you."

He took a step forward, but Quintus put his hand on his chest and stopped him. "Arms up!" he commanded, and he nodded to the guards. Rufus hastily raised both hands while Titus Sextus searched him. "I expect he's come to spy on us," said Quintus, who had never cared much for Rufus and often asked me why I thought his brother tolerated the presence of such a tearaway.

"I've not come to spy. I've come to warn: Catilina's back."

Cicero banged his fist on the table. "I knew it! Put your hands down, Rufus. When did he return?"

"This evening."

"And where is he now?"

"At the home of Marcus Laeca, on the street of the scythe-makers."

"Who's with him?"

"Sura, Cethegus, Bestia—the whole gang. I've only just got away."

"And?"

"They're going to kill you at sunrise."

Terentia put her hand to her mouth.

"How?" demanded Quintus.

"Two men, Vargunteius and Corenelius, will call on you at dawn to pledge their loyalty and claim they've deserted Catilina. They'll be armed. There'll be others at their backs to overpower your guards. You mustn't admit either of them."

"We won't," said Quintus.

"But I'd have admitted them," said Cicero. "A senator and a knight—of course I would. I'd have offered them the hand of friendship." He seemed amazed at how close to disaster he had come despite all his precautions.

"How do we know the lad isn't lying?" said Quintus. "It could be a trick to divert us from the real threat."

"He has a point, Rufus," said Cicero. "Your loyalty is about as fixed as a weathercock."

"It's the truth."

"Yet you support their cause?"

"Their cause, yes, not their methods—not any longer."

"What methods are these?"

"They've agreed to carve up Italy into military regions. The moment you're dead Catilina will go to the rebel army in Etruria. Parts of Rome will be set alight. There'll be a massacre of senators on the Palatine, and then the city gates will be opened to Manlius and his mob."

"And Caesar? Does he know all this?"

"He wasn't there tonight but I sense he knows what's planned. Catilina talks to him quite often."

This was the first time Cicero had received direct intelligence of Catilina's intentions. His expression was appalled. He bent his head and rubbed his temples with his knuckles. "What to do?" he muttered.

"We need to get you out of this house tonight," said Quintus, "and hide you somewhere they can't get at you."

"You could go to Atticus," I suggested.

Cicero shook his head. "That's the first place they'd look. The only safe refuge is out of Rome. Terentia and Marcus at least could go to Tusculum."

"I'm not going anywhere," said Terentia, "and neither should you. The Roman people will respect many kinds of leader, but they'll never respect a coward. This is your home and your father's home before you—stay in it and dare them to do their worst. I know I should if I were a man."

She glared at Cicero, and I feared we were about to be treated to another of their stupendous rows which had so often split that modest house like claps of thunder. But then Cicero nodded. "You're right. Tiro, send a message to Atticus telling him we need reinforcements urgently. We'll barricade the doors."

"And we should get some barrels of water on the roof," added Quintus, "in case they try to burn us out."

"I'll stay and help," said Rufus.

"No, my young friend," said Cicero, "you've done your part, and I'm grateful for it. But you should leave the city at once. Go back to your father's house in Interamna until all this is settled, one way or the other." Rufus started to protest, but Cicero cut him off. "If Catilina fails to kill me tomorrow he may suspect you of betraying him; if he succeeds, you'll be sucked into the whirlpool. Either way you're better off a long way from Rome."

Rufus tried to argue but to no avail. After he had gone, Cicero said, "He's probably on our side, but who can tell? In the end, the only safe place to put a Trojan horse is outside your walls."

I dispatched one of the slaves to Atticus with a plea for help. Then we barred the door and dragged a heavy chest and a couch across it. The rear entrance was also locked and bolted; as a second line of defense we wedged an upended table to block the passageway. Together with Sositheus and Laurea I carried up bucket after bucket of water to the roof, along with carpets and blankets to smother any fires. Within this makeshift citadel we had, to protect the consul, a garrison of three bodyguards, Quintus, myself, Sargon and his handler, a gatekeeper, and a few male slaves armed with knives and sticks. And I must not forget Terentia, who carried a heavy iron candleholder at all times, and who would probably have been more effective than any of us. The maids cowered in the nursery with Marcus, who had a toy sword.

Cicero put on a display of great calmness. He sat at his desk, thinking and making notes and writing out letters in his own hand. From time to time he asked me whether there was any reply yet from Atticus. He wanted to know the moment the extra men appeared, so I armed myself with a kitchen knife, went up onto the roof again, wrapped myself in a blanket, and kept watch on the street. It was dark and silent; nothing moved. As far as I could tell the whole of Rome was slumbering. I thought back to the night that Cicero won the consulship, and how I had joined the family up here to dine by starlight in celebration. He had realized from the start that his position was weak and that power would be fraught with dangers; he could hardly have imagined such a scene as this.

Several hours passed. I heard dogs bark occasionally but no human voices, apart from the watchman down in the valley, calling the divisions of the night. The cocks crowed as usual, then fell silent, and the air actually seemed to grow darker and very cold. Laurea called up that the consul wanted to see me. I went downstairs and found him seated in his curule chair in the atrium, with a drawn sword resting across his knees.

"You're sure you definitely requested those extra men from Atticus?"

"Of course."

"And you stressed the urgency?"

"Yes."

"And the messenger was trustworthy?"

"Very."

"Well then," said Cicero, "Atticus won't let me down; he never has." But he sounded as if he was trying to reassure himself, and I am sure that he was remembering the circumstances of their last meeting, and their chilly parting. It was nearly dawn. The dog started barking wildly again. Cicero looked at me with exhausted eyes. His face was very strained. "Go and see," he said.

I climbed back up to the roof and peered carefully over the parapet. At first I could make out nothing. But gradually I realized that the shadows on the far side of the street were moving. A line of men was approaching, keeping close to the wall. My first thought was that our reinforcements had arrived. But then Sargon set up his infernal barking again. The shadows halted and a man's voice whispered. I hurried back down to Cicero. Quintus was standing next to him with his sword unsheathed. Terentia clutched her candlestick.

"The attackers are here," I said.

"How many?" asked Quintus.

"Ten. Perhaps twelve."

There was a loud knock on the front door. Cicero swore. "If a dozen men are determined to get into this house, they'll do it."

"The door will hold them for a while," said Quintus. "It's fire that worries me."

"I'll go back to the roof," I said.

There was a very faint gray tinge to the sky by this time, and when I looked down into the street I could see the dark shapes of heads huddled around the front of the house. They seemed intent on something. There was a flash, and abruptly they all drew back as a torch flared. Someone must have seen my face looking down, because a man shouted, "Hey, you up there! Is the consul in?" I pulled back out of sight.

Another man called up, "This is Senator Lucius Vargunteius, to see the consul! I have urgent information for him!"

Just then I heard a crash and voices from the back of the house. A second group was trying to break in at the rear. I was halfway across the roof when suddenly a torch sailed over the edge of the parapet, twisting and roaring in flight. It buzzed close to my ear and clattered onto the tiles next to me, the burning pitch breaking and scattering into a dozen flaming pieces. I shouted down the stairwell for help, grabbed a heavy carpet, and just about managed to throw it over the little fires, stamping out the ones I missed as best I could. Another torch roared through the air, landed with a crash, and disintegrated; then another, and another. The roof, which was made of old timber as well as terra-cotta, glimmered in the darkness like a field of stars, and I saw that Quintus was right: if this went on much longer they would burn us out and slaughter Cicero in the street.

Filled with a fury born of fear, I seized the handle of the nearest torch which still had a sizable piece of burning pitch attached to it, darted to the edge of the roof, took careful aim, and hurled it at the men below. It hit one fellow square on the head, setting his hair on fire. While he was screaming I ran back for another. By now Sositheus and Laurea had come up onto the roof to help stamp out the fires, and they must have thought I was demented as I jumped up onto the parapet, screaming with rage, and threw another burning missile at our attackers. Out of the corner of my eye I saw that more shadowy figures with torches were pouring into the street. I thought we were certain to be overwhelmed. But suddenly from beneath me came the sound of angry cries, the ring of steel on steel, and the echo of running feet. "Tiro!" shouted a voice, and by the flaring yellow light I recognized the upturned face of Atticus. The street was jammed with his men. "Tiro! Is your master safe? Let us in!"

I ran downstairs and along the passageway, with the consul and Terentia at my heels, and together with Quintus and the Sextus brothers we dragged away the chest and the couch and unbarred the door. The moment it was open Cicero and Atticus fell into each other's arms, to the cheers and applause from the street of some thirty members of the Order of Knights.

By the time it was fully light the approaches to Cicero's house were blocked and guarded. Any visitor wishing to see him, even senior members of the Senate, had to wait at one of the armed checkpoints until word had been sent to the consul. Then if Cicero wanted to meet them I would go out to confirm their identity and escort them into his presence. Catulus, Isauricus, Hortensius, and both of the Lucullus brothers were all admitted in this way, along with the consuls-elect, Silanus and Murena. They brought with them the news that throughout Rome Cicero was now regarded as a hero. Sacrifices had been made in his honor and prayers of thanks offered up for his safety, while rocks had been hurled at Catilina's empty house. All morning a steady procession of gifts and goodwill messages was carried up the Esquiline Hill—flowers, wine, cakes, olive oil— until the atrium looked like a market stall. Clodia sent him a basket of luxuriant fruit from her orchard on the Palatine. But this was intercepted by Terentia before it reached her husband, and I watched a look of suspicion darken her face as she read Clodia's note; she ordered the steward to throw the fruit away, "for fear of poison."

A warrant was issued by Cicero for the arrest of Vargunteius and Cornelius. The leaders of the Senate also urged him to order the capture of Catilina, dead or alive. But Cicero hesitated. "It's all very well for them," he said to Quintus and Atticus after the deputation had gone, "their names wouldn't be on the warrant. But if Catilina is killed illegally on my orders I'll be fighting off prosecutors for the rest of my days. Besides, it would only be a short-term remedy. It would still leave his supporters in the Senate."

"You're not suggesting he should be allowed to carry on living in Rome?" protested Quintus.

"No, I just want him to leave—leave and take his treasonous friends with him, and let them all join the rebel army and be killed on the field of battle, preferably a hundred miles away from me. By heavens, I'd give them a pass of safe conduct and a guard of honor to escort them out of the city if they wanted it—anything they liked so long as they'd just clear out."

But however much he paced around he could not see a way of bringing this about, and in the end he decided his only course was to call a meeting of the Senate. Quintus and Atticus immediately objected that this would be dangerous: How could they guarantee his safety? Cicero pondered further and then came up with a clever idea. Rather than convene the Senate in its usual chamber, he gave orders that the benches should be carried across the Forum to the Temple of Jupiter the Protector. This had two advantages. First, because the temple was on the lower slopes of the Palatine, it could more easily be defended against an attack by Catilina's supporters. Second, it would have great symbolic value. According to legend the temple had been vowed to Jupiter by Romulus himself at a critical juncture in the war against the Sabine tribes. Here was the very spot on which Rome had stood and rallied in her earliest hour of danger: here she would stand and rally in her latest, led by her new Romulus.

By the time Cicero set off for the temple, tightly protected by lictors and bodyguards, an atmosphere of real dread hung over the city, as tangible as the gray November mist rising from the Tiber. The streets were deathly quiet. Nobody applauded or jeered; they simply hid indoors. In the shadows of their windows the citizenry gathered, white-faced and silent, to watch the consul pass.

When we reached the temple we found it ringed by members of the Order of Knights, some quite elderly, all armed with lances and swords. Within this security perimeter several hundred senators stood around in muted groups. They parted to let us through, and a few patted Cicero on the back and whispered their good wishes. Cicero nodded in acknowledgment, took the auspices very quickly, and then he and the lictors led the way into the large building. I had never set foot inside before and it presented a most somber scene. Centuries old, every wall and corner was crammed with relics of military glory from the earliest days of the republic—bloodied standards, dented armor, ships' beaks, legionary eagles, and a statue of Scipio Africanus painted up to look so lifelike it actually seemed he stood among us. I was some distance back in Cicero's retinue, the senators pouring in behind me, and because I was so busy craning my neck at all the memorabilia I must have dawdled a little. At any rate it wasn't until I had nearly reached the dais that I became aware, to my embarrassment, that the only sound in the building was the *click click* of my footsteps on the stone floor. The Senate, I realized, had fallen entirely still.

Cicero was fiddling with a roll of papyrus. He turned to find out what was happening, and I saw his face become transfixed with astonishment. I spun around in alarm myself—only to see Catilina calmly taking his place on one of the benches. Almost everyone else was still on their feet watching him. Catilina sat, whereupon all the men nearest to him started edging away, as if he had leprosy. I never saw such a demonstration in my life. Even Caesar wouldn't go near him. Catilina took no notice, but folded his arms and thrust out his chin. The silence lengthened until eventually I heard Cicero's voice, very calm behind me.

"How much longer, Catilina, will you try our patience?"

All my life people have asked me about Cicero's speech that day. "Did he write it out beforehand?" they want to know. "Surely he must at least have planned what he was going to say?" The answer to both questions is "no." It was entirely spontaneous. Fragments of things he had long wanted to say, lines he had practiced in his head, thoughts that had come to him in the sleepless nights of the last few months—all of it he wove together while he was on his feet.

"How much longer must we put up with your madness?"

He descended from his dais and started to advance very slowly along the aisle to where Catilina was sitting. As he walked he extended both his arms and briefly gestured to the senators to take their places, which they did, and somehow that schoolmasterly gesture, and their instant compliance, established his authority. He was speaking for the republic.

"Is there no end to your arrogance? Don't you understand that we know what you're up to? Don't you appreciate your conspiracy is uncovered? Do you think there's a man among us who doesn't know what you did last night—where you were, who came to your meeting, and what you agreed?" He stood at last in front of Catilina, his arms akimbo, looked him up and down, and shook his head. "Oh, what times are these," he said in a voice of utter disgust, "and oh, what morals! The Senate knows everything, the consul knows everything, and yet—*this man is still alive!*"

He wheeled around. "Alive? Not just alive, gentlemen," he cried, moving on down the aisle from Catilina and addressing the packed benches from the center of the temple, "he attends the Senate! He takes part in our debates. He listens to us. He watches us—and all the time he's deciding who he's going to kill! Is this how we serve the republic—simply by sitting here, hoping it's not going to be us? How very brave we are! It's been twenty days since we voted ourselves the authority to act. We have the sword—but we keep it sheathed! You ought to have been executed immediately, Catilina. Yet still you live! And as long as you live, you don't give up your plotting—you increase it!"

I suppose by now even Catilina must have realized the size of his mistake in coming into the temple. In terms of physical strength and sheer effrontery he was much more powerful than Cicero. But the Senate was not the arena for brute force. The weapons here were words, and no one ever knew how to deploy words as well as Cicero. For twenty years, whenever the courts were in session, scarcely a day had gone by which hadn't seen Cicero practicing his craft. In a sense, his whole life had been but a preparation for this moment.

"Let's go over the events of last night. You went to the street of the scythe-makers—I'll be precise—to the house of Marcus Laeca. There you were joined by your criminal accomplices. Well, do you deny it? Why the silence? If you deny it, I'll prove it. In fact, I see some of those who were with you here in the Senate. In heaven's name, where in the world are we? What country is this? What city are we living in? Here, gentlemen—here in our very midst, in this, the most sacred and important council in the world, there are men who want to destroy us, destroy our city, and extend that destruction to the entire world!

"You were at the house of Laeca, Catilina. You carved up the regions of Italy. You decided where you wanted each man to go. You said you would go yourself as soon I was dead. You chose parts of the city to be burned. You sent two men to kill me. So I say to you, why don't you finish the journey you have begun? At long last really leave the city! The gates are open. Be on your way! The rebel army awaits its general. Take all your men with you. Cleanse the city. Put a wall between us. You cannot remain among us any longer—I cannot, I will not, I *must not* permit it!"

He thumped his right fist against his chest and cast his eyes to the roof of the temple as the Senate came to its feet, bellowing its approval. "Kill him!" someone shouted. "Kill him! Kill him!" The cry was passed from man to man. Cicero waved them back down onto their benches.

"If I give an order for you to be killed, there will remain in the state the rest of the conspirators. But if, as I have long been urging, you leave the city, you will drain from it that flood of sewage that for you are your accomplices and for the rest of us our deadly enemies. Well, Catilina? What are you waiting for? What's left that can give you any pleasure in this city now? Beyond that conspiracy of ruined men there isn't a single person who doesn't fear you, not one who doesn't hate you."

There was much more in this vein, and then Cicero moved into his peroration. "Let the traitors, then, depart!" he concluded. "Go forth, Catilina, to your iniquitous and wicked war, and so bring sure salvation to the republic, disaster and ruin on yourself, and destruction to those who have joined you. Jupiter, you will protect us," he thundered, reaching out his hand to the statue of the deity, "and visit on these evil men, alive or dead, your punishment eternal!"

Cicero turned away and stalked up the aisle to the dais. Now the chant was "Go! Go! Go!" In an effort to retrieve the situation Catilina leapt to his feet and began waving his arms about and shouting at Cicero's back. But it was far too late for him to undo the damage, and he didn't have the skill. He was flayed, humiliated, exposed, finished. I caught the words "immigrant" and "exile," but the din was too great for him to be heard and in any case his fury rendered him almost incomprehensible. As the cacophony of sound raged around him he fell silent, breathing deeply, and stood there for a short while longer, turning this way and that, like a once great ship lashed by a terrible storm, mastless and twisting at anchor, until something in him seemed to give way. He shuddered and stepped out into the aisle, at which point several senators, including Quintus, jumped across the benches to protect the consul. But even Catilina was not that demented: had he lunged at his enemy he would have been torn to pieces. Instead, with a final contemptuous glance around him—a glance that no doubt took in all those ancient glories in which his ancestors had played their part—he marched out of the Senate. Later that same day, accompanied by twelve followers whom he called his lictors, and preceded by the silver eagle that had once belonged to Marius, he left the city and went to Arretium, where he formally proclaimed himself consul.

There are no lasting victories in politics, there is only the remorseless grinding forward of events. If my work has a moral, this is it. Cicero had scored an oratorical triumph over Catilina that would be talked about for years. With the whip of his tongue he had driven the monster from Rome. But the sewage, as he called it, did not, as he had hoped, drain away with him. On the contrary, after their leader had departed, Sura and the others remained calmly in their places, listening to the rest of the debate. They sat together, presumably on the principle of safety in numbers: Sura, Cethegus, Longinus, Annius, Paetus, the tribune-elect Bestia, the Sulla brothers, even Marcus Laeca, from whose house the assassins had been dispatched. I could see Cicero staring at them and I wondered what was going through his mind. Sura actually rose at one point and suggested in his sonorous voice that Catilina's wife and children be placed under the protection of the Senate! The discussion meandered on. Then the tribune-elect Metellus Nepos demanded the floor. Now that Catilina had left the city, he said, presumably to lead the insurrection, surely the most prudent course would be to invite Pompey the Great back to Italy to take charge of the senatorial forces? Caesar quickly stood and seconded the proposal. Nimble-witted as ever, Cicero saw a chance to drive a wedge between his opponents, and with an innocent air of genuine interest, he asked Crassus, who had been consul alongside Pompey, for his opinion. Crassus got up reluctantly.

"Nobody has a higher opinion of Pompey the Great than I," he began, and then had to stop for a while, tapping his foot irritably as the temple shook with mocking laughter. "Nobody has a higher opinion than I," he repeated, "but I have to say to the tribune-elect, in case he hasn't noticed, that it's nearly winter, the very worst time to transport troops by sea. How can Pompey possibly be here before the spring?"

"Then let us have Pompey the Great without his army," countered Nepos. "Traveling with a light escort he can be with us in a month. His name alone is worth a dozen legions."

This was too much for Cato. He was on his feet in an instant. "The enemies we face will not be defeated by *names*," he mocked, "even *names* which end in 'Great.' What we need are armies: armies in the field—armies like the one being raised at this very moment by the tribune-elect's own brother. Besides, if you ask me, Pompey has too much power as it is."

That drew a loud and shocked "Oh!" from the assembly.

"If this Senate will not vote Pompey the command," said Nepos, "then I give you fair warning that I shall lay a bill before the people as soon as I take office as tribune demanding his recall."

"And I give you fair warning," retorted Cato, "that I shall veto your bill."

"Gentlemen, gentlemen!" cried Cicero, having to shout to make himself heard, "we shall do neither the state nor ourselves any good by bickering at a time of national emergency! Tomorrow there will be a public assembly. I shall report to the people on our deliberations, and I hope," he added, staring hard at Sura and his cronies, "those senators whose bodies may be with us but whose loyalties lie elsewhere will search their hearts overnight and act accordingly. This house stands adjourned."

Normally after a session ended Cicero liked to stand outside for a while so that any senator who wished to speak to him could do so. It was one of those tools by which he exerted his control over the chamber, this knowledge he had of every man, however minor—his strengths and weaknesses, what he desired and what he feared, what he would put up with and what he would not stomach under any circumstances. But that afternoon he hurried away, his face rigid with frustration. "It's like fighting the Hydra!" he complained furiously when we got home. "No sooner do I lop off one head than another two grow back in its place! So while Catilina storms out, his henchmen all sit there as calm as you please, and now Pompey's faction are starting to stir! I have one month," he ranted, "just one month—if I can survive that long—before the new tribunes come into office. Then the agitation for Pompey's recall will really get started. And in the meantime we can't even be sure we'll actually have two new consuls in January because of this *fucking lawsuit*!" And with that he swept his arm across his desk and sent all the documents relating to Murena's prosecution flying across the floor.

In such a mood he was quite unreasonable, and I had learned from long experience there was no point in attempting to reply. He waited irritably for me to respond and then, failing to get satisfaction, he stamped out in search of someone else to shout at, while I knelt and calmly gathered up all the rolls of evidence. I knew he would come back sooner or later in order to prepare his address to the people for the following day, but the hours passed, dusk fell, and the lamps and candles were lit, and I began to feel alarmed. Afterward I discovered he had gone with his guards and lictors to the nearby gardens and spent the time pacing around and around so ceaselessly they thought he would wear a groove in the stones. When at last he came back his face was very pale and grim. He had devised a plan, he told me, and he did not know which frightened him more: the thought that it might fail or the possibility that it might succeed.

• • •

The following morning he invited Quintus Fabius Sanga to come and see him. Sanga, you may recall, was the senator to whom he had written on the day the murdered boy's body was discovered, requesting information about human sacrifice and the religion of the Gauls. Sanga was about fifty and immensely rich from his investments in Nearer and Further Gaul. He had never aspired to rise beyond the backbenches and treated the Senate purely as a place in which he could protect his business interests. He was very respectable and pious, lived modestly, and was rumored to be strict with his wife and children. He spoke only in debates about Gaul, on which he was, to be frank, an immense bore: once he started talking about its geography, climate, tribes, customs, and so forth, he could empty the chamber quicker than a shout of "Fire!"

"Are you a patriot, Sanga?" asked Cicero the moment I showed him in.

"I like to think I am, Consul," replied Sanga cautiously. "Why?"

"Because I wish you to play a vital part in the defense of our beloved republic."

"Me?" Sanga looked very alarmed. "Oh dear. I am rather afflicted by gout—"

"No, no, nothing like that. I merely want you to ask a man to speak to a man, and then to tell me what he replies."

Sanga noticeably relaxed. "Well yes, I believe I could do that. Who are these men?"

"One is Publius Umbrenus, a freedman of Lentulus Sura, who often acts as his secretary. He used to live in Gaul, I believe. Perhaps you know him?"

"I do indeed."

"The other fellow simply needs to be a Gaul of some sort. I don't mind from what region of Gaul especially. Someone known to you. An emissary of one of the tribes would be ideal. A credible figure here in Rome, whom you trust absolutely."

"And what do you want this Gaul to do?"

"I want him to contact Umbrenus and offer to organize an uprising against Roman rule."

When Cicero had first explained his plan to me the night before I had been privately appalled, and I anticipated that the straitlaced Sanga would feel the same way: that he would throw up his hands and perhaps even storm out of the room at hearing such a monstrous suggestion. But businessmen, I have since come to realize, are the least shockable of characters, far less so than soldiers and politicians. You can propose almost anything to a businessman and he will usually be willing at least to think about it. Sanga merely raised his eyebrows. "You want to lure Sura into an act of treason?"

"Not necessarily treason, but I do want to discover if there are any limits to the wickedness that he and his confederates are willing to envisage. We already know they cheerfully plot assassination, massacre, arson, and armed rebellion. The only heinous crime left that I can think of is collusion with Rome's enemies—not," he added quickly, "that I regard the Gauls as enemies, but you understand what I mean."

"Do you have any particular tribe in mind?"

"No. I'll leave that up to you."

Sanga was silent, turning the matter over. He had a very crafty face. His thin nose twitched. He tapped at it and pulled at it. You could tell he was smelling money. "I have many trading interests in Gaul, and trade depends on peaceful relations. The last thing I want is to make my Gallic friends any less popular in Rome than they are already."

"I can assure you, Sanga, if they help me expose this conspiracy, then by the time I've finished they'll be national heroes."

"And I suppose there's also the question of my own involvement—"

"Your role will be kept entirely secret, except of course, with your permission, from the governors of Further and Nearer Gaul. They're both good friends of mine and I'm sure they'll want to recognize your contribution."

At the prospect of money, Sanga smiled for the first time that morning. "Well, seeing as you put it like that, there *is* a tribe that might fit the bill. The Allobroges, who control the Alpine passes, have just sent a delegation to the Senate to complain about the level of taxes they have to submit to Rome. They arrived in the city a couple of days ago."

"Are they warlike?"

"Very. If I could hint to them that their petition might be looked at favorably, I'm sure they'd be willing to do something in return . . ."

After he had gone, Cicero said to me: "You disapprove?"

"It's not my place to pass judgment, Consul."

"Oh, but you do disapprove! I can see it in your face! You think it's somehow dishonorable to lay a trap. But shall I tell you what's dishonorable, Tiro? What's dishonorable is to go on living in a city that you are secretly plotting to destroy! If Sura has no treasonous intentions, he will send those Gauls packing. But if he agrees to consider their proposals, I shall have him, and then I shall take him personally to the gates of the city and fling him out, and let Celer and his armies finish him off! And no one can say there is anything dishonorable about that!"

He spoke with such vehemence he almost convinced me.

X

THE TRIAL OF the consul-elect, Lucius Murena, on a charge of
electoral corruption began on the Ides of November and was scheduled to last two weeks. Servius and Cato led for the prosecution; Hortensius, Cicero, and Crassus for the defense. It was a huge affair, staged in the
Forum, the jury alone numbering nine hundred. These jurors were made
up of equal proportions of senators, knights, and respectable citizens;
there were too many members for the jury to be rigged, which was the
intention behind having such a large number, but it also made it hard to
tell which way they would vote. The prosecution certainly laid out a formidable case. Servius had plenty of evidence of Murena's bribery which
he presented in his dry legal manner, and he went on at great length
about Cicero's betrayal of their friendship by appearing for the accused.
Cato took the Stoic line and inveighed against the rottenness of an age in
which office could be bought by feasts and games. "Did you not," he
thundered at Murena, "seek supreme power, supreme authority, the very
government of the state, by pandering to men's senses, bewitching their
minds, and plying them with pleasures? Did you think you were asking a
gang of spoiled youths for a job as a pimp or the Roman people for world
dominion?"

Murena was not at all happy with this and had to be calmed throughout by young Clodius, his campaign manager, who sat beside him day
after day and tried to keep his spirits up by witty remarks. As for his defense counsel—well, Murena could hardly have hoped for better. Hortensius, still bruised from his mauling during the trial of Rabirius, was
determined to show he could still command a court, and he had a great
deal of sport at Servius's expense. Crassus, it was true, was not much of an
advocate, but his mere presence on the defense's bench carried weight in
itself. As for Cicero, he was being kept in reserve for the final day of the
trial, when he was due to make the summing-up to the jury.

Throughout the hearing he sat on the rostra, reading and writing, and
only occasionally looking up and pretending to be shocked or amused by

what had just been said. I squatted behind him, handing him documents and receiving instructions. Little of this was to do with the case, for as well as having to attend the court each day Cicero was now in sole charge of Rome and was sunk up to his ears in administration. From the entire length of Italy came reports of disturbances: in the heel and in the toe, in the knee and in the thigh. Celer had his hands full arresting malcontents in Picenum. There were even rumors that Catilina might be about to take the ultimate step and recruit slaves to the rebel army in return for emancipation—if that happened the whole country would soon be in flames. More troops had to be levied, and Cicero persuaded Hybrida to take command of a new army. He did this partly to show a united front but chiefly to get Hybrida out of the city, for he was still not entirely convinced of his colleague's loyalty and did not want him in Rome if Sura and the other conspirators decided to make their move. It seemed to me madness to give an entire army to a man he did not trust, but Cicero was no fool. He appointed a senator with almost thirty years' military experience, Marcus Petreius, as Hybrida's second-in-command, and gave Petreius sealed orders which were to be opened only in the event that the army looked likely to have to fight.

As the winter arrived the republic seemed to be on the brink of collapse. At a public assembly Metellus Nepos made a violent attack on Cicero's consulship, accusing him of every possible crime and folly— dictatorship, weakness, rashness, cowardice, complacency, incompetence. "How long," he demanded, "must the people of Rome be denied the services of the one man who could deliver them from this miserable situation—Gnaeus Pompey, so rightly surnamed 'the Great'?" Cicero did not attend the assembly but was given a full report of what was said.

Just before the end of Murena's trial—I think it must have been the first day of December—Cicero received an early morning visit from Sanga. He came in with his little eyes shining, as well they might because he brought momentous news. The Gauls had done as he had requested and had approached Sura's freedman, Umbrenus, in the Forum. Their conversation had been entirely friendly and natural. The Gauls had bemoaned their lot, cursed the Senate, and declared that they agreed with the words of Catilina: death was preferable to living in this condition of slavery. Pricking up his ears, Umbrenus had suggested they continue their discussion somewhere more private and had taken them to the home of Decimus Brutus, which was close by. Brutus himself—an aristocrat who had been consul some fourteen years previously—had nothing to do with the conspiracy and was away from Rome, but his wife, a clever and sinuous woman, was one of Catilina's many amours, and it was she who suggested they should make common cause. Umbrenus went off to fetch one of the leaders of the plot and returned with the knight Capito, who swore the Gauls to secrecy and said the uprising in the city would be starting any day now. As soon as Catilina and the rebels were close to Rome, the newly elected tribune Bestia would call a public assembly and demand that Cicero be arrested. This would be the signal for a general uprising. Capito and a fellow knight, Statilius, at the head of a large body of arsonists, would start fires in twelve locations. In the ensuing panic the young senator Cethegus would lead the death squad that had volunteered to murder Cicero; others would assassinate the various victims allotted to them; many young men would kill their fathers; the Senate House would be stormed.

"And how did the Gauls respond?" asked Cicero.

"As instructed, they asked for a list of men who supported the conspiracy," replied Sanga, "so they could gauge its chances of success." He produced a wax tablet, crammed with names written in tiny letters. "Sura," he read, "Longinus, Bestia, Sulla—"

"We know all this," interrupted Cicero, but Sanga held up his finger.

"—Caesar, Hybrida, Crassus, Nepos—"

"But this is a fantasy, surely?" Cicero took the tablet from Sanga's hand and scanned the list. "They want to make themselves sound stronger than they are."

"That I can't judge. I can only tell you those were the names that Capito provided."

"A consul, the chief priest, a tribune, and the richest man in Rome, who has already denounced the conspiracy? I don't believe it." Nevertheless, Cicero threw the tablet to me. "Copy them out," he ordered, and then he shook his head. "Well, well—be careful of what questions you ask, for fear of what answers you may receive." It was one of his favorite maxims from the law courts.

"What should I tell the Gauls to do next?" asked Sanga.

"If that list is correct, I should advise them to join the conspiracy! When exactly did this meeting take place?"

"Yesterday."

"And when are they due to meet again?"

"Today."

"So obviously they are in a hurry."

"The Gauls got the impression matters would come to a head in the next few days."

Cicero fell silent, thinking. "Tell them they should demand written proof of the involvement of as many of these men as possible: letters, fixed with personal seals, that they can take back and show to their fellow countrymen."

"And if the conspirators refuse?"

"The Gauls should say it will be impossible for their tribe to take such a hazardous step as going to war with Rome without hard evidence."

Sanga nodded, and then he said: "I'm afraid that after this my involvement in this affair will have to end."

"Why?"

"Because it's becoming far too dangerous to remain in Rome."

As a final favor he agreed to return with the conspirators' answer as soon as the Gauls had received it; then he would leave. In the meantime Cicero had no alternative but to go down to Murena's trial. Sitting on the bench next to Hortensius he put on an outward show of calm, but from time to time I would catch his gaze drifting around the court, resting occasionally on Caesar—who was one of the jurors—on Sura, who was sitting with the praetors, and finally and most often on Crassus, who was only two places farther along the bench. He must have felt extremely lonely, and I noticed for the first time that his hair was flecked with gray, and that there were ridges of dark skin under his eyes. The crisis was aging him. At the seventh hour, Cato finished his summing-up of the prosecution case, and the judge, whose name was Cosconius, asked Cicero if he would like to conclude for the defense. The question seemed to catch him by surprise, and after a moment or two of shifting through his documents he rose and requested an adjournment until the next day, so that he could gather his thoughts. Cosconius looked irritable but conceded that the hour was getting late. He grudgingly agreed to Cicero's request, and the conclusion of Murena's trial was postponed.

We hurried home in the now-familiar cocoon of guards and lictors, but there was no sign of Sanga, nor any message from him. Cicero went silently into his study and sat with his elbows on his desk, his thumbs pressed hard to his temples, surveying the piles of evidence laid across it, rubbing at his flesh, as if he might somehow drive into his skull the speech he needed to deliver. I had never felt sorrier for him. But when I took a step toward him to offer my help he flicked his hand at me without looking up, wordlessly dismissing me from his presence. I did not see him again that evening. Instead Terentia drew me to one side to express her worries about the consul's health. He was not eating properly, she said, or sleeping. Even the morning exercises he had practiced since he was a young man had been abandoned. I was surprised she should talk to me in this intimate way, as the truth was she had never much liked me, and took out on me much of the frustration she felt with her husband. I was the one who spent the most time sequestered with him, working. I was the one who disturbed their rare moments of leisure together by bringing him piles of letters and news of callers. Nevertheless, for once she spoke to me politely and almost as a friend. "You must reason with him," she said. "I sometimes believe you are the only one he will listen to, while I can only pray for him."

When the next morning arrived and there was still no word from Sanga, I began to fear that Cicero would be too nervous to make his speech. Remembering Terentia's plea, I even suggested he might ask for a further postponement. "Are you mad?" he snapped. "This isn't the time to show weakness. I'll be fine. I always am." Despite his bravado, I never saw him shake more at the start of a speech or begin more inaudibly. The Forum was packed and noisy, even though great masses of cloud were rolling over Rome, releasing occasional flurries of rain across the valley. But as it turned out Cicero put a surprising amount of humor into that speech, memorably contrasting the claims of Servius and Murena for the consulship.

"You are up before dawn to rally your clients," he said to Servius, "he to rally his army. You are woken by the call of cocks, he by the call of trumpets. You draw up a form of proceedings, he a line of battle. He understands how to keep off the enemy's forces, you rainwater. He has been engaged in extending boundaries, you in defining them." The jury loved that. And they laughed even longer when he poked fun at Cato and his rigid philosophy. "Rest assured that the superhuman qualities we see in Cato are innate; his failings due not to Nature but to his master. For there was a man of genius called Zeno, and the disciples of his teaching are called Stoics. Here are some of his precepts: the wise man is never moved by favor and never forgives anyone's mistakes; only a fool feels pity; all misdeeds are equal, the casual killing of a cock no less a crime than strangling one's father; the wise man never assumes anything, never regrets anything, is never wrong, never changes his mind. Unfortunately, Cato has seized on this doctrine not just as a topic for discussion but as a way of life."

"What a droll fellow our consul is," sneered Cato in a loud voice as everybody laughed. But Cicero hadn't finished yet.

"Now I must admit when I was younger I also took some interest in philosophy. My masters, though, were Plato and Aristotle. They don't hold violent or extreme views. They say that favor can sometimes influence the wise man; that a good man can feel pity; that there are different degrees of wrongdoing and different punishments; that the wise man often makes assumptions when he doesn't know the facts, and is sometimes angry, and sometimes forgives, and sometimes changes his mind; that all virtue is saved from excess by a so-called mean. If you had studied these masters, Cato, you might not be a better man or braver—that would be impossible—but you might be a little more kind.

"You say that the public interest led you to start these proceedings. I don't doubt it. But you slip up because you never stop to think. I am defending Lucius Murena not because of friendship, but for the sake of peace, quiet, unity, liberty, our self-preservation—in short the very lives of us all. Listen, gentlemen," he said, turning to the jury, "listen to a consul who spends all his days and nights in nonstop thinking about the republic. It is vital that there are two consuls in the state on the first day of January. Plans have been laid by men among us now to destroy the city, slaughter the citizens, and obliterate the name of Rome. I give you warning. My consulate is reaching its dying days. Don't take from me the man whose vigilance should succeed mine." He rested his hand on Murena's shoulder. "Don't remove the man to whom I wish to hand over the republic still intact, for him to defend against these deadly perils."

He spoke for three hours, stopping only now and again to sip a little diluted wine or to mop the rain from his face. His delivery became more and more powerful as he went on, and I was reminded of some strong and graceful fish that had been tossed, apparently dead, back into the water—inert at first and belly-up; but then suddenly, on finding itself returned to its natural element, with a flick of its tail, it revives. In the same way Cicero gathered strength from the very act of speaking, and he finished to prolonged applause not only from the crowd but from the jury. It proved to be a good omen: when their ballots were counted Murena was acquitted by a huge majority. Cato and Servius left at once in a state of great dejection. Cicero lingered on the rostra just long enough to congratulate the consul-elect, and to receive many slaps on the back from Clodius, Hortensius, and even Crassus, and then we headed home.

The instant we came into the street we noticed a fine carriage drawn up outside the house. As we came closer we saw that it was crammed with silver plate, statues, carpets, and pictures. A wagon just behind it was similarly laden. Cicero hurried forward. Just inside the front door Sanga was waiting, his face as gray as an oyster.

"Well?" demanded Cicero.

"The conspirators have written their letters."

"Excellent!" Cicero clapped his hands. "Have you brought them with you?"

"Wait, Consul. There's more to it than that. The Gauls don't actually have the letters yet. They've been told to go to the Fontinalian Gate at midnight and be ready to leave the city. They'll be met there by an escort who'll give them the letters."

"And why do they need an escort?"

"He'll take them to meet Catilina. And then from Catilina's camp they are to go directly to Gaul."

"By the gods, if we can get hold of those letters we will have them at last!" Cicero strode up and down the narrow passageway. "We must lay an ambush," he said to me, "and catch them red-handed. Send for Quintus and Atticus."

"You'll need soldiers," I said, "and an experienced man to command them."

"He must be someone we can trust absolutely."

I took out my notebook and stylus. "What about Flaccus? Or Pomptinus?" Both men were praetors with long experience in the legions, and both had proved steadfast throughout the crisis.

"Good. Get them both here now."

"And the soldiers?"

"We could use that century from Reate. They're still in their barracks. But they're to be told nothing of their mission. Not yet."

He called for Sositheus and Laurea and rapidly issued the necessary instructions, then he turned to say something to Sanga but the passageway behind him was empty, the front door open, and the street deserted. The senator had fled.

• • •

Quintus and Atticus arrived within the hour, and shortly afterward the two praetors also turned up, greatly bemused by this dramatic summons. Without going into details Cicero said simply that he had information that a delegation of Gauls would be leaving the city at midnight, together with an escort, and that he had reason to believe they were on their way to Catilina with incriminating documents. "We need to stop them at all costs, but we need to let them get far enough along the road that there can be no doubt that they're leaving the city."

"In my experience an ambush at night is always more difficult than it sounds," said Quintus. "In the darkness some are bound to escape—taking your evidence with them. Are you sure we can't simply seize them at the gate?"

But Flaccus, who was a soldier of the old school, having seen service under Isauricus, said immediately, "What rubbish! I don't know what army you served in, but it should be easy enough. In fact I know just the spot. If they're taking the Via Flaminia they'll have to cross the Tiber at the Mulvian Bridge. We'll trap them there. Once they're halfway across there's no chance of escape, unless they're willing to throw themselves into the river and drown."

Quintus looked very put out and from that moment on effectively washed his hands of the whole operation, so much so that when Cicero suggested he should join Flaccus and Pomptinus at the bridge, he replied sulkily that it was clear his advice was not needed.

"In that case I shall have to go myself," said Cicero, but everyone immediately objected to that on the grounds it was not safe. "Then it will have to be Tiro," he concluded, and seeing my look of horror, he added: "Someone has to be there who isn't a soldier. I shall need a clear account written up by an eyewitness that I can give to the Senate tomorrow, and Flaccus and Pomptinus will be too busy directing operations."

"What about Atticus?" I suggested—somewhat impertinently, I realize now, but fortunately for me Cicero was too preoccupied to notice.

"He'll be in charge of my security in Rome, as usual." Behind his back Atticus shrugged at me apologetically. "Now, Tiro, make sure you write down everything they say, and above all else secure those letters with their seals unbroken."

• • •

We set off on horseback well after darkness fell: the two praetors, their eight lictors, another four guards, and finally and reluctantly, me. To add to my woes I was a terrible rider. I bounced up and down in my saddle, an empty document case banging against my back. We clattered over the stones and through the city gate at such speed I had to wind my fingers into the mane of my poor mare to stop myself falling off. Fortunately she was a tolerant beast, no doubt especially reserved for women and idiots, and as the road stretched down the hill and across the plain she plunged on without requiring guidance from me, and so we managed to keep pace with the horses ahead of us.

It was one of those nights when the sky is an adventure all to itself, a brilliant moon racing through motionless oceans of silvery cloud. Beneath this celestial odyssey the tombs lining the Via Flaminia silently flickered as if in a lightning storm. We trotted along steadily until, after about two miles, we came to the river. We drew to a halt and listened. In the darkness I could hear rushing water, and looking ahead I could just make out the flat roofs of a couple of houses and the silhouettes of trees, sharp against the hurtling sky. From somewhere close by a man's voice demanded the password. The praetors replied—"Aemilius Scaurus!"— and suddenly, from both sides of the road, the men of the Reate century rose out of the ditches, their faces blackened with charcoal and mud. The praetors quickly divided this force in two. Pomptinus with his men was to remain where he was while Flaccus led forty legionnaires over to the opposite bank. For some reason it seemed to me safer to be with Flaccus, and I followed him onto the bridge. The river was wide and shallow and flowing very fast across the big flat rocks. I peered over the edge of the parapet to where the waters crashed and foamed against the pillars more than forty feet below, and I realized what an effective trap the bridge made, that jumping in to avoid capture would be an act of suicide.

In the house on the far bank there was a family asleep. At first they refused to let us in, but their door soon flew open when Flaccus threatened to break it down. They had irritated him, so he locked them in the cellar. From the upstairs room we had a clear view of the road, and here we settled down to wait. The plan was that all travelers, from whichever direction, would be allowed onto the bridge, but once they reached the other side they would be challenged and questioned before being allowed off it. Long hours passed and not a soul approached, and the conviction steadily grew in me that we must have been tricked. Either there was no party of Gauls heading out of the city that night, or they had already gone, or they had chosen a different route. I expressed these doubts to Flaccus, but he shook his grizzled head. "They will come," he said, and when I asked why he was so certain, he replied: "Because the gods protect Rome." Then he folded his large hands over his broad stomach and went to sleep.

I must have drifted off myself. At any rate the next thing I remember is a hand on my shoulder and a voice hissing in my ear that there were men on the bridge. Straining my eyes into the darkness, I heard the sound of the horses' hooves before I could make out the shapes of the riders— five, ten men or more, crossing at a leisurely pace. "This is it!" whispered Flaccus, jamming on his helmet, and with surprising speed for a man of his girth he jumped down the stairs three at a time and ran out onto the road. As I ran after him I heard whistles and a trumpet blaring, and legionnaires with drawn swords and some with torches began appearing from all directions and surging onto the bridge. The oncoming horses shied and stopped. A man yelled out that they must fight their way through. He spurred his horse and charged our line, heading straight for the spot where I was standing, slashing right and left with his sword. Someone next to me reached out to grab his reins, and to my amazement I saw the outstretched hand cleanly severed and land almost at my feet. Its owner screamed and the rider, realizing there were too many to hack his way past, wheeled around and headed back the way he had come. He shouted to the others to follow, and the entire party now attempted to retreat toward Rome. But Pomptinus's men were flooding onto the bridge from the opposite side. We could see their torches and hear their excited cries. All of us ran in pursuit—even I, my fear entirely forgotten in my desire to seize those letters before they could be thrown into the river.

By the time we reached the middle of the bridge the fighting was almost over. The Gauls, distinctive by their long hair and beards and their wild dress, were throwing down their weapons and dismounting; they must have been expecting an ambush such as this. Soon only the impetuous rider who had tried to break past us was still in his saddle, urging his fellow companions to show some resistance. But it turned out they were slaves, with no stomach for a fight: they knew that even to raise a hand

against a Roman citizen would mean crucifixion. One by one they surrendered. Eventually their leader also threw down his bloodied sword,
then I saw him bend and hurriedly begin unfastening the straps of his
saddlebags, at which I had the rare presence of mind to dart forward and
seize the bag. He was young and very strong and almost managed to hurl
it into the river, and would have done so had not other willing hands
reached up and dragged him off his horse. I guess these men must have
been friends of the soldier whose hand he had cut off, for they gave him
quite a kicking before Flaccus wearily intervened and told them to stop.
He was dragged up by his hair and Pomptinus, who knew him, identified
him as Titus Volturcius, a knight from the town of Croton. I meanwhile
had his bag in my hand, and I called over a soldier with a torch so that I
could search it properly. Inside were six letters, all sealed.

I sent a messenger at once to Cicero to tell him that our mission had
borne fruit. Then, once our prisoners had all been bound with their hands
behind their backs and roped in a line at the neck—all except the Gauls,
who were treated with the respect due to ambassadors—we started back
to Rome.

We entered the city just before dawn. A few people were already up.
They stopped and gawped at our sinister little procession as we crossed the
Forum and headed up the hill to Cicero's house. We left the prisoners
outside in the street under close guard. Inside, the consul received us
flanked by Quintus and Atticus. He listened to the praetors' accounts,
thanked them warmly, and then asked to see Volturicius. He was pushed
and dragged in, looking bruised and frightened, and immediately launched
into some absurd story about being asked by Umbrenus to convey the
Gauls out of the city, and at the last moment being given some letters to
carry, and not knowing their contents.

"Then why did you put up such a fight on the bridge?" demanded
Pomptinus.

"I thought you were highwaymen."

"Highwaymen in army uniform? Commanded by praetors?"

"Take the villain away," ordered Cicero, "and don't bring him back
until he's ready to tell the truth."

After the prisoner had been dragged out Flaccus said, "We need to act
quickly, before the news is all over Rome."

"You're right," agreed Cicero. He asked to see the letters and we examined them together. Two I easily recognized as belonging to the urban praetor, Lentulus Sura: his seal included a portrait of his grandfather, who had been consul a century earlier. The other four we worked out from the names on our lists as probably having come from the young senator Cornelius Cethegus and the three knights Capito, Statilius, and Caeparius. The praetors watched us impatiently.

"Surely there's an easy way to settle this?" said Pomptinus. "Why don't we just open the letters?"

"That would be tampering with evidence," replied Cicero, continuing his minute perusal of the letters.

"With respect, Consul," growled Flaccus, "we're wasting time."

I realize now of course that wasting time was precisely Cicero's intention. He knew how awkward his position would be if he had to decide the conspirators' fate. He was giving them a final chance to flee. His preferred solution was still for them to be dealt with by the army in battle. But he could only delay for so long, and eventually he told us to go and fetch them. "Mind you, I don't want them arrested," he cautioned. "Simply tell them the consul would be grateful for an opportunity to clear up a few matters, and ask them to come and see me."

The praetors clearly thought he was being feeble, but they did as they were commanded. I was sent to accompany Flaccus to the homes of Sura and Cethegus, who lived on the Palatine; Pomptinus went off to locate the others. I remember how odd it felt to approach Lentulus Sura's grand ancestral house and discover life there going on entirely as normal. He had not fled; quite the opposite. His clients were waiting patiently in the public rooms to see him. When he heard we were at the door he sent out his stepson, Mark Antony, to discover what we wanted. Antony was then just twenty, very tall and strong, with a fashionable goatee beard and a face still thickly covered in pimples. It was the first time I had ever met him, and I wish I could remember more about this encounter, but I'm afraid all I can recall are his spots. He went off and gave his stepfather the message and returned to say the praetor would call on the consul as soon as he had finished his morning levee.

It was the same story at the home of Caius Cethegus, that fiery young patrician who, like his kinsman Sura, was a member of the Cornelian clan. Petitioners were queuing to talk to him, but he at least paid us the compliment of coming into the atrium himself. He looked Flaccus up and down as if he were a stray dog, heard what he had to say, and replied that it was not his habit to go running to anyone when called, but out of respect for the office if not the man he would attend on the consul very shortly.

We went back to Cicero, who was clearly amazed to hear that the two senators were still in Rome. "What are they thinking of?" he muttered to me.

In fact it turned out that only one of the five—Caeparius, a knight from Terracina—had actually run away from the city. The rest all arrived separately at Cicero's house over the next hour or so, such was their supreme confidence that they were untouchable. I often wonder when it was that they started to realize they had made an appalling miscalculation. Was it when they reached the street where Cicero lived and discovered it jammed with armed men, prisoners, and curious onlookers? Was it when they went inside to find not just Cicero but the two consuls-elect, Silanus and Murena, and the principal leaders of the Senate—Catulus, Isauricus, Hortensius, Lucullus, and several others—all of whom Cicero had summoned to witness the proceedings? Or was it, perhaps, when they saw their letters laid out on the table, with the seals unbroken? Or noticed the Gauls being treated as honored guests in an adjoining room? Or was it when Volturcius abruptly changed his mind and decided to save himself by testifying against them, in return for the promise of a pardon? I imagine it might have felt rather like drowning—a dawning realization that they had ventured out of their depth and were being carried farther and farther away from the shore with every passing moment. Only when Volturcius accused Cethegus to his face of boasting that he would murder Cicero and then storm the Senate House did Cethegus at last jump to his feet and declare he would not stay here and listen to this a moment longer. But he found his exit blocked by two legionnaires of the Reate century, who returned him very forcefully to his chair.

Cicero turned to his new star witness. "And what about Lentulus Sura? What exactly did he say to you?"

"He said that the Sibylline Books had prophesied that Rome would be ruled by three members of the Cornelian family; that Cinna and Sulla had been the first two; and that he himself was the third and would soon be master of the city."

"Is this true, Sura?" But Sura made no reply and merely stared straight ahead, blinking rapidly. Cicero sighed. "An hour ago you could have left the city unmolested. Now I'd be as guilty as you are if I dared to let you go." He beckoned to the soldiers standing in the atrium. They filed in and stationed themselves in pairs behind the conspirators.

"Open Sura's letters!" cried Catulus, who could not contain his fury any longer at this betrayal of the republic by the direct descendant of one of the six founding families of Rome. "Open the letters and let's discover how far the treasonous swine was prepared to go!"

"Not yet," said Cicero. "We'll do that in front of the Senate." He looked sadly at the conspirators who were now his prisoners. "Whatever happens I don't want anyone ever to be able to say I forged evidence or coerced testimony."

It was now the middle of the morning. Incongruously, the house was starting to fill with flowers and greenery in preparation for the annual ceremony of the Good Goddess, over which Terentia was due to preside that night as the wife of the senior magistrate. As slaves carried in baskets of mistletoe, myrtle, and winter roses, Cicero issued a decree that the Senate should meet that afternoon not in their usual chamber but in the Temple of Concordia, so that the spirit of the goddess of national harmony might guide their deliberations. He also gave orders that a newly completed statue of Jupiter, originally destined for the Capitol, should be put up at once in the Forum in front of the rostra. "I shall surround myself with a bodyguard of deities," he said to me. "Because, mark my words, by the time this is over I may well have need of all the protection I can get."

The five conspirators were kept under guard in the atrium while Cicero went to his study to question the Gauls. Their testimony was, if anything, even more damning than that of Volturcius, for it turned out that just before leaving Rome the ambassadors had been taken to the house of Cethegus and shown a stockpile of weapons that were to be distributed when the signal for the massacre was given. I was sent along with Flaccus to make an inventory of this arsenal, which we discovered in the tablinum stacked in boxes from floor to ceiling. The swords and knives were unused, gleaming and of a curious, curved design, with strange carvings on their hilts. Flaccus said they looked foreign-made to him. I rested my thumb on the blade of one sword. It was as sharp as a razor, and I thought with a shiver that not only might Cicero's throat have been cut with it but very probably mine as well.

By the time I had finished examining the boxes and returned to Cicero's house, it was time to leave for the Senate. The downstairs rooms were festooned with sweet-smelling flora, and numerous amphorae of wine were being carried in from the street. Clearly, whatever other mysteries it might entail, the ceremony of the Good Goddess was not abstemious. Terentia drew her husband to one side and embraced him. I could not hear what she said, nor did I try to, but I did see her take his arm and grip it fiercely, and then we set off, surrounded by legionnaires, with each conspirator escorted down to the Temple of Concordia by a man of consular rank. They were all very subdued now; even Cethegus had lost his arrogance. None of us knew what to expect. As we entered the Forum Cicero took Sura by the hand as a mark of respect, but the patrician appeared too dazed by events to notice. I was walking just behind them carrying the box of letters. What was remarkable was not so much the size of the crowds—needless to say, almost the entire population had flocked to the Forum to watch what was going on—but their complete silence.

The temple was ringed by armed men. The waiting senators looked on in amazement as they saw Cicero leading Sura. Once inside, the conspirators were locked into a small storeroom near the entrance while Cicero went straight to the makeshift dais where his chair had been placed beneath the statue of Concordia. "Gentlemen," he began, "earlier today, shortly before first light, the gallant praetors Lucius Flaccus and Gaius Pomptinus, acting on my orders, at the head of a large body of armed men, apprehended a group of riders on the Mulvian Bridge heading in the direction of Etruria . . ." Nobody whispered; nobody even coughed. It was a silence such as I had never heard before in the Senate—fearful, ominous, oppressive. Occasionally I was able to glance up from my notetaking at Caesar and Crassus. Both men were leaning forward in their seats, concentrating on Cicero's every word: "Thanks to the loyalty of our allies, the envoys of the Gauls, who were appalled by what was proposed, I had already received warning of the treasonous activities of some of our fellow citizens and was able to take the necessary precautions . . ."

When the consul finished his account, which included a description of the plot to set fire to parts of the city and massacre many senators and other prominent figures, there was a kind of collective sigh or groan.

"The question now arises, gentlemen, of what we are supposed to do with these villains. I propose that as a first step we consider the evidence against the accused, and hear what they have to say for themselves. Send in the witnesses!"

The four Gauls entered first. They looked around them in wonder at the long rows of white-robed senators, whose appearance was such a dramatic contrast with their own. Titus Volturcius came in next, trembling so much he could hardly walk down the aisle. Once they were in position Cicero called out to Flaccus, who was stationed at the entrance: "Bring in the first of the prisoners!"

"Which do you wish to question first?" Flaccus shouted in reply.

"Whichever is to hand," said Cicero grimly, and so it was that Cethegus, escorted by a pair of guards, was brought from the storeroom to the far end of the temple where Cicero waited. Finding himself before an audience of his peers, the young senator recovered some of his old spirit. He almost sauntered down the aisle, and when the consul showed him the letters and asked him to identify which seal was his, he picked it up casually.

"This one is mine I believe."

"Give it to me."

"If you insist," said Cethegus, handing it over. "I must say I was always taught it was the height of bad manners for one gentleman to read another gentleman's mail."

Cicero ignored him, broke open the letter, and read it out loud: *"From Caius Cornelius Cethegus to Catugnatus, chief of the Allobroges—greetings! By this letter I give you my word that I and my companions will keep the promises we have made to your envoys, and that if your nation rises against your unjust oppressors in Rome it will have no more loyal allies than us.'"*

On hearing this, the assembled senators let out a great bellow of outrage. Cicero held up his hand. "Is this your writing?" he asked Cethegus.

The young senator, clearly taken aback by his reception, mumbled something I could not hear.

"Is this your writing?" repeated Cicero. "Speak up!"

Cethegus hesitated, then said quietly, "It is."

"Well, young man, clearly we had different tutors, for I was always .taught that the true height of bad manners was not reading another man's mail but plotting treason with a foreign power! Now," continued Cicero, consulting his notes, "at your house this morning we discovered an armory of a hundred swords and the same number of daggers. What do you have to say for yourself?"

"I'm a collector of weapons—" began Cethegus. He may have been trying to be witty; if he was, it was a foolish joke, and also his last. The rest of his words were lost in the angry protests that came from every corner of the temple.

"We've heard enough from you," said Cicero. "Your guilt is self-confessed. Take him away and bring in the next."

Cethegus was led off, not quite so jaunty now, and Statilius was marched down the aisle. The same process was repeated: he identified his seal, the letter was broken open and read (the language was almost identical to that used by Cethegus), he confirmed the handwriting was his, but, when asked to explain himself, claimed it was not meant seriously.

"Not meant seriously?" repeated Cicero in wonder. "An invitation to an alien tribe to slaughter Roman men, women, and children—not meant seriously?" Statilius could only hang his head.

Capito's turn followed, with the same result, and then Caeparius made a disheveled appearance. He was the one who had tried to escape at dawn, but he had been captured on his way to Apulia with messages for the rebel forces. His confession was the most abject of all. Finally there remained only Lentulus Sura to confront, and this was a moment of great drama, for you must remember that Sura was not only the urban praetor, and therefore the third most powerful magistrate in the state, but also a former consul: a man in his middle-fifties of the most distinguished lineage and appearance. As he entered he looked around with appealing eyes at colleagues he had sat with for a quarter of a century in the highest council of the state, but none would meet his gaze. With great reluctance he identified the last two letters, both of which bore his seal. The one to the Gauls was the same as those that had been read out earlier. The second was addressed to Catilina. Cicero broke it open.

" 'You will know who I am from the bearer of this message,' " he read. " 'Be a man. Remember how critical your position is. Consider what you must now do and enlist aid wherever you find it—even from the lowest of the low.' " Cicero held out the letter to Sura. "Your writing?"

"Yes," replied Sura with great dignity, "but there's nothing criminal about it."

"This phrase, 'the lowest of the low'—what do you mean by it?"

"Poor people—shepherds, tenant farmers, and suchlike."

"Isn't it rather a lordly way for a so-called champion of the poor to refer to our fellow citizens?" Cicero turned to Volturcius: "You were supposed to convey this letter to Catilina at his headquarters, were you not?"

Volturcius lowered his eyes. "I was."

"What precisely does Sura mean by this phrase, 'the lowest of the low'? Did he tell you?"

"Yes he did, Consul. He means that Catilina should encourage an uprising of slaves."

The roars of fury that greeted this revelation were almost physical in their force. To encourage an uprising of slaves so soon after the havoc wrought by Spartacus and his followers was worse even than making an alliance with the Gauls. "Resign! Resign! Resign!" the Senate chorused at the urban praetor. Several senators actually ran across the temple and began wrenching off Sura's purple-bordered toga. He fell to the ground and briefly disappeared in a crowd of assailants and guards. Large pieces of his toga were borne away, and very quickly he was reduced to his undergarments. His nose was bleeding, and his hair, normally oiled and coiffed, was standing up on end. Cicero called out for a fresh tunic to be brought, and when one was found, he actually went down and helped Sura put it on.

After some kind of calm had been restored Cicero took a vote on whether or not Sura should be stripped of his office. The Senate roared back an overwhelming "Aye!" which was of great significance, as it meant Sura was no longer immune from punishment. Sura, dabbing at his nose, was taken away, and the consul resumed his questioning of Volturicius: "We have here five conspirators, fully revealed at last, unable any longer to hide from public gaze. To your certain knowledge, are there more?"

"There are."

"And what are their names?"

"Autronius Paetus, Servius Sulla, Cassius Longinus, Marcus Laeca, Lucius Bestia."

Everyone looked around the temple to see if any of the named men were present; none was.

"The familiar roll call," said Cicero. "Does the house agree that these men should also be arrested?"

"Aye!" they chorused back.

Cicero turned back to Volturcius. "And were there any others?"

"I did hear of others."

"And their names?"

Volturcius hesitated and glanced nervously around the Senate. "Gaius Julius Caesar," he said quietly, "and Marcus Licinius Crassus."

There were gasps and whistles of astonishment. Both Caesar and Crassus angrily shook their heads.

"But you have no actual evidence of their involvement?"

"No, Consul. It was only ever rumors."

"Then strike their names from the record," Cicero instructed me. "We shall deal in evidence, gentlemen," he said, having to raise his voice to be heard above the swelling murmur of excitement, "evidence and not speculation!"

It was a while before he could continue. Caesar and Crassus continued to shake their heads and protest their innocence with exaggerated gestures to the men seated around them. Occasionally they turned to look at Cicero, but it was hard to read their expressions. The temple was gloomy even on a sunny day. But now the winter afternoon light was fading fast, and even faces quite close by were becoming difficult to see.

"I have a proposal!" shouted Cicero, clapping his hands to try to regain order. "I have a proposal, gentlemen!" At last the noise began to die away. "It's obvious that we cannot settle the fate of these men today. Therefore they must be kept guarded overnight until we can agree on a course of action. To keep them all in the same place would invite a rescue attempt. Therefore what I propose is this. The prisoners should be separated and each entrusted to the custody of a different member of the Senate, a man of praetorian rank. Does anyone have any objections to that?" There was silence. "Very well." Cicero squinted around the darkening temple. "Who will volunteer for this duty?" Nobody raised his hand. "Come now, gentlemen—there's no danger! Each prisoner will be guarded! Quintus Cornificius," he said at last, pointing to a former praetor of impeccable reputation, "will you be so good as to take charge of Cethegus?"

Cornificius glanced around, then got to his feet. "If that is what you want, Consul," he replied reluctantly.

"Spinther, will you take Sura?"

Spinther stood. "Yes, Consul!"

"Terentius—would you house Caeparius?"

"If that is the will of the Senate," replied Terentius in a glum voice.

Cicero continued to peer around for more potential custodians, and finally his gaze alighted on Crassus. "In which case," he said, as if the idea had only just occurred to him, "Crassus, what better way for you to prove your innocence—not to me, who requires no proof, but to that tiny number who might doubt it—than for you to take custody of Capito? And by the same token, Caesar—you are a praetor-elect—perhaps you will take Statilius into the residence of the chief priest?" Both Crassus and Caesar looked at him with their mouths agape. But what else could they do except nod their assent? They were in a trap. Refusal would have been tantamount to a confession of guilt; so would allowing their prisoners to escape. "Then that is settled," declared Cicero, "and until we reconvene tomorrow, this house stands adjourned."

"Just a moment, Consul!" came a sharp voice, and with a discernible cracking of his elderly knees, Catulus got to his feet. "Gentlemen," he said, "before we depart to our homes for the night to ponder how we may vote tomorrow, I feel it necessary to recognize that one among us has been consistent in his policy, has been consistently attacked for it, and has also, as events have proved, been consistently wise. Therefore I wish to propose the following motion: 'In recognition of the fact that Marcus Tullius Cicero has saved Rome from burning, its citizens from massacre, and Italy from war, this house decrees a three-day public Thanksgiving at every shrine to all the immortal gods for having favored us at such a time with such a consul.' "

I was stunned. As for Cicero, he was quite overwhelmed. This was the first time in the history of the republic that a public thanksgiving had been proposed for anyone other than a victorious general. There was no need to put the motion to a vote. The house rose in acclamation. One man alone remained frozen in his seat, and that was Caesar.

XI

I COME NOW TO the crux of my story, that hinge around which Cicero's life, and the lives of so many of us, was to revolve forever after—the decision about the fate of the prisoners.

Cicero left the Senate with the applause, as it were, still ringing in his ears. The senators poured out after him, and he went immediately across the Forum to the rostra to deliver a report to the people. Hundreds of citizens were still standing around in the chilly twilight, hoping to discover what was going on, and among them I noticed many friends and family of the accused. In particular I recognized young Mark Antony going from group to group trying to rouse support for his stepfather, Sura.

The speech which Cicero afterward had published was very different from the one he actually delivered—a matter I shall come to in due course. Far from singing his own praises, he gave an entirely matter-of-fact report, almost identical to the one he had just relayed to the Senate. He told the crowd about the conspirators' plot to set fire to the city and to murder the magistrates, about their desire to make a pact with the Gauls and the ambush on the Mulvian Bridge. Then he described the opening of the letters and the reactions of the accused. The people listened in a silence that was either rapt or sullen depending on how one chose to interpret it. Only when Cicero announced that the Senate had just voted a three-day national holiday to celebrate his achievement did they finally break into applause. Cicero mopped the sweat from his face and beamed and waved, but he must have known that the cheers were really for the holiday rather than for him. He finished by pointing to the large statue of Jupiter, which he had arranged to have put up quickly that morning. "Surely the very fact that this statue was being erected when the conspirators and witnesses were taken on my orders through the Forum to the Temple of Concordia is clear proof of the intervention of Jupiter Best and Greatest. If I were to say that I foiled them entirely alone I would be taking too much credit for myself. It was Jupiter, the mighty

Jupiter, who foiled them; it was Jupiter who secured the salvation of the Capitol, of these temples, of the whole city, and of you all."

The respectful applause that greeted this remark was no doubt intended for the deity rather than the speaker but at least it meant that Cicero was able to leave the platform with a semblance of dignity. Wisely, he did not linger. As soon as he came down the steps his bodyguard closed around him, and with the lictors clearing the way, we pushed and struggled across the Forum in the direction of the Quirinal Hill. I mention this in order to show that the situation in Rome as night fell was very far from stable, and that Cicero was not nearly as sure of what he ought to do as he later pretended. He would have liked to have returned home and consulted Terentia, but as chance would have it this was the one occasion in his entire life when he was not allowed to cross his own threshold: during the nocturnal rites of the Good Goddess no member of the male sex was allowed under the same roof as the priestesses of the cult; even little Marcus had been sent away. Instead we had to climb the Via Salutaris to the house of Atticus, where it had been arranged that the consul would spend the evening.

Here it was, therefore, with armed guards ringing the house and with all manner of people—senators, knights, Treasury officials, lictors, messengers—bustling in and out from the crowded atrium, that Cicero issued various orders to protect the city. He also sent a note to Terentia to inform her of what had happened. Then he retreated to the quiet of the library to try to decide what to do with the five conspirators. From the four corners of the room, freshly garlanded busts of Aristotle and Plato, Zeno and Epicurius gazed down on his deliberations, unperturbed.

"If I sanction the execution of the traitors, I shall be pursued by their supporters for the rest of my days—you saw how sullen that crowd was. On the other hand, if I let them simply go into exile, those same supporters will agitate constantly for their return; I shall never know safety, and this whole fever will quickly recur." He gazed dejectedly at the head of Aristotle. "The philosophy of the golden mean does not seem to fit this particular predicament."

Exhausted, he sat on the edge of his chair, leaning forward, with his hands clasped behind the back of his neck, staring at the floor. He did not lack advice. His brother, Quintus, urged a hard line: the conspirators were so clearly guilty, the whole of Rome—the whole world, come to that—would think him a weakling if he didn't punish them with death.

This was a time of war! The gentle Atticus's view was entirely the opposite: if Cicero had stood for anything throughout his political career, it was surely the rule of law. For centuries every citizen had had the right of appeal against arbitrary sentence. What else had the Verres case been about if not this? *Civis Romanus sum!* As for me, I am afraid that when my turn came to speak, I advocated the coward's way out. Cicero had only another twenty-six days in office. Why not lock the prisoners away somewhere and leave it to his successors to determine their fate? Both Quintus and Atticus threw up their hands at this, but Cicero could see the merits in it, and years later he told me that actually I had been right. "But that is with hindsight," he said, "which is of course the irredeemable flaw of history. If you remember the circumstances of the time, with soldiers on the streets and armed bands congregating, and with rumors that Catilina might attack the city at any moment in an attempt to free his associates— how could I have avoided taking a stand?"

The most extreme advice of all came from Catulus, who turned up late in the evening, just as Cicero was about to retire to bed, with a group of former consuls, including the two Lucullus brothers, Lepidus, Torquatus, and the former governor of Nearer Gaul Gaius Piso. They came to demand that Caesar be arrested.

"On what evidence?" asked Cicero, rising wearily to his feet to greet the delegation.

"Treason, of course," replied Catalus. "Do you have the least particle of doubt that he's had a hand in this business from the start?"

"None. But that's not the same as having evidence."

"Then make the evidence," said the senior Lucullus smoothly. "All that's required is a more detailed statement from Volturcius implicating Caesar, and we shall have him at last."

"I guarantee you a majority of the Senate will vote to arrest him," said Catulus. His companions murmured in agreement.

"And then what?"

"Execute him along with the others."

"Execute the head of the state religion on a trumped-up charge? There'll be a civil war!"

Lucullus said, "There's likely to be a civil war one day anyway, thanks to Caesar, but if you act now, you can prevent it. Remember your authority. You've just been granted a thanksgiving. Your prestige in the Senate has never been higher."

"I was not granted a thanksgiving in order to go around like a tyrant butchering my opponents!"

"You were granted it," retorted Catulus, "because I proposed it."

"And you are so blinded with hatred for Caesar because he robbed you of the pontificate that you can no longer see straight!" I had never heard Cicero speak in such a way to one of the old patricians, and Catulus's whole body seemed to give a jerk, as if he had stepped on something sharp. "Now listen to me," the consul continued, pointing his finger. "Listen to me, all of you. I have Caesar precisely where I want him. I have that Leviathan by the tail at last. If he lets his prisoner escape tonight, I agree—we can arrest him, because he will have given us proof of his guilt. But for that very reason he won't let him escape. He'll obey the will of the Senate for a change. And I mean to make sure it's a habit he gets used to."

"Until he does the same thing again," said Piso, who had only recently survived an attempt by Caesar to have him exiled for corruption.

"Then we'll just have to outwit him again," said Cicero. "And again. And again. And we'll have to go on doing it for as long as is necessary. But I believe I have his measure now, and my handling of this crisis over the past year has shown that my judgment about such matters is not usually wrong."

His visitors lapsed into silence. He was the man of the hour. His prestige was at its zenith. For once nobody felt able to contradict him, not even Lucullus. Eventually Piso said, "And the conspirators?"

"That is for the Senate to decide, not for me."

"They will look to you for a lead."

"Then they will look in vain. Dear gods, have I not done enough?" Cicero shouted suddenly. "I have exposed the conspiracy. I have stopped Catilina from becoming consul. I have driven him from Rome. I have foiled an attempt to burn down half the city and massacre us in our homes. I have delivered the traitors into custody. Now am I supposed to shoulder all the opprobrium for killing them as well? It's time you gentlemen started playing your part."

"What is it you want us to do?" asked Torquatus.

"Stand up in the Senate tomorrow and say what you want done with the conspirators. Show a lead to the rest of them. Don't expect me to carry the whole burden any longer. I'll call you one by one. State your view—death it must be, I suppose: I can't see any way out of it—but state it loud and clear so that at least when I go before the people I can say I am the instrument of the Senate and not a dictator."

"You can rely on us for that," said Catulus, glancing around at the others. They all nodded in agreement. "But you're wrong about Caesar. We'll never get a better chance than this to stop him. Think on it overnight, I urge you."

After they had gone, certain grim contingencies needed to be faced. If the Senate voted for the death penalty, when would the condemned men be killed, and how, and where, and by whom? There was no precedent for such an action. When was easy enough: immediately after judgment was passed, to forestall a rescue. And by whom was also obvious: the public executioner would do the dispatching, to establish that they were common criminals. Where and how were harder. They could scarcely be flung from the Tarpeian Rock—that would invite a riot. Cicero consulted the head of his official bodyguard, the proximate lictor, who told him that the best place—because the most easy to protect—would be the execution chamber beneath the Carcer, which was conveniently next door to the Temple of Concordia. The space was too cramped and the light too poor for decapitation, he announced, so by a process of elimination it was settled that the conspirators would have to be strangled. The lictor went off to make sure that the carnifex and his assistants would be standing by.

I could tell Cicero was upset by this conversation. He refused to eat, saying he had no appetite. He did consent to drink a little of Atticus's wine, from one of his exquisite Neapolitan glass beakers, but unfortunately his hand was shaking so much he dropped it, shattering the glass on the mosaic floor. After that had been cleared up Cicero decided he needed some fresh air. Atticus called for a slave to unlock the doors and we stepped out from the library onto the narrow terrace. Down in the valley, the effect of the curfew was to make Rome seem as dark and fathomless as a lake. Only the Temple of Luna, lit up by torches on the slopes of the Palatine, was distinctly visible. It seemed to hover, suspended in the night, like some white-hulled vessel descended from the stars to inspect us. We leaned against the balustrade and vainly contemplated what we could not see.

Cicero sighed and said, more to himself than to any of us, "I wonder what men will make of us a thousand years from now. Perhaps Caesar is right—this whole republic needs to be pulled down and built again. I tell you, I have grown to dislike these patricians as much as I dislike the mob—and they haven't the excuse of poverty or ignorance." And then again, a few moments later: "We have so much—our arts and learning, laws, treasure, slaves, the beauty of Italy, dominion over the entire earth—and yet why is it that some ineradicable impulse of the human mind always impels us to foul our own nest?" I surreptitiously made a note of both remarks.

That night I slept very badly, in a cubicle adjoining Cicero's room. The tramp of the sentries' boots as they patrolled the garden and their whispered voices intermingled with my dreams. Seeing Lucullus had stirred a remembrance of Agathe, and I had a nightmare in which I asked him about her and he told me he had no idea whom I meant but that all his slaves in Misenum were dead. When I woke exhausted to the gray dawn, I had a heavy feeling of dread, as if a rock had been laid on my chest. I looked into Cicero's room but his bed was empty. I found him sitting motionless in the library, with the shutters closed and only a small lamp beside him. He asked if it was dawn yet. He wanted to go home to speak with Terentia.

We left soon afterward, escorted by a new detachment of bodyguards under the command of Clodius. Ever since the crisis began, this notorious reprobate had regularly volunteered to accompany the consul, and these demonstrations of his loyalty, matched by Cicero's stout defense of Murena, had strengthened the bond between them. I guess what drew Clodius to Cicero was the opportunity to learn the art of politics from a master—he intended to stand for the Senate himself the following year—while Cicero was amused by Clodius's youthful indiscretions. At any rate, much as I distrusted him, I was glad to see him on duty that morning, for I knew he would lift the consul's mood by some distracting gossip. Sure enough, he started at once.

"Have you heard that Murena's getting married again?"

"Really?" said Cicero in surprise. "To whom?"

"Sempronia."

"Isn't Sempronia already married?"

"She's getting divorced. Murena will be her third husband."

"Three husbands! What a hussy."

They walked on a little farther. "She has a fifteen-year-old daughter from her first marriage," said Clodius thoughtfully. "Did you know that?"

"I did not."

"I'm considering marrying the girl. What do you think?"

"So Murena would become your stepfather-in-law?"

"That's it."

"Not a bad idea. He can help your career a lot."

"She's also immensely rich. She's the heiress of the Gracchi estate."

"Then what are you waiting for?" asked Cicero, and Clodius laughed.

By the time we reached Cicero's house the female worshippers were emerging blearily into the cold morning, led by the vestal virgins. A crowd of bystanders had gathered to watch them go. Some, like Caesar's wife, Pompeia, looked very unsteady and had to be supported by their maids. Others, including Caesar's mother, Aurelia, seemed entirely unmoved by whatever it was they had experienced. She swept by Cicero, stone-faced, without a glance in his direction, which suggested to me that she knew what had happened in the Senate the previous afternoon. In fact, an amazing number of the women coming out of the house had some connection with Caesar. In all I counted at least three of his former mistresses—Mucia, the wife of Pompey the Great; Postumia, the wife of Servius; and Lollia, who was married to Pompey's lieutenant, Aulus Gabinius. Clodius looked on agog at this perfumed parade. Finally, Caesar's current and greatest amour, Servilia, the wife of the consul-elect Silanus, stepped over the doorstep and into the street. She was not especially beautiful: her face was handsome—mannish, I suppose one would call it—but full of intelligence and strength of character. And it was typical of her that she, alone of all the wives of the senior magistrates, actually stopped to ask Cicero what he thought would happen that day.

"It will be for the Senate to decide," he replied guardedly.

"And what do you think their decision will be?"

"That is up to them."

"But you will give them a lead?"

"If I do—forgive me—I shall announce it later in the Senate rather than now on the street."

"You don't trust me?"

"I do indeed, madam. But others may somehow get to hear of our conversation."

"I don't know what you mean by that!" Her voice sounded offended, but her piercing blue eyes shone with malicious humor.

"She is by far the cleverest of his women," observed Cicero once she had moved on, "even shrewder than his mother, and that's saying some-thing. He'd do well to stick with her."

The rooms of Cicero's house were still warm from the women's pres-ence, the air moist with the scent of perfume and incense, of sandalwood and juniper. Female slaves were sweeping the floors and clearing away leftovers; on the altar in the atrium was a pile of white ash. Clodius made no attempt to hide his curiosity. He went around picking up objects and examining them and was obviously bursting to ask all manner of ques-tions, especially when Terentia appeared. She was still wearing the robes of the high priestess, but even these were forbidden to the eyes of men, so she concealed them beneath a cloak which she kept tightly clasped at her throat. Her face was flushed; her voice was high and strange.

"There was a sign," she announced, "not an hour ago, from the Good Goddess herself!" Cicero looked dubious but she was too enraptured to notice. "I have received a special dispensation from the vestal virgins to inform you of what we saw. There"—she gestured dramatically—"on the altar, the fire had entirely burned out. The ash was quite cold. But then a great bright flame shot up. It was the most extraordinary portent anyone could ever remember."

"And what do they think it means, this portent?" inquired Cicero, clearly interested despite himself.

"It is a sign of favor, sent directly to your home on a day of great im-portance, to promise you safety and glory."

"Is it indeed?"

"Be bold," she said, taking his hand. "Do the brave thing. You will be honored forever. And no harm will come to you. That is the message from the Good Goddess."

I have often wondered in the years since whether this affected Cicero's judgment at all. True, he had repeatedly derided auguries and omens to me as childish nonsense. But then I have found that even the greatest skeptics, in extremis, will pray to every god in the firmament if they think it might help them. Certainly I could tell that Cicero was pleased. He kissed Terentia's hand and thanked her for her piety and concern for his interests. Then he went upstairs to prepare for the Senate as news of the portent was spread, on his instructions, to the crowd in the street. Clo-dius, meanwhile, had found a woman's shift lying beneath one of the couches, and I watched him put it to his nose and inhale deeply.

• • •

On the orders of the consul the prisoners were not brought to the Senate but were left where they had been confined overnight. Cicero said this was for reasons of security, but in my opinion it was because he could not bear to look at their faces. Once again the session was held in the Temple of Concordia, and all the leading men of the republic attended except for Crassus, who sent word that he was ill. In reality he wished to avoid casting a vote either for or against the death penalty. He may also have been fearful of assault: there were plenty among the patricians and the Order of Knights who thought he too should have been arrested. Caesar, however, turned up as cool as you please, his sharp wide shoulders pushing past the guards, ignoring their oaths and insults. He squeezed into his seat on the front bench, settled back and thrust out his legs far into the gangway. Cato's narrow skull was directly opposite him: his head was bent reading the Treasury accounts, as usual. It was very cold. The doors at the far end of the temple had been left wide open for the crowd of spectators, and a veritable gale was blowing down the aisle. Isauricus wore a pair of old gray mittens, there was much coughing and sneezing, and when Cicero stood to call the house to order his breath billowed out like steam from a cooking pot.

"Gentlemen," he declared, "this is the most solemn assembly of our order that I can ever remember. We meet to determine what should be done with the criminals who have threatened our republic. I intend that every man here who desires to speak shall have the chance to do so. I do not mean to express a view myself—" He held up his hand to quell the objections. "No one can say I have not played the part of leader in this matter. But henceforth I wish to be the Senate's servant, and whatever you decide you may be sure I shall put into effect. I would rule only that your decision must be reached today, before nightfall. We cannot delay. Your punishment, whatever form it takes, must be a swift one. I now call Decimus Junius Silanus to give his opinion."

It was the privilege of the senior consul-elect always to speak first in debates, but I am sure that on that particular day it was an honor Silanus would happily have forgone. Up to now I have not had much to say about Silanus, in part because I find it hard to remember him: in an age of giants, he was a dwarf—respectable, gray, dull, prone to bouts of ill health and enervating gloom. He would never have won the prize in a thousand years but for the energy and ambition of Servilia, who was so determined that her three daughters should have a consul for a father she made herself Caesar's mistress to further her husband's career. Glancing occasionally with nervous eyes along the front bench to the man who was cuckolding him, Silanus spoke haltingly of the competing claims of justice and mercy, of security and liberty, of his friendship with Lentulus Sura and his hatred of traitors. What was he driving at? It was impossible to tell. Finally Cicero had to ask him directly what penalty he was recommending. Silanus took a deep breath and closed his eyes. "Death," he said.

The Senate stirred as the dreadful word was spoken. Murena was called next. I could see why Cicero had favored him to be consul over Servius at a time of crisis. There was something solid and four-square about him as he stood with his legs apart and his pudgy hands on his hips. "I am a soldier," he said. "Rome is at war. Out in the countryside women and children are being ravished, temples pillaged, crops destroyed; and now our vigilant consul has discovered that similar chaos was being plotted in the mother city. If I found men in my camp planning to set it afire and murder my officers, I would not hesitate for an instant to order their execution. The penalty for traitors is always, must be—and can only be—death."

Cicero worked his way along the front bench, calling one ex-consul after another. Catulus made a blood-curdling speech about the horrors of butchery and arson and also came out firmly in support of death; so did the two Lucullus brothers, Piso, Curio, Cotta, Figulus, Volcacius, Servilius, Torquatus, and Lepidus; even Caesar's cousin Lucius came down reluctantly for the supreme penalty. Taken together with Silanus and Murena, that made fourteen men of consular rank all arguing for the same punishment. No voice was raised against. It was so one-sided Cicero later told me he feared he might be accused of rigging the vote. After several hours during which nothing had been heard except demands for death, he rose and asked if there was any man who wished to propose a different sentence. All heads naturally turned to Caesar. But it was an ex-praetor, Tiberius Claudius Nero, who was the first on his feet. He had been one of Pompey's commanders in the war against the pirates, and he spoke on his chief's behalf. "Why are we in such a hurry, gentlemen? The conspirators are safely under lock and key. I believe we should summon Pompey the Great home to deal with Catilina. Once the leader is defeated then we can decide at our leisure what to do with his minions."

When Nero had finished, Cicero asked, "Does anyone else wish to speak against an immediate sentence of death?"

That was when Caesar slowly uncrossed his legs and rose to his feet. Immediately a great cacophony of shouts and jeering rang out, but Caesar had obviously anticipated this and had prepared his response. He stood with his hands behind his back, patiently waiting until the noise had died down. "Whoever, gentlemen, is pondering a difficult question," he said in his quietly threatening voice, "ought to clear his mind of all hatred and anger, as well as affection and compassion. It isn't easy to discern the truth if one gives way to emotion." He uttered the last word with such stinging contempt it had the effect of briefly silencing his opponents. "You may ask why I oppose the death penalty—"

"Because you're also guilty!" someone shouted.

"If I were guilty," retorted Caesar, "how better to hide it than to clamor for death with all the rest of you? No, I don't oppose death because these men were once my friends—in public life one must set aside such feelings. Nor do I oppose it because I regard their offenses as trivial. Frankly, I think that any torture would be less than these men deserve. But people have short memories. Once criminals have been brought to justice, their guilt is soon forgotten, or becomes a matter of dispute. What's never forgotten is their punishment, especially if it's extreme. I'm sure Silanus makes his proposal with the best interests of his country at heart. Yet it strikes me—I won't say as harsh, for in dealing with such men nothing could be too harsh—but as out of keeping with the traditions of our republic.

"All bad precedents have their origins in measures which at the time seem good. Twenty years ago, when Sulla ordered the execution of Brutus and other criminal adventurers, who among us did not approve his action? The men were villains and troublemakers; it was generally agreed they deserved to die. But those executions proved to be the first step on the path to a national calamity. Before long, anyone who coveted another man's land or villa—or in the end merely his dishes and clothes—could have him killed by denouncing him as a traitor. So those who rejoiced in the death of Brutus found themselves being hauled off to execution, and the killings didn't stop till Sulla had glutted all his followers with riches. Of course I'm not afraid that any such action will be taken by Marcus

Cicero. But in a great nation like ours there are many men, with many different characters, and it may be that on some future occasion, when another consul has, like him, an armed force at his disposal, a false report will be accepted as true. If so, with this precedent set, who will there be to restrain him?"

At the mention of his own name, Cicero intervened. "I have been listening to the remarks of the chief priest with great attention," he said. "Is he proposing that the prisoners simply be released to join Catilina's army?"

"By no means," responded Caesar. "I agree they have forfeited the right to breathe the same air and see the same light as the rest of us. But death has been ordained by the immortal gods not as a means of punishment but as a relief from our toil and woe. If we kill them, their suffering ceases. I therefore propose a harsher fate: *that the prisoners' goods shall be confiscated and that they shall be imprisoned, each in a separate town, for the remainder of their lives; against this sentence the condemned shall have no right of appeal, and any attempt by any person to make an appeal on their behalf shall be regarded as an act of treason.* Life, gentlemen," he concluded, "will mean life."

What an astonishing piece of effrontery this was—but also how clever and effective! Even as I wrote Caesar's motion down and handed it up to Cicero I could hear the excited whispers running around the Senate. The consul took it from me with a worried expression. He sensed his enemy had made a cunning move but was not quite sure of all its implications, or how to respond. He read Caesar's proposal aloud and asked if anyone wished to comment upon it, whereupon who should stand up but consul-elect and cuckold-in-chief Silanus.

"I have been deeply moved by the words of Caesar," he declared, with an unctuous rubbing of his hands, "so moved, in fact, that I shall not vote for my own proposal. Instead of death I too believe that a more appropriate punishment would be imprisonment for life."

That provoked a low exclamation of surprise followed by a kind of rustling along the benches which I recognized immediately as the wind of sensible opinion changing its direction. In a choice between death and exile, most senators favored death. But if the choice became one between death and incarceration for life, they were able to adjust their calculation. And who could blame them? It seemed to offer the perfect solution: the conspirators would be punished horribly but the Senate would escape the odium of having blood on its hands. Cicero looked around him anxiously for supporters of the death penalty, but now speaker after speaker rose to urge the merits of perpetual imprisonment. Hortensius supported Caesar's motion; so, surprisingly, did Isauricus. Metellus Nepos declared that execution without the right of appeal would be illegal, and echoed Nero's demands for Pompey to be recalled. After this had gone on for another hour or two, with only a few voices now hankering after death, Cicero called a brief adjournment before the vote to allow some senators to go outside and relieve themselves and others to take refreshment. In the meantime he held a quick private conclave with Quintus and me. It was already starting to get gloomy again, and there was nothing we could do to alleviate it—lighting a fire or any kind of lamp within the walls of a temple was of course forbidden. Suddenly I realized there was not much time left. "Well," Cicero asked us softly, leaning out of his chair, "what do you think?"

"Caesar's motion will pass," answered Quintus in a whisper, "no question of it. Even the patricians are weakening."

Cicero groaned. "So much for their promises . . ."

"Surely this is good for you," I said eagerly, for I was all in favor of a compromise. "It lets you off the hook."

"But his proposal is a nonsense!" hissed Cicero, with an angry glance in Caesar's direction. "No Senate can pass a law that will bind its successors in perpetuity, and he well knows it. What if a magistrate lays a motion next year to say it isn't treason to agitate for the prisoners' release after all, and it passes through a public assembly? He just wants to keep the crisis alive for his own ends."

"Then at least it will become your successors' problem," I answered, "and not yours."

"You'll look weak," warned Quintus. "What will history say? You'll have to speak."

Cicero's shoulders sagged. This was precisely the predicament he had dreaded. I had never seen him in such an agony of indecision. "You're right," he concluded, "although I can see no outcome from this that isn't ruinous to me."

Accordingly, when the adjournment ended, he announced that he would give his view after all. "I see that your faces and eyes, gentlemen, are all turned upon me, so I shall say what as consul I must say. We have before us two proposals: one of Silanus—though he will no longer vote for it—urging death for the conspirators; the other of Caesar for life imprisonment—an exemplary punishment for a heinous crime. It is, as he says, far worse than death, for Caesar removes even hope, the sole consolation of men in their misfortune. He further orders that their property be confiscated, to add poverty to their other torments. The only thing he leaves these wicked men is their life—whereas if he had taken that from them he would in one painful act have relieved them of much mental and bodily suffering.

"Now, gentlemen, it is clear to me where my own interest lies. If you adopt the motion of Caesar, since he is a populist, I shall have less reason to fear the attacks of the people, because I shall be doing what he has proposed. Whereas if you adopt the alternative, I fear that more trouble may be brought down upon my head. But let the interests of the republic count for more than considerations of danger to myself. We must do what is right. Answer me this: if the head of a household were to find his children killed by a slave, his wife murdered, and his house burned, and to not inflict the supreme penalty in return, would he be thought kindly and compassionate or the most inhuman and cruel of men not to avenge their suffering? To my mind a man who does not soften his own grief and suffering by inflicting similar distress upon the man responsible is unfeeling and has a heart of stone. I support the proposal of Silanus."

Caesar quickly rose to intervene. "But surely the flaw in the consul's argument is that the accused have not committed any such acts—they are being condemned for their intentions, rather than for anything they have done."

"Exactly!" cried a voice from the other side of the chamber, and all heads turned to Cato.

If the vote had been taken at this point I have little doubt that Caesar's proposal would have carried the day, regardless of the consul's view. The prisoners would have been packed off across Italy, to rot or be reprieved according to the caprices of politics, and Cicero's future would have worked out very differently. But just as the outcome seemed assured, there arose from the benches near the back of the temple a familiar gaunt and ill-kempt apparition, his hair all awry, his shoulders bare despite the cold, his sinewy arm stretched out to indicate his desire to intervene.

"Marcus Porcius Cato," said Cicero uneasily, for one could never be sure which way Cato's rigid logic would lead him. "You wish to speak?"

"Yes, I wish to speak," said Cato. "I wish to speak because someone has to remind this house of exactly what it is we're facing. The whole point, gentlemen, is precisely that we're *not* dealing with crimes that have been committed, but with crimes that are *planned*. For that very reason it will be no good trying to invoke the law afterward—we shall all have been slaughtered!" There was a murmur of acknowledgment: he spoke the truth. I glanced up at Cicero. He was also nodding. "Too many sitting here," proclaimed Cato, his voice rising, "are more concerned for their villas and their statues than they are for their country. In heaven's name, men, wake up! Wake up while there's still time and lend a hand to defend the republic! Our liberty and lives are at stake! At such a time does anyone here dare talk to me of clemency and compassion?"

He came down the gangway barefoot and stood in the aisle, that harsh and remorseless voice grating away like a blade on a grindstone. It was as if his famous great-grandfather had just stepped out of his grave and was shaking his furious gray locks at us.

"Do not imagine, gentlemen, that it was by force of arms that our ancestors transformed a petty state into this great republic. If it were so, it would now be at the height of its glory, since we have more subjects and citizens, more arms and horses, than they ever had. No, it was something else entirely that made them great—something we entirely lack. They were hard workers at home, just rulers abroad, and to the Senate they brought minds that were not racked by guilt or enslaved by passion. That is what we've lost. We pile up riches for ourselves while the state is bankrupt, and we idle away our lives so that when an assault is made upon the republic there's no one left to defend it.

"A plot has been hatched by citizens of the highest rank to set fire to their native city. Gauls, the deadliest foes of everything Roman, have been called to arms. The hostile army and its leader are ready to descend upon us. And you're still hesitating and unable to decide how to treat public enemies taken within your own walls?" He literally spat out his sarcasm, showering the senators nearest him with phlegm. "Why then, I suggest you take pity on them—they are young men led astray by ambition. Armed though they are, let them go. But mind what you're doing with your clemency and compassion—if they draw the sword it will be too late to do anything about it. Oh yes, you say, the situation is certainly ugly, but you're not afraid of it. Nonsense! You're quaking in your shoes! But you're so indolent and weak that you stand irresolute, each waiting for someone else to act—no doubt trusting to the gods. Well, I tell you, vows and womanish supplications won't secure divine aid. Only vigilance and action can achieve success.

"We're completely encircled. Catilina and his army are ready to grip us by the throat. Our enemies are living in the very heart of the city. That is why we must act quickly. This therefore is my proposal, Consul. Write it down well, scribe: *Whereas by the criminal designs of wicked citizens the republic has been subjected to serious danger; and whereas, by testimony and confession, the accused stand convicted of planning massacre, arson, and other foul atrocities against their fellow citizens: that, having admitted their criminal intention, they should be put to death as if they had been caught in the actual commission of capital offenses, in accordance with ancient custom.*"

For thirty years I attended debates in the Senate and I witnessed many great and famous speeches. But I never saw one—not one: not even close—that rivaled in its effects that brief intervention by Cato. What is great oratory, after all, except the distillation of emotion into exact words? Cato said what a majority of men were feeling but had not the language to express, even to themselves. He admonished them, and they loved him for it. All across the temple senators rose from their seats applauding and went to stand beside their hero to indicate he had their support. He was no longer the eccentric on the back bench. He was the rock and bone and sinew of the old republic. Cicero looked on in astonishment. As for Caesar, he jumped up demanding the right to reply, and actually started making a speech. But everyone could see that his true intention was to talk out Cato's motion and prevent a vote, for the light was very low now and shadows were deep across the chamber. There were shouts of rage from those around Cato, and some jostling, and several of the knights who had been watching from the doorway rushed in with their swords drawn. Caesar was twisting his shoulders back and forth to throw off the hands that were trying to pull him down, and still he kept on speaking. The knights looked to Cicero for instruction. All it would have taken was a nod from him, or a raised finger, and Caesar would have been run through on the spot. And for the briefest of instants he did hesitate. But then he shook his head. Caesar was released, and in the chaos he must have rushed from the temple, for I lost sight of him after that. Cicero came down off his dais. Striding along the aisle, shouting at the senators, he and his lictors separated the combatants and pushed a few of them back into their places, and when some sort of order had been restored he returned to his chair.

"Gentlemen," he said, his face as white as milk in the darkness, his voice very thin and strained, "the sentiment of the house is clear. Marcus Cato's motion passes. The sentence is death."

Speed was now vital. The condemned men had to be moved quickly to the execution chamber before their friends and supporters realized their fate. To fetch each prisoner Cicero placed a former consul at the head of a detachment of guards: Catulus went for Cethegus, Torquatus for Capito, Piso for Caeparius, and Lepidus for Statilius. After settling the details and requesting that the other senators remain in their places while the deed was done, he himself went off last of all to collect the most senior of the accused, Lentulus Sura.

Outside, the sun had just gone down. The Forum was ominously crowded yet the people parted at once to let us through. They reminded me of spectators at a sacrifice—solemn, respectful, filled with awe at the mysteries of life and death. We went with our escort up onto the Palatine, to the home of Spinther, who was a kinsman of Sura, and found our prisoner in the atrium playing dice with one of the men assigned to guard him. He had just made his throw: the dice clattered onto the board as we came in. He must have realized at once from Cicero's expression that it was all over for him. He glanced down to inspect his score, then looked back up at us and gave a bleak smile. "I seem to have lost," he said.

I cannot reproach Sura for his behavior. His grandfather and his great-grandfather had both been consuls, and they would have been proud of his conduct in this last hour at least. He handed over a purse with some money to be distributed among his guards, then walked out of the house as calmly as if he were going to take a bath. He offered only the mildest of reproaches. "I believe you laid a trap for me," he said.

"You trapped yourself," replied Cicero.

Sura didn't say another word as we crossed the Forum but trod steadily with his chin thrust out. He still wore the plain tunic he had been given the previous day. Yet from their demeanors one would have guessed that the deathly pale Cicero, despite his consular purple, was the condemned man and Sura his captor. I felt the eyes of the vast crowd upon us; they were as curious and docile as sheep. At the foot of the steps leading up to the Carcer, Sura's stepson, Mark Antony, ran out in front of the guards crying out to know what was happening.

"I have a short appointment," replied Sura calmly. "It will all be over soon. Go and comfort your mother. She will have more need of you now than I."

Antony bellowed with grief and anger and tried to reach out to touch Sura, but he was pushed out of the way by the lictors. We passed on up the steps between the pickets of troops and ducked through a doorway that was low but very thick, almost like a tunnel, and into a windowless circular stone chamber lit by torches. The air was close, noxious with the stink of death and human waste. As my eyes adjusted to the gloom I recognized Catulus, Piso, Torquatus, and Lepidus, with the folds of their togas pressed to their noses, and also the short and broad figure of the state executioner, the carnifex, in his leather apron, attended by half a dozen assistants. The other prisoners were already lying on the ground with their arms tightly pinioned behind their backs. Capito, who had spent the day with Crassus, was crying softly. Statilius, who had been held at Caesar's official residence, was insensible from the effects of wine. Caeparius was lost to the world, curled up in a ball with his eyes closed. Cethegus was protesting loudly that this was illegal and demanding the right to address the Senate; someone kicked him in the ribs and he went quiet. The carnifex seized Sura's arms and bound them quickly at the wrists and elbows.

"Consul," said Sura, wincing as he was trussed, "will you give me your word that no harm will befall my wife and family?"

"Yes, I promise you that."

"And will you surrender our bodies to our families for burial?"

"I will." (Afterward Mark Antony claimed Cicero had denied this final request: yet another of his innumerable lies.)

"This was not supposed to be my destiny. The auguries were quite clear."

"You allowed yourself to be suborned by wicked men."

Moments later the tying-up was finished and Sura looked around him. "I die a Roman nobleman," he shouted defiantly, "and a patriot!"

That was too much even for Cicero. "No," he said curtly, nodding to the carnifex, "you die a traitor."

At those words Sura was dragged toward the large black hole in the center of the floor which was the only means of entrance to the execution chamber beneath us. Two powerful fellows lowered him into it and I had a last glimpse of his handsome, baffled, stupid face in the torchlight. Then strong hands must have taken hold of him from beneath, for abruptly he disappeared. Statilius's limp form was let down immediately after Sura; then it was quickly the turn of Capito, who was shaking so much his teeth were rattling; then Caeparius, still in a swoon of terror; and finally Cethegus, who screamed and sobbed and put up such a tremendous struggle that two men had to sit on him while a third tied his wildly thrashing legs—in the end they tipped him through the hole headfirst and he fell with a thud. Nothing more was to be heard after that, apart from some occasional scuffling sounds; eventually those also ceased. I was told later they were hanged in a row from hooks fixed in the ceiling. After what seemed an eternity the carnifex called up that the job was done and Cicero went reluctantly to the hole and peered down. A torch was flourished over the victims. The five strangled men lay in a row, gazing up at us with bulging sightless eyes. I felt no pity: I was remembering the violated body of the boy they had sacrificed to seal their pact. Cato was right, I thought: they deserved to die; and that remains my opinion to this day.

Once he had assured himself that the conspirators were dead, Cicero could not wait to get away from that "antechamber to hell," as he afterward called it. We squeezed back out through the narrow tunnel of a doorway and straightened into the fresh night air—only to find that a most amazing sight awaited us. In the dusk the whole of the Forum was lit by torches—a great carpet of flickering yellow light. In every direction people were standing, motionless and silent, including the whole of the Senate, which had now emerged from the Temple of Concordia, just next door to the prison. Everyone was looking toward Cicero. Obviously he had to announce what had happened, although he had no idea what the reaction might be, and he also had another peculiar difficulty, which showed the unprecedented nature of what had just occurred: it was a superstition in those days that a magistrate must never utter the words "death" or "died" in the Forum, lest he bring down a curse on the city. So Cicero thought for a moment, cleared his throat of whatever thick bile had accumulated in the Carcer, threw back his shoulders, and proclaimed, very loudly, *"They have lived!"*

His voice echoed off the buildings and was followed by a silence so profound that I feared the vast crowd might be hostile after all and we would be the next to be hanged. But I suppose they were just working out what he meant. A few senators started clapping. Others joined in. The clapping turned to cheers. And slowly the cheers began spreading across the vast throng. "Hail Cicero!" they called. "Hail Cicero!" "Thank the gods for Cicero!" "Cicero—the savior of the republic!"

Standing only a foot away from him, I saw the tears well up into his eyes. It was as if some dam had broken in him and all the emotions that had been accumulating behind it, not only during the past few hours but throughout his consulship, were suddenly allowed to burst forth. He tried to say something but could not, which only increased the volume of applause. Finally there was nothing for it but to descend the steps, and by the time he reached the level of the Forum, with the cheers of friends and opponents alike ringing in his ears, he was weeping freely. Behind us the bodies of the prisoners were being dragged out by hooks.

The story of Cicero's last few days as consul may be swiftly told. No civilian in the history of the republic had ever been as lauded as he was at this time. After months of holding its breath, the city seemed to let out a great sigh of relief. On the night the conspirators were executed, the consul was escorted home from the Forum by the whole of the Senate in a great torchlit procession and was cheered every step of the way. His house was brilliantly illuminated to welcome him back; the entrance where Terentia waited for him with his children was decked with laurel; his slaves lined up to applaud him into the atrium. It was a strange homecoming. He was too exhausted to sleep, too hungry to eat, too eager to forget the horrible business of the executions to be capable of talking about anything else. I assumed he would recover his equilibrium in a day or two. Only later did I realize that something in him had changed forever: had snapped, like an axle. The following morning the Senate bestowed upon him the title "Father of his Country." Caesar chose not to attend the session, but Crassus came and voted with the rest, and praised him to the skies.

Not every voice was raised in acclamation. Metellus Nepos, on taking up his tribunate a few days later, continued to insist that the executions were illegal. He predicted that when Pompey returned to Italy to restore order he would deal not only with Catilina but with this petty tyrant Cicero as well. Despite his immense popularity Cicero was sufficiently worried to go to Clodia and ask her to tell her brother-in-law privately that if he persisted in this course, Cicero would prosecute him for his own links to Catilina. Clodia's lustrous brown eyes widened in delight at this opportunity to meddle in affairs of state. But Nepos coolly ignored the warning, reasoning correctly that Cicero would never dare to move against Pompey's closest political ally. All now depended, therefore, on how swiftly Catilina could be defeated.

When the salutory news of the execution of Sura and the others reached Catilina's camp, a large number of his followers at once deserted him. (I doubt they would have done so if the Senate vote had been for life imprisonment.) Realizing that Rome was now secure against them, he and Manlius decided to take the rebel army north, with the intention of crossing the Alps into Further Gaul and creating a mountainous enclave in which they might hold out for years. But winter was coming and the lower passes were blocked by Metellus Celer at the head of three legions. Meanwhile, in hard pursuit at his rear was the Senate's other army, under the command of Hybrida. This was the opponent Catilina chose to turn and fight, picking his ground in a narrow plain to the east of Pisae.

Not surprisingly, suspicions arose, which persist to this day, that he and his old ally Hybrida had been in secret contact all along. Cicero had foreseen this, and when it became clear that battle was to be joined, Hybrida's veteran military legate, Marcus Petreius, opened the sealed orders he had been given in Rome. These appointed him the operational commander and directed that Hybrida should plead illness and take no part in the fighting; if he refused, Petreius was to arrest him. When the matter was put to Hybrida he swiftly agreed and announced that he was suffering from gout. In this way Catilina unexpectedly found himself facing one of the most able commanders in the Roman army, who was at the head of a force much larger and better equipped than his own.

On the morning of the battle Catilina addressed his soldiers, many of whom were armed only with pitchforks and hunting spears, in the following terms: "Men, we fight for our country, our freedom, and our life, whereas our opponents fight for a corrupt oligarchy. Their numbers may be greater but our spirit is stronger, and we will prevail. But if for any reason we do not, and Fortune turns against us, do not allow yourselves to be slaughtered like cattle, but fight like men and make sure that bloodshed and mourning are the price that the enemy will pay for victory." The trumpets then sounded and the front lines advanced toward one another.

It was a terrible carnage and Catilina was in the thick of it all day. Not one of his lieutenants surrendered. They fought with the ferocious abandon of men with nothing to lose. Only when Petreius sent in a crack praetorian cohort did the rebel army finally collapse. Every one of Catilina's followers, including Manlius, died where he stood; afterward their wounds were found to be entirely in the front and none in the back. At nightfall after the battle Catilina was discovered deep inside his opponents' lines, surrounded by the corpses of the enemies he had hacked to pieces. He was still just breathing but died soon afterward from terrible wounds. His head was sent back to Rome in a barrel of ice on Hybrida's instructions and presented to the Senate. But Cicero, who had left the consulship a few days earlier, refused to look at it, and thus ended the conspiracy of Lucius Sergius Catilina.

PART TWO

PATER PATRIAE

62–58 B.C.

Nam Catonem nostrum non tu amas plus quam ego; sed
tamen ille optimo animo utens et summa fide nocet interdum
rei publicae; dicit enim tamquam in Platonis politeia, non
tamquam in Romuli faece, sententiam.

As for our friend Cato, I have as warm a regard
for him as you. But the fact remains that with
all his patriotism and integrity he is sometimes a
political liability. He speaks in the Senate as
though he were living in Plato's Republic rather
than Romulus's shit hole.

CICERO, LETTER TO ATTICUS, 3 JUNE 60 B.C.

XII

FOR THE FIRST few weeks after he ceased to be consul, everyone clamored to hear the story of how Cicero had foiled the conspiracy of Catilina. There was not a fashionable dinner table in Rome that was not open to him. He went out often; he hated to be alone. Frequently I would accompany him, standing with other members of his entourage behind his couch as he regaled his fellow diners with extracts from his speeches, or the story of how he had escaped assassination on polling day on the Field of Mars, or the trap he had set on the Mulvian Bridge for Lentulus Sura. Usually he illustrated these tales by moving plates and cups around, in the manner of Pompey describing an old battle. If someone interrupted him or tried to raise another subject he would wait impatiently for a gap in their conversation, give them a hard look, and then resume: "*As I was saying* . . ." Every morning the grandest of the grand families would flock to his levees, and he would point to the very spot where Catilina had stood on the day he offered to be his prisoner, or to the exact pieces of furniture which had been used to barricade the door when the conspirators laid siege to the house. In the Senate whenever he rose to speak a respectful hush fell over the assembly, and he never missed a chance to remind them that they were meeting together at all only because he had saved the republic. He became, in short—and whoever would have imagined saying this of Cicero?—a bore.

It would have been so much better for him if he had left Rome for a year or two to govern a province; his mystique would have grown with his absence; he would have become a legend. But he had given away his governorships to Hybrida and Celer, and there was nothing for him to do except to stay in the city and resume his legal practice. Familiarity makes even the most fascinating figure dull: one would probably be bored with Jupiter Himself if one passed Him on the street every day. Slowly Cicero's luster faded. For several weeks he busied himself dictating to me an immense report on his consulship which he wanted to present to Pompey. It was the size of a book and justified his every action in minute detail. I knew it was a mistake and tried all the tactics I could think of to delay sending it—to no avail. Off it went by special courier to the East, and while he awaited the great man's reply, Cicero set about editing and publishing the speeches he had delivered during the crisis. He inserted many purple passages about himself, especially in the public address he had made from the rostra on the day the plotters were arrested. I was sufficiently worried that one morning, when Atticus was leaving the house, I drew him aside and read out a couple of sections.

"This day on which we are saved is, I believe, as bright and joyous as the day on which we were born. And just as we thank the gods for the man who founded this city, so you and your descendants will be able to hold in honor the man who has saved the city."

"What?" exclaimed Atticus. "I don't remember his saying that."

"Well, he didn't," I replied. "For him to have compared himself to Romulus at such a moment would have seemed absurd. And listen to this." I lowered my voice and looked around to make sure Cicero was nowhere near. *"In recognition of such great services, citizens, I shall demand of you no reward for my valor, no signal mark of distinction, no monument in my honor, except that this day be remembered for all time, and that the immortal gods should be thanked that there have arisen at such a moment in our history two men, one of whom has carried your empire to the limits not of earth but of heaven, and one who has preserved the home and seat of this empire . . ."*

"Let me see that," demanded Atticus. He grabbed the speech from my hands and read it through, shaking his head in disbelief. "Putting yourself on the same level as Romulus is one thing: comparing yourself with Pompey is quite another. It would be dangerous enough if someone else said it about him, but for him to say it about *himself* . . . ? Let's just hope Pompey doesn't get to hear of it."

"He's bound to."

"Why?"

"I've been ordered to send him a copy." Once again I checked that no one was listening. "Forgive me, sir, if I am speaking out of turn," I said, "but I'm becoming quite concerned about him. He's not been the same since the executions. He isn't sleeping well, he won't listen to anyone, and yet he can't bear to spend even an hour by himself. I think the sight of the dead men has affected him—you know how squeamish he is."

"It's not his delicate stomach that's troubling him, it's his conscience.

If he were entirely satisfied that what he did was right he wouldn't feel the need to justify himself so endlessly."

It was a shrewd remark and I feel sorrier for Cicero in retrospect than I did at the time, for it must be a lonely business, trying to turn oneself into a public monument. However, by far his greatest folly was not the vainglorious letter to Pompey, or the endless boasting, or the amended speeches: it was a house.

Cicero was not the first politician, and I am sure he will not be the last, to covet a house beyond his means. In his case the property was the boarded-up mansion on the Palatine next to Celer's on Victory Rise that he had noticed when he went to persuade the praetor to take command of the army against Catilina. It now belonged to Crassus, but before that it had been the property of the immensely wealthy tribune Marcus Livius Drusus. The story went that the architect who built it had promised Drusus he would make sure he was not overlooked by any of his neighbors. "No," responded Drusus, "rather construct it so that all my fellow citizens may see everything I do." That was the sort of place it was: high up on the hill, tall, wide, and ostentatious, easily visible from every part of the Forum and the Capitol. Celer's house was on one side of it and on the other were a large public garden and a portico that had been put up by Catulus's father. I do not know who planted the idea of buying it in Cicero's head. I fancy it might have been Clodia. Certainly she told him over dinner one night that it was still on the market and that it would be "wonderfully amusing" to have him as a next-door neighbor. Naturally that was enough to set Terentia dead against the purchase from the start.

"It is modern and it is vulgar," she told him. "It is a parvenu's idea of where a gentleman might live."

"I am the Father of the Nation. The people will like the idea that I am looking down on them in a paternal manner. And it's where we deserve to be, up there among the Claudii, the Aemilii Scauri, the Metelli—the Ciceros are a great family now. Besides, I thought you hated this place."

"It's not moving in principle I object to, husband; it's moving *there*. And how can you possibly afford it? It's one of the largest houses in Rome—it must be worth at least ten million."

"I shall go and talk to Crassus. Maybe he'll let me have it cheap."

Crassus's own mansion, which was also on the Palatine, was deceptively modest on the outside, especially for a man who was rumored to have eight thousand amphorae filled with silver coin. Inside he sat with his abacus and his account books and the team of slaves and freedmen who ran his business interests. I accompanied Cicero when he went to see him, and after a little preliminary talk about the political situation, Cicero broached the subject of the Drusus house.

"Do you want to buy it?" asked Crassus, suddenly alert.

"I might. How much is it?"

"Fourteen million."

"Ouch! That's too expensive for me, I fear."

"I'd let you have it for ten."

"That's generous but it's still out of my range."

"Eight?"

"No, really, Crassus—I appreciate it, but I should never have brought the subject up." Cicero started to rise from his chair.

"Six?" offered Crassus. "Four?"

Cicero sat down again. "I could possibly manage three."

"Shall we settle on three and a half?"

Afterward as we were walking home I tried gently to suggest that taking possession of such a house for a quarter of its true value would not go down well with the voters. They would smell something fishy about it. "Who cares about the voters?" replied Cicero. "I'm barred from standing for the consulship for the next ten years whatever I do. In any case, they need never know how much I paid for it."

"It will get out somehow," I warned.

"For gods' sake, will you stop lecturing me about how I am to live? It is bad enough hearing it from my wife without taking it from my secretary! Haven't I earned the right to some luxury, at long last? Half this town would be nothing but charred brick and ashes if it weren't for me! Which reminds me—have we heard back from Pompey yet?"

"No," I said, bowing my head.

I let the matter drop, but I continued to be troubled. I was absolutely certain that Crassus would expect something in return for his money; either that or he hated Cicero so much he was willing to forfeit ten million simply to make the people envy and resent him. My secret hope was that Cicero would come to his senses in a day or two, not least because I knew that he did not have three and a half million sesterces, or anything like it. But Cicero always took the view that income should adjust to meet expenditure rather than the other way around. He had set his heart on moving up to Victory Rise to dwell among the pantheon of the great names of the republic and was determined to find the cash somehow. He soon discovered a way.

Almost every day at this time one of the surviving conspirators was to be found on trial in the Forum. Autronius Paetus; Cassius Longinus; Marcus Laeca; the two would-be assassins, Vargunteius and Vorenelius; and many more passed through the courts in a dismal procession. In each case Cicero was a witness for the prosecution, and such was his prestige that a word from him was invariably sufficient to sway the court. One after another they were found guilty—although, fortunately for them, because the emergency was now over, they were not sentenced to death. Instead, each was stripped of his citizenship and property and sent destitute into exile. Cicero was feared and hated by the conspirators and their families almost more than ever, and it remained necessary for him to go around with guards.

Perhaps the most keenly awaited trial of all was that of Publius Cornelius Sulla, who had been immersed in the conspiracy right up to his noble neck. As the date for his hearing approached, his advocate—inevitably it was Hortensius—came to see Cicero.

"My client has a favor to ask of you," he said.

"Don't tell me: he would like me to refuse to appear as a witness against him."

"That's right. He's entirely innocent and has always had the highest regard—"

"Oh, spare me all the hypocrisy. He's guilty and you know it." Cicero scrutinized Hortensius's bland face, weighing him up. "Actually, you can tell him I might be willing to hold my tongue in his particular case, but on one condition."

"And what is that?"

"He gives me a million sesterces."

I was making my usual note of the conversation, but I must say my hand froze when I heard that. Even Hortensius, who after thirty years at the Roman bar was not shocked by much, looked taken aback. Still, he went off and saw Sulla and came back later that same day.

"My client wishes to make a counteroffer. If you are willing to give the closing speech in his defense, he will pay you two million."

"Agreed," said Cicero without any hesitation.

There is little doubt that if Cicero had not struck this bargain, Sulla would have been condemned to exile like all the rest; indeed it was said he had already transferred a large part of his fortune abroad. So when, on the opening day of the trial, Cicero turned up and sat on the bench reserved for the defense, the prosecuting counsel, Torquatus, an old ally of Cicero, could hardly contain his fury and disappointment. In the course of his summing-up he made a bitter attack on Cicero, accusing him of being a tyrant, of setting himself up as judge and jury, of having been the third foreign-born king of Rome, after Tarquin and Numa. It was painful to hear, and worse, it drew some applause from the spectators in the Forum. This expression of popular opinion penetrated even Cicero's carapace of self-regard, and when the time came for him to deliver the closing speech he did venture a kind of apology. "Yes," he said, "I suppose my achievements have made me too proud and bred in me a sort of arrogance. But of those glorious and deathless achievements, I can say only this: I shall be amply rewarded for saving this city and the lives of all its citizens if no danger falls upon my person for this great service to all mankind. The Forum is full of those men whom I have driven from your throats, gentlemen, but have not removed from mine."

The speech was effective and Sulla was duly acquitted. But Cicero would have done well to heed these signals of a coming storm. Instead, such was his delight at raising most of the money he needed to buy his new house that he quickly shrugged off the incident. He was now only one and a half million short of the full sum, and for this he turned to the moneylenders. They required security, and therefore he told at least two of them, in confidence, of his agreement with Hybrida and his expectation of a share of the revenues from Macedonia. It was good enough to clinch the deal, and toward the end of the year we moved into Victory Rise.

The house was as grand inside as out. Its dining room had a paneled ceiling with gilded rafters. In the hall were golden statues of young men, whose outstretched hands were designed to hold flaming torches. Cicero swapped his cramped study, where we had spent so many memorable hours, for a fine library. Even I had a larger room, which, though it was belowground, was not at all damp and had a small barred window through which I could smell the flowers in the garden and hear the birdsong early in the morning. I would have preferred to have had my freedom, of course, and a place of my own, but Cicero had never mentioned it and I was too bashful—and in a curious way, too proud—to ask.

After I had laid out my few belongings and found a hiding place for my life savings, I went and joined Cicero on a tour of the grounds. The colonnaded path took us past a fountain and a summer house, under a pergola, and into a rose garden. The few blooms left were fleshy and faded; when Cicero reached out to pluck one the petals came away. I felt that we were under inspection from the whole of the city: it made me uncomfortable, but that was the price one paid for the open view, which was indeed amazing. Beyond the Temple of Castor one could clearly see the rostra, and beyond that the Senate House itself, and if one looked in the other direction one could just about make out the back of Caesar's official residence. "I have done it at last," said Cicero, gazing down at it with a slight smile. "I have a better house than he has."

The ceremony of the Good Goddess fell as usual on the fourth day of December. It was exactly a year since the arrest of the conspirators and just a week after we had moved into our new quarters. Cicero had no appointments in court; the Senate's order of business was dull. He told me that for once we would not be going down into the city. Instead we would spend the day working on his memoirs.

He had decided to write one version of his autobiography in Latin, for the general reader, and another in Greek, for more restricted circulation. He was also trying to persuade a poet to turn his consulship into a verse epic. His first choice, Archias, who had done a similar job for Lucullus, was reluctant to take it on; he said he was too old at sixty to do justice to such an immense theme. Cicero's preferred alternative, the fashionable Thyillus, replied humbly that his meager skills as a versifier were simply not up to the task. "Poets!" grumbled Cicero. "I don't know what is the matter with them. The story of my consulship is an absolute gift to anyone with the slightest spark of imagination. It is beginning to look," he continued darkly, in a phrase that struck fear into my heart, "as though I shall have to write this poem myself."

"Is that altogether wise?" I asked.

"What do you mean?"

I felt myself beginning to sweat. "Well, after all, even Achilles needed his Homer. His story might not have had quite the same—what should one say?—*epic resonance* if he had told it from his own point of view."

"I solved that problem in bed last night. My plan is to tell my tale in the voices of the gods, each taking it in turn to recount my career to me as they welcome me as an immortal onto Mount Olympus." He jumped up and cleared his throat. "I'll show you what I mean:

Torn from your studies in youth's early dawn, your country recalled
    you,
Giving you place in the thick of the struggle for public preferment;
Yet in seeking release from the worries and cares that oppress you,
Time that the State leaves free you devote to us and to learning . . ."

Dear heavens, it was terrible stuff! The gods must have wept to hear it. But when the mood seized him Cicero could lay down hexameters as readily as a bricklayer could throw up a wall: three, four, even five hundred lines a day was nothing to him. He paced around the great open space of his library, acting out the roles of Jupiter and Minerva and Urania, the words pouring out of him so freely I had difficulty keeping up, even in shorthand. When eventually Sositheus tiptoed in and announced that Clodius was waiting outside, I must confess I was greatly relieved. By now it was quite late in the morning—the sixth hour at least—and Cicero was so seized by inspiration he almost sent his visitor packing. But he knew that Clodius would probably be bearing some choice morsel of gossip, and curiosity got the better of him. He told Sositheus to show him in, and Clodius duly strolled into the library, his golden curls elegantly coiffed, his goatee trimmed, his bronzed limbs trailing a scent of crocus oil. He was thirty by now, a married man, having wed the fifteen-year-old heiress Fulvia in the summer, at the same time as he was elected a magistrate. Not that married life detained him much. Her dowry had bought them a large house on the Palatine, and there she sat alone most evenings while he continued with his roisterous ways in the taverns of Subura.

"Tasty news," announced Clodius. He held up a finger with a highly polished nail. "But you mustn't tell a soul."

Cicero gestured to him to take a seat. "You know how discreet I am."

"You will simply adore this," said Clodius, settling himself down. "This will make your day."

"I hope it lives up to its billing."

"It will." Clodius tugged at his little beard with glee. "The Warden of Land and Sea is divorcing."

Cicero had been lounging back in his chair with a half smile on his face, his usual posture when gossiping with Clodius. But now he slowly straightened. "Are you absolutely sure?"

"I just heard it from your next-door neighbor, my darling sister—who sends her love, by the way—who received the news by special messenger from husband Celer last night. Apparently Pompey has written to Mucia telling her not to be in the house by the time he gets back to Rome."

"Which will be when?"

"In a few weeks. His fleet is off Brundisium. He may even have landed by now."

Cicero let out a low whistle. "So he's coming home at last. After six years I was beginning to think I'd never see him again."

"Hoping you'd never see him again, more like."

It was an impertinent remark, but Cicero was too preoccupied with Pompey's impending return to notice. "If he's divorcing, that must mean he's remarrying. Does Clodia know whom he has in mind?"

"No, only that Mucia's out on her pretty little pink ear and the children go with Pompey, even though he hardly knows them. Her brothers are both up in arms, as you can imagine. Celer swears he's been betrayed. Nepos swears it even more. Clodia naturally finds it very funny. But still, what an insult, eh, after all they've done for him—to have their sister publicly cast aside for adultery?"

"And was she an adulteress?"

"*Was she an adulteress?*" Clodius gave a surprisingly high-pitched giggle. "My dear Cicero, the bitch has been rolling around on her back waving her legs in the air ever since he left! Don't tell me you haven't had her? If so, you must be the only man in Rome who hasn't!"

"Are you drunk?" demanded Cicero. He leaned across and sniffed at Clodius, then wrinkled his nose. "You are, damn you. I suggest you go away and sober up, and mind your manners in future."

For a moment I thought Clodius might hit him. But then he smirked and started wiggling his head from side to side derisively. "Oh, I am a terrible man. A terrible, terrible man . . ."

He looked so comical that Cicero forgot his anger and started laughing at him. "Go on," he said, "clear off and take your mischief somewhere else."

That was Clodius before he changed: a moody boy—a moody, spoiled, charming boy. "That fellow amuses me," Cicero remarked after the young patrician had gone, "but I can't say I really care for him. Still," he added,

"I'll forgive any man a coarse remark who brings me such intriguing news." From then on he was too preoccupied trying to work out all the implications of Pompey's homecoming and potential remarriage to resume dictating his poem. I was grateful to Clodius for that at least, and thought no more about his visit for the remainder of the day.

A few hours later Terentia came into the library to say goodbye to her husband. She was leaving to celebrate the Good Goddess's nocturnal rites, and she would not be back until the morning. Relations between her and Cicero were cool. Despite the elegance of her private apartments on the upper floor, she still hated the house, especially the late-night comings and goings of Clodia's louche salon next door, and the proximity of the noisy crowds in the Forum who gaped up at her whenever she went onto the terrace with her maids. To try to placate her, Cicero was going out of his way to be friendly.

"And where is the Good Goddess to be worshipped tonight? If," he added with a smile, "a mere man can be entrusted with such sacred information." (The ritual was always held in the house of a senior magistrate, whose wife was responsible for organizing it; they took it in turns.)

"At Caesar's house."

"Aurelia presiding?"

"Pompeia."

"I wonder if Mucia will be there."

"I expect so. Why shouldn't she be?"

"She might be too ashamed to show her face."

"Why?"

"It seems Pompey is divorcing her."

"No?" Despite herself, Terentia was unable to conceal her interest. "Where did you hear that?"

"Clodius came around to tell me."

Immediately her lips compressed into a thin line of disapproval. "Then it probably isn't true. You really ought to keep better company."

"I shall keep what company I like."

"No doubt, but do you really have to inflict it on the rest of us? It's bad enough living so close to the sister, without having the brother under our roof as well."

She turned without saying goodbye and stalked off across the marble floor. Cicero pulled a face at her narrow back. "First the old house was too far away from everyone, now the new one is too close. You're lucky you're not married, Tiro."

I was tempted to reply that I had been given little choice in the matter.

He had been invited weeks ago to dine that evening with Atticus. Quintus had also been asked, and so, curiously enough, had I: our host's plan was that the four of us should reassemble in exactly the same place and at exactly the same time as last year, and drink a toast in celebration of the fact that we, and Rome, had survived. Cicero and I turned up at his house as darkness fell. Quintus was already there. But although the food and the wine were good enough, and there was Pompey to gossip about, and the library was conducive to conversation, the occasion was not a success. Everyone seemed out of sorts. Cicero had been put into a bad mood by his encounter with Terentia and was perturbed at the thought of Pompey's return. Quintus was coming to the end of his term as praetor and was heavily in debt and apprehensive about what province he might draw in the forthcoming lottery. Even Atticus, whose Epicurean sensibilities were normally unruffled by the outside world, was preoccupied with something. As usual I took my mood from theirs and spoke only when asked a question. We drank to the glorious fourth of December, but for once not even Cicero could bring himself to reminisce. Suddenly it did not seem appropriate to celebrate the deaths of five men, however villainous. The past fell like a clammy shadow across us, chilling all conversation. Finally, Atticus said, "I'm thinking of going back to Epirus."

For a moment or two nobody spoke.

"When?" asked Cicero quietly.

"Directly after Saturnalia."

"You're not *thinking* of going," said Quintus with a nasty edge to his voice, "you've already made up your mind. You're *telling* us."

Cicero said, "Why do you want to go now?"

Atticus played around with the stem of his glass. "I came back to Rome two years ago to help you win the election. I've stayed ever since to support you. But now that things seem to have settled down, I don't think you need me anymore."

"I most certainly do," insisted Cicero.

"Besides, I have business interests over there I have to attend to."

"Ah," said Quintus into his glass, "*business interests*. Now we get to the bottom of it."

"What do you mean by that?" asked Atticus.

"Nothing."

"No, please—say what's in your mind."

"Leave it, Quintus," warned Cicero.

"Only this," said Quintus, "that somehow Marcus and I seem to run all the dangers of public life, and shoulder all the hard work, while you are free to flit between your estates and attend to your *business interests* at will. You prosper through your connection with us, yet we seem permanently short of money. That's all."

"But you enjoy the rewards of a public career. You have fame and power and will be remembered by history, whereas I am a nobody."

"A nobody! A nobody who knows everybody!" Quintus took another drink. "I don't suppose there's any chance of your taking your sister back with you to Epirus, is there?"

"Quintus!" cried Cicero.

"If your marriage is unhappy," said Atticus mildly, "then I am sorry for you. But that is hardly my fault."

"And there we are again," said Quintus. "You've even managed to avoid marriage. I swear this fellow has the secret of life! Why don't you bear your share of domestic suffering, like the rest of us?"

"That's enough," said Cicero, getting to his feet. "We should leave you, Atticus, before any more words are uttered that aren't really meant. Quintus?" He held out his hand to Quintus, who scowled and looked away. "Quintus!" he repeated angrily, and thrust out his hand again. Quintus turned reluctantly and glanced up at his elder brother, and just for an instant I saw such a flash of hatred in his eyes it made me catch my breath. But then he threw aside his napkin and stood. He swayed a little and almost fell back onto the table, but I grabbed his arm and he recovered his balance. He lurched out of the library and we followed him into the atrium.

Cicero had ordered a litter to take us home, but now he insisted that Quintus have it. "You ride home, Brother. We shall walk." We helped him into his chair and Cicero told the bearers to carry him to our old house on the Esquiline, next to the Temple of Tellus, into which Quintus had moved when Cicero moved out. Quintus was asleep even before the litter set off. As we watched him go I reflected that it was no easy matter being the younger brother of a genius, and that all the choices in Quintus's life—his career, his home, even his wife—had been made in accordance with the demands of his brilliant, ambitious sibling, who could always talk him into anything.

"He means no harm," said Cicero to Atticus. "He's worried about the future, that's all. Once the Senate has decided which provinces are to be put into this year's ballot and he knows where he's going, he'll be happier."

"I'm sure you're right. But I fear he believes at least some of what he says. I hope he doesn't speak for you as well."

"My dearest friend, I am perfectly aware that our relationship has cost you far more than you have ever profited from it. We have simply chosen to tread different paths, that's all. I have sought public office while you have yearned for honorable independence, and who's to say which of us is right? But in every quality that really matters I put you second to no man, myself included. There now—are we clear?"

"We are clear."

"And you will come and see me before you leave, and write to me often afterward?"

"I shall."

With that Cicero kissed him on the cheek and the two friends parted, Atticus retreating into his beautiful house with its books and treasures while the former consul trudged down the hill toward the Forum with his guards. On this question of the good life and how to lead it—purely theoretical in my own case, of course—my sympathies were all with Atticus. It seemed to me at that time—and still does now, only even more so—an act of madness for a man to pursue power when he could be sitting in the sunshine and reading a book. But then, even if I had been born into freedom, I know I would not have possessed that overweening force of ambition without which no city is created, no city destroyed.

As chance would have it, our route home took us past the scenes of all Cicero's triumphs, and he fell very quiet as we walked, no doubt pondering his conversation with Atticus. We passed the locked and deserted Senate House, where he had made such memorable speeches; passed the curving wall of the rostra, surmounted by its multitude of heroic statues, from which he had addressed the Roman people in their thousands; and finally we passed the Temple of Castor, where he had presented his case to the extortion court in the long legal battle against Verres that had launched his career. The great public buildings and monuments, so quiet and massive in the darkness, nevertheless seemed to me that night as substantial as air. We heard voices in the distance and occasional scuffling noises closer by, but it was only rats in the heaps of rubbish.

We left the Forum, and ahead of us were the myriad lights of the Palatine, tracing the shape of the hill—the yellow flickering of the torches and braziers on the terraces, the dim pinpricks of the candles and lamps in the windows amid the trees. Suddenly Cicero halted. "Isn't that our house?" he asked, pointing to a long cluster of lights. I followed his outstretched arm and replied that I thought it was. "But that's very odd," he said. "Most of the rooms seem to be lit. It looks as though Terentia is home."

We set off quickly up the hill. "If Terentia has left the ceremony early," said Cicero breathlessly over his shoulder, "it won't be of her own volition. Something must have happened." He almost ran along the street toward the house and hammered on the door. Inside, we found Terentia standing in the atrium surrounded by a cluster of maids and womenfolk who seemed to twitter and scatter like birds at Cicero's approach. Once again she was wearing a cloak fastened tightly at the throat to conceal her sacred robes. "Terentia?" he demanded, advancing toward her. "What's wrong? Are you all right?"

"I am well enough," she replied, her voice cold and trembling with rage. "It is Rome that is sick!"

That so much harm could flow from so farcical an episode will doubtless strike future generations as absurd. In truth it often seemed absurd at the time: fits of public morality generally do. But human life is bizarre and unpredictable. Some joker cracks an egg and from it hatches tragedy.

The basic facts were simple. Terentia recounted them to Cicero that night, and the story was never seriously challenged. She had arrived at Caesar's residence to be greeted by Pompeia's maid, Abra—a girl of notoriously easy virtue, as befitted the character of her mistress and of her master, too, for that matter, although he of course was not on the premises at the time. Abra showed Terentia into the main part of the house, where Pompeia, the hostess for the evening, and the vestal virgins were already waiting, along with Caesar's mother, Aurelia. Within the hour, most of the senior wives of Rome were congregated in this spot and the ritual began. What exactly they were doing Terentia would not say, only that most of the house was in darkness when suddenly they were interrupted by screams. They ran to discover the source and immediately came across one of Aurelia's freedwomen having a fit of hysterics. Between sobs she cried out that there was an intruder in the house. She had approached what she thought was a female musician, only to discover that the girl was actually a man in disguise! It was at this point Terentia realized that Pompeia had disappeared.

Aurelia at once took charge of the situation and ordered that all the holy things be covered and that the doors be locked and watched. Then she and some of the braver females, including Terentia, began a thorough search of the huge house. In due course, in Pompeia's bedroom, they found a veiled figure dressed in women's clothes, clutching a lyre and trying to hide behind a curtain. They chased him down the stairs and into the dining room, where he fell over a couch and his veil was snatched away. Nearly everyone recognized him. He had shaved off his small beard and had put on rouge, black eye makeup, and lipstick, but that was hardly sufficient to disguise the well-known pretty-boy features of Publius Clodius Pulcher—"Your friend Clodius," as Terentia bitterly described him to Cicero.

Clodius, who was plainly drunk, realizing he was discovered, then jumped onto the dining table, pulled up his gown, exposed himself to all the assembled company, including the vestal virgins, and, finally, while his audience was shrieking and swooning, ran out of the room and managed to escape from the house via a kitchen window. Only now did Pompeia appear with Abra, whereupon Aurelia accused her daughter-in-law and her maid of collusion in this sacrilege. Both denied it tearfully, but the senior vestal virgin announced their protests did not matter: a desecration had occurred, the sacred rites would have to be abandoned, and the devotees must all disperse to their homes at once.

Such was Terentia's story, and Cicero listened to it with a mixture of incredulity, disgust, and painfully suppressed amusement. Obviously, he would have to take a stern moral line in public and in front of Terentia—it *was* shocking, he agreed with her absolutely—but secretly he also thought it one of the funniest things he had ever heard. In particular the image of Clodius waving his private parts in the horrified faces of Rome's stuffiest matrons made him laugh until his eyes watered. But that was for the seclusion of his library. As far as the politics were concerned, he thought Clodius had finally shown himself to be an irredeemable idiot—"he's thirty, in the name of heaven, not thirteen"—and that his career as a magistrate was finished before it had even started. He also sus-pected, gleefully, that Caesar might be in trouble as well: the scandal had happened in his house, it had involved his wife; it would not look good.

This was the spirit in which Cicero went down to the Senate the fol-lowing morning, one year to the day after the debate on the fate of the conspirators. Many of the senior members had heard from their wives what had happened, and as they stood around in the senaculum waiting for the auspices to be taken there was only one topic of discussion, or at least there was by the time Cicero had finished his rounds. The Father of the Nation moved solemnly from group to group wearing an expression of piety and grave seriousness, his arms folded inside his toga, shaking his head, and reluctantly spreading the news of the outrage to those who had not already heard it. "Oh look," he would say in conclusion, with a glance across the senaculum, "there's poor Caesar now—this must be a terrible embarrassment for him."

And Caesar did indeed look gray and grim, the young chief priest, standing alone on that bleak day in December, at the absolute nadir of his fortunes. His praetorship, now drawing to its close, had not been a suc-cess: at one point he was actually suspended, and had been lucky not to be hauled into court along with Catilina's other supporters. He was anx-iously waiting to hear which province he would be allotted: it would need to be lucrative, as he was greatly in debt to the moneylenders. And now this ludicrous affair involving Clodius and Pompeia threatened to turn him into a figure of ridicule. It was almost possible to feel sorry for him as he watched, with hawkish eyes, Cicero going around the senaculum, relaying the gossip. Rome's cuckolder in chief: a cuckold! A lesser man would have stayed away from the Senate for the day, but that was never Caesar's style. When the auspices were read he walked into the chamber and sat on the praetors' bench, two places along from Quintus, while Cicero went over to join the other ex-consuls on the opposite side of the aisle.

The session had barely begun when the former praetor Cornificius, who regarded himself as a custodian of religious probity, jumped up on a point of order to demand an emergency debate on the "shameful and im-moral" events that were said to have occurred overnight at the official residence of the chief priest. Looking back, this could have been the end for Clodius right then and there. He was not yet even eligible to take his seat in the Senate. But fortunately for him, the consul presiding in December was none other than his stepfather-in-law, Murena, and whatever his private feelings on the subject, he had no intention of adding to the family's embarrassment if he could avoid it.

"This is not a matter for the Senate," ruled Murena. "If anything has happened it is the responsibility of the religious authorities to investigate."

This brought Cato to his feet, his eyes ablaze with excitement at the thought of such decadence. "Then I propose that this house asks the College of Priests to conduct an inquiry," he said, "and report back to us as soon as possible."

Murena had little choice except to put the motion to the vote, and it passed without discussion. Earlier, Cicero had told me he was not going to intervene ("I'll let Cato and the others make hay if they want to; I'm going to keep out of it; it's more dignified"). However, when it came to the point, he could not resist the opportunity. Rising gravely to his feet, he looked directly at Caesar. "As the alleged outrage occurred under the chief priest's own roof, perhaps he could save us all the trouble of waiting for the outcome of an inquiry and tell us now whether or not an offense was committed."

Caesar's face was so clenched that even from my old position by the door—to which I had been obliged to return now that Cicero was no longer consul—I could see the muscle twitching in his jaw as he got up to reply. "The rites of the Good Goddess are not a matter for the chief priest, as he is not even allowed to be present at the time they are celebrated." He sat down.

Cicero put on a puzzled expression and rose again. "But surely the chief priest's own wife was presiding over the ceremony? He must have at least some knowledge of what occurred." He lapsed back into his seat.

Caesar hesitated for a fraction, then got up and said calmly, "That woman is no longer my wife."

An excited whisper went around the chamber. Cicero got up again. Now he sounded genuinely puzzled. "So we may take it, therefore, that an outrage *did* occur."

"Not necessarily," replied Caesar, and once again sat down.

Cicero stood. "But if an outrage did not occur, then why is the chief priest divorcing his wife?"

"Because the wife of the chief priest must be above suspicion."

There was a good deal of amusement at the coolness of this reply, and

Cicero did not rise again but signaled to Murena that he no longer wished to pursue the matter. Afterward, as we were walking home, he said to me, not without a hint of admiration, "That was the most ruthless thing I ever saw in the Senate. How long would you say Caesar and Pompeia have been married?"

"It must be six or seven years."

"And yet I'm certain he only made up his mind to divorce her when I asked him that question. He realized it was the best way to get himself out of a tight corner. You have to hand it to him—most men wouldn't abandon their dog so casually."

I thought sadly of the beautiful Pompeia and wondered if she was aware yet that her husband had just publicly ended their marriage. Knowing how swiftly Caesar liked to act, I suspected she would be out of his house by nightfall.

When we got home Cicero went at once to his library to avoid running into Terentia and lay down on a couch. "I need to hear some pure Greek to wash away the dirt of politics," he said. Sositheus, who normally read to him, was ill, so he asked if I would do the honors, and at his request I fetched a copy of Euripides from its compartment and unrolled it beside the lamp. It was *The Suppliant Women* he asked to hear, I suppose because on that day the execution of the conspirators was uppermost in his mind, and he hoped that at least in yielding up the bodies of his enemies for an honorable burial he had played the part of Theseus. I had just gotten to his favorite lines—*Rashness in a leader causes failure; the sailor of a ship is calm, wise at the proper time. Yes, and forethought: this too is bravery*—when a slave came in and said that Clodius was in the atrium.

Cicero swore. "Go and tell him to get out of my house. I can't be seen to have anything more to do with him."

This was not a job I relished, but I laid aside Euripides and went out into the atrium. I had expected to find Clodius in a state of some distress. Instead he wore a rueful smile. "Good day, Tiro. I thought I had better come and see my teacher straightaway and get my punishment over and done with."

"I'm afraid my master is not in."

Clodius's smile faltered a little, because of course he guessed that I was lying. "But I have worked the whole thing up for him into the most wonderful story. He simply has to hear it. No, this is ridiculous. I won't be sent away."

He pushed past me and walked across the wide hall and into the library. I followed, wringing my hands. But to his surprise and mine the room was empty. There was a small door in the opposite corner for the slaves to come and go, and even as we looked it closed gently. The Euripides lay where I had left it. "Well," said Clodius, sounding suddenly uneasy, "make sure you tell him I called."

"I certainly shall," I replied.

XIII

AROUND THIS TIME, exactly as Clodius had predicted, Pompey the Great returned to Italy, making land at Brundisium. The Senate's messengers raced in relays nearly three hundred miles to Rome to bring the news. According to their dispatches, twenty thousand of his legionnaires had disembarked with him, and the following day he addressed them in the town's forum. "Men," he was reported to have said, "I thank you for your service. We have put an end to Mithridates, the republic's greatest enemy since Hannibal, and performed heroic deeds together that the world will remember for a thousand years. It is a bitter day that sees us part. But ours is a nation of laws, and I have no authority from the Senate and people to maintain an army in Italy. Disperse to your native cities. Go back to your homes. I promise you your services will not go unrewarded. There will be money and land for all of you. You have my word. And in the meantime, stand ready for my summons to join me in Rome, where you will receive your bounty and we shall celebrate the greatest triumph the mother city of our newly enlarged empire has ever seen!"

With that, he set off on the road to Rome accompanied by only his official escort of lictors and a few close friends. As news of his humble entourage spread, it had the most amazing effect. People had feared he would move north with his army, leaving a swathe of countryside behind them stripped bare as if by locusts. Instead, the Warden of Land and Sea merely ambled along in a leisurely fashion, stopping to rest in country inns, as if he were nothing more grand than a sightseer returning from a foreign holiday. In every town along the route—in Tarentum and in Venusia, across the mountains and down onto the plains of Campania, in Capua and in Minturnae—the crowds turned out to cheer him. Hundreds decided to leave their homes and follow him, and soon the Senate was receiving reports that as many as five thousand citizens were on the march with him to Rome.

Cicero read of all this with increasing alarm. His long letter to Pompey was still unacknowledged, and even he was beginning to perceive that his boasting about his consulship might have done him harm. Worse, he now learned from several sources that Pompey had formed a bad impression of Hybrida, having traveled through Macedonia on his journey back to Italy, witnessing firsthand his corruption and incompetence, and that when he reached Rome he would press for the governor's immediate recall. Such a move would threaten Cicero with financial ruin, not least because he had yet to receive a single sesterce from Hybrida. He called me to his library and dictated a long letter to his former colleague: *"I shall try to protect your back with all my might, provided I do not seem to be throwing my trouble away. But if I find that it gets me no thanks, I shall not let myself be taken for an idiot—even by you."* A few days after Saturnalia there was a farewell dinner for Atticus, at the end of which Cicero gave him the letter and asked him to deliver it to Hybrida personally. Atticus swore to discharge this duty the moment he reached Macedonia, and then, amid many tears and embraces, the two best friends said their farewells. It was a source of deep sadness to both men that Quintus had not bothered to come and see Atticus off.

With Atticus gone from the city, worries seemed to press in on Cicero from every side. He was deeply concerned, and I even more so, by the worsening health of his junior secretary, Sositheus. I had trained this lad myself, in Latin grammar, Greek, and shorthand, and he had become a much-loved member of the household. He had a melodious voice, which was why Cicero came to rely on him as a reader. He was twenty-six or thereabouts and slept in a small room next to mine in the cellar. What started as a hacking cough developed into a fever, and Cicero sent his own doctor down to examine him. A course of bleeding did no good; nor did leeches. Cicero was very much affected, and most days he would sit for a while beside the young man's cot, holding a cold wet towel to his burning forehead. I stayed up with Sositheus every night for a week, listening to his rambling nonsense talk and trying to calm him down and persuade him to drink some water.

It is often the case with these dreadful fevers that the final crisis is preceded by a lull. So it was with Sositheus. I remember it very well. It was long past midnight. I was stretched out on a straw mattress beside his cot, huddled against the cold under a blanket and a sheepskin. He had gone very quiet, and in the silence and the dim yellow light cast by the lamp, I nodded off myself. But something woke me and when I turned I saw that he was sitting up and staring at me with a look of great terror.

"The letters," he said.

It was so typical of him to be worried about his work, I nearly wept. "The letters are taken care of," I replied. "Everything is up to date. Go back to sleep now."

"I copied out the letters."

"Yes, yes, you copied out the letters. Now go to sleep." I tried gently to press him back down, but he wriggled beneath my hands. He was nothing but sweat and bone by this time, as feeble as a sparrow. Yet he would not lie still. He was desperate to tell me something.

"Crassus knows it."

"Of course Crassus knows it." I spoke soothingly. But then I felt a sudden sense of dread. "Crassus knows what?"

"The letters."

"What letters?" Sositheus made no reply. "You mean the anonymous letters? The ones warning of violence in Rome? *You* copied those out?" He nodded. "How does Crassus know?" I whispered.

"I told him." His fragile claw of a hand scrabbled at my arm. "Don't be angry."

"I'm not angry," I said, wiping the sweat from his forehead. "He must have frightened you."

"He said he knew already."

"You mean he tricked you?"

"I'm so sorry—" He stopped and gave an immense groan—a terrible noise, for one so frail—his whole body trembled. His eyelids drooped, then opened wide for one last time, and he gave me such a look as I have never forgotten—there was a whole abyss in those staring eyes—and then he fell back in my arms unconscious. I was horrified by what I saw, I suppose because it was like gazing into the blackest mirror—nothing to see but oblivion—and I realized at that instant that I too would die like Sositheus, childless and leaving behind no trace of my existence. From then on I redoubled my resolve to write down all the history I was witnessing, so that my life might at least have this small purpose.

Sositheus lingered on all through that night and into the next day, and on the last evening of the year he died. I went at once to tell Cicero.

"The poor boy," he sighed. "His death grieves me more than perhaps the loss of a slave should. See to it that his funeral shows the world how much I valued him." He turned back to his book, then noticed that I was still in the room. "Well?"

I was in a dilemma. I felt instinctively that Sositheus had imparted a great secret to me, but I could not be absolutely sure if it was true or merely the ravings of a fevered man. I was also torn between my responsibility to the dead and my duty to the living—to respect my friend's confession, or to warn Cicero? In the end, I chose the latter. "There's something you should know," I said. I took out my tablet and read to him Sositheus's dying words, which I had taken the precaution of writing down.

Cicero studied me as I spoke, his chin in his hand, and when I finished, he said, "I knew I should have asked you to do that copying."

I had not quite been able to bring myself to believe it until that moment. I struggled to hide my shock. "And why didn't you?"

He gave me another appraising look. "Your feelings are bruised?"

"A little."

"Well, they shouldn't be. It's a compliment to your honesty. You sometimes have too many scruples for the dirty business of politics, Tiro, and I would have found it hard to carry off such a deception under your disapproving gaze. So I had you fooled then, did I?" He sounded quite proud of himself.

"Yes," I replied, "completely," and he had: when I remembered his apparent surprise on the night Crassus brought the letters around with Scipio and Marcellus, I was forced to marvel at his skills as an actor, if nothing else.

"Well, I regret I had to trick you. However, it seems I didn't trick Old Baldhead—or at least he isn't tricked any longer." He sighed again. "Poor Sositheus. Actually, I'm fairly sure I know when Crassus extracted the truth from him. It must have been on the day I sent him over to collect the title deeds to this place."

"You should have sent me!"

"I would have done, but you were out and there was no one else I trusted. How terrified he must have been when that old fox trapped him into confessing! If only he had told me what he'd done—I could have set his mind at rest."

"But aren't you worried what Crassus might do?"

"Why should I be worried? He got what he wanted, all except the command of an army to destroy Catilina—that he should even have *thought* of asking for that amazed me! But as for the rest—those letters Sositheus wrote at my dictation and left on his doorstep were a gift from the gods as far as he was concerned. He cut himself free of the conspiracy and left me to clear up the mess and stop Pompey from intervening. In fact I should say Crassus derived far more benefit from the whole affair than I did. The only ones who suffered were the guilty."

"But what if he makes it public?"

"If he does, I'll deny it—he has no proof. But he won't. The last thing he wants is to open up that whole stinking pit of bones." He picked up his book again. "Go and put a coin in the mouth of our dear dead friend, and let us hope he finds more honesty on that side of the eternal river than exists on this."

I did as he commanded, and the following day Sositheus's body was burned on the Esquiline Field. Most of the household turned out to pay their respects, and I spent Cicero's money freely on flowers and flautists and incense. All in all it was as well done as these occasions ever can be: you would have thought we were bidding farewell to a freedman, or even a citizen. Thinking over what I had learned, I did not presume to judge Cicero for the morality of his action, nor did I feel much wounded pride that he had been unwilling to trust me. But I did fear that Crassus would try to seek revenge, and as the thick black smoke rose from the pyre to merge with the low clouds rolling in from the east I felt full of apprehension.

Pompey approached the city on the Ides of January. The day before he was due, Cicero received an invitation to attend upon the imperator at the Villa Publica, which was then the government's official guesthouse. It was respectfully phrased. He could think of no reason not to accept. To have refused would have been seen as a snub. "Nevertheless," he confided to me as his valet dressed him the next morning, "I cannot help feeling like a subject, being summoned out to greet a conqueror, rather than a partner in the affairs of state arranging to meet another on equal terms."

By the time we reached the Field of Mars, thousands of citizens were already straining for a glimpse of their hero, who was now rumored to be only a mile or two away. I could see that Cicero was slightly put out by the fact that for once the crowds all had their backs to him and paid him no attention, and when we went into the Villa Publica his dignity received another blow. He had assumed he was going to meet Pompey privately, but instead he discovered several other senators with their attendants already waiting, including the new consuls, Pupius Piso and Valerius Messalla. The room was gloomy and cold, in that way of official buildings that are little used, and yet although it smelled strongly of damp no one had troubled to light a fire. Here Cicero was obliged to settle down to wait on a hard gilt chair, making stiff conversation with Pupius, a taciturn lieutenant of Pompey's whom he had known for many years and did not like.

After about an hour the noise of the crowd began to grow and I realized that Pompey must have come into view. Soon the racket was so intimidating the senators gave up trying to talk and sat mute, like strangers thrown together by chance while seeking shelter from a thunderstorm. People ran to and fro outside, and cried and cheered. A trumpet sounded. Eventually we heard the clump of boots filling the antechamber next door and a man said, "Well, you can't say the people of Rome don't love you, Imperator!" And then Pompey's booming voice could be heard clearly in reply: "Yes, that went well enough. That certainly went well enough."

Cicero rose along with the other senators, and a moment later into the room strode the great general, in full uniform of scarlet cloak and glittering bronze breastplate on which was carved a sun spreading its rays. He handed his plumed helmet to an aide as his officers and lictors poured in behind him. His hair was as improbably thick as ever and he ran his meaty fingers through it, pushing it back in the familiar cresting wave that peaked above his broad, sunburned face. He had changed little in six years except to have become—if such a thing were possible—even more physically imposing. His torso was immense. He shook hands with the consuls and the other senators, and exchanged a few words with each while Cicero looked on awkwardly. Finally he moved on to my master. "Marcus Tullius!" he exclaimed. Taking a step backward, Pompey appraised him carefully, gesturing in mock wonder first at Cicero's polished red shoes and then up the crisp lines of his purple-bordered toga to his neatly trimmed hair. "You look very well. Come then," he said, beckoning him closer, "let me embrace the man but for whom I would have no country left to return to!" He flung his arms around Cicero, crushing him to his breastplate in a hug, and winked at us over his shoulder. "I know that must be true because it's what he keeps on telling me!" Everyone laughed and Cicero tried to join in. But Pompey's clasp had squeezed all the air out of him, and he could manage only a mirthless wheeze. "Well, gentlemen," continued Pompey, beaming around the room, "shall we sit?"

A large chair was carried in for the imperator, and he settled himself into it. An ivory pointer was placed in his hand. A carpet was unrolled at his feet into which was woven a map of the East, and as the senators gazed down he began gesturing at it to illustrate his achievements. I made some notes as he talked, and afterward Cicero spent a long while studying them with an expression of disbelief. In the course of his campaign, Pompey claimed to have captured one thousand fortifications, nine hundred cities, and fourteen entire countries, including Syria, Palestine, Arabia, Mesopotamia, and Judea. The pointer flourished again. He had established no fewer than thirty-nine new cities, only three of which had he allowed to name themselves Pompeiopolis. He had levied a property tax on the East which would increase the annual revenues of Rome by two-thirds. From his personal funds he proposed to make an immediate donation to the Treasury of two hundred million sesterces. "I have doubled the size of our empire, gentlemen. Rome's frontier now stands on the Red Sea."

Even as I was writing this down, I was struck by the singular tone in which Pompey gave his account. He spoke throughout of "my" this and "my" that. But were all these states and cities, and these vast amounts of money, really his, or were they Rome's?

"I shall require a retrospective bill to legalize all this, of course," he concluded.

There was a pause. Cicero, who had just about recovered his breath, raised an eyebrow. "Really? Just *one* bill?"

"One bill," affirmed Pompey, handing his ivory stick to an attendant, "which need be of just one sentence: *'The Senate and people of Rome hereby approve all decisions made by Pompey the Great in his settlement of the East.'* Naturally, you can add some lines of congratulation if you wish, but that will be the essence of it."

Cicero glanced at the other senators. None met his gaze. They were happy to let him do the talking. "And is there anything else you desire?"

"The consulship."

"When?"

"Next year. A decade after my first. Perfectly legal."

"But to stand for election you will need to enter the city, which will mean surrendering your imperium. And surely you intend to triumph?"

"Of course. I shall triumph on my birthday, in September."

"But then how can this be done?"

"Simple. Another bill. One sentence again: *'The Senate and people of Rome hereby permit Pompey the Great to seek election to the office of consul in absentia.'* I hardly need to canvass for the post, I think. People know who I am!" He smiled and looked around him.

"And your army?"

"Disbanded and dispersed. They will need rewarding, of course. I've given them my word."

The consul Messalla spoke up. "We received reports you promised them land."

"That's right." Even Pompey could detect the hostility in the silence that followed. "Listen, gentlemen," he said, leaning forward in his thronelike chair, "let's talk frankly. You know I could have marched with my legionnaires to the gates of Rome and demanded whatever I wanted. But it's my intention to serve the Senate, not to dictate to it, and I've just traveled up through Italy in the most humble manner to demonstrate exactly that. And I want to go on demonstrating it. You have all heard that I've divorced?" The senators nodded. "Then how would it be if I made a marriage that tied me to the senatorial party forever?"

"I think I speak for us all," said Cicero cautiously, checking with the others, "when I say that the Senate desires nothing more than to work with you, and that a marriage alliance would be of the greatest help. Do you have a candidate in mind?"

"I do, as a matter of fact. I'm told Cato is a force in the Senate these days, and Cato has nieces and daughters of marriageable age. My plan is that I should take one of these girls as my wife and my eldest son should take another. There." He sat back contentedly. "How does that strike you?"

"It strikes us very well," responded Cicero, again after a quick glance around at his colleagues. "An alliance between the houses of Cato and Pompey will secure peace for a generation. The populists will all be prostrated with shock and the good men will all rejoice." He smiled. "I congratulate you on a brilliant stroke, Imperator. What does Cato say?"

"Oh, he doesn't know of it yet."

Cicero's smile became fixed. "You have divorced Mucia and severed your connections with the Metelli in order to marry a connection of Cato—but you have not yet inquired what Cato's reaction might be?"

"I suppose you could put it that way. Why? Do you think there'll be a problem?"

"With most men I would say no, but with Cato—well, one can never be sure where the undeviating arrow-flight of his logic may lead him. Have you told many other people of your intentions?"

"A few."

"In that case, might I suggest, Imperator, that we suspend our discussions for the time being while you send an emissary to Cato as quickly as possible?"

A dark cloud had passed over Pompey's hitherto sunny expression—it had obviously never entered his mind that Cato might refuse him: if he did, it would mean a terrible loss of face—and in a distracted tone he agreed to Cicero's suggestion. By the time we left, he was already holding an urgent consultation with Lucius Afranius, his closest confidante. Outside, the crowds were as dense as ever and even though Pompey's guards opened the gates only just wide enough to let us depart, they very nearly found themselves overwhelmed by the numbers pressing to get in. People shouted out to Cicero and the consuls as they struggled back toward the city. "Have you spoken to him?" "What does he say?" "Is it true he has become a god?"

"He was not a god the last time I looked," replied Cicero cheerfully, "although he is not far off it! He is looking forward to rejoining us in the Senate. What a farce," he added to me, out of the corner of his mouth. "Plautus could not have come up with a more absurd scenario."

It did indeed turn out exactly as Cicero had feared. Pompey sent that very day for Cato's friend Munatius, who conveyed the great man's offer of a double marriage to Cato's house, where as it happened his family were all gathered for a feast. The womenfolk were overjoyed at the prospect, such was the status of Pompey as Rome's greatest war hero, and the renown of his magnificent physique. But Cato flew into an immediate rage, and without pausing for thought or consulting anyone made the following reply: "Go, Munatius: go and tell Pompey that Cato is not to be captured by way of women's apartments. He greatly prizes Pompey's goodwill and if Pompey behaves properly will grant him a friendship more to be relied upon than any marriage connection. But he will not give hostages for the glory of Pompey to the detriment of his country!"

Pompey, by all accounts, was stunned by the rudeness of the reply ("if Pompey behaves properly!") and quit the Villa Publica at once in a very ill humor to go to his house in the Alban Hills. But even here he was pursued by tormenting demons determined to puncture his dignity. His daughter, then age nine, whom he had not seen since she could barely speak, had been coached by her tutor, the famous grammarian Aristodemus of Nyssa to greet her father with some passages from Homer. Unfortunately, the first line she spoke as he came through the door was that of Helen to Paris: "You came back from the war; I wish you had died there." Too many people witnessed the episode for it not to become public, and I am afraid that Cicero found it so funny he too played his part in spreading the story across Rome.

In the midst of all this tumult it was possible to believe that the affair of the Good Goddess might be forgotten. More than a month had now passed since the outrage, and Clodius had been careful to keep out of public view. People had started to talk of other things. But a day or two after the return of Pompey the College of Priests finally handed its judgment on the incident to the Senate. Pupius, who was the leading consul, was a friend of Clodius and keen to hush up the scandal. Nevertheless he was obliged to read out the priests' report, and their verdict was unambiguous. Clodius's action was a clear case of nefas—an impious deed, a sin, a crime against the Goddess, an abomination.

The first senator on his feet was Lucullus, and what a sweet moment this must have been for him as, with great solemnity, he declared that his former brother-in-law had besmirched the traditions of the republic and had risked bringing the wrath of the gods down upon the city. "Their anger can only be appeased," he said, "by the sternest punishment of the offender," and he formally proposed that Clodius be charged with violating the sanctity of the vestal virgins—an offense for which the penalty was to be beaten to death. Cato seconded the motion. The two patrician leaders, Hortensius and Catulus, both rose in support, and it was clear that the mood of the house was strongly with them. They demanded that the most powerful magistrate in Rome after the consuls, the urban prae-

tor, should convene a special court, appoint a handpicked jury drawn
from the Senate, and try the case as speedily as possible. With such men
in control the result would be preordained. Pupius agreed reluctantly to
draw up a bill to this effect, and by the time the session was over Clodius
looked to be a dead man.

Late that night, when I heard someone knock on Cicero's front door,
I was sure in my bones it must be Clodius. Despite his snub on the day
after the Good Goddess fiasco, the young man had continued to make
regular return visits to the house in the hope of a meeting with Cicero.
But I was under strict instructions to refuse him admittance: much to his
irritation he had never gotten farther than the atrium. Now, as I crossed
the hall, I braced myself for another unpleasant scene. But to my astonishment, when I unlocked the door, the person I found standing on the
step was Clodia. Normally she voyaged around the city, amid a flotilla of
maids, but on this night she was unescorted. She asked in a very cool
voice if my master was in, and I replied that I would check. I showed her
into the hall and invited her to wait, and then almost ran into the library
where Cicero was working. When I announced who had come to see him
he laid down his pen and thought for a moment or two.

"Has Terentia gone up to her room?"

"I believe so."

"Then show her in." I was amazed that he should take such a risk, and
he must have realized the dangers himself, for just as I was leaving he said,
"Make sure you don't leave us alone together."

I went and fetched her. The moment she entered the library she
crossed to where Cicero was standing and quickly knelt at his feet. "I have
come to plead for your support," she said, bowing her head. "My poor
brother is beside himself with fear and remorse, yet he is too proud to try
to ask you for help again, so I am here alone." She took the hem of his
toga in her hands and kissed it. "My dear friend, it takes a great deal for a
Claudian to kneel, but I am begging for your help."

"Get up off the floor, Clodia," replied Cicero, glancing anxiously at
the door. "Someone may see you, and the story will be all over Rome."
When she did not respond, he added, more gently, "I won't even talk to
you unless you get on your feet!" Clodia rose, her head bowed. "Now
listen to me," said Cicero. "I'll say this once and then you must leave. You
want me to help your brother, yes?" Clodia nodded. "Then tell him he
must do precisely what I say. He must write letters to every one of those

women whose honor he has outraged. He must tell them he is sorry, it was a fit of madness, he is no longer worthy to breathe the same air as them and their daughters, and so on and so forth—believe me, he cannot be too obsequious. Then he must renounce his quaestorship. Leave Rome. Go into exile. Stay away from the city for a few years. When things calm down, he can come back and start again. It's the best advice I can offer. Goodbye."

He began to turn away from her but she grabbed his arm.

"Leaving Rome will kill him!"

"No, madam, staying in Rome will kill him. There is bound to be a trial and he is bound to be found guilty. Lucullus will see to that. But Lucullus is old and lazy, and your brother is young and energetic. Time is his greatest ally. Tell him I said that, and that I wish him well, and tell him to go tomorrow."

"If he stays in Rome, will you join in the attacks on him?"

"I will do my best to keep out of it."

"And if it comes to a trial," she said, still holding his arm, "will you defend him?"

"No, that is completely impossible."

"Why?"

"Why?" Cicero gave an incredulous laugh. "Any one of a thousand reasons."

"Is it because you believe he is guilty?"

"My dear Clodia, the whole world *knows* he is guilty!"

"But you defended Cornelius Sulla, and the whole world knew he was guilty, too."

"But this is different."

"Why?"

"My wife, for one thing," said Cicero softly, with another glance at the door. "My wife was present. She witnessed the entire episode."

"You are saying your wife would divorce you if you defended my brother?"

"Yes, I believe she would."

"Then take another wife," said Clodia, and stepping back but still staring at him, she quickly untied her cloak and let it fall from her shoulders. Beneath it she was naked. The dark smoothness of her oiled skin glistened in the candlelight. I was standing almost directly behind her. She knew I was watching, yet she no more minded my presence than if I had been a table or a footstool. The air seemed to thicken. Cicero stood perfectly still. Thinking back on it I am reminded of that moment in the Senate, in the chaos after the debate on the conspirators, when a single word or gesture of assent from him would have led to Caesar's death, and the world—our world—would have been entirely different. So it was now. After a long pause he gave the very slightest shake of his head, and, stooping, he retrieved her cloak and held it out to her.

"Put it back on," he said quietly.

She ignored it. Instead she put her hands on her hips. "You really prefer that pious old broomstick to me?"

"Yes." He sounded surprised by his own answer. "When it comes to it, I believe I do."

"Then what a fool you are," she said, and turned around so that Cicero could drape the cloak across her shoulders. The gesture was as casual as if she were going home after a dinner party. She caught me looking at her, and her eyes flashed me such a look that I quickly dropped my gaze. "You will think back on this moment," she said, briskly fastening her cloak, "and regret it for the rest of your life."

"No I won't, because I shall put it out of my mind, and I suggest you do the same."

"Why should I want to forget it?" She smiled and shook her head. "How my brother will laugh when he hears about it."

"You'll tell him?"

"Of course. It was his idea."

"Not a word," said Cicero after Clodia had gone. He held up a warning hand. He did not want to discuss it, and we never did. Rumors that something had occurred between them circulated for many years, but I always refused to comment on the gossip. I have kept this secret for half a century.

Ambition and lust are often intertwined. In some men, such as Caesar and Clodius, they are as tightly plaited as a rope. With Cicero it was the opposite case. I believe he had a passionate nature, but it frightened him. Like his stutter or his youthful illnesses or his unsteady nerves, he viewed passion as a handicap, to be overcome by discipline. He therefore learned to separate this strand in his nature, and to avoid it. But the gods are implacable, and despite his resolution not to have anything to do with Clodia and her brother, he soon found himself being sucked into the quickening whirlpool of the scandal.

It is hard to comprehend at this great distance how completely the Good Goddess affair gripped public life in Rome, so that eventually all government business came to a halt. On the surface Clodius's cause seemed hopeless. Plainly he had committed this ludicrous offense, and almost the whole of the Senate was set on his punishment. But sometimes in politics a great weakness can be turned into a strength, and from the moment Lucullus's motion was passed the Roman people began to mutter against it. What was the young man guilty of, after all, except an excess of high spirits? Was a fellow to be beaten to death merely because of a lark? When Clodius ventured into the Forum he found that the citizens, rather than wanting to pelt him with ordure, actually wished to shake his hand.

There were still thousands of plebeians in Rome who were disaffected with the renewed authority of the Senate and who looked back with nostalgia to the days when Catilina ruled the streets. Clodius attracted these people by the score. They would gather around him in crowds. He took to jumping up onto a nearby cart or trader's stall and inveighing against the Senate. He had learned well from Cicero the tricks of political campaigning: keep your speeches short, remember names, tell jokes, put on a show; above all, render an issue, however complex, into a story anyone can grasp. Clodius's tale was the simplest possible: he was the lone citizen unjustly persecuted by the oligarchs. "Take care, my friends!" he would cry. "If it can happen to me, a patrician, it could happen to any one of you!" Soon he was holding daily public meetings at which order was kept by his friends from the taverns and the gambling dens, many of whom had been supporters of Catilina.

Clodius attacked Lucullus, Hortensius, and Catulus repeatedly by name, but when it came to Cicero he confined himself merely to repeating the old joke that the former consul had kept himself "fully informed." Cicero was often tempted to respond, and Terentia urged him to do so, yet he was mindful of his promise to Clodia and managed to keep his temper in check. However, the controversy kept on swelling regardless of his silence. I was with him on the day the Senate's bill to set up the special court was laid before the people in a popular assembly. Clodius's gangs of toughs took control of the meeting, occupying the gangways and seizing the ballot boxes. Their clamor so unnerved the consul Pupius that he actually spoke against his own bill—in particular the clause that allowed the urban praetor to select the jury. Many senators turned to Cicero, expecting him to take control of the situation, but he remained on his bench, glowering with anger and embarrassment, and it was left to Cato to deliver a lashing attack on the consul. The meeting was abandoned. The senators promptly trooped back to their chamber and voted by four hundred votes to fifteen to press on with the bill despite the dangers of civil unrest. A tribune, Fufius, who was sympathetic to Clodius, promptly announced that he would veto the legislation. The affair was now seriously out of hand, and Cicero hurried out of the chamber and up to his house, crimson in the face.

The turning point came when Fufius decided to convene a public assembly outside the city walls so that Pompey could be summoned and asked his views on the affair. Grumbling mightily at this intrusion on his time and dignity, the Warden of Land and Sea had no choice but to lumber over from the Alban Hills to the Circus Flaminius and submit himself to a series of insolent questions from the tribune, watched by a huge market-day crowd that temporarily set aside their bargaining and clustered around to gawk at him.

"Are you aware of the so-called outrage committed against the Good Goddess?" asked Fufius.

"I am."

"Do you support the Senate's proposal that Clodius be prosecuted?"

"I do."

"Do you believe he should be tried by a jury of senators selected by the urban praetor?"

"I do."

"Even though the urban praetor will also be his judge?"

"I suppose so, if that is the procedure the Senate has settled on."

"And where is the justice in that?"

Pompey glared at Fufius as if he were some buzzing insect that would not leave him alone. "I hold the Senate's authority in the highest respect," he declared, and proceeded to deliver a lecture on the Roman constitution that might have been written for him by a fourteen-year-old. I was standing with Cicero at the front of the huge throng and could sense the audience behind us losing interest as he droned on. Soon they started shuffling about and talking. The vendors of hot sausages and pastries on the edge of the crowd began doing a busy trade. Pompey was a boring speaker at the best of times, but standing on that platform he must have felt as if he were in a bad dream. All those visions of a triumphant home-coming he had entertained as he lay at night in his tent beneath the burn-ing stars of Arabia—and in the end what had he returned to? A Senate and a people obsessed not with his achievements but with a young man dressed in women's clothes!

When the public assembly was mercifully over Cicero conducted Pompey across the Circus Flaminius to the Temple of Bellona, where the Senate had convened specially to greet him. The ovation he received was respectful, and he sat down next to Cicero on the front bench and waited for the praise to begin. Instead, he found himself once again cross-examined from the chair about his views on the sacrilege issue. He re-peated what he had just said outside, and when he resumed his place I saw him turn and mutter something irritably to Cicero. (His actual words, Cicero told me afterward, were "I hope we can now talk about something else.") I had been keeping an eye throughout all this on Crassus, who was sitting on the edge of his bench ready to jump up the moment he got a chance. There was something about his determination to speak, and a kind of happy craftiness in his expression, for which I did not much care.

"How wonderful it is, gentlemen," he said when at last he was called, "to have with us beneath this sacred roof the man who has expanded our empire, and sitting next to him the man who has saved our republic. May the gods be blessed who have brought this to pass. Pompey I know stood ready with his army to come to the aid of the fatherland if it was necessary—but praise the heavens he was spared the task by the wisdom and foresight of our consul at that time. I hope I take nothing away from Pompey when I say that it is to Cicero that I feel I owe my status as a senator and a citizen; to him I owe my freedom and my life. Whenever I look upon my wife and my house, or upon the city of my birth, what I see is a gift that was granted me by Cicero . . ."

There was a time when Cicero would have spotted such an obvious trap a mile off. But I fear there is in all men who achieve their life's ambi-tion only a narrow line between dignity and vanity, confidence and delu-sion, glory and self-destruction. Instead of staying in his seat and modestly disavowing such praise, Cicero rose and made a long speech agreeing with Crassus's every word, while beside him Pompey gently cooked in a stew of jealousy and resentment. Watching from the door, I wanted to run forward and cry out to Cicero to stop, especially when Crassus stood and asked him, as the Father of the Nation, if he recognized in Clodius a second Catilina.

"How can I not," responded Cicero, unable to resist this opportunity to rekindle the glory days of his leadership of the Senate in front of Pompey, "when the same debauched men who followed the one now flock to the other, and when the same tactics are daily employed? Unity, gentlemen, is our only hope of salvation, now as it was then—unity between this Senate and the Order of Knights; unity between all classes; unity across Italy. As long as we remember that glorious concord that existed under my consulship we need have no fear, for the spirit that saw off Sergius Catilina will most assuredly see off his bastard son!"

The Senate cheered, and Crassus sat back on his bench beaming at a job well done, because of course the news of what Cicero had said spread across Rome immediately and quickly reached the ears of Clodius. At the end of the session, when Cicero walked back home with his entourage, Clodius was waiting in the Forum surrounded by a gang of his own supporters. They blocked our path and I was sure some heads were going to be broken, but Cicero remained calm. He halted his procession. "Offer them no provocation!" he called out. "Give them no excuse to start a riot." And, turning to Clodius, he said, "You would have done well to have heeded my advice and gone into exile. The road you have started down can only end in one place."

"And where is that?" sneered Clodius.

"Up there," said Cicero, pointing at the Carcer, "at the end of a rope."

"Not so," responded Clodius, and he gestured in the other direction, to the rostra, with its ranks of life-size statues. "One day I shall be up there, among the heroes of the Roman people."

"Really? And, tell me, will you be sculpted wearing women's clothing and carrying a lyre?" We all started to laugh. "Publius Clodius Pulcher: the first hero of the Order of Transvestites? I rather doubt it. Get out of my way."

"Willingly," said Clodius with a smile. But as he stood aside to let Cicero pass I was struck by how much he had changed. It was not merely that he seemed physically bigger and stronger: there was a glint of resolution in his eyes that had not been there before. He was feeding on his notoriety, I realized: drawing energy from the mob. "Caesar's wife was one of the best I ever had," he said softly as Cicero went by, "almost as good as

Clodia." He seized his elbow and added loudly, "I was willing to be your friend. You should have been mine."

"Claudians make unreliable friends," replied Cicero, pulling himself free.

"Yes, but we make very reliable enemies."

He proved to be as good as his word. From that day on, whenever he spoke in the Forum he would always gesture to Cicero's new house, sitting on the Palatine high above the heads of the crowd, as a perfect symbol of dictatorship. "Look how mightily the tyrant who butchered citizens without a proper trial has prospered by his handiwork—no wonder he is thirsty for fresh blood!" Cicero responded in kind. The mutual insults grew more and more deadly. Sometimes Cicero and I used to stand on the terrace and watch the tyro demagogue at work, and although we were too far away to hear exactly what he said, the applause of the crowd was audible and I recognized what we were seeing: the monster Cicero thought he had slain had begun to twitch back into life.

XIV

AROUND THE MIDDLE of March, Hortensius came to see Cicero. He trailed Catulus after him, and when the old patrician shuffled in he looked more than ever like a tortoise without its shell. Catulus had recently had the last of his teeth removed, and the trauma of the extraction, the long months of agony that had preceded it, and the distortion of his mouth that had resulted all combined to make him look every one of his sixty years. He seemed unable to stop drooling and carried a large handkerchief that was sodden and yellowish. He reminded me of someone: I could not think whom at first, and then I remembered—Rabirius. Cicero sprang up to help him to a chair but Catulus waved him away, mumbling that he was perfectly all right.

"This wretched affair with Clodius cannot be allowed to drag on any longer," Hortensius began.

"I agree with you," said Cicero, who privately, I knew, was beginning to feel uncomfortable about the damaging war of words he was locked in with Clodius. "The government is at a standstill. Our enemies are laughing at us."

"We need to bring it to trial as soon as possible. I propose we should give up our insistence that the jury be selected by the urban praetor."

"So how would it be selected?"

"In the usual way, by lot."

"But might we not then find ourselves with quite a few dubious characters on the jury? We don't want the rascal to be acquitted. That really would be a disaster."

"Acquittal is utterly impossible. Once any jury sees the weight of the evidence against him, he's bound to be convicted. All we need is a bare majority. We must have some faith in the good sense of the Roman people."

"He must be crushed by the facts," put in Catulus, holding his stained handkerchief to his mouth, "and the sooner the better."

"Will Fufius agree to drop his veto if we give up the clause about the jury?"

"He assures me he will, on condition we also reduce the penalty from death to exile."

"What does Lucullus say?"

"He just wants a trial on any terms. You know he's been preparing for this day for years. He has all manner of witnesses lined up ready to testify to Clodius's immorality—even the slave girls who changed the sheets on his bed in Misenum after he had intercourse with his sisters."

"Dear gods! Is it wise to have that kind of detail aired in public?"

"I never heard of such disgusting behavior," drooled Catulus. "The whole Augean stable needs cleaning out, or it will be the ruin of us."

"Even so—" Cicero frowned and did not complete the sentence. I could see he was not convinced, and for the first time I believe he sniffed danger to himself. Exactly what it was he could not say, simply that something about it smelled ominous. He continued to raise objections for a little longer—"Wouldn't it be better just to drop the whole bill? Haven't we made our point? Don't we risk making a martyr of the young fool?"— before reluctantly giving Hortensius his assent. "Well, I suppose you will have to do whatever you think is right. You've taken the lead in this thing from the start. However, I must make one thing clear—I want no part in it."

I was vastly relieved to hear him utter those words: it seemed to me almost the first sensible decision he had made since leaving the consulship. Hortensius looked disappointed, having doubtless hoped that Cicero would lead for the prosecution, but he did not try to argue the matter, and duly went off to make the deal with Fufius. Thus the bill was passed, and the people of Rome licked their lips and prepared for what promised to be the most scandalous trial in the republic's history.

The normal business of government was now able to resume, beginning with the drawing of lots by the praetors for their provinces. A few days before the ceremony, Cicero went out to the Alban Hills to see Pompey and asked him as a favor not to press for the recall of Hybrida.

"But the man is a disgrace to our empire," objected Pompey. "I have never heard of such thievery and incompetence."

"I am sure he is not as bad as all that."

"Are you doubting my word?"

"No. But I would be grateful if you could oblige me in this matter. I gave him my assurance that I'd support him."

"Ah, so I assume he's cutting you in?" Pompey winked and rubbed his thumb and forefinger together.

"Certainly not. I simply feel honor-bound to protect him, in return for all the help he gave me in saving the republic."

Pompey looked unconvinced. But then he grinned and clapped Cicero on the shoulder. What was Macedonia, after all? A mere vegetable plot to the Warden of Land and Sea! "All right, let him have another year. But in return I expect you to do everything in your power to get my three bills through the Senate."

Cicero agreed, and thus when the lot-drawing took place in the chamber of the Senate, Macedonia, the most valuable prize, was not on the table. Instead there were just five provinces to be divided among the eight former praetors. The rivals all sat in a row on the front bench, Caesar at the end farthest from Quintus. Vergilius went first, if I remember rightly, and drew Sicily, and Caesar was the next to step up to try his luck. This was an important moment for him. Because of his divorce he had been obliged to hand back Pompeia's dowry and was being hard-pressed by his creditors; there was talk he was no longer solvent and might even be forced to leave the Senate. He put his hand into the urn and gave the token to the consul. When the result was read out—"Caesar draws Further Spain!"—he grimaced. Unfortunately for him, there was no war to be had in that distant land; he would much have preferred Africa or even Asia, where there was a greater chance of making money. Cicero managed to suppress a smile of triumph, but only for a moment or two, because shortly afterward Asia went to Quintus, and Cicero was the first on his feet to congratulate his brother. Once again he let his tears of relief flow freely. There seemed every possibility that Quintus might return from his province and become consul in his turn. Theirs was a dynasty in the making, and joyous was the family celebration that evening, to which I was once again invited. Cicero and Caesar were now on opposite sides of Fortune's wheel, with Cicero at the top and Caesar very firmly at the bottom.

Normally, the new governors would have set off for their provinces immediately; in fact, they should have left months earlier. But on this occasion the Senate refused to allow them to leave Rome until the trial of Clodius had been concluded, in case they might be needed to restore public order.

The court duly convened in May, the prosecution being mounted by three young members of the Cornelius Lentulus family—Crus, Marcellinus, and Niger, the latter being also the chief priest of Mars. They were great rivals of the Claudian clan and had a particular grudge against Clodius, who had seduced several of their womenfolk. As his chief defender Clodius relied upon a former consul, Gaius Scribonius Curio, who was the father of one of his closest friends. Curio had made his fortune in the East as a soldier under Sulla but was rather slow-witted, with a poor memory. As an orator he was known as "the Fly-Swatter" because of his habit of throwing his arms around when he spoke. To weigh the evidence was a jury of fifty-six citizens, drawn by lot. They were of all types and conditions, from patrician senators down to such notorious low-life figures as Talna and Spongia. Originally eighty jurors had been impaneled, but the defense and prosecution each had twelve challenges which they quickly used up, the defense rejecting the respectable and the prosecution the rough. Those who had survived this winnowing sat uneasily together.

A sex scandal will always draw a crowd, but a sex scandal involving the ruling classes is titillating beyond measure. To accommodate the numbers who wished to watch, it was necessary to hold the trial in front of the Temple of Castor. A special section of seats was set aside for the Senate, and that was where Cicero took his place on the opening day, on the bench next to Hortensius. Caesar's ex-wife had prudently withdrawn from Rome to avoid giving evidence, but the chief priest's mother, Aurelia, and his sister, Julia, both came forward to act as witnesses and identified Clodius as the man who had invaded the sacred rites. Aurelia made an especially strong impression, as she pointed her talonlike finger at the accused, sitting no more than ten feet from her, and insisted in her hard voice that the Good Goddess must be placated by his exile or disaster would descend on Rome. That was the first day.

On the second, Caesar followed her onto the witness stand, and I was struck again by the similarities between mother and son—tough and sinewy, and confident beyond mere arrogance, to a point where all men, aristocrat or plebeian, were deemed equally beneath them in their gaze. (This, I think, was why he was always so popular with the people: he was far too superior to be a snob.) Under cross-examination he responded that he could not say what had happened that night, as he had not been present. He added, very coldly, that he bore no particular ill will toward Clodius—in whose direction, however, he did not once look—because he had no idea whether he was guilty or not; clearly, he loathed him. As to his divorce, he could only repeat the answer he had given Cicero in the Senate: he had set Pompeia aside not necessarily because she was guilty but because, as the chief priest's wife, she could not be tainted by suspicion. As everyone in Rome knew of Caesar's own reputation, not least his conquest of Pompey's wife, this fine piece of casuistry provoked long and mocking laughter, which he had to endure behind his habitual mask of supreme indifference.

He finished giving evidence and stepped down from the tribunal, coincidentally at exactly the same moment Cicero rose to leave the audience. They almost walked into each other, and there was no chance of avoiding at least a brief exchange.

"Well, Caesar, you must be glad your testimony is over."

"Why do you say that?"

"I presume it must have been awkward for you."

"I never feel awkward. But yes, you're right, I am delighted to put this absurd affair behind me, because now I can set off for Spain."

"When are you planning to leave?"

"Tonight."

"But I thought the Senate had forbidden the new governors to leave for their provinces until the trial was over."

"True, but I haven't a moment to lose. The moneylenders are after me. Apparently I somehow have to make twenty-five million sesterces just to own nothing." He gave a shrug—a gambler's shrug: I remember he seemed quite unconcerned—and sauntered off toward his official residence. Within the hour, accompanied by a small entourage, he was gone, and it was left to Crassus to stand surety for his debts.

Caesar's evidence was entertaining enough. But the real highlight of the proceedings came on the third day of Clodius's trial, with the appearance of Lucullus. It is said that at the entrance to Apollo's shrine at Delphi three things are written: "Know thyself"; "Desire nothing too much"; and "Never go to law." Did ever a man so willfully ignore these precepts as Lucullus in this affair? Forgetting that he was supposed to be a military hero, he ascended onto the platform trembling with his desire to ruin Clodius, and very soon began to describe how he had surprised his wife in bed with her brother during a vacation when Clodius had been a guest in his house on the Bay of Naples more than a decade earlier. By then he had been watching them together for many weeks, said Lucullus—oh yes, the way they touched each other, and whispered when they thought his back was turned: they took him for a fool—and he had ordered his wife's maids to bring her sheets to him each morning for his inspection and report to him everything he saw. These female slaves, six in all, were summoned into court, and as they filed in, clearly nervous and with their eyes lowered, I saw among them my beloved Agathe, whose image had rarely left my mind in the two years since we were together.

They stood meekly as their depositions were produced, and I willed her to look up and glance in my direction. I waved. I even whistled. The people standing around me must have thought I had gone mad. Finally I cupped my hands to my mouth and yelled her name. She did raise her eyes at that, but there were so many thousands of spectators crammed into the Forum, and the noise was so intense, and the glaring sunshine so bright, there can have been little chance of her seeing me. I tried to struggle forward through the packed crowd, but the people in front of me had queued for hours for their places, and they refused to let me through. In an agony I heard Clodius's counsel announce that they did not wish to challenge these witnesses, as their testimony was not relevant to the case, and the maids were ordered to leave the platform. I watched Agathe turn with the others and descend out of sight.

Lucullus resumed giving evidence, and I felt a great hatred well up in me at the sight of this decaying plutocrat who unthinkingly possessed a treasure for which, at that moment, I would have given my life. I was so preoccupied that I briefly lost track of what he was saying, and it was only when I realized that the crowd had started to gasp and laugh with delight that I took notice of his evidence. He was describing how he had concealed himself in his wife's bedchamber and observed her and her brother in the act of fornication: "dog on bitch," as he put it. Nor, continued Lucullus, ignoring the noise of the crowd, did Clodius confine his base appetites to one sister, but boasted of his conquests of the other two. Bearing in mind that Clodia's husband, Celer, had just returned from Nearer Gaul to stand for the consulship, this allegation caused a particular sensation. Clodius sat through it all smiling broadly at his former brother-in-law, clearly aware that whatever damage Lucullus imagined he was doing to him, he was actually inflicting far more harm on his own reputation. That was the third day, and at the end of it the prosecution rested its case. I lingered after the court had been adjourned in the hope of seeing Agathe again, but she had been taken away.

On the fourth day, the defense began the job of trying to extricate Clodius from this morass of filth. It seemed a hopeless task, for no one, not even Curio, was in serious doubt of his client's guilt of the actual offense. Nevertheless, he did his best. The core of his case was that the whole episode had been a simple matter of mistaken identity. The lights had been dim, the women hysterical, the intruder disguised—how could anyone be sure it was Clodius? It was hardly a convincing line. But then, just as the morning was nearing its end, Clodius's side produced a surprise witness. A man named Gaius Causinius Schola, a seemingly respectable citizen from the town of Interamna, some ninety miles from Rome, came forward to say that on the night in question Clodius had actually been with him in his home. Even under cross-examination he was quite unshakable on this point, and although his was only one voice set against a dozen on the other side, including the firm testimony of Caesar's own mother, he cut a strangely believable figure.

Cicero, who was watching from the senators' benches, beckoned me over to him. "This fellow is either lying or insane," he whispered. "On the day of the Good Goddess ceremony surely Clodius came to see me? I recall having an argument about his visit with Terentia."

Now that he mentioned the occasion, I remembered it as well, and I confirmed he was correct.

"What's all this?" asked Hortensius, who was, as usual, sitting next to Cicero and had been trying to listen in to our conversation.

Cicero turned to him. "I was saying that Clodius was in my house that day, so how could he possibly have reached Interamna by nightfall? His alibi is preposterous." He spoke entirely without premeditation; had he thought about the implications of what he was saying he would have been more cautious.

"Then you must testify," responded Hortensius at once. "This witness needs to be destroyed."

"Oh no," said Cicero quickly, "I told you at the start, I want no part of it," and beckoning to me to follow he got up at once and left the Forum, accompanied by the two well-muscled slaves who these days acted as his guard. "That was stupid of me," he said as we climbed the hill to his house. "I must be getting old." Behind us I could hear the crowd laughing at some point made by one of Clodius's supporters: the weight of evidence might be against him but the mob was all on his side. I sensed that Cicero was uneasy with the day's proceedings. Quite unexpectedly, the defense seemed to be taking charge.

Once the trial had adjourned for the day, all three of the prosecutors came to see Cicero, along with Hortensius. The instant I saw them I knew what they wanted, and I secretly cursed Hortensius for putting Cicero in this position. I showed them into the garden, where he was sitting with Terentia watching little Marcus play with a ball. It was a perfect late afternoon in late spring. The air was fragrant with blossom, and the sounds rising from the Forum were as drowsy and indistinct as insects humming in a meadow.

"We need you to testify," began Crus, who was the lead counsel.

"I suspected you were going to say that," replied Cicero, with an angry look at Hortensius. "And I think you can guess my reply. There must be a hundred people apart from me who saw Clodius in Rome earlier that day."

"None that we can find," said Crus, "at least none that is willing to testify."

"Clodius has frightened them off," said Hortensius.

"And certainly none that has your authority," added Marcellinus, who had always been a supporter of Cicero, right back to the days of the Verres prosecution. "If you can do this favor for us tomorrow and confirm that Clodius was with you, the jury will have no choice except to convict him. That alibi is the only thing standing between him and exile."

Cicero looked at them in disbelief. "Just a moment, gentlemen. Are you telling me that without my testimony you think he might *walk free*?" They hung their heads. "How has this happened? Never has a more guilty man been set before a court." He rounded on Hortensius. "Acquittal you said was 'utterly impossible.' 'Trust the good sense of the Roman people'—wasn't that what you told me?"

"He has become very popular. And those who don't actually love the man at the very least fear his supporters."

"We were also damaged by Lucullus," said Crus. "All that business about sheets and hiding behind screens has turned us into a laughing-stock. Even some of the jury are saying that Clodius is no more perverted than the men prosecuting him."

"So now it is my responsibility to make good your damage?" Cicero threw up his hands in exasperation.

Terentia had been nursing Marcus on her lap. Suddenly she set him down and told him to go indoors. Turning to her husband, she said, "You may not like it but you must do it—if not for the republic's sake, then for your own."

"I said before: I want no part of it."

"But nobody stands to gain more from sending Clodius into exile than you. He has become your greatest enemy."

"Yes he has—indeed he has!—and whose fault is that?"

"Yours—for encouraging his career in the first place!"

They argued back and forth for a while longer as the senators watched, bemused. It was already widely known in Rome that Terentia was not the usual humble, obedient kind of wife, and this scene was bound to be widely reported. But although Cicero must have resented her for contradicting him in front of his colleagues, I knew that he would have to agree with her in the end. His anger stemmed from his recognition that he had no choice: he was trapped. "Very well," he said finally. "I'll do my duty for Rome, as always, although it may be at some cost to my personal safety. But then I suppose I should be used to that. I shall see you in the morning, gentlemen." And with an irritated wave of his hand he dismissed them.

After they had gone, he sat brooding. "You realize that this is a trap."

"A trap for whom?" I asked.

"For me, of course." He turned to Terentia. "Consider it: out of the whole of Italy it finally turns out only one man is in a position to challenge Clodius's alibi—and that man is Cicero. Do you think that is a coincidence?" Terentia did not respond; nor had it occurred to me until he mentioned it. He said to me, "This witness of theirs from Interamna—this Causinius Schola, or whatever his name is—we ought to find out more about him. Whom do we know from Interamna?"

I thought for a moment, and then with a sick feeling in my heart I said, "Caelius Rufus."

"Caelius Rufus," repeated Cicero, striking the side of his chair, "of course."

"Another man you should never have brought into our house," said Terentia.

"When was the last time we saw him?"

"Months ago," I answered.

"Caelius Rufus! He was a drinking and whoring companion of Clodius back when he first became my pupil." The longer Cicero pondered it, the more certain he became. "First he runs with Catilina and then he takes up with Clodius. What a snake that boy has been to me! This wretched witness from Interamna will turn out to be a client of his father's, you can rely upon it."

"So you think Rufus and Clodius have plotted between them to entrap you?"

"Do you doubt they're capable of it?"

"No. But I wonder why they would go to all the trouble of creating a false alibi purely in order to lure you onto the witness stand to destroy it. Clodius wants his alibi to go unchallenged, surely?"

"So you think that someone else is behind it?"

I hesitated.

"Who?" demanded Terentia.

"Crassus."

"But Crassus and I are entirely reconciled," said Cicero. "You heard the way he praised me to the skies in front of Pompey. And then he let me have this house so cheaply—" He was going to say something else, but then he stopped.

Terentia turned the full force of her scrutiny onto me. "Why would Crassus go to such lengths to cause your master trouble?"

"I don't know," I lied. I could feel my face turning red.

Cicero said quietly, "You might as well ask, why does the scorpion sting? Because that is what scorpions do."

The conversation broke up soon afterward. Terentia went off to attend to Marcus. I retired to the library to attend to the senator's correspondence. Only Cicero remained on the terrace, staring thoughtfully across the Forum to the Capitol as the shades of evening began to spread.

The following morning, pale and silent with nerves—for he knew full well what kind of reception he was likely to receive—Cicero went down into the Forum, escorted by the same number of bodyguards he used to have around him in the days of Catilina. Word had got out that the prosecution was unexpectedly calling him as a witness, and the moment Clodius's supporters saw him pushing his way toward the platform they set up a gale of booing and catcalling. As he climbed the temple steps toward the tribunal some eggs and dung were thrown, which provoked the most remarkable counterdemonstration. Almost the whole of the jury got to their feet and formed a cordon to protect Cicero from the missiles. Some even turned to the crowd, pulled down their collars, and pointed to their bare throats, as if to say to Clodius's lynch mob, "You will have to kill us before you can kill him."

Cicero was well used to giving evidence on the witness stand. He had done it in at least a dozen cases against Catilina's coconspirators in the last year alone. But never had he faced a cockpit such as this, and the urban praetor had to suspend the court until order could be restored. Clodius sat looking at him with his arms folded and a grim expression on his face: the behavior of the jury must have been deeply troubling to him. Sitting by Clodius's side for the first time in the trial was his wife, Fulvia. It was a cunning move on the defense's part to produce her, for she was only sixteen and looked more like his daughter than like a married woman— exactly the sort of vulnerable young girl guaranteed to melt a jury's heart. She was also a descendant of the Gracchi family, who were immensely popular with the people. She had a hard, mean face, but then, being married to Clodius would surely have been enough to curdle even the sweetest nature.

When at last the chief prosecutor, Lentulus Crus, was called on to examine the witness, an anticipatory silence fell. He crossed the court to Cicero. "Although the whole world knows who you are, would you please state your name?"

"Marcus Tullius Cicero."

"Do you swear by all the gods to tell the truth?"

"I swear."

"You are familiar with the accused?"

"I am."

"Where was he between the sixth and seventh hours on the day of the ritual of the Good Goddess last year? Can you give the court that information?"

"I can. I remember it very well." Cicero turned from his questioner to the jury. "He was in my house."

An excited murmur ran around the spectators and the jury. Clodius said very loudly, "Liar!" and his claque set up a fresh chorus of jeering. The praetor, whose name was Voconius, called for order. He gestured to the prosecutor to continue.

"There is no doubt about this?" asked Crus.

"None whatever. Others in my household saw him, as well as I."

"What was the purpose of the visit?"

"It was a social call."

"Would it have been possible, in your opinion, for the accused to have left your house and been in Interamna by nightfall?"

"Not unless he put on wings as well as women's clothes."

There was much laughter at this. Even Clodius smiled.

"Fulvia, the wife of the accused, who is also sitting there, claims to have been with her husband in Interamna that same evening. What do you say to that?"

"I would say that the delights of married life have obviously so affected her judgment that she no longer knows what day of the week it is."

The laughter was even more prolonged, and again Clodius joined in, but Fulvia stared ahead of her with a face that was like a child's fist, small and white and clenched: she was a terror even then.

Crus had no further questions and returned to the prosecutors' bench, yielding the floor to Clodius's advocate, Curio. He was no doubt a brave man on the battlefield, but the courtroom was not his natural arena, and he approached the great orator in the manner of a nervous schoolboy poking a snake with a stick. "My client has long been an enemy of yours, I believe?"

"Not at all. Until he committed this act of sacrilege we enjoyed friendly relations."

"But then he was accused of this crime and you deserted him?"

"No, his senses deserted him, and then he committed the crime."

Again there was laughter. The defense counsel looked annoyed. "On the fourth day of December last year you say that my client came to see you?"

"I do."

"It is suspiciously convenient, is it not, that you should suddenly remember that Clodius came to see you on that date?"

"I should have said the convenience in the matter of dates was all on his side."

"What do you mean by that?"

"Well, I doubt he spends many nights of the year in Interamna. But by a remarkable coincidence the one night he does happen to find himself in that distant spot is also the night a dozen witnesses swear to have seen him cavorting in women's dress in Rome."

As the amusement spread, Clodius stopped smiling. Clearly he had had enough of watching his advocate batted around the court, and he gestured to him to come over to his bench for a consultation. But Curio, who was nearing sixty and unused to ridicule, was losing his temper and had started waving his arms around.

"Some fools no doubt will think this is all very witty wordplay, but I put it to you that you have made a mistake, and that my client came to see you on another day entirely."

"I have no doubt about the date—and for a very good reason. It was the first anniversary of my salvation of the republic. Believe me, I shall always have particular reason for remembering the fourth day of December."

"And so will the wives and children of the men you had murdered!" shouted Clodius. He leapt to his feet. Voconius at once appealed for order, but Clodius refused to sit and continued yelling insults. "You behaved as a tyrant then, as you do now!" Turning to his supporters standing in the Forum, he gestured to them to join in. They needed little encouragement. Almost to a man they surged forward, jeering. A fresh flight of missiles raked the platform. For the second time that morning, the jury came to Cicero's aid, surrounding him and trying to cover his head. The urban praetor shouted out to Curio, demanding to know if the defense had any further questions for the witness. Curio, who looked utterly dismayed at the way the jury were again protecting Cicero, signaled he had finished, and the court was hastily adjourned. A combination of jurymen, bodyguards, and clients cleared a path for Cicero through the Forum and up the Palatine Hill to his home.

I had expected to find Cicero badly shaken by the whole experience, and certainly at first sight he looked it. His hair was standing up in tufts, his toga streaked with dirt. But otherwise he was unscathed. Indeed, he was exultant, striding around his library, reliving the highlights of his testimony. He felt he had defeated Catilina for a second time. "Did you see the way that jury closed ranks around me? If ever you wished for a symbol of all that is best about Roman justice, Tiro, you saw it this morning." Still, he decided against going back to the court to hear the closing speeches, and it was not until two days later, when the verdict was due to be delivered, that he ventured down to the Temple of Castor to see Clodius sentenced.

The jury by this time had requested armed protection from the Senate, and a century of troops guarded the steps up to the platform. As Cicero approached the section of seats reserved for senators, he raised his arm to the jury and a few saluted him back, but many glanced nervously in the other direction. "I suppose they must be afraid of showing their feelings in front of Clodius's mob," Cicero said to me. "After they have cast their votes, do you think I should go and stand with them, to show my support? There is bound to be trouble, even with an armed guard." I was not at all sure this was wise, but there was no time for me to reply, as the praetor was already coming out of the temple. I left Cicero to take his place on the bench and went to join the crowd nearby.

The prosecution and defense having rested their cases, it now remained only for Voconius to sum up their arguments and direct the jury on points of law. Clodius was once again seated beside Fulvia. He turned and whispered to her occasionally while she stared hard at the men who would shortly decide her husband's fate. Everything in court always takes longer than one expects—questions have to be answered, statutes consulted, documents found—and it must have been at least an hour later that the court officials finally began handing out the wax voting tokens to the jurymen. On one side was scratched an *A* for acquittal, and on the other a *C* for condemn. The system was designed for maximum secrecy: it was the work of a moment to use one's thumb to wipe a letter clear and then drop the vote into the urn as it was handed round. When every token had been collected, the urn was carried over to the table in front of the praetor and emptied out. All around me the crowd stood on tiptoe, straining to see what was happening. For some, the tension of the silence was too much, and they felt compelled to puncture it by shouting out banalities—"Come on, Clodius!" "Long live Clodius!"—cries which produced little flurries of applause in the teeming multitude. An awning had been set up above the court to keep off the weather, and I remember how the canvas snapped like a sail in the stiff May breeze. At last the reckoning was done and the tally was handed to the praetor. He stood, and the court all did the same. Fulvia gripped Clodius's arm. I closed my eyes tight shut and prayed. We needed just twenty-nine votes to send Clodius into exile for the rest of his life.

"There voted in favor of condemnation twenty-five, and in favor of acquittal thirty-one. The verdict of this court is therefore that Publius Clodius Pulcher is not guilty of the charges laid against him and the case—"

The praetor's final words were lost in the roar of approval. For me, the earth seemed to tilt. I felt myself sway and when I opened my eyes, blinking in the glare, Clodius was making his way around the court shaking hands with the jurors. The legionnaires had linked arms to prevent anyone's storming the platform. The mob were cheering and dancing. On either side of me Clodius's supporters insisted on shaking my hand, and I tried to force a smile as I did so, otherwise they might have beaten me up, or worse. In the midst of this noisy jubilation the senatorial benches sat as white and still as a field of freshly fallen snow. I could make out a few expressions—Hortensius stricken, Lucullus uncomprehending, Catulus slack-mouthed with dismay. Cicero wore his professional mask and gazed, statesmanlike, into the distance.

After a few moments Clodius came to the front of the platform. He ignored the praetor's shouts that this was a court of law and not a public assembly and held up his hands for quiet. At once the noise fell away.

"My fellow citizens," he said, "this is not a victory for me. This is a victory for you, the people." Another great swell of applause carried forward and broke against the temple, and he turned his face toward it, Narcissus to his mirror. This time he let the adulation go on for a long time. "I was born a patrician," he continued eventually, "but the members of my own class turned against me. It is you who have supported and sustained me. It is to you I owe my life. I am of you. I wish to be among you. And henceforth I shall dedicate myself to you. Let it be known, therefore, on the day of this great victory, that it is my resolve to disavow my inheritance of blood as a patrician, and to seek adoption as a plebeian." I glanced at Cicero. The statesmanlike look had vanished. He was staring at Clodius in open astonishment. "And if I am successful, I shall follow a path of ambition not through the Senate—filled as it is with the bloated and the corrupt—but as a people's representative—as one of you—as a tribune!" More massive applause followed, which again he quieted with a stroke of his hand. "And if you the people choose me as a tribune, I make you this pledge and this promise, my friends—those who took the lives of Roman citizens without trial will very soon know what it is to taste the people's justice!"

Afterward Cicero retired to his library to mull over the verdict with Hortensius, Catulus, and Lucullus, while Quintus went off to see if he could discover what had happened. As the senators sat in shock Cicero told me to fetch some wine. "Four votes," he murmured. "Just four votes cast the other way, and that irresponsible reprobate would even now be on his way out of Italy forever. *Four votes!*" He could not stop repeating it.

"Well, this is the end for me, gentlemen," announced Lucullus. "I shall retire from public life." From a distance he seemed still to possess his usual cold demeanor, but when one came close to him, as I did when I handed him a cup of wine, one could see that he was blinking uncontrollably. He had been humiliated. It was intolerable to him. He drank the wine quickly and held out his cup for more.

"Our colleagues will be in a panic," observed Hortensius.

Catulus said, "I feel quite faint."

"Four votes!"

"I shall tend my fish, study philosophy, and compose myself for death. This republic holds no place for me any longer."

Presently, Quintus arrived with news from the court. He had spoken to the prosecutors, he said, and to three of the jurors who had voted to condemn. "It seems there has never been such bribery in the history of Roman justice. There are rumors that some of the key men were offered four hundred thousand to make sure the verdict went Clodius's way."

"Four hundred thousand?" repeated Hortensius in disbelief.

"But where did Clodius get such sums?" demanded Lucullus. "That little bitch of a wife is rich, but even so—"

Quintus said, "The rumor is that the money was put up by Crassus."

For the second time that day, the solid earth seemed to melt beneath my feet. Cicero glanced briefly in my direction.

"I find that hard to believe," said Hortensius. "Why would Crassus want to pay out a fortune to rescue Clodius, of all people?"

"Well, I can only report what is being said," replied Quintus. "Crassus had twenty of the jury around to his house last night, one after the other, and asked each of them what they wanted. He settled bills for some. To others he gave contracts. The rest took cash."

"That is still not a majority of the jury," pointed out Cicero.

"No, the word is that Clodius and Fulvia were also busy," said Quintus, "and not just with their gold. Beds were creaking in some noble houses in Rome last night, for those jurors who chose to take their payment in a different coin—male or female. I'm told that Clodia herself worked hard for several votes."

"Cato has been right all along," exclaimed Lucullus. "The core of our republic is utterly rotten. We're finished. And Clodius is the maggot who will destroy us."

"Can you imagine a *patrician* transferring to the *plebs*?" asked Hortensius in a tone of wonder. "Can you imagine *wanting* to do such a thing?"

"Gentlemen, gentlemen," said Cicero, "we've lost a trial, that's all—don't let's lose our nerve. Clodius isn't the first guilty man to walk free from a court of law."

"He will come after you, Brother," warned Quintus. "If he transfers to the plebs, you can be sure he will be elected tribune—he's too popular now to be stopped—and once he has the powers of that office at his disposal he can cause you a great deal of trouble."

"It will never happen," said Cicero. "He will never be allowed to transfer by the state authorities. And if by some amazing mischance he were, do you really think that I—after all that I've achieved in this city, starting from nothing—do you honestly believe that I can't handle a giggling puerile pervert such as our Little Miss Beauty? I could snap his spine in a single speech!"

"You're right," said Hortensius, "and I want you to know that we will never abandon you. If he does dare to attack you, you will always have our complete support. Is that not true, Lucullus?"

"Of course."

"Don't you agree, Catulus?" But Catulus did not answer. "Quintus?" Again there was no reply. Hortensius sighed. "I'm afraid he's grown very old of late. Wake him, will you, Tiro?"

I put my hand on Catulus's shoulder and shook him gently. His head lolled over to one side and I had to grab him to stop his sliding to the floor. His head flopped back so that his leathery old face was suddenly staring up into mine. His eyes were open. His mouth hung loose, leaking spit. I snatched away my hand in shock, and it was Quintus who had to step forward and feel his neck and pronounce him dead.

Thus passed from this world Quintus Lutatius Catulus, in the sixty-first year of his life: consul, pontiff, and fierce upholder of the prerogatives of the Senate. He was of an earlier, sterner era, and I look back on his death, as I do that of Metellus Pius, as a milestone in the demise of the republic. Hortensius, who was Catulus's brother-in-law, took a candle from Cicero and held it to the old man's face, and softly tried to call him back to life. Never have I seen the point of the ancient tradition more clearly than at that moment, for it really did seem as if Catulus's spirit had just slipped out of the room and could easily return if properly summoned. We waited to see if he might revive but of course he did not, and after a while Hortensius kissed his forehead and closed his eyes. He wept a little, and even Cicero looked red-eyed, for although he and Catulus had started out as enemies they had ended up making common cause, and he had come to respect the old man for his integrity. Only Lucullus appeared unmoved, but by then I believe he had reached a stage where he preferred fish to human beings.

Naturally, all discussion of the trial was ended. Catulus's slaves were summoned to carry their master's corpse the short distance to his house, and once this had been done, Hortensius went off to break the news to his own household, while Lucullus retired to dine alone, no doubt on larks' wings and the tongues of nightingales, in his vast Room of Apollo. As for Quintus, he announced that he was to depart at dawn the next morning on the start of his long journey to Asia. Cicero knew he was under orders to leave as soon as the jury returned its verdict, but even so I could tell that this was the hardest of all the blows he had endured that day. He summoned Terentia and little Marcus to say goodbye, and then abruptly withdrew to his library alone, leaving me to accompany Quintus to the door.

"Goodbye, Tiro," he said, taking my hand in both of his. He had hard, calloused palms; not like Cicero's soft lawyer's hands. "I shall miss your counsel. Will you write to me often and tell me how my brother is faring?"

"Gladly."

He seemed about to step into the street, but then he turned and said,

"He should have given you your freedom when he ceased to be consul. That was his intention. Did you know that?"

I was stunned by this revelation. "He had stopped talking about it," I stammered. "I assumed he had changed his mind."

"He says he is frightened of how much you know."

"But I would never utter a word I had learned in confidence to anyone!"

"I know that, and in his heart so does he. Don't be concerned. It's really just an excuse. The truth is he's scared of the thought that you might leave him too, just as Atticus and I are doing. He relies on you more than you know."

I was too overcome to speak.

"When I return from Asia," he continued, "you shall have your freedom, I promise you. You belong to the family, not just to my brother. In the meantime, look out for his safety, Tiro. There's something happening in Rome that I don't like the smell of."

He raised his hand in farewell and, accompanied by his attendants, set off down the street. I stood on the step and watched his familiar sturdy figure, with his broad shoulders and his steady tread, stride down the hill until he was out of sight.

XV

CLODIUS WAS SUPPOSED to go straight off to Sicily as a junior magistrate. Instead he chose to linger in Rome to savor his victory. He even had the nerve to take his seat in the Senate, to which he was now entitled. It was the Ides of May, two days after the trial, and the house was debating the political situation in the aftermath of the fiasco. Clodius entered the chamber just as Cicero was speaking. Greeted by loud hisses, he smiled to himself as if he found their hostility amusing, and when no senator would budge along their bench to make room for him he leaned against the wall and folded his arms, regarding the speaker with a smirk. Crassus, sitting in his usual place in the front row, looked distinctly uncomfortable and pretended to examine a scratch on his red leather shoe. Cicero simply ignored Clodius and continued with his speech.

"Gentlemen," he said, "we must not flag or falter because of a single blow. I agree we have to recognize that our authority has been weakened, but that doesn't mean we should panic. We would be fools to ignore what has happened, but cowards to let it frighten us. The jury may have let loose an enemy upon the state—"

Clodius called out, "I was acquitted not as an enemy of the state but as the man to clean up Rome!"

"Clodius, you are mistaken," said Cicero calmly, not even deigning to look at him. "The jury has preserved you not for the streets of Rome but for the death cell. They don't want to keep you with us, but rather to deprive you of the chance of exile." He resumed his speech. "And so, gentlemen, take heart and maintain your dignity—"

"And where's *your* dignity, Cicero?" shouted Clodius. "You take bribes!"

"The political consensus of honest men still holds—"

"You took a bribe so that you could buy a house!"

Now Cicero turned to face him. "At least," he said, "I didn't buy a jury."

The Senate rang with laughter, and I was reminded of an old lion cuffing an unruly cub. Still, Clodius pressed on: "I'll tell you why I was acquitted—because your evidence was a lie, and the jury didn't credit it."

"On the contrary, twenty-five members of that jury gave me credit and thirty-one gave you none—they demanded their money in advance."

It may not sound especially funny now, but at the time one would have thought that Cicero had made the wittiest remark in history. I suppose the Senate laughed so much because they wanted to show him their support, and each time Clodius tried to respond they laughed even louder, so that in the end he gave up irritably and left the chamber. This sally was considered a great success for Cicero, especially as a couple of days later Clodius left Rome to go off to Sicily, and for the next few months he was able to put "Little Miss Beauty" out of his mind.

It was made clear to Pompey the Great that if he wanted to stand for a second consulship he would have to give up his hopes of a triumph and come into Rome to campaign, and this he could not bring himself to do, for much as he relished the substance of power he loved the show of it even more—the gaudy costumes, the blaring trumpets, the roar and stink of the wild beasts in their cages, the tramping boots and raucous cheers of his soldiers, the adulation of the crowd.

So he abandoned the idea of becoming consul, and the date of his triumphal entry into the city was fixed, at his request, to coincide with his forty-fifth birthday, at the end of September. Such was the scale of his achievement, however, that the parade—which it was reckoned would extend for at least twenty miles—had to be spread over two whole days. Therefore it was actually on the eve of the imperator's birthday that Cicero and the rest of the Senate went out to the Field of Mars to greet the conqueror formally. Not only had Pompey colored his face red for the occasion, he had dressed himself in the most fabulous golden armor and was wearing a magnificent cloak that had once belonged to Alexander the Great. Drawn up around him were thousands of his veterans guarding hundreds of wagons laden with booty.

Until this point, Cicero had not really grasped the extent of Pompey's wealth. As he remarked to me: "One million, or ten million, or a hundred million—what are these? Mere words. The imagination cannot comprehend their meaning." But Pompey had gathered these riches all in one place and by doing so revealed his power. For example, a skilled man at that time might work an entire day in Rome and at the end of it count himself lucky if he had earned one silver drachma. Pompey had laid out open chests on glistening display that morning which contained *seventy-five million* silver drachmae: more than the annual tax revenue of the entire Roman world. And that was just the cash. Towering over the parade, and requiring a team of four oxen to pull it, was a solid gold statue of Mithridates that was twelve feet tall. There was Mithridates's throne and his scepter, also gold. There were thirty-three of his crowns made of pearl, and three golden statues of Apollo, Minerva, and Mars. There was a mountain shaped like a pyramid and made of gold, with deer and lions and fruit of every variety, and a golden vine entwined all around it. There was a checkered gaming board, three feet long by four feet broad, made of precious green and blue stones, with a solid gold moon upon it weighing thirty pounds. There was a sundial made of pearls. Another five wagons were required to carry the most precious books from the royal library. It made a profound impression on Cicero, who recognized that such wealth was bound to have unforeseeable consequences for Rome and its politics. He took great delight in going over to Crassus and teasing him. "Well, Crassus, you once had the distinction of being the richest man in Rome—but not anymore, I fancy. After this even you will be applying to Pompey for a loan!" Crassus gave a crooked smile; one could tell the sight was choking him.

Pompey sent all this into the city on the first day, but remained himself outside the gates. On the second day, his birthday, the triumphal parade proper began with the prisoners he had brought back from the East: first the army commanders, then the officials of Mithridates's household, then a group of captured pirate chiefs, then the King of the Jews, followed by the King of Armenia with his wife and son, and, finally, as the highlight of this part of the procession, seven of Mithridates's children and one of his sisters. The thousands of Romans in the Forum Boarium and the Circus Maximus jeered and flung lumps of shit and earth at them, so much so that by the time they finally stumbled down the Via Sacra toward the Carcer they looked like clay figures come to life. There they were made to wait beneath the gaze of the carnifex and his assistants, trembling at the thought of their fate, while the distant roars from the direction of the Triumphal Gate signaled that at last their conqueror had entered the city.

Cicero waited too, with the rest of his colleagues, outside the Senate

House. I was on the opposite side of the Forum, and as the parade passed between us I kept losing sight of him amid all that torrent of glory. There were wagons with gaudy tableaux depicting each of the nations Pompey had subdued—Albania, Syria, Palestine, Arabia, and so forth—followed by some of the eight hundred heavy bronze ramming beaks of the pirate ships he had captured, and the glittering heaps of armor and shields and swords he had seized from Mithridates's armies. Behind all this tramped Pompey's soldiers, chanting bawdy verses about their commander, and then at last Pompey himself came into the Forum, riding in his jewel-studded chariot, wearing a purple toga embroidered with golden stars, and of course the cloak of Alexander. Clinging onto the platform behind him was the slave traditionally charged with intoning in his ear that he was only human. I did not envy that poor fellow his job, and he was clearly starting to get on Pompey's nerves, because the moment the chari-oteer pulled up the horses outside the Carcer and the parade came to a halt, Pompey pushed him roughly off the platform and turned his broad red-painted face to address the muddy apparitions of the prisoners.

"I, Pompey the Great, conqueror of three hundred and twenty-four nations, having been granted the power of life and death by the Senate and people of Rome, do hereby declare that you, as vassals of the Roman empire, shall immediately"—he paused—"be granted a full pardon and set free to return to the lands of your birth. Go, and tell the world of my mercy!"

It was as magnificent as it was unexpected, for Pompey had been known in his youth as "the Butcher Boy" and had seldom shown much clemency to anyone. The crowd seemed disappointed at first but then began to applaud, while the prisoners, when they were told what he had said, stretched out their hands and cried out to Pompey in their babble of foreign tongues. Pompey acknowledged their gratitude with a twirling gesture of his hand, then jumped down from his chariot and walked to-ward the Capitol, where he was due to sacrifice to Jupiter. The Senate, Cicero included, trailed after him, and I was about to follow when I made a most remarkable discovery.

Now that the parade had ended, the wagons laden with arms and ar-mor were queuing to leave the Forum, and for the first time I saw at close quarters some of the swords and knives. I was no expert when it came to soldiering, but even I could recognize that these brand-new weapons, with their curved oriental blades and mysterious engravings on their hilts, were exactly the same as the weapons which Cethegus had been hoarding in his house, and of which I had made an inventory on the eve of his execution. I made a move to pick one up, intending to take it back and show it to Cicero, but the legionnaire who was guarding the wagon shouted at me roughly to keep my distance. I was on the point of telling him who I was and why I needed it when good sense checked my tongue. I turned without a word and hurried away, and when I looked back the legionnaire was still watching me suspiciously.

Cicero had been obliged to attend Pompey's great official banquet following the sacrifice, and it was not until late in the evening that he returned home—in a bad mood, as he usually was after spending much time with Pompey. He was surprised to find me waiting up for him and listened intently as I explained my discovery. I was inordinately pleased with my cleverness and expected him to congratulate me. Instead, he became increasingly irritated. "Are you trying to tell me," he demanded, after he had heard me out, "that Pompey sent back captured weapons from Mithridates in order to arm Catilina's conspiracy?"

"All I know is that the markings and the design were identical—"

Cicero cut me off. "This is treasonous talk! I cannot have you say such things! You've seen how powerful Pompey is. Don't ever mention it again, do you hear me?"

"I'm sorry," I said, gulping with embarrassment. "Forgive me."

"Besides, how would Pompey have gotten them to Rome? He was a thousand miles away."

"I wondered if perhaps they came back with Metellus Nepos."

"Go to bed," he said angrily. "You're talking nonsense." But he obviously must have thought about it overnight, because the next morning his attitude was more subdued. "I suppose you could be right that the weapons came from Mithridates. After all, the entire royal arsenal was captured, and it's plausible that Nepos might have brought a consignment with him to Rome. However, that's not the same thing as saying that Pompey was actively assisting Catilina."

"Of course not," I said.

"That would simply be too appalling to contemplate. Those blades were intended to cut my throat."

"Pompey would never do anything to harm either you or the state," I assured him.

The following day Pompey asked Cicero to come and see him.

• • •

The Warden of Land and Sea had taken up residence again in his old house on the Esquiline Hill. Over the summer its appearance had been transformed. Dozens of the ramming beaks from the captured pirates' warships now bristled from the walls. Some were fashioned in bronze to look like gorgons' heads. Others bore the snouts and horns of animals. Cicero had not seen them before and regarded them with great distaste. "Imagine having to sleep here every night," he said as we waited for the porter to open the door. "It's like the death chamber of a pharaoh." And from this time on he often privately referred to Pompey as "the Pharaoh" or sometimes as "the Shah."

A large crowd stood outside, admiring the house. Inside, the public rooms were thronged with petitioners hoping to find space to feed at Pompey's golden trough. Some were bankrupt senators looking to sell their votes. Others were businessmen with schemes in which they hoped to persuade Pompey to invest. There were shipowners and horse trainers and furniture makers and jewelers, and some who were plainly just beggars, out to catch Pompey's sympathy with a hard-luck story. Much to their envy, we were shown straight past all these mendicants and into a large private room. In one corner was a tailor's dummy displaying Pompey's triumphal toga and the cloak of Alexander, in another a large head of Pompey made entirely of pearls, which I recognized from the triumphal parade. And in the center, set up on two trestles, was an architect's model of an immense complex of buildings, over which loomed Pompey, holding a pair of toy wooden temples in either hand. A group of men behind him seemed to be waiting anxiously for his decision.

"Ah," he said, looking up, "here is Cicero. He's a clever fellow. He will have a view. What do you think, Cicero? Should I build four temples here, or three?"

"I always build my temples in fours," replied Cicero, "providing I have the space."

"Excellent advice!" exclaimed Pompey. "Four it will be," and he set them down in a row, to the applause of his audience. "We shall decide which gods they are to be dedicated to later. Well?" he said to Cicero, gesturing to the model. "What do you think?"

Cicero peered down at the elaborate construction. "Most impressive. What is it? A palace?"

"A theater, with seating for ten thousand. Here will be public gardens, surrounded by a portico. And here temples." He turned to one of the men behind him, who I realized must be architects. "Remind me again: How big is it going to be?"

"The whole construction will extend for a quarter of a mile, excellency."

Pompey grinned and rubbed his hands. "A building a quarter of a mile in length! Imagine it!"

"And where is it to be built?" asked Cicero.

"On the Field of Mars."

"But where will the people vote?"

"Oh, here somewhere," said Pompey, waving his hand vaguely, "or down here by the river. There'll still be plenty of room. Take it away, gentlemen," he ordered, "take it away and start digging the foundations, and don't worry about the cost."

After they had gone, Cicero said, "I don't wish to sound pessimistic, Pompey, but I fear you may have trouble over this with the censors."

"Why?"

"They've always forbidden the building of a permanent theater in Rome, on moral grounds."

"I've thought of that. I shall tell them I'm building a shrine to Venus. It will be incorporated into the stage somehow—these architects know what they're doing."

"You think the censors will believe you?"

"Why wouldn't they?"

"A shrine to Venus a quarter of a mile long? They might think you're taking your piety to extreme lengths."

But Pompey was in no mood for teasing, especially not by Cicero. All at once his generous mouth shrank into a pout. His lips quivered. He was famous for his short temper, and for the first time I witnessed just how quickly he could lose it. "This city!" he cried. "It's so full of *little* men— just jealous *little* men! Here I am, proposing to donate to the Roman people the most marvelous building in the history of the world, and what thanks do I receive? None. *None!*" He kicked over one of the trestles. I was reminded of little Marcus in his nursery after he had been made to put away his games. "And speaking of little men," he said menacingly, "why hasn't the Senate given me any of the legislation I asked for? Where's the

bill to ratify my settlements in the East? And the land for my veterans—
what's become of that?"

"These things take time—"

"I thought we had an understanding: I would support you in the matter of Hybrida, and you would secure my legislation for me in the Senate.
Well, I've done my part. Where's yours?"

"It is not an easy matter. I can hardly carry these bills on my own. I'm
only one of six hundred senators, and unfortunately you have plenty of
opponents among the rest."

"Who? Name them!"

"You know who they are better than I. Celer won't forgive you for
divorcing his sister. Lucullus is still resentful that you took over his command in the East. Crassus has always been your rival. Cato feels you act
like a king—"

"Cato! Don't mention that man's name in my presence! It's entirely
thanks to Cato I have no wife!" The roar of Pompey's voice was carrying
through the house, and I noticed that some of his attendants had crept up
to the door and were standing, watching. "I put off raising this with you
until after my triumph, in the hope you'd have made some progress. But
now I am back in Rome and I demand that I am given the respect I'm
due! Do you hear me? I demand it!"

"Of course I hear you. I should imagine the dead can hear you. And I
shall endeavor to serve your interests, as your friend, as I always have."

"Always? Are you sure of that?"

"Name me one occasion when I was not loyal to your interests."

"What about Catilina? You could have brought me home then to defend the republic."

"And you should thank me I didn't, for I spared you the odium of
shedding Roman blood."

"I could have dealt with him like *that*!" Pompey snapped his fingers.

"But only after he had murdered the entire leadership of the Senate,
including me. Or perhaps you would have preferred that?"

"Of course not."

"Because you know that was his intention? We found weapons stored
within the city for that very purpose."

Pompey glared at him, and this time Cicero stared him out: indeed, it
was Pompey who turned away first. "Well, I know nothing about any
weapons," he muttered. "I can't argue with you, Cicero. I never could.

You've always been too nimble-witted for me. The truth is I'm more used to army life than politics." He forced a smile. "I suppose I must learn I can no longer simply issue a command and expect the world to obey it. 'Let arms to toga yield, laurels to words'—isn't that your line? 'O, happy Rome, born in my consulship'—there, you see? There's another. You can tell what a student I have become of your work."

Pompey was not normally a man for poetry, and it was immediately clear to me that the fact that he could recite these lines from Cicero's consular epic—which had just started to be read all over Rome—was proof that he was dangerously jealous. Still, he somehow managed to bring himself to pat Cicero on the arm, and his courtiers exhaled with relief. They drifted away from the entrance and gradually the sounds of the house resumed, whereupon Pompey—whose bonhomie could be as abrupt and disconcerting as his rages—suddenly announced that they should drink some wine. It was brought in by a very beautiful woman, whose name, I discovered afterward, was Flora. She was one of the most famous courtesans in Rome and was living under Pompey's roof while he was between wives. She always wore a scarf around her neck, to conceal, she said, the bite marks Pompey inflicted when he was making love. She poured the wine demurely, and then withdrew while Pompey showed us Alexander's cloak, which had, he said, been found in Mithridates's private apartments. It looked very new to me, and I could see that Cicero was having difficulty keeping a straight face. "Imagine," he said in a hushed voice, feeling the material with great reverence, "three hundred years old and yet it looks as though it was made less than a decade ago."

"It has magical properties," said Pompey. "As long as I keep it by me I am told no harm can befall me." He became very serious as he showed Cicero to the door. "Speak to Celer, will you, and the others, on my behalf? I promised my veterans that I would give them land, and Pompey the Great can't be seen to go back on his word."

"I'll do everything I can."

"I'd prefer to work through the Senate, but if I have to find my friends elsewhere, I shall. You can tell them I said that."

As we walked home, Cicero said, "Did you hear him? 'I know nothing about any weapons!' Our Pharaoh may be a great general but he is a terrible liar."

"What are you going to do?"

"What else can I do? Support him, of course. I don't like it when he says he might try to find his friends elsewhere. At all costs I must try to keep him out of the arms of Caesar."

And so Cicero put aside his distaste and his suspicions and did the rounds on Pompey's behalf, just as he had done years before when he was merely a rising senator. It was yet another lesson to me in politics—an occupation which, if it is to be pursued successfully, demands the most extraordinary reserves of self-discipline, a quality that the naive often mistake for hypocrisy.

First, Cicero invited Lucullus to dinner and spent several fruitless hours trying to persuade him to abandon his opposition to Pompey's bills; but Lucullus would never forgive the Pharaoh for taking all the credit for the defeat of Mithridates, and he flatly refused to cooperate. Next Cicero tried Hortensius, and received the same answer. He even went to see Crassus, who, despite clearly wishing to destroy his visitor, nevertheless received him very civilly. He sat back in his chair with the tips of his fingers pressed together and his eyes half-closed, listening to Cicero's appeal and relishing every word.

"So," he summarized, "Pompey fears he will lose face if his bills don't pass, and he asks me to set aside past enmities and give him my support, for the sake of the republic?"

"That's it."

"Well, I have not forgotten the way he tried to take the credit for defeating Spartacus—a victory that was entirely mine—and you can tell him that I would not raise a hand to help him even if my life depended on it. How is your new house, by the way?"

"Very fine, thank you."

After that, Cicero decided to approach Metellus Celer, who was now consul-elect. It took him a while to summon up the nerve to go next door: this would be the first time he had stepped over the threshold since Clodius committed his outrage at the Good Goddess ceremony. In fact, like Crassus, Celer could not have been friendlier. The prospect of power suited him—he had been bred for it, like a racehorse—and he too listened judiciously as Cicero made out his case.

"I no more care for Pompey's hauteur than you do," concluded Cicero, "but the fact remains that he is by far the most powerful man in the world, and it will be a disaster if he ends up alienated from the Senate. And that is what will happen if we don't try to give him his legislation."

"You think he will retaliate?"

"He says he will have no option except to find his friends elsewhere, which obviously means the tribunes or, even worse, Caesar. And if he follows that route we'll have popular assemblies, vetoes, riots, paralysis, the people and the Senate at each other's throats—in short, a disaster."

"That's a grim picture, I agree," said Celer, "but I'm afraid I cannot help you."

"Even for the sake of the country?"

"By divorcing my sister in such a public fashion Pompey humiliated her. He also insulted me, my brother, and all my family. I've learned the sort of man he is: utterly untrustworthy, interested only in himself. You should beware of him, Cicero."

"You have good cause for grievance, no one can doubt that. But think what magnanimity it would show if you were able to say in your inaugural address that for the good of the nation Pompey should be accommodated."

"It would not show magnaminity. It would show weakness. The Metelli may not be the oldest family in Rome, or the grandest, but we have become the most successful, and we have done it by never yielding an inch to our enemies. Do you know what creature we have as our heraldic symbol?"

"The elephant?"

"The elephant, that's right. We have it because our ancestors beat the Carthaginians, but also because an elephant is the animal our family most resembles. It is massive, it moves slowly, it never forgets, and it always prevails."

"Yes, and it is also quite stupid, and therefore easily caught."

"Maybe," agreed Celer with a twitch of annoyance. "But then you set too great a store by cleverness, in my opinion," and he stood to signal that the interview was over.

He led us into the atrium with its huge display of consular death masks, and as we crossed the marbled floor he gestured to his ancestors, as if all those massed, bland, dead faces proved his point more eloquently than any words. We had just reached the entrance hall when Clodia appeared with her maids. I have no idea whether this was coincidental or deliberate, but I suspect the latter, for she was very elaborately coiffed and made up considering the hour of the morning: "In full nighttime battle rig," as Cicero said afterward. He bowed his head to her.

"Cicero," she responded, "you have become a stranger to me."

"True, alas, but not by choice."

Celer said, "I was told you two had become great friends while I was away. I'm glad to see you speaking again." When I heard those words, and the casual way he uttered them, I knew at once he had no idea of his wife's reputation. He possessed that curious innocence about the civilian world which I have noticed in many professional soldiers.

"You are well, I trust, Clodia?" inquired Cicero politely.

"I am prospering." She looked at him from under her long lashes. "And so is my brother in Sicily—despite your efforts."

She flashed him a smile that was as warm as a blade and swept on, leaving the faintest wash of perfume in her wake. Celer shrugged and said, "Well, there it is. I wish she talked to you as much as she does this damned poet who's always trailing after her. But she's very loyal to Clodius."

"And does he still plan to become a plebeian?" asked Cicero. "I wouldn't have thought having a pleb in the family would have gone down at all well with your illustrious ancestors."

"It will never happen." Celer checked to see that Clodia was out of earshot. "Between you and me, I think the fellow is an absolute disgrace."

This exchange, at least, cheered Cicero, but otherwise all his politicking had come to nothing, and the following day, as a last resort, he went to see Cato. The Stoic lived in a fine but artfully neglected house on the Aventine, which smelled of stale food and unwashed clothes and offered nothing to sit on except hard wooden chairs. The walls were undecorated. There were no carpets. Through an open door I caught a glimpse of two plain and solemn teenage girls at work on their sewing, and I wondered if those were the daughters or nieces Pompey had wanted to marry. How different Rome would have been if only Cato had consented to the match! We were shown by a limping porter into a small and gloomy chamber where Cato conducted his official business beneath a bust of Zeno. Once again Cicero laid out the case for making a compromise with Pompey, but Cato, like the others before him, would have none of it.

"He has too much power as it is," said Cato, repeating his familiar complaint. "If we let his veterans form colonies throughout Italy he'll have a standing army at his beck and call. And why in the name of heaven should we be expected to confirm all his treaties without examining them one by one? Are we the supreme governing body of the Roman republic or little girls to be told where to sit and what to do?"

"True," said Cicero, "but we have to face reality. When I went to see him he could not have made his intentions plainer: if we won't work with him, he'll get a tribune to lay the legislation he wants before a popular assembly, and that will mean endless conflict. Or, worse, he'll throw in his lot with Caesar when he gets back from Spain."

"What are you afraid of? Conflict can be healthy. Nothing good comes except through struggle."

"There's nothing good about a struggle between people and Senate, believe me. It will be like Clodius's trial, only worse."

"Ah!" Cato's fanatical eyes widened. "You are confusing separate issues there. Clodius was acquitted not because of the mob but because of a bribed jury. And there's an obvious remedy for jury bribing, which I intend to pursue."

"What do you mean by that?"

"I intend to lay a bill before the house that will remove from all jurors who are not senators their traditional immunity to prosecution for bribery."

Cicero clutched his hair. "You can't do *that*!"

"Why not?"

"Because it will look like an attack by the Senate on the people!"

"It's no such thing. It's an attack by the Senate on dishonesty and corruption."

"Maybe so, but in politics how things look is often more important than what they are."

"Then politics needs to change."

"At least, I beg you, don't do it now—not on top of everything else."

"It's never too soon to right a wrong."

"Now listen to me, Cato. Your integrity may be second to none but it obliterates your good sense, and if you carry on like this your noble intentions will destroy our country."

"Better destroyed than reduced to a corrupt monarchy."

"But Pompey doesn't want to be a monarch! He's disbanded his army. All he's ever tried to do is work with the Senate, yet all he's received is rejection. And far from corrupting Rome, he has done more to extend its power than any man alive!"

"No," said Cato, shaking his head, "no, you are wrong. Pompey has subjugated peoples with whom we had no quarrel, he has entered lands in which we have no business, and he has brought home wealth we have not earned. He is going to ruin us. It is my duty to oppose him."

From this impasse not even Cicero's agile brain could devise a means of escape. He went to see Pompey later that afternoon to report his failure and found him in semidarkness, brooding over the model of his theater. The meeting was too short even for me to take a note. Pompey listened to the news, grunted, and as we were leaving called after Cicero, "I want Hybrida recalled from Macedonia at once."

This threatened Cicero with a serious personal crisis, for he was being hard-pressed by the moneylenders. Not only did he still owe a sizable sum for the house on the Palatine but he had also bought several new properties, and if Hybrida stopped sending him a share of his spoils in Macedonia—which he had at last begun to do—Cicero would be seriously embarrassed. His solution was to arrange for Quintus's term as governor of Asia to be extended for another year. He was then able to draw from the Treasury the funds which should have gone to defray his brother's expenses (he had full power of attorney) and hand the whole lot over to his creditors to keep them quiet. "Now don't give me one of your reproachful looks, Tiro," he warned me as we came out of the Temple of Saturn with a Treasury bill for half a million sesterces safely stowed in my document case. "He wouldn't even *be* a governor if it weren't for me, and besides, I shall pay him back." Even so, I felt very sorry for Quintus, who was not enjoying his time in that vast, alien, and disparate province and was very homesick.

Over the next few months everything played out as Cicero had predicted. An alliance of Crassus, Lucullus, Cato, and Celer blocked Pompey's legislation in the Senate and Pompey duly turned to a friendly tribune named Fulvius, who laid a new land bill before the popular assembly. Celer then attacked the proposal with such violence that Fulvius had him committed to prison. The consul responded by having the back wall of the jail dismantled so that he could continue to denounce the measure from his cell. This display of resolution so delighted the people and discredited Fulvius that Pompey actually abandoned the bill. Cato then alienated the Order of the Knights entirely from the Senate by stripping them of jury immunity and also refusing to cancel the debts many had incurred by unwise financial speculation in the East. In both of these actions he was absolutely right morally while being at the same time utterly wrong politically.

Throughout all this, Cicero made few public speeches but confined himself entirely to his legal practice. He was very lonely without Quintus and Atticus and I often caught him sighing and muttering to himself when he thought he was alone. He slept badly, waking in the middle of the night and lying there with his mind churning, unable to nod off again until dawn. He confided to me that during these intervals, for the first time in his life, he was plagued with thoughts of death, as men of his age—he was forty-six—frequently are. "I am so utterly forsaken," he wrote to Atticus, "that my only moments of relaxation are those I spend with my wife, my little daughter, and my darling Marcus. My worldly, meretricious friendships may make a fine show in public, but in the home they are barren things. My house is crammed of a morning, I go down to the Forum surrounded by droves of friends, but in all the crowds I cannot find one person with whom I can exchange an unguarded joke or let out a private sigh."

Although he was too proud to admit it, the specter of Clodius also disturbed his rest. At the beginning of the new session, a tribune by the name of Herennius introduced a bill on the floor of the Senate proposing that the Roman people should meet on the Field of Mars and vote on whether or not Clodius should be permitted to become a pleb. That did not alarm Cicero: he knew the measure would swiftly be vetoed by the other tribunes. What did disturb him was that Celer spoke up in support of it, and after the Senate was adjourned he sought him out.

"I thought you were opposed to Clodius transferring to the plebs?"

"I am, but Clodia nags me morning and night about it. The measure won't pass in any case, so I hope this will give me a few weeks' peace. Don't worry," he added quietly. "If ever it comes to a serious fight I shall say what I really feel."

This answer did not entirely reassure Cicero and he cast about for some means of binding Celer to him more closely. As it happened, a crisis was developing in Further Gaul. A huge number of Germans—one hundred and twenty thousand, it was reported—had crossed the Rhine and settled on the lands of the Helvetii, a warlike tribe, whose response was to move westward in their turn, into the interior of Gaul, looking for fresh territory. This situation was deeply troubling to the Senate, and it was decided that the consuls should at once draw lots for the province of Further Gaul in case military action proved necessary. It promised to be a glittering command, full of opportunities for wealth and glory. Because both consuls were competitors for the prize—Pompey's clown, Afranius, was Celer's colleague—it fell to Cicero to conduct the ballot, and while I will not go so far as to say he rigged it—as he had once before for Celer—nevertheless, it was Celer who drew the winning token. He quickly repaid the debt. A few weeks later, when Clodius returned to Rome from Sicily after his quaestorship was over and stood up in the Senate to demand the right to transfer to the plebs, it was Celer who was the most violent in his opposition.

"You were born a patrician," he declared, "and if you reject your birthright you will destroy the very codes of blood and family and tradition on which this republic rests!"

I was standing at the door of the Senate when he made his about-face, and Clodius's expression was one of total surprise and horror. "But although I may have been born a patrician," he protested, "I do not wish to die one."

"You most assuredly will die a patrician," retorted Celer, "and if you continue on your present course, I tell you frankly, that inevitability will befall you sooner rather than later."

The Senate murmured with astonishment at this threat, and although Clodius tried to brush it off he must have known that his chances of becoming a pleb, and thus a tribune, lay at that moment in ruins.

Cicero was delighted. He lost all fear of Clodius and from then on foolishly took every opportunity to taunt him and jeer at him. I remember in particular an occasion not long after this when he and Clodius found themselves walking together into the Forum to introduce candidates at election time. Unwisely, for plenty around them were listening, Clodius took the opportunity to boast that he had now taken over from Cicero as the patron of the Sicilians and henceforth would be providing them with seats at the Games. "I don't believe you were ever in a position to do that," he sneered.

"I was not," conceded Cicero.

"Mind you, space is hard to come by. Even my sister, as consul's wife, says she can only give me one foot."

"Well, I wouldn't grumble about one foot in your sister's case," replied Cicero. "You can always hoist the other."

I had never before heard Cicero make a dirty joke, and afterward he rather regretted it as being "unconsular." Still, it was worth it at the time for the roars of laughter it elicited from everyone standing around and also for the effect it had on Clodius, who turned a fine shade of senatorial purple. The remark became famous and was repeated all over the city, although mercifully no one had the courage to relay it back to Celer.

And then, in an instant, everything changed, and as usual the man responsible was Caesar—who, although he had been away from Rome for almost exactly a year, had never been far from Cicero's thoughts.

One afternoon toward the end of May Cicero was sitting on the front bench in the Senate House next to Pompey. He had arrived late for some reason, otherwise I am sure he would have gotten wind of what was coming. As it was, he heard it at the same time as everyone else. After the auguries had been taken, Celer got to his feet to declare that a dispatch had just arrived from Caesar in Further Spain, which he now proposed to read.

"To the Senate and people of Rome from Gaius Julius Caesar, imperator—"

At the word "imperator" a stir of excitement went around the chamber, and I saw Cicero abruptly sit up and exchange looks with Pompey.

"From Gaius Julius Caesar, *imperator,*" repeated Celer, with greater emphasis, "greetings. The army is well. I have taken a legion and three cohorts across the mountains called Herminius and pacified the lands on either side of the river Durius. I have dispatched a flotilla from Gades seven hundred miles north and captured Brigantium. I have subdued the tribes of Callaecia and Lusitania and been saluted imperator in the field by the army. I have concluded treaties which will yield annual revenues of twenty million sesterces to the Treasury. The rule of Rome now extends to the farthermost shores of the Atlantic sea. Long live our republic."

Caesar's language was always terse, and it took a moment for the Senate to grasp the momentous nature of what they had just been told. Caesar had been sent out merely to govern Further Spain, a province thought to be more or less pacified, but had somehow contrived to conquer the neighboring country! His financial backer Crassus immediately jumped to his feet and·proposed that Caesar's achievement be rewarded with three days of national thanksgiving. For once even Cato was too dazed to object, and the motion was carried unanimously. Afterward, the senators spilled out into the bright sunshine. Most were talking excitedly about this brilliant feat. Not so Cicero: in the midst of that animated throng he walked with the slow tread and downcast eyes of a man at a funeral. "After all his scandals and near bankruptcies, I thought he was finished," he muttered to me as he reached the door, "at least for a year or two."

He beckoned me to follow, and we went and stood in a shady spot in the senaculum, where presently we were joined by Hortensius, Lucullus, and Cato; all three looked equally mournful.

"So, what is next for Caesar?" asked Hortensius gloomily. "Will he try for the consulship?"

"I should say it's certain, wouldn't you?" replied Cicero. "He can easily afford the campaign—if he's giving twenty million to the Treasury you can be sure he's keeping much more for himself."

At that moment Pompey walked past, looking thoughtful, and the group fell silent until he was far enough away not to be able to hear them.

Cicero said quietly, "There goes the Pharaoh. I expect that great ponderous mind of his will be grinding like a mill wheel. I certainly know what conclusion I'd come to in his place."

"What's that?" asked Cato.

"I'd make a deal with Caesar."

The others all shook their heads in disagreement. "That will never happen," said Hortensius. "Pompey can't abide to see another man getting a share of the glory."

"He'll put up with it this time, though," said Cicero. "You gentlemen won't help him get his laws through, but Caesar will promise him the earth—anything in return for Pompey's support in the elections."

"Not this summer, at least," said Lucullus firmly. "There are too many mountains and rivers between here and the Atlantic. Caesar can't get back in time to put his name on the ballot."

"And there's another thing," added Cato. "Caesar will want to triumph and he'll have to stay outside the city until he does."

"And we can hold him up for years," said Lucullus, "just as he made me wait for half a decade. My revenge for that insult is going to taste better than any meal."

Cicero, however, did not look convinced. "Well, maybe, but I have learned by hard experience never to underestimate our friend Gaius."

It was a wise remark, because about a week later a second dispatch reached the Senate from Further Spain. Again, Celer read it aloud to the assembled senators: in view of the fact that his newly conquered territory was entirely subdued, Caesar announced that he was returning to Rome.

Cato got up to object. "Provincial governors should remain at their posts until this house gives them permission to do otherwise," he said. "I move that we tell Caesar to stay where he is."

"It's a bit late for that!" someone next to me shouted from the doorway. "I've just seen him on the Field of Mars!"

"That is impossible," insisted Cato, looking flustered. "The last time we heard from him, he was boasting that he was on the Atlantic coast."

Nevertheless, Celer took the precaution of sending a slave out onto the Field of Mars to check the rumor, and he returned an hour later to announce that it was true: Caesar had overtaken his own messenger and was staying at the home of a friend outside the city.

The news threw Rome into a frenzy of hero worship. The next day Caesar sent an emissary to the Senate to ask that he be granted his triumph in September, and that in the interim he be permitted to stand for the consulship in absentia. There were plenty in the Senate willing to grant him his wish, for they recognized that Caesar's renown combined with his new wealth had made his candidacy well-nigh unstoppable. If a vote had been called, his supporters would probably have won it. Accordingly, day after day, whenever the motion was brought before the house, Cato rose and talked it out. He droned on about the overthrow of the kings of Rome. He bored away about the ancient laws. He wearied everyone with the importance of asserting senatorial control over the legions. He repeatedly warned of the dangerous precedent it would set if a candidate were allowed to seek office at election time while still holding military imperium: "Today Caesar asks for the consulship, tomorrow, he may demand it."

Cicero did not take part himself but signaled his support for Cato by coming into the chamber whenever he spoke and sitting on the front bench nearest to him. Time was running out for Caesar, and it looked certain that he would miss the deadline for submitting his nomination.

Naturally everyone expected that he would choose to triumph rather than become a candidate: Pompey had done that; every victorious general in Rome's history had done it; there was surely nothing to equal the glory of a triumph. But Caesar was never a man to mistake power's show for its substance. Late one afternoon on the fourth day of Cato's filibuster, when the chamber was almost empty and the long green summer shadows were creeping over the deserted benches, into the Senate House strolled Caesar. The twenty or so senators who were present could not believe their eyes. He had taken off his uniform and put on a toga.

Caesar bowed to the chair and took his place on the front bench opposite Cicero. He nodded politely across the aisle to my master and settled down to listen to Cato. But for once the great didact was lost for words. Having no further motivation to talk, he sat down abruptly, and the following month Caesar was elected consul by a unanimous vote of all the centuries—the first candidate to achieve this feat since Cicero.

XVI

THE WHOLE OF Rome now waited to see what Caesar would do. "The only thing we can expect," said Cicero, "is that it will be unexpected." And so it was. It took five months, but when Caesar made his move it was masterly.

One day toward the end of the year, in December, actually shortly before Caesar was due to be sworn in, Cicero received a visit from the eminent Spaniard Lucius Cornelius Balbus.

This remarkable creature was then forty years old. Born in Gades of Phoenician extraction, he was a trader, and very rich. His complexion was dark, his hair and beard as black as jet, his teeth and the whites of his eyes as bright as polished ivory. He had a very quick way of talking and he laughed a lot, throwing back his small neat head in delight, so that the most boring men in Rome all fancied themselves great wits after a short time in his company. He had a particular gift for attaching himself to powerful figures—first to Pompey, under whom he served in Spain and who arranged to make him a Roman citizen, and then to Caesar, who picked him up in Gades when he was governor, appointed him his chief engineer during his conquest of Lusitania, and then brought him back to Rome to run his errands. Balbus knew everyone, even if at first they did not know him, and he bustled in to see Cicero on that December morning with his hands held wide as if he were meeting his closest friend.

"My dear Cicero," he said in his thickly accented Latin, "how are you? You look as well as I have ever seen you—and I have never seen you looking anything other than well!"

"Then I suppose I am very much the same as ever." He gestured to Balbus to take a seat. "And how is Caesar?"

"He is marvelous," replied Balbus, "completely marvelous. He asks me to give you his very warmest regards and his absolute assurance that he is your greatest and most sincere friend in the world."

"Time for us to start counting our spoons, then, Tiro," said Cicero, and Balbus clapped his hands and pulled up his knees and literally rocked with laughter.

"Well, that is very funny—'count the spoons' indeed!—I shall tell him you said that, and he will be most amused. The spoons!" He wiped his eyes and recovered his breath. "Oh dear! But seriously, Cicero, when Caesar offers his friendship to a man it is not an empty thing. He takes the view that deeds, not words, are what count in this world."

Cicero had a mountain of legal documents to read. "Balbus," he said wearily, "you have obviously come here to say something—so would you kindly just say it?"

"Of course. You are busy, I can see that. Forgive me." He pressed his hand to his heart. "Caesar wishes me to tell you that he and Pompey have reached an agreement. They intend to settle this question of land reform once and for all."

Cicero gave me a quick look: it was exactly as he predicted. To Balbus he said: "On what terms is this to be settled?"

"The public lands in Campania will be divided between Pompey's de-mobbed legionnaires and those among the Roman poor who wish to farm. The whole scheme will be administered by a commission of twenty. Caesar hopes very much to have your support."

Cicero laughed in disbelief. "But this is almost precisely the bill he tried to bring in at the start of my consulship and which I opposed!"

"There will be one great difference," said Balbus with a grin. "This is between us, please. Yes?" His eyebrows danced in delight. He ran his small pink tongue over the edges of his large white teeth. "The official commission will be of twenty, but there will be an inner commission of just five magistrates who will make all the decisions. Caesar would be most honored—most honored indeed—if you would agree to join it."

That caught Cicero off his guard. "Would he indeed? And who would be the other four?"

"Apart from yourself, there would be Caesar, Pompey, one other still to be decided, and"—Balbus paused for effect, like a conjurer about to produce an exotic bird from an empty basket—"and Crassus."

Up to that point Cicero had been treating the Spaniard with a kind of friendly disdain—as a joke figure: one of those self-important go-betweens who often crop up in politics. Now he gazed at him in wonder. *"Crassus?"* he repeated. "But Crassus can barely abide to be in the same *city* as Pompey. How is he going to sit beside him on a committee of five?"

"Crassus is a dear friend of Caesar. And also Pompey is a dear friend of Caesar. So Caesar played the marriage broker, in the interests of the state."

"The interests of themselves more like! It will never work."

"It most certainly will work. The three have met and agreed it. And against such an alliance, nothing else in Rome will stand."

"If it has already been agreed, why am I needed?"

"As Father of the Nation, you have a unique authority."

"So I am to be brought in at the last moment to provide a covering of respectability?"

"Not at all, not at all. You would be a full partner, absolutely. Caesar authorizes me to say that no major decision in the running of the empire would be made without consulting you first."

"So this inner commission would, in effect, act as the executive government of the state?"

"Precisely."

"And how long would it exist?"

"I am sorry?"

"When will it dissolve?"

"It will never dissolve. It will be permanent."

"But this is outrageous! There is no precedent in our history for such a body. It would be the first step on the road to a dictatorship!"

"My dear Cicero, really!"

"Our annual elections would become meaningless. The consuls would be puppets, the Senate might as well not exist. This inner group would control the allocation of all land and taxes—"

"It would bring stability—"

"It would be a kleptocracy!"

"Are you actually *rejecting* Caesar's offer?"

"Tell your master I appreciate his consideration and I have no desire to be anything other than his friend, but this is not something I can countenance."

"Well," said Balbus, plainly shocked, "he will be disappointed—indeed he will be sorrowful—and so will Pompey and Crassus. Obviously they would like your assurance you will not oppose them."

"I am sure they would!"

"Yes, they would. They desire no unpleasantness. But if opposition is offered, you must understand, it will have to be met."

With great effort, Cicero controlled his temper. "You can tell them I have struggled for more than a year on Pompey's behalf to secure a fair settlement for his veterans—in the teeth, I might add, of strenuous opposition from Crassus. You can tell them I won't go back on that. But I want no part of any secret deal to establish a government by cabal. It would make a mockery of everything I have ever stood for in my public life. You can see yourself out, I think."

After Balbus had gone, Cicero sat silent in his library as I tiptoed around him arranging his correspondence into piles. "Imagine," he said eventually, "sending that Mediterranean carpet salesman to offer me a fifth share of the republic at a bargain price! Our Caesar fancies himself to be a great gentleman, but really he is the most awful vulgar crook."

"There may be trouble," I warned.

"Well then, let there be trouble. I am not afraid." But clearly he was afraid, and suddenly here it was again, that quality I admired the most about him—his reluctant, nervous resolution in the end to do the right thing. Because from this time on he must have known that his position in Rome would start to become untenable. After another long period of reflection, he said: "All the time that Spanish pimp was talking I kept thinking of what Calliope says to me in my poetic autobiography. Do you recall her lines?" He closed his eyes and recited:

> *Meantime the paths which you from earliest days did seek—*
> *Yes, and when Consul too, as mood and virtue called—*
> *These hold, and foster still your fame and good men's praise.*

"I have my faults, Tiro—you know them better than any man: no need to point them out—but I am not like Pompey, or Caesar, or Crassus. Whatever I've done, whatever mistakes I've made, I've done for my country; and whatever they do, they do for themselves, even if it means helping a traitor like Catilina." He gave a long sigh. He seemed almost surprised at his own principled stand. "Well, there it all goes, I suppose—a peaceful old age, reconciliation with my enemies, power, money, popularity with the mob . . ." He folded his arms and contemplated his feet.

"It's a lot to throw away," I said.

"It is a lot. Perhaps you should run after Balbus and tell him I've changed my mind."

"Shall I?" My tone was eager—I was desperate for a quiet life—but Cicero did not seem to hear me. He continued to brood on history and heroism, and after a while I went back to arranging his correspondence.

I had thought that "the Beast with Three Heads," as the triumvirate of Caesar, Pompey, and Crassus came to be known, might renew its offer, but Cicero heard no more. The following week Caesar became consul and quickly laid his land bill before the Senate. I was watching from the door with a large crowd of jostling spectators when he started asking the senior members for their opinions on the proposed law. He began with Pompey. Naturally the great man approved at once, and so did Crassus. Cicero was called on next, and with Caesar watching him keenly, and with many reservations, added his assent. Hortensius rejected it. Lucullus rejected it. Celer rejected it. And when eventually Caesar worked his way down the list of the great and the good and came to Cato, he too stated his disapproval. But instead of simply giving his view like the others and then sitting down, Cato continued with his denunciation, reaching far back into antiquity for precedents to argue that common land was held in trust for all the nation and was not to be parceled out by unscrupulous "here today and gone tomorrow" politicians for their own gain. After an hour it became clear he had no intention of resuming his place and was resorting to his old trick of talking out the day's business.

Caesar grew more and more irritated, tapping his foot impatiently. At last he stood. "We have heard enough from you," he said, interrupting Cato in midsentence. "Sit down, you damned sanctimonious windbag, and let someone else speak."

"Any senator has the right to talk for as long as he wishes," retorted Cato. "You should look up the laws of this house if you want to preside over it," and so saying, he carried on talking.

"Sit down!" bellowed Caesar.

"I shall not be intimidated by you," replied Cato, and he refused to yield the floor.

Have you ever seen a bird of prey tilt its head from one side to the other, as it detects a potential kill? Well, that was very much how Caesar looked at that instant. His avian profile bent first to the left and then to the right, and then he extended a long finger and beckoned to his chief lictor. He pointed to Cato. "Remove him," he rasped. The proximate lictor looked unwilling. "I said," repeated Caesar in a terrible voice, *"remove him!"*

The terrified fellow did not need telling twice. Gathering half a dozen of his colleagues, he set off down the aisle toward Cato, who continued to speak even as the lictors clambered over the benches to seize him. Two men took hold of each of his arms and dragged him toward the door, and another picked up all his Treasury accounts while the Senate watched in horror.

"What shall we do with him?" called the proximate lictor.

"Throw him in the Carcer," commanded Caesar, "and let him address his wisdom to the rats for a night or two."

As Cato was bundled from the chamber some senators began objecting to his treatment. The great Stoic was carried directly past me, unresisting but continuing to shout out some obscure point about the Scantian forests. Celer rose from the front bench and hurried out after him, closely trailed by Lucullus, and then by Caesar's own consular colleague, Marcus Bibulus. I should think thirty or forty senators must have joined this demonstration. Caesar came down off his dais and tried to intercept a few of those departing. I remember his catching hold of the arm of old Petreius, the commander who had defeated Catilina's army at Pisae. "Petreius!" he said. "You are a soldier like me. Why are you leaving?"

"Because," said Petreius, pulling himself free, "I would rather be in prison with Cato than here with you!"

"Go then!" Caesar shouted after him. "Go, all of you! But remember this: as long as I am consul the will of the people will not be frustrated by procedural tricks and ancient customs! This bill will be placed before the people, whether you gentlemen like it or not, and it will be voted on by the end of the month." He strode back up the aisle to his chair and glared around the chamber, defying anyone else to challenge his authority.

Cicero stayed uncomfortably in his place as the roll call resumed, and after the session was over he was intercepted outside the Senate House by Hortensius, who demanded to know in a reproachful voice why he had not walked out with the others. "Don't blame me for the mess you have landed us in," replied Cicero. "I warned you what would happen if you continued to treat Pompey with contempt." Nevertheless, I could tell he was embarrassed, and as soon as he could he escaped to his home. "I have contrived the worst of all worlds for myself," he complained to me as we climbed the hill. "I gain no benefit from supporting Caesar, yet I am denounced by his enemies as a turncoat. What a political genius I have turned out to be!"

In any normal year Caesar would have either failed with his bill or at the very least been obliged to compromise. His measure was opposed, first and foremost, by his fellow consul, Marcus Bibulus, a proud and irascible patrician whose misfortune throughout his career had been to hold office at the same time as Caesar, and who in consequence had been so entirely overshadowed that people usually forgot his name. "I am tired of playing Pollux to his Castor," he declared angrily, and he vowed that now that he was consul it would be different. Also ranged against Caesar were no fewer than three tribunes: Ancharius, Calvinus, and Fannius, each of whom wielded a veto. But Caesar was determined to get his way, whatever the price, and now began his deliberate destruction of the Roman constitution—an act for which I trust he will be cursed by humanity until the end of time.

First, he inserted into the bill a clause requiring every senator to swear an oath—on pain of death—that they would never try to repeal the law once it was on the statute book. Then he called a public assembly at which both Crassus and Pompey appeared. Cicero stood with the other senators and watched as Pompey, for the first time in his long career, was prevailed upon to issue a direct threat. "This bill is just," he declared. "My men have shed their blood for Roman soil, and it is only right that when they return they should be given a share of that soil as their reward."

"And what," Caesar asked him disingenuously, "if those who oppose this bill resort to violence?"

"If anyone comes with the sword I shall bring my shield," responded Pompey, before adding with menacing emphasis, "and I shall also bring a sword of my own."

The crowd roared in delight. Cicero could not bear to watch anymore. He turned and pushed his way past his fellow senators and out of the public assembly.

Pompey's words were effectively a call to arms. Within days Rome began to fill with his veterans. He paid for them to come from all over Italy, and he put them up in tents outside the city or in cheap lodgings around the town. They smuggled in illegal weapons which they kept concealed, in anticipation of the last day in January, when the law was to be voted upon by the people. Senators who were known to oppose the legislation were jeered at in the street and their houses stoned.

The man who organized this intimidation on behalf of the Three-Headed Beast was the tribune Publius Vatinius, who was known as the ugliest man in Rome. He had contracted scrofula as a boy and his face and neck were covered in pendulous purplish-blue lumps. His hair was sparse and his legs were rickety, so that he walked with his knees wide apart, as if he had just dismounted after a long ride or had soiled himself. Curiously, he also had great charm and did not care at all what anyone said about him: he would always cap an enemy's joke about his appearance with a funnier one of his own. Pompey's men were devoted to him, and so were the plebs. He called many public meetings in support of Caesar's law and on one occasion summoned the consul Bibulus to be cross-examined on the tribunes' platform. Bibulus was bad-tempered at the best of times, and Vatinius, knowing this, got his followers to lash together some wooden benches and run a bridge from the tribunes' platform straight up to the Carcer. When in due course under questioning Bibulus denounced the land bill in violent language—"You will not have your law this year, not even if you all want it!"—Vatinius arrested him and had him paraded along the bridge to the jail, like a prisoner of the pirates being made to walk the plank.

Cicero watched much of this from his garden, huddled in a cloak against the January chill. He felt very wretched and tried to keep out of it. Besides, he soon had more pressing problems of his own.

One morning in the midst of these tumultuous events I opened the door to find Antonius Hybrida waiting outside in the street. It was more than three years since I had last set eyes on him, and at first I did not recognize him. He had grown very stout on the meats and vines of Macedonia and even more florid, as if he had been coated in an extra layer of mottled red fat. When I took him into the library Cicero jumped as if he had seen a ghost, which in a sense he had, for this was his past come back to haunt him—and with a vengeance. At the start of his consulship, when the two men had concluded their deal, Cicero had given a written undertaking to Hybrida that if he was ever prosecuted, he would appear as his advocate: now his former colleague had come to collect on that promise. He had brought a slave with him who carried the indictment, and Hybrida passed it across to Cicero with a hand that trembled so violently

I thought he was having a seizure. Cicero took it over to the light to study it.

"When was this served?"

"Today."

"You realize what this is, don't you?"

"No. That's why I've brought the wretched thing straight to you. I never could get the hang of all this legal talk."

"This is a writ for treason." Cicero scanned the document with an expression of increasing puzzlement. "Odd. I would have thought they would have come after you for corruption."

"I say, Cicero, there's no chance of some wine, is there?"

"Just a moment. Let's just try to keep our heads clear for business for a little while longer. It says here that you lost an army in Histria."

"Only the infantry."

"Only the infantry!" Cicero laughed. "When was that?"

"A year ago."

"Who is the prosecutor? Has he been appointed yet?"

"Yes, he was sworn in yesterday. He's that protégé of yours—young Caelius Rufus."

The news came as a complete shock. That Rufus had become completely estranged from his former mentor was no secret. But that he should choose as his first significant foray into public life the prosecution of Cicero's consular colleague—that was an act of real treachery. Cicero actually sat down, he was so taken aback. He said, "I thought it was Pompey who was most determined to have you put on trial."

"He is."

"Then why is he letting Rufus cut his teeth on such an important case?"

"I don't know. What about that wine now?"

"Forget the damned wine for a minute." Cicero rolled up the writ and sat tapping it against the palm of his hand. "I don't like the sound of this. Rufus knows a lot about me. He could bring up all kinds of things." He threw it back into Hybrida's lap. "I think you should get someone else to defend you."

"But I want you! You're the best. We had an agreement, remember? I would give you a share of the money and you would shield me from prosecution."

"I agreed to defend you if ever you were charged with corruption. I never said anything about treason."

"That's not true. You're breaking your word."

"Look, Hybrida, I'll appear as a witness in your support, but this could be an ambush—laid by Caesar, probably, or Crassus—and I'd be a fool to walk straight into it."

Hybrida's eyes, though now buried deep in his flesh, were still very blue, like sapphires pressed into a lump of red clay. "People tell me you've come up in the world," he said. "Houses everywhere."

Cicero made a weary gesture. "Don't try to threaten me."

"All this," said Hybrida, pointing around the library. "Very nice. Do people know how you got the money to pay for it?"

"I warn you: I could as readily appear as a witness for the prosecution as for the defense."

But the threat sounded hollow and Cicero must have known it, for he suddenly wiped his hand across his face, as if trying to expunge some disturbing vision.

"I think you should join me in that cup of wine," said Hybrida with deep satisfaction. "Things always look better after a little drink."

On the evening before the vote on Caesar's land bill we could hear loud noises rising from the Forum—hammering and sawing, drunken singing, cheers, cries, the breaking of pots. At dawn a shroud of brown smoke hung over the area beyond the Temple of Castor where the voting was to take place.

Cicero dressed carefully and went down to the Forum, accompanied by two guards, two members of his household staff—myself and another secretary—and half a dozen clients who wished to be seen with him. All the streets and alleys leading to the voting ground were crammed with citizens. Many, when they recognized Cicero, stood out of the way to let him through. But at least an equal number deliberately blocked his path and had to be pushed out of the way by his guards. It was a struggle for us to make progress, and by the time we found a spot with a view of the temple steps, Caesar was already speaking. It was impossible to hear more than a few words. A great press of bodies, thousands of them, stretched between us and him. The majority looked to be old soldiers who had been there all night and who had lit fires to cook and keep themselves warm.

"These men are not attending this assembly," Cicero observed, "they are occupying it."

After some time we became aware of scuffling in the direction of the Via Sacra, on the opposite side of the crowd to where we were standing, and the word quickly went around that Bibulus had arrived with the three tribunes who were intending to veto the bill. It was a tremendously brave action on their part. All around us men began pulling out from beneath their clothing knives and even swords. Bibulus and his supporters were clearly having difficulty reaching the temple steps. We could not see them; we could follow their progress only by the origin of the shouts and the line of flailing fists. The tribunes were felled early on and carried away, but somehow Bibulus—and behind him Cato, who had been released from prison—did at last manage to reach his objective.

Shaking off the hands that were trying to restrain him, he climbed up onto the platform. His toga had been torn away, leaving his shoulder bare, and blood was running down his face. Caesar glanced at him briefly and carried on speaking. The fury of the crowd was deafening. Bibulus pointed to the heavens and made a cutting gesture across his throat. He repeated this several times until his meaning was obvious—as consul he had observed the heavens and was declaring that the auguries were unfavorable and no public business could be transacted. Still Caesar ignored him. And then two stout fellows climbed onto the platform carrying a big half barrel, of the sort used to collect rainwater. They hoisted it above Bibulus's head and tipped it over him. I guess the crowd must have been shitting into it all night, for it was brimful of noxious brown liquid and Bibulus was completely drenched. He tried to back away, skidded, his legs shot out from under him, and he fell heavily on his backside. For a moment he was too winded to move. But then he saw that another barrel was being carried up onto the platform and he scrambled away—I did not blame him—to the derisive laughter of thousands of citizens. He and his followers escaped from the Forum and eventually found sanctuary in the Temple of Jupiter the Protector—the same building from which Cicero by his oratory had driven Sergius Catilina.

Thus, in the most contemptible of circumstances, was carried onto the statute book Caesar's great land reform act, which awarded farms to twenty thousand of Pompey's veterans and afterward to those among the urban poor who could show they had more than three children. Cicero did not stay for the voting, which was a forgone conclusion, but slunk back to his house, where—such was his depression—he shunned all company, even Terentia's.

The following day Pompey's soldiers were back on the streets again. They had spent the night celebrating and now they had shifted their attention to the Senate House, crowding into the Forum, waiting to see if the Senate would dare to challenge the legality of what had happened. They left a narrow gangway through their ranks, wide enough for three or four men to walk abreast, and I found it intimidating to pass among them beside Cicero, even though the greetings they called out were friendly enough: "Come on, Cicero!" "Cicero—don't forget us!" Inside I had never seen a more dejected assembly. It was the first day of the new month, and Bibulus, who had a bandage around his forehead, was in the chair. He rose at once and demanded that the house condemn the disgraceful violence of the previous day. He further insisted that the law be declared invalid because the auguries had been unfavorable. But nobody was willing to take such a step—not with several hundred armed men outside. Confronted by their silence, Bibulus lost his temper.

"The government of this republic has become a travesty," he shouted, "and I shall take no further part in it! You have shown yourselves unworthy of the name of the Roman Senate. I shall not summon you to meet on any day when I am consul. Stay in your homes, gentlemen, as I shall do, and look into your souls, and ask yourselves if you have played your parts with honor."

Many of his listeners bowed their heads in shame. But Caesar, who was sitting between Pompey and Crassus and who had been listening to this with a faint smile, immediately rose and said, "Before Marcus Bibulus and his soul depart the chamber and this house is adjourned for a month, I would remind you gentlemen that this law obliges us all to swear an oath to uphold it. I therefore propose that we should go together now, as a body, to the Area Capitolina and take that oath, so that we may show publicly our unity with the people."

Cato jumped up. He had his arm in a sling. "This is an outrage!" he protested, no doubt stung to find the moral high ground temporarily taken from him by Bibulus. "I shan't sign your illegal law!"

"And nor shall I," echoed Celer, who had delayed setting out for Further Gaul in order to oppose Caesar. Several others called out the same—among them I noticed young Marcus Favonius, who was an acolyte of Cato's, and the ex-consul Lucius Gellius, who was well into his seventies.

"Then on your own heads be it," said Caesar with a shrug. "But remember: the penalty for refusing to comply with the law may be death."

I had not expected Cicero to speak, but very slowly he got to his feet, and it was a tribute to his authority that the whole chamber was immediately stilled. "I do not mind this man's law," he said, staring directly at Caesar, "although I deplore and condemn absolutely the methods by which he has forced it upon us. Nevertheless," he continued, turning to the rest of the chamber, "the law it is, and the people want it, and it requires us to take this oath. Therefore I say to Cato and to Celer, and to any other of my friends who contemplate making dead heroes of themselves: the people will not understand your action, for you cannot oppose illegality by illegality and hope to command respect. Hard times lie ahead, gentlemen, and although you may not feel you need Rome anymore, Rome has need of you. Preserve yourselves for the battles yet to come rather than sacrifice yourselves uselessly in one that is already lost."

It was a most effective speech, and when the senators filed out of the chamber almost all of them followed the Father of the Nation toward the Capitol, where the oath was to be sworn. Once Pompey's soldiers saw what the Senate intended to do, they cheered them loudly (Bibulus, Cato, and Celer went up later, when no one was looking). The sacred stone of Jupiter, which had fallen from the heavens many centuries earlier, was fetched out from the great temple and the senators lined up to place their hands on it and promise to obey the law. But Caesar, even though they were all doing what he wanted, was clearly troubled. I saw him go up to Cicero and take him to one side and speak to him with great seriousness. Afterward I asked Cicero what he had said. "He thanked me for my leadership in the Senate," Cicero replied, "but said he did not care for the tone of my remarks and hoped that I did not plan to cause him and Pompey and Crassus any trouble, for if I did he would be obliged to retaliate, and that would pain him. He had given me my chance, he said, to join his administration and I had rejected it and now I must bear the consequences. How do you like that for a piece of effrontery?" He swore roundly, which was unusual for him, and added, "Catulus was right: I should have beheaded that snake when I had the chance."

XVII

DESPITE HIS RESENTMENT, Cicero kept out of public life for the whole of the next month—an easy matter, as it turned out, as the Senate did not meet. Bibulus locked himself away in his house and refused to move, whereupon Caesar declared that he would govern through assemblies of the people, which Vatinius, as tribune, would summon on his behalf. Bibulus retaliated by letting it be known that he was perpetually on his roof, studying the auguries, and that they were consistently unfavorable—thus no official business could legally be transacted. Caesar responded by organizing noisy demonstrations in the street outside Bibulus's home and by continuing to pass his laws via the public assemblies regardless of what his colleague said. (Cicero wittily remarked that Rome seemed to be living under the joint consulship of Julius and Caesar.) It sounded legitimate when one put it that way—governing through the people: What could be fairer?—but really "the people" were the mob, controlled by Vatinius, and any who opposed what Caesar wanted were quickly silenced. Rome had become a dictatorship in all but name, and most respectable senators were appalled. But with Pompey and Crassus supporting Caesar, few dared speak out against him.

Cicero would have preferred to stay in his library and continue to avoid trouble. But in the midst of all this turmoil, toward the end of March, he was obliged to go down to the treason tribunal in the Forum to defend Hybrida. To his huge embarrassment the hearing was scheduled to be held in the comitium itself, just outside the Senate House. The curved steps of the rostra, rising like the seats of an amphitheater, had been cordoned off to form the court, and a large crowd was already clustered around it, eager to see what possible defense the famous orator could come up with for a client who was so manifestly guilty. "Well, Tiro," he said to me under his breath as I opened the document case and handed him his notes, "here is the proof that the gods have a sense of humor—that I should have to appear in this place, as the advocate for this rogue!" He turned and smiled at Hybrida, who was himself at that moment climbing laboriously up onto the platform. "Good morning to you, Hybrida. I trust you have avoided the wine at breakfast, as you promised? We shall need to keep clear wits about us today."

"Of course," replied Hybrida. But it was obvious from the way he stumbled on the steps, as well as from his slurred speech, that he had not been as abstemious as he claimed.

Apart from me and his usual team of clerks, Cicero had also brought along his son-in-law, Frugi, to act as his junior. Rufus, in contrast, appeared alone, and the moment I saw him striding across the comitium toward us, with only one secretary in attendance, I felt what little confidence I had evaporate. He was not yet twenty-three and had just completed a year in Africa on the staff of the governor. A youth had gone out; a man had returned, and I reckoned the contrast between this tall and sunburned prosecutor and the fleshy, ruined Hybrida was worth a dozen jury votes even before the trial had started. Nor did Cicero come well out of the comparison. He was twice the age of Rufus, and when he went over to his opponent to shake his hand and wish him good luck he appeared stooped and careworn. It was like a tableau on the wall of the baths: Juventus versus Senex, with sixty jurymen arrayed in tiers behind them and the praetor, the haughty Cornelius Lentulus Clodianus, seated between them in the judge's chair.

Rufus was called on first to lay out his case, and it was soon obvious that he had been a more attentive pupil in Cicero's chambers than any of us had realized. The burden of his prosecution was fivefold: first, that Hybrida had concentrated all his energies on extorting as much money as he could from Macedonia; second, that the revenue which should have gone to his army had been diverted into his own pocket; third, that he had neglected his duties as military commander during an expedition to the Black Sea to punish rebellious tribes; fourth, that he had demonstrated cowardice on the field of battle by fleeing from the enemy; and finally fifth, that as a result of his incompetence the empire had lost the region around Histria on the Lower Danube. He laid these charges with a mixture of moral outrage and malicious humor that was worthy of the master at his best. I remember in particular his graphic account of Hybrida's dereliction of duty on the morning of the battle against the rebels. "They found the man himself stretched out in a drunken stupor," he said, walking around the back of Hybrida and gesturing to him as if he were an exhibit, "snoring with all the force of his lungs, belching repeatedly, while the distinguished ladies who shared his quarters sprawled over every couch, and the other women were lying on the floor all around. Half dead with terror, and aware now of the enemy's approach, they tried to rouse up Hybrida; they shouted his name and tried in vain to hoist him up by his neck; some whispered blandishments in his ear; one or two gave him an energetic slap. He recognized all their voices and their touch and tried to put his arms around the neck of whoever was nearest to him. He was too much aroused to sleep, and too drunk to stay awake; dazed and half asleep, he was thrown around in the arms of his centurions and his concubines."

And all this, mark you, delivered without a note. It was murderous enough for the defense by itself. But the prosecution's main witnesses—including several of Hybrida's army commanders, a pair of his mistresses, and his quartermaster—were even worse. At the end of the day Cicero congratulated Rufus on his performance, and that evening he frankly advised his gloomy client to sell his property in Rome for the best price he could get and to convert his assets into jewelry or anything portable that he could carry into exile. "You must brace yourself for the worst."

I shall not describe all the details of the trial. Suffice it to say that even though Cicero tried every trick he knew to discredit Rufus's case, he barely left a scratch on it, and the witnesses Hybrida produced in his own defense were uniformly feeble—mostly his old drinking companions, or officials he had bribed to lie. By the end of the fourth day, the only question was: Should Cicero call on Hybrida to testify, in the hope at least of eliciting some sympathy from the jury; or should Hybrida cut his losses, leave Rome quietly before the verdict, and thus spare himself the humiliation of being jeered out of the city? Cicero took Hybrida into his library to make a decision.

"What do you think I should do?" asked Hybrida.

"I would leave," answered Cicero, who was desperate to put an end to his own ordeal. "It's possible your testimony could make matters even worse. Why give Rufus the satisfaction?"

Hybrida broke down. "What did I ever do to that young man that he should seek to destroy me in such a fashion?" Tears of self-pity trickled down his plump cheeks.

"Now, Hybrida, compose yourself and remember your illustrious ancestors." Cicero reached across and patted his knee. "Besides, it's nothing personal. He's simply a clever young man from the provinces, ambitious to rise in the world. In many ways, he reminds me of myself at that age. Unfortunately, you just happen to provide him with the best means of making his name—just as Verres did for me."

"Damn him," said Hybrida suddenly, straightening his back. "I shall testify."

"Are you certain you are up to it? Cross-examination can be a brutal business."

"You undertook to defend me," said Hybrida, at last showing some of his old spirit, "and I want to put up a defense, even if I lose."

"Very well," said Cicero, doing his best to disguise his disappointment. "In that case we must rehearse your testimony, and that will take us some time. Tiro, you had better bring the senator some wine."

"No," said Hybrida firmly. "No wine. Not tonight. I spent my entire career drunk; I shall at least end it sober."

And so we worked late into the night, practicing what Cicero would ask and how Hybrida would respond. After that, Cicero played the part of Rufus and threw the most unpleasant questions he could devise at his former colleague, and helped him frame the least incriminating answers. I was surprised by how quick on the uptake Hybrida was when he put his mind to it. The two men went to bed at midnight—Hybrida sleeping under Cicero's roof—and got up at dawn to resume their preparation. Afterward, as we were walking down to the court with Hybrida and his attendants ahead of us, Cicero said, "I begin to see why he rose so high in the first place. If only he could have shown such grip earlier, he would not now be facing ruin."

When we reached the comitium, Hybrida called out cheerfully, "This is how it was in the time of our joint consulship, Cicero, when we stood shoulder to shoulder to save the republic!" The two men then went up onto the platform where the court was waiting, and when Cicero announced that he would be calling Hybrida as his final witness, a stir of anticipation ran through the jury. I saw Rufus sit forward on his bench and whisper something in the ear of his secretary, and the man picked up his stylus.

Hybrida was quickly sworn in and Cicero took him through the questions they had rehearsed, beginning with his military experience under Sulla a quarter of a century before, and dwelling especially on his loyalty to the state at the time of Catilina's conspiracy.

"You laid aside considerations of past friendship, did you not," asked Cicero, "to take command of the Senate's legions that finally crushed the traitor?"

"I did."

"And you sent back the monster's head to the Senate as proof of your actions?"

"I did."

"Mark that well, gentlemen," said Cicero, addressing the jury. "Is that the action of a traitor? Young Rufus over there supported Catilina—let him deny it—and then fled from Rome to avoid sharing in his fate. Yet now he has the nerve to come creeping back into the city and accuse of treason the very man who rescued us from ruin!" He turned back to Hybrida. "After crushing Catilina, you relieved me of the burden of governing Macedonia, so that I could devote myself to extinguishing the last embers of the conspiracy?"

"I did."

And so it went on, with Cicero leading his client through his testimony like a father leading a child by the hand. He prompted him to describe how he had raised revenue in Macedonia through entirely legal means, accounted for every penny, raised and equipped two legions, and led them on a hazardous expedition eastward through the mountains to the Black Sea. He painted a terrifying picture of warlike tribes—Getians, Bastarns, Histrians—harrying the Roman column as it marched along the Danube valley.

"The prosecution alleges that when you heard there was a large enemy force ahead, you split your force in two, taking the cavalry with you to safety and leaving the infantry undefended. Is that true?"

"Not at all."

"You were in fact bravely pursuing the Histrian army, is that correct?"

"That's right."

"And while you were away, the Bastarn forces crossed the Danube and attacked the infantry from the rear?"

"True."

"And there was nothing you could do?"

"I am afraid there was not." Hybrida lowered his head and wiped his eyes, as Cicero had instructed him.

"You must have lost many friends and comrades at the hands of the barbarians."

"I did. A great many."

After a long pause, during which there was complete silence in the court, Cicero turned to the jury. "The fortunes of war, gentlemen," he said, "can be cruel and capricious. But that is not the same as treason."

As he resumed his seat there was prolonged applause, not only from the crowd but among the jury, and for the first time I dared to hope that Cicero's skill as an advocate might once again have saved the day. Rufus smiled to himself and took a sip of wine and water before getting to his feet. He had an athlete's way of loosening his shoulders by linking his hands behind his head and rotating his upper torso from side to side. Watching him do it then, just before he started his cross-examination, the years seemed to fall away and suddenly I remembered how Cicero used to send him running errands across the city and tease him for the looseness of his clothes and the length of his hair. And I recalled how the boy would steal money from me and stay out all night drinking and gambling, and yet how hard it was to feel angry with him for long. What pattern of ambition's twisting paths had brought us each to this place?

Rufus sauntered over to the witness stand. He was entirely without nerves. He might have been meeting a friend at a tavern. "Do you have a good memory, Antonius Hybrida?"

"I do."

"Well then, I expect you remember a slave of yours who was murdered on the eve of your consulship."

A look of great mystification passed across Hybrida's face, and he glanced across in puzzlement toward Cicero. "I'm not sure that I do. One's had so many slaves over the years—"

"But you must remember this slave?" persisted Rufus. "A Smyrnan? Twelve years old or thereabouts? His body was dumped in the Tiber. Cicero was there when his remains were discovered. His throat had been cut and his intestines removed."

There was a gasp of horror around the court and I felt my mouth go dry, not only at the memory of that poor lad but at the realization of where this chain of questioning might lead. Cicero saw it, too. He jumped up in alarm and appealed to the praetor, "This is irrelevant, surely? The death of a slave more than four years ago can have nothing to do with a lost battle on the shores of the Black Sea."

"Let the prosecutor ask his question," ruled Clodianus, and then added philosophically: "I have found in life that all sorts of things are often linked."

Hybrida was still looking hopelessly at Cicero. "I believe perhaps I do remember something of the sort."

"I should hope so," responded Rufus. "It's not every day that a human sacrifice is performed in one's presence! Even for you, I would have thought, with all your abominations, that must have been a rarity!"

"I know nothing about any human sacrifice," muttered Hybrida.

"Catilina did the killing and then required you and others present to swear an oath."

"Did he?" Hybrida screwed up his face as if he were trying to remember some long-forgotten acquaintance. "No, I don't think so. No, you are mistaken."

"Yes he did. You swore an oath on the blood of that slaughtered child to murder your own colleague as consul—the man who now sits beside you as your advocate!"

These words produced a fresh sensation, and when the cries had died away, Cicero got up. "Really, this is a pity," he said, with a regretful shake of his head, "a great pity, because my young friend was not doing a bad job as prosecutor up to this moment—he was my pupil once, gentlemen, so actually I flatter myself as well as him by conceding it. Unfortunately, now he has gone and ruined his own case with an insane allegation. I fear I shall have to take him back to the classroom."

"I know it is true, Cicero," retorted Rufus, smiling even more broadly, "because you told me about it yourself."

For the barest flicker of an instant, Cicero hesitated, and I saw to my horror that he had forgotten his conversation with Rufus all those years ago. "You ungrateful wretch," he spluttered. "I did no such thing."

"In the first week of your consulship," said Rufus, "two days after the Latin Festival you called me to your house and asked if Catilina had ever talked in my presence of killing you. You told me that Hybrida had confessed to swearing an oath with Catilina on a murdered boy to do precisely that. You asked me to keep my ears open."

"That is a complete lie!" shouted Cicero, but his bluster did little to dispel the effect of Rufus's cool and precise recollection.

"This is the man you took into your confidence as consul," continued Rufus with deadly calmness, pointing at Hybrida. "This is the man you foisted on the people of Macedonia as their governor—a man you knew to have taken part in a bestial murder, and who had desired your own death. And yet this is the man you defend today. Why?"

"I don't have to answer your questions, boy."

Rufus strolled over to the jury. "That is the question, gentlemen: Why does Cicero, of all men, who made his reputation attacking corrupt provincial governors, now destroy his good name by defending this one?"

Once again Cicero stretched out a hand to the praetor. "Clodianus, I am asking you, for heaven's sake, to control your court. This is supposed to be a cross-examination of my client, not a speech about me."

"That is true, Rufus," said the praetor. "Your questions must relate to the case in hand."

"But they do. My case is that Cicero and Hybrida came to an agreement."

Cicero said, "There is no proof of that."

"Yes there is," retorted Rufus. "Less than a year after you dispatched Hybrida to the long-suffering people of Macedonia, you bought yourself a new house. There," said Rufus. He gestured to it, gleaming on the Palatine in the spring sunshine, and the jurymen all turned their heads to look. "One much like it sold soon afterward for fourteen million sesterces. *Fourteen million!* Ask yourselves, gentlemen: Where did Cicero, who prided himself on his humble origins, acquire such a fortune, if not from the man he both blackmailed and protected, Antonius Hybrida? Is that not the truth," he demanded, turning back to the accused, "that you diverted part of the money you extorted from your province to your partner in crime in Rome?"

"No, no," protested Hybrida. "I may have sent Cicero a gift or two from time to time, but that is all." (This was the explanation they had agreed on the previous evening, in case Rufus had evidence of money passing between them.)

"*A gift?*" repeated Rufus. With exaggerated slowness he looked once more at Cicero's house, raising his hand to protect his eyes from the sun. A woman with a parasol was strolling along the terrace, and I realized it must be Terentia. "That is quite a gift!"

Cicero sat very still. He watched Rufus closely. Several members of the jury were shaking their heads. From the audience in the comitium came the sound of jeering.

"Gentlemen," said Rufus, "I believe I have made my case. I have shown how Hybrida lost a whole region from our empire by his treason-able negligence. I have proved his cowardice and incompetence. I have revealed how money that should have gone to the army went instead into his own coffers. The ghosts of his legionnaires, abandoned by their chief and cruelly murdered by the barbarians, cry out to us for justice. This monster should never have been permitted to hold such a high position, and would not have done so without the collusion of his consular colleague. His career is soaked in blood and depravity—the murder of that child is but a small part of it. It is too late to bring the dead back to life, but let us at least remove this man and his stench from Rome. Let us send him into exile tonight."

Rufus sat down to prolonged applause. The praetor looked somewhat surprised and asked if that was the conclusion of the prosecution's case. Rufus signaled that it was.

"Well, well. I thought we had at least another day to go," said Clodianus. He turned to Cicero. "Do you wish to make your closing speech for the defense immediately, or would you prefer the court to adjourn overnight so that you can prepare your remarks?"

Cicero was looking very flushed, and I knew at once it would be a grave mistake for him to speak before he had had a chance to calm down. I was sitting in the space set aside for the clerks, just below the podium, and I actually rose and went up the couple of steps to plead with him to accept the adjournment. But he waved me aside before I could utter a word. There was a curious light in his eyes. I am not sure he even saw me.

"Such lies," he said with utter disgust. He rose to his feet. "Such lies are best squashed dead at once, like cockroaches, and not left alive to breed overnight."

The area in front of the court had been full before, but now people began to stream into the comitium from all across the Forum. Cicero on his feet was one of the great sights of Rome, and no one wanted to miss it. Not one of the three Heads of the Beast was present, but here and there in the crowd I could see their surrogates: Balbus for Caesar, Afranius for Pompey, Arrius for Crassus. I did not have time to look for anyone else: Cicero had started speaking and I had to take down his words.

"I must confess," he said, "I had not much relished the prospect of coming down to this court to defend my old friend and colleague Antonius Hybrida, for such obligations as these are numerous and rest heavily on a man who has been in public life as long as I have. Yes, Rufus: 'obligations'—that is a word you do not understand, otherwise you would not have addressed me in such a fashion! But now I welcome this duty—I relish it, I am glad for it—because it enables me to say something that has needed to be said for years. Yes, I made common cause with Hybrida, gentlemen—I do not deny it. I sought him out. I overlooked the differences in our styles of life and views. I overlooked many things, in fact, because I had no choice. If I was to save this republic I needed allies, and could not be too particular about where they came from.

"Cast your minds back to that terrible time. Do you think that Catilina acted alone? Do you think that one man, however energetic and inspired in his depravity, could have proceeded as far as Catilina did—could have brought this city and our republic to the edge of destruction—if he had not had powerful supporters? And I do not mean that ragbag of bankrupt noblemen, gamblers, drunkards, perfumed youths, and layabouts who flocked around him—among whom, incidentally, our ambitious young prosecutor was once numbered.

"No, I mean men of substance in our state—men who saw in Catilina an opportunity to advance their own dangerous and deluded ambitions. These men were not justly executed on the orders of the Senate on the fifth day of December, nor did they die on the field of battle at the hands of the legions commanded by Hybrida. They were not sent into exile as a result of my testimony. They walk free today. No, more than that: *they control this republic!*"

Up to this point in his speech, Cicero had been heard in silence. But now a great many people drew in their breath, or turned to their neighbors to express their astonishment. Balbus had started making notes on a wax tablet. I thought to myself, *Does he realize what he is doing?* and I risked a glance at Cicero. He barely seemed conscious of where he was— oblivious to the court, to his audience, to me, to political calculation: he was intent only on getting out his words.

"These men made Catilina what he was. He would have been nothing without them. They gave him their votes, their money, their assistance, and their protection. They spoke up for him in the Senate and in the law courts and in the popular assemblies. They shielded him and they nurtured him and they even supplied him with the weapons he needed to slaughter the government." (Here my notes record more loud exclamations from the audience.) "Until this moment, gentlemen, I did not realize the extent to which there were two conspiracies I had to fight. There was the conspiracy which I destroyed, and then there was the conspiracy behind that conspiracy—and that inner one prospers still. Look around you, Romans, and you can see how well it prospers! Rule by secret conclave and by terror on the streets. Rule by illegal methods and by bribery on a massive scale—dear gods, you accuse Hybrida of corruption? He is as guileless and as helpless as a baby by comparison with Caesar and his friends!

"This trial itself is the proof. Do you think that Rufus is the sole author of this prosecution? This neophyte who has barely grown his first beard? What nonsense! These attacks—this so-called evidence—all of it is designed to discredit not just Hybrida alone but me—my reputation, my consulship, and the policies I pursued. The men behind Rufus seek to destroy the traditions of our republic for their own wicked ends, and to accomplish that—forgive me if I flatter myself: it is not the first time, I know—to achieve that aim they need to destroy me first.

"Well, gentlemen, here in this court, on this day, at this defining hour, you have a chance for immortal glory. That Hybrida made mistakes I do not doubt. That he has indulged himself more than was wise for him, I sadly concede. But look beyond his sins and you will see the same man who stood with me against the monster who threatened this city four years ago. Without his support, I would have been struck down by an assassin very early in my term. He did not desert me then, and I shall not abandon him now. Acquit him by your votes, I pray you; keep him here in Rome, and by the grace of our ancient gods we shall once again restore the light of liberty to this city of our forefathers!"

Thus spoke Cicero, but when he sat down there was very little applause—mostly just a buzz of amazement around the court at what he had said. Those who agreed with him were too frightened to be seen to support him. Those who disagreed with him were too cowed by the impact of his rhetoric to protest. The rest—the majority, I should say—were simply bewildered. I looked for Balbus in the crowd but he had slipped away. I went up to Cicero with my notebook and congratulated him on the force of his remarks.

"Did you get it all down?" he asked, and when I replied that I had, he told me to copy out the speech as soon as we got home and hide it in a safe place. "I expect a version is on its way to Caesar even now," he added. "I saw that reptile Balbus writing almost as quickly as I could speak. We must make sure we have an accurate transcript in case this is raised in the Senate."

I could not stay to talk to him further, as the praetor was ordering that the jury should be balloted at once. I glanced at the sky. It was the middle of the day; the sun was high and warm. I returned to my place and watched the urn as it was passed from hand to hand and filled with tokens. Cicero and Hybrida sat watching as well, side by side, too nervous to speak, and I thought of all the other trials I had sat through and how they always ended in exactly this way, with this horrible period of waiting. Eventually the clerks completed their tally and the result was passed up to the praetor. He stood and we all followed suit.

"The question before the court is whether Gaius Antonius Hybrida is to be condemned for treason in connection with his governorship of the province of Macedonia. There voted in favor of condemnation forty-seven, and in favor of acquittal twelve." There was a great cheer from the crowd. Hybrida bowed his head. The praetor waited until the sounds had died away. "Gaius Antonius Hybrida is therefore stripped of all rights of property and citizenship in perpetuity, and from midnight is to be denied fire and water anywhere within the lands, cities, and colonies of Italy, and any who seek to assist him shall be subject to the same punishment. This court is adjourned."

Cicero did not lose many cases, but on the rare occasions that he did he was usually scrupulous in congratulating his opponents. Not this time. When Rufus came over to commiserate, Cicero pointedly turned his back on him, and I was pleased to see that the young rogue was left with his hand extended in midair, looking a fool. Eventually he shrugged and turned away. As for Hybrida, he was philosophical. "Well," he said to Cicero in my hearing, as he was preparing to be led away by the lictors, "you warned me the way the wind was blowing, and thankfully I have a little money put by to see me through my old age. Besides, I am told that the southern coast of Gaul looks very like the Bay of Naples. So do not concern yourself with my fate, Cicero. After that speech it is your own you ought to worry about."

It must have been about two hours later—certainly no more—that the door to Cicero's house was suddenly thrown open and Metellus Celer appeared in a state of great agitation demanding to see my master. Cicero was dining with Terentia, and I was still transcribing his speech. But I could see it was supremely urgent, so I took him through at once.

Cicero was reclining on a couch describing the end of Hybrida's trial when Celer burst into the room and interrupted him.

"What did you say in court about Caesar this morning?"

"Good day to you, Celer. I told a few truths, that's all. Will you join us?"

"Well, they must have been pretty dangerous truths, for Gaius is exacting a mighty revenge."

"Is he really?" replied Cicero, with an attempt at sangfroid. "And what is to be my punishment?"

"He is in the Senate House as we speak, arranging for that swine of a brother-in-law of mine to become a plebeian!"

Cicero sat up in such alarm he knocked his glass over. "No, no," he said, "that cannot be right. Caesar would never lift a finger to help Clodius—not after what Clodius did to his wife."

"You are wrong. He is doing it right now."

"How do you know?"

"My own darling wife just took great pleasure in telling me."

"But how is it possible?"

"You forget Caesar is the chief priest. He has summoned an emergency meeting of the curia to approve an adoption."

Terentia said, "Is that legal?"

"Since when did legality matter," asked Cicero bitterly, "when Caesar is involved?" He started rubbing his forehead very hard, as if he could somehow magic forth a solution. "What about getting Bibulus to pronounce the auguries unfavorable?"

"Caesar's thought of that. He has Pompey with him—"

"Pompey?" Cicero looked stunned. "This gets worse every moment!"

"Pompey is an augur. He's observed the skies and declared all's well."

"But you're an augur. Can't you overrule him?"

"I can try. At the very least we ought to get down there."

Cicero needed no further urging. Still wearing his slippers, he hurried out of the house after Celer while I panted along at their backs with their attendants. The streets were quiet: Caesar had moved so quickly no word of what was happening had filtered through to the people. Unfortunately, by the time we had sprinted across the Forum and thrown open the doors of the Senate House the ceremony was just finishing—and what a shameful scene it was that met our eyes! Caesar was on the dais at the far end of the chamber, dressed in his robes as chief priest and surrounded by his lictors. Pompey was beside him, absurd in his augural cap and carrying a divining wand. Several other pontiffs were also standing around, among them Crassus, who had been co-opted into the college at Caesar's behest to replace Catulus. Clustered together on the wooden benches, like penned sheep, was the curia, the thirty elderly grayheads who were the chiefs of the tribes of Rome. And finally to complete the picture was the golden-curled Clodius, kneeling in the aisle next to another man. Everyone turned at the noise of our entrance, and never have I forgotten the smirk of triumph on Clodius's face when he realized Cicero was watching—it was a look of almost childish devilment—although it was quickly replaced by an expression of terror as his brother-in-law strode toward him, followed by Cicero.

"What the in the name of fucking Jupiter is going on here?" shouted Celer.

"Metellus Celer," responded Caesar in a firm voice, "this is a religious ceremony. Do not profane it."

"A religious ceremony! With Rome's profaner in chief kneeling here—the man who fucked your own wife!" He aimed a kick at Clodius, who scrambled away from him toward Caesar's feet. "And who is this boy?" he demanded, looming over the other cowering man. "Let's see who's joined the family!" He hauled him to his feet by the scruff of his neck and turned him around to show us—a shivering pimply youth of twenty or so.

"Show some respect to my adopted father," said Clodius, who, despite his fear, could not stop himself laughing.

"You disgusting—" Celer dropped the youth and returned his attention to Clodius, drawing back his huge fist to strike him, but Cicero caught his arm. "No, Celer. Don't give them an excuse to arrest you."

"Wise advice," said Caesar.

After a moment, Celer reluctantly lowered his hand. "So your father is younger than you are? What a farce this is!"

Clodius smirked. "He was the best that could be found at short notice."

Precisely what the tribal elders—none of whom was under fifty—must have made of this spectacle I cannot imagine. Many were old friends of Cicero. We learned later they had been turfed from their homes and places of business by Caesar's henchmen, frog-marched to the Senate House, and more or less ordered to approve Clodius's adoption.

"Have we finished here yet?" asked Pompey. He not only looked ridiculous in his augural outfit but plainly was embarrassed.

"Yes, we have finished," said Caesar. He held out a hand as if bestowing a blessing at a wedding. "Publius Clodius Pulcher, by the powers of my office as pontifex maximus I declare you are now the adopted son of Publius Fonteius, and will be entered into the state's records as a plebeian. Your change of status having immediate effect, you may therefore contest the elections for tribune if you wish. Thank you, gentlemen." Caesar nodded their dismissal, the curia rose to their feet, and the first consul and chief priest of Rome lifted his robes a fraction and stepped down from his dais, his afternoon's work done. He moved past Clodius with his head averted in distaste, as one might pass a carcass in the street. "You should have heeded my warning," he hissed at Cicero as he went by. "Now look what you've forced me to do." He processed with his lictors toward the door, followed by Pompey, who still could not bring himself to meet Cicero's eyes; only Crassus permitted himself a slight smile.

"Come along, Father," said Clodius, putting his arm around Fonteius's shoulders, "let me help you home." He gave another of his unnerving, girlish laughs, and after a bow to Cicero and his brother-in-law they joined the end of the cortege.

"*You* may have finished, Caesar," Celer called after them, "but I have not! I am the governor of Further Gaul, remember, and I command legions, whereas you have none! *I* have not even started yet!"

His voice was loud. It must have carried halfway across the Forum. Caesar, however, passed from the chamber and into the daylight without giving any sign he had heard. Once he and the rest had gone and we were alone, Cicero slumped heavily onto the nearest bench and put his head in his hands. Up in the rafters the pigeons flapped and cooed—to this day I cannot hear those filthy birds without thinking of the old Senate House— while the sounds of the street outside seemed strangely disconnected from me: unearthly, as if I were already in prison.

"No despairing, Cicero," said Celer briskly after some time had passed. "He's not even a tribune yet—and won't be, if I can help it."

"Crassus I can beat," replied Cicero. "Pompey I can outwit. Even Caesar I have managed to hold in check in the past. But all three combined, and with Clodius as their weapon?" He shook his head wearily. "How am I to live?"

• • •

That evening Cicero went to see Pompey, taking me with him, partly to show that this was a business call and not in any way social, and also I suspect to bolster his nerve. We found the great man drinking in his bachelor den with his old army comrade and fellow Picenian Aulus Gabinius. They were examining the model of Pompey's theater complex when we were shown in, and Gabinius was gushing with enthusiasm. He was the man who, as an ambitious tribune, had proposed the laws that secured Pompey his unprecedented military powers, and he had duly been rewarded with a legateship under Pompey in the East. He had been away for several years, during which time—unknown to him—Caesar had been conducting an affair with his wife, the blowsy Lollia (at the same time as Caesar had been sleeping with Pompey's wife, come to think of it). But now Gabinius was back in Rome—just as ambitious, a hundred times as rich, and determined to become consul.

"Cicero, my dear fellow," said Pompey, rising to embrace him, "will you join us for some wine?"

"I shall not," said Cicero stiffly.

"Oh dear," said Pompey to Gabinius, "do you hear his tone? He's come to upbraid me for that business this afternoon I was telling you about," and, turning back to Cicero, he said, "Do I really need to explain to you that it was all Caesar's idea? I tried to talk him out of it."

"Really? Then why didn't you?"

"He was of the view—and I must say I have to agree with him—that the tone of your remarks in court today was grossly offensive to us and merited a public rebuke of some kind."

"So you open the way for Clodius to become a tribune—knowing that his stated intention once he gains that office is to bring a prosecution against me?"

"I would not have gone that far, but Caesar was set on it. Are you sure I cannot tempt you to some wine?"

"For many years," said Cicero, with a terrible calmness, "I have supported you in everything you wanted. I have asked for nothing in return except your friendship, which has been more precious to me than anything in my public life. And now at last you have shown your true regard for me to all the world—by helping to give my deadliest enemy the weapon he needs to destroy me!"

Pompey's lip quivered and his oyster eyes filled with tears. "Cicero, I am appalled. How can you say such things? I would never stand aside and see you destroyed. My position is not an easy one, you know—trying to exert a calming influence on Caesar is a sacrifice I make on behalf of the republic every day of my life!"

"But not today, apparently."

"He felt his dignity and authority were threatened by what you said."

"Not half as threatened as they will be if I reveal all I know about this Three-Headed Beast and its dealings with Catilina!"

Gabinius broke in. "I don't think you should speak to Pompey the Great in that tone."

"No, no, Aulus," said Pompey sadly, "what Cicero says is right. Caesar has gone too far. The gods know I have tried to do as much as I can to moderate his actions behind the scenes. When Cato was flung in prison, I had him released at once. And poor Bibulus would have suffered a much worse fate than having a barrel of shit poured over him if it hadn't been for me. But on this occasion I failed. I was bound to one day. I'm afraid Caesar is just so . . . *relentless*." He sighed and picked up one of the toy temples from his model theater and contemplated it thoughtfully. "Perhaps the time is coming," he said, "when I shall have to break with him." He gave Cicero a crafty look—his eyes had quickly dried, I noticed. "What do you think of that?"

"I think it cannot come soon enough."

"You may be right." Pompey took the temple between his fat thumb and forefinger and replaced it with surprising delicacy in its former position. "Do you know what his new scheme is?"

"No."

"He wishes to be awarded a military command."

"I'm sure he does! But the Senate has already decreed there will be no provinces for the consuls this year."

"The Senate has, yes. But Caesar doesn't care about the Senate. He is going to get Vatinius to propose a law in the popular assembly."

"What?"

"A law granting him not just one province, but two—Nearer Gaul and Bithynia—with the authority to raise an army of two legions. And it won't just be a one-year appointment, either—he wants five years."

"But the award of provinces has always been decided by the Senate, not the people," protested Cicero. "And *five years*! This will smash our constitution to pieces."

"He says not. Caesar says to me, 'What is wrong with trusting the people?' "

"It isn't the people! It's a mob, controlled by Vatinius."

"Well," said Pompey, "now perhaps you can understand why I agreed to watch the skies for him this afternoon. Of course I should have refused. But I have to keep a larger picture in view. Someone must control him."

Cicero put his head in his hands in despair. Eventually he said, "May I tell some of my friends your reasons for going along with him today? Otherwise they will think I no longer have your support."

"If you must—in the strictest confidence. And you may tell them—with Aulus here as a witness—that no harm will befall Marcus Tullius Cicero as long as Pompey the Great still breathes in Rome."

Cicero was very silent and thoughtful as we walked home. Instead of going straight to his library he took several turns around his garden in the darkness, while I sat at a table nearby with a lamp and quickly wrote down as much of Pompey's conversation as I could remember. When I had finished, Cicero told me to come with him, and we went next door to see Metellus Celer.

I was worried Clodia might be present, but there was no sign of her. Instead Celer was sitting in his dining room alone, lit by a solitary candelabrum, chewing morosely on a cold chicken leg with a jug of wine beside him. Cicero refused a drink for the second time that evening and asked me to read out what Pompey had just said. Celer was predictably outraged.

"So I shall have Further Gaul—which is where the fighting will have to be done—and he Nearer, yet each of us is to have two legions?"

"Yes, except that he will hold his province for an entire lustrum, while you will have to give up yours by the end of the year. You may be sure if there's any glory to be had Caesar will have it all."

Celer let out a bellow of rage and shook his fists. "He *must* be stopped! I don't care if there *are* three of them running this republic. There are hundreds of us!"

Cicero sat down on the couch beside him. "We don't need to beat all three," he said quietly. "Just one will do. You heard what Pompey said. If we can somehow take care of Caesar, I don't think he'll do much about it. All Pompey cares about is his own dignity."

"And what about Crassus?"

"Once Caesar is off the scene he and Pompey won't be allies for another hour—they can't abide each other. No: Caesar is the stone that holds this arch together. Remove him and the structure falls."

"So what do you propose we should do?"

"Arrest him."

Celer gave Cicero a sharp look. "But Caesar's person is inviolable, not once but twice—first as chief priest and then as consul."

"You really think he'd worry about the law if he were in our place? When his every act as consul has been illegal? We either stop him now, while there's time, or we leave it until he's picked us all off one by one and there's nobody left to oppose him."

I was amazed by what I was hearing. Until that afternoon I am sure that Cicero would never have entertained for a moment the thought of such a desperate action. It was a measure of the chasm he now saw opening up before him that he should actually have given voice to it.

"How would this be done?" asked Celer.

"You're the one with an army. How many men do you have?"

"I have two cohorts camped outside the city, preparing to march with me to Gaul."

"How loyal are they?"

"To me? Absolutely."

"Would they be willing to seize Caesar from his residence after dark and hold him somewhere?"

"No question, if I gave the order. But surely it would be better just to kill him?"

"No," said Cicero. "There would have to be a trial. On that I insist. I want no 'accidents.' We would have to put through a bill to set up a special tribunal to try him for his illegal actions. I'd lead for the prosecution. Everything would have to be open and clear."

Celer looked dubious. "As long as you agree there could only be one verdict."

"And Pompey would have to approve—don't imagine for a moment you could go back to your old habit of opposing him on everything he wants. We would have to guarantee his men could keep their farms, confirm his Eastern settlements—maybe even give him a second consulship."

"That's a lot to swallow. Wouldn't we just be swapping one tyrant for another?"

"No," said Cicero with great force. "Caesar is of a different category of man altogether. Pompey merely wants to rule the world. Caesar longs to smash it to pieces and remake it in his own image. And there's something else." He paused, searching for the words.

"What? He's cleverer than Pompey, I'll give him that."

"Oh yes, yes, of course, he's a hundred times cleverer. No, it's not that—it's more—I don't know—there's a kind of divine recklessness about him—a contempt, if you like, for the world itself—as if he thinks it's all a joke. Anyway, this—whatever it is: this quality—it makes him hard to stop."

"That's all very philosophical, but I'll tell you how we stop him. It's easy. We put a sword through his throat and you'll find he'll die the same as any man. But we have to do it to him as he would do it to us—fast, and ruthlessly, and when he least expects it."

"When would you suggest?"

"Tomorrow night."

"No, that's too soon," said Cicero. "We can't do this entirely alone. We shall have to bring in others."

"Then Caesar is bound to get to hear of it. You know how many informants he has."

"I'm only talking about half a dozen men, if that. All reliable."

"Who?"

"Lucullus. Hortensius. Isauricus—he still carries a lot of weight, and he's never forgiven Caesar for becoming chief priest. Possibly Cato."

"Cato!" scoffed Celer. "We'll still be discussing the ethics of the matter long after Caesar has died of old age!"

"I'm not so sure. Cato was the loudest in his clamor for action against Catilina's gang. And the people respect him almost as much as they love Caesar."

A floorboard creaked, and Celer put a warning finger to his lips. He called out, "Who's there?" The door opened. It was Clodia. I wondered how long she had been listening and how much she might have heard. The same thought had obviously occurred to Celer. "What are you doing?" he demanded.

"I heard voices. I was on my way out."

"Out?" he said suspiciously. "At this time? What are you going out for?"

"Why do you think? To see my brother, the plebeian. To celebrate!"

Celer cursed and grabbed the wine jug and hurled it at her. But she had already gone, and it smashed harmlessly against the wall. I held my breath to see if she would respond, but then I heard the front door open and close.

"How soon can you get the others together?" asked Celer. "Tomorrow?"

"Better make it the day after," replied Cicero, who was plainly still marveling at this exchange, "otherwise it will seem as if there's some emergency, and Caesar may get wind of it. Let us meet at my house, at close of public business, the day after tomorrow."

The following morning Cicero wrote out the invitations himself and had me go around the city delivering them in person into the hands of the recipients. All four were mightily intrigued, especially because by then everyone had heard of Clodius's transfer to the plebs. Lucullus actually said to me, with one of his bleak supercilious smiles, "What is it your master wishes to plot with me? A murder?" But each agreed to come— even Cato, who was not normally very sociable—for they were all alarmed by what was happening. Vatinius's bill proposing that Caesar be given two provinces and an army for five years had just been posted up in the Forum. The patricians were enraged, the populists jubilant, the mood in the city stormy. Hortensius took me aside and told me that if I wanted to know how bad things were becoming, I should go and look at the tomb of the Sergii, which stands at the crossroads just outside the Capena Gate. This was where the head of Catilina had been interred. I went and found it piled high with fresh flowers.

I decided not to tell Cicero about these floral tributes: he was tense enough as it was. On the day of the meeting he shut himself away in his library and did not emerge until the appointed hour approached. Then he bathed, dressed in clean clothes, and fussed about the arrangement of the chairs in the tablinum. "The truth is I am too much of a lawyer for this kind of thing," he confided in me. I murmured my assent, but actually I

don't think it was the legality that was troubling him—it was his squeamishness again.

Cato was the first to arrive, in his usual malodorous rig of unwashed
toga and bare feet. His nose twitched with distaste at the luxury of the
house, but he readily consented to take some wine, for he was a heavy
drinker: it was his only vice. Hortensius came next, full of sympathy for
Cicero's deepening worries about Clodius; he assumed this was what the
meeting had been called to discuss. Lucullus and Isauricus, the two old
generals, arrived together. "This is quite a conspiracy," said Isauricus,
glancing at the others. "Is anyone else coming?"

"Metellus Celer," replied Cicero.

"Good," said Isauricus. "I approve of him. I reckon he's our best hope
in the times to come. At least the fellow knows how to fight."

The five sat in a circle. I was the only other person in the room. I went
around with a jug of wine, and then retreated to the corner. Cicero had
ordered me not to take notes but to try to remember as much as I could
and write it up afterward. I had attended so many meetings with these
men over the years that no one any longer even noticed me.

"May we know what this is about?" asked Cato.

"I think we can guess," said Lucullus.

Cicero said, "I suggest we wait until Celer arrives. He is the one with
the most to contribute."

The group sat in silence until at last Cicero could stand it no longer
and told me to go next door and find out why Celer was delayed.

I do not pretend to possess powers of divination, but even as I approached Celer's house I sensed that something was wrong. The exterior
was too quiet; there was none of the normal coming and going. Inside,
there was that awful hush that always accompanies catastrophe. Celer's
steward, whom I knew tolerably well, met me with tears in his eyes and
told me that his master had been seized by terrible pains the previous day,
and that although the doctors were unable to agree what was wrong with
him, they concurred it could well be fatal. I felt sick myself at the news
and begged him to go to Celer and ask if he had any message for Cicero,
who was waiting at home to see him. The steward went away and came
back with a single word, which apparently was all that Celer had been
able to gasp: "Come!"

I ran back to Cicero's house, and when I went into the tablinum naturally the senators all turned to look at me, assuming I was Celer. There were groans of impatience when I gestured to Cicero that I needed to speak with him in private.

"What are you playing at?" he whispered angrily when I got him into the atrium. His nerves were clearly stretched to the breaking point. "Where's Celer?"

"Gravely ill," I replied. "Perhaps dying. He wants you to come at once."

Poor Cicero. That must have been a blow. He seemed literally to stagger back from it. Without exchanging a word we went straight to Celer's house, where the steward was waiting for us, and he led us toward the private apartments. I shall never forget those gloomy passageways, with their dim candles and the sickly smell of incense being burned to cover the still more powerful odors of vomit and bodily decay. So many doctors had been called to attend upon Celer they blocked the door to his bedchamber, talking quietly in Greek. We had to force our way inside. It was stiflingly hot and so dark Cicero was obliged to pick up a lamp and take it over to where the senator lay. He was naked apart from the bandages which marked where he had been bled. Dozens of leeches were attached to his arms and the insides of his legs. His mouth was black and frothy: I learned afterward he had been fed charcoal as part of some crackpot cure. It had been necessary to tie him to his bed because of the force of his convulsions.

Cicero knelt beside him. "Celer," he said in a voice of great tenderness, "my dear friend, who has done this to you?"

Hearing Cicero's voice, Celer turned his face to him and tried to speak, but all that emerged was an unintelligible gurgle of black bubbles. He surrendered after that. He closed his eyes and by all accounts he never opened them again.

Cicero lingered for a little while and asked the doctors various questions. They disagreed about everything, in the way of medical men, but on one point they were unanimous: none had ever seen a healthy body succumb to a disease more quickly.

"A disease?" said Cicero incredulously. "Surely he has been poisoned?"

Poisoned? The doctors recoiled at the very word. No, no—this was a ravaging sickness, a virulent distemper, the result of a snakebite: anything except poisoning, which was simply too appalling a possibility to be discussed. Besides, who would want to poison the noble Celer?

Cicero left them to it. That Celer had been murdered he never doubted, although whether Caesar had a hand in it, or Clodius, or both, he never discovered, and the truth remains a mystery to this day. There was, however, no question in his mind as to who had administered the fatal dose, for as we left that house of death we met coming in through the front door Clodia, accompanied by—of all people—young Caelius Rufus, fresh from his triumph over Hybrida. And although they both hastily assumed grave expressions, one could tell they had been laughing a moment earlier; and although they quickly stood apart, it was clear that they were lovers.

XVIII

CELER'S BODY WAS burned on a funeral pyre set up in the Forum as a mark of national mourning. His face in death was tranquil, that coal-black mouth as clean and pink as a rosebud. Caesar and all the Senate attended. Clodia looked beautiful in mourning and shed many a widow's tear. Afterward his ashes were interred in the family mausoleum, and Cicero sank into a deep gloom. He sensed that any hopes of stopping Caesar had died with Celer.

Seeing her husband's depression, Terentia insisted on a change of scene. Cicero had acquired a new property out on the coast at Antium, a day and a half's journey from Rome, and that was where the family went for the start of the spring recess. On the way we passed close to Solonium, where the Claudian family had long owned a great country estate. Behind its high ocher walls Clodius and Clodia were said to be closeted together in a family conference with their two brothers and two sisters. "Six of them all together," said Cicero, as we rattled past in our carriage, "like a litter of puppies—the litter from hell! Imagine them in there, tumbling around in bed with one another and plotting my destruction." I did not contradict him, although it was hard to imagine those two stiff-necked older brothers, Appius and Gaius, getting up to any such mischief.

When we reached Antium, the weather was inclement, with squalls of rain blowing in off the sea. Cicero sat out on the terrace regardless of the conditions, gazing over the thundering waves at the gray horizon, trying to find a way out of his predicament, and eventually after a day or two of that, with his head much clearer, he retreated to his library. "What are the only weapons I possess, Tiro?" he asked me, and then he answered his own question. "These," he said, gesturing to his books. "Words. Caesar and Pompey have their soldiers, Crassus his wealth, Clodius his bullies on the street. My only legions are my words. By language I rose, and by language I shall survive."

Accordingly we began work on what he called *The Secret History of My Consulship*—the fourth and final version of his autobiography, and by far the truest, a book which he intended to be the basis of his defense if he was put on trial, which has never been published, and which I have drawn on to write this memoir. In it, he set out all the facts about Caesar's relationship with Catilina; about the way in which Crassus had defended Catilina and financed him and finally betrayed him; and how Pompey had used his lieutenants to try to prolong and worsen the crisis so that he could use it as an excuse to come home with his army. It took us two weeks to compile, and I made an extra copy as we went along. When we had finished I wrapped each roll of the original in a linen sheet and then in oilcloth and put them in an amphora which we sealed tight with wax. Then Cicero and I rose early one morning, while the rest of the household was asleep, and took it into the nearby woods and buried it between a hornbeam and an ash. "If anything happens to me," Cicero instructed, "dig it up and give it to Terentia and tell her to use it as she thinks fit."

As far as he could see he had only one real hope left of avoiding being put on trial: that Pompey's disenchantment with Caesar would widen into an open breach. Given their characters, it was not an unreasonable expectation, and he was constantly on the lookout for any scrap of promising news. All letters from Rome were eagerly opened. All acquaintances on their way south to the Bay of Naples were closely questioned. There were bits of intelligence that seemed encouraging. As a gesture to Cicero, Pompey had asked Clodius to undertake a mission to Armenia rather than stand for tribune. Clodius had refused. Pompey had thereupon taken offense and fallen out with Clodius. Caesar had sided with Pompey. Clodius had argued with Caesar, even to the extent of threatening, when he became tribune, to rescind the triumvirate's legislation. Caesar had lost his temper with Clodius. Pompey had rebuked Caesar for landing them with this ungovernable patrician-cum-plebeian in the first place. Some even whispered that the two great men had stopped speaking. Cicero was delighted. "Mark my words, Tiro: all regimes, however popular or powerful, pass away eventually." There were signs this one might be collapsing already. And perhaps it would have done if Caesar had not taken a dramatic step to preserve it.

The blow fell on the first day of May. It was in the evening, after dinner, and Cicero had just nodded off on his couch when a letter arrived from Atticus. I should explain that we were in the villa in Formiae by this time, and that Atticus had returned briefly to his house in Rome, whence he was sending Cicero more or less daily all the intelligence he could discover. Of course it was no substitute for actually seeing Atticus, but nevertheless it was agreed between them that he should stay there, for he was of more service picking up gossip than counting waves on the seashore. Terentia was doing her embroidery in a corner of the room, all was peaceful, and I debated whether or not to wake Cicero. But he had already heard the noise of the messenger, and his hand rose imperiously from the couch. "Give it me," he said. I handed him the letter and went out onto the terrace. I could see a tiny light on a boat out at sea, and I was wondering what manner of fish had to be caught in darkness or if this was the setting of traps for lobsters or whatnot—I am a terrible landlubber— when I heard a great groan from the couch behind me.

Terentia looked up in consternation. "Whatever is it?" she asked.

I went inside. Cicero had the letter crumpled on his chest. "Pompey has married again," he said in a hollow voice. *"He has married Caesar's daughter!"*

Against the workings of history he could deploy many weapons: logic, cunning, irony, wit, oratory, experience, his profound knowledge of law and men. But against the alchemy of two naked bodies in a bed in the darkness, and against all the complex longings and attachments and commitments which such intimacy might arouse, he had nothing with which to fight. Strange as it may seem, the prospect of a marriage between the two had never occurred to him. Pompey was nearly forty-seven. Julia was fourteen. Only Caesar, raged Cicero, could have prostituted his child in a manner so cynical and repulsive and depraved. He railed against it for an hour or two—"Imagine it: *him,* and *her: together!*"—and then, when he had calmed down, wrote a letter of congratulations to the bride and groom, and as soon as he returned to Rome went to see them with a gift. I carried it in for him in a sandalwood box, and after he had delivered his prepared speech about the celestial radiance of their union I placed it in his hands.

"Now who is in charge of receiving the presents in this household?" he asked with a smile, and he took half a step toward Pompey, who naturally reached out to take it before Cicero abruptly turned away and gave the box to Julia with a bow. She laughed, and so after a moment or two did Pompey, although he wagged his finger at Cicero and called him a mischievous fellow. I must say that Julia had grown up to be a most charming young woman—pretty, graceful, and obviously kind, and yet the peculiar thing was that one could see her father in every line of her face and gesture of her body. It was as if all the gaiety had been sucked out of him and blown into her. And the other amazing thing was that she was very clearly in love with Pompey. She opened the box and took out Cicero's gift—it was an exquisite silver dish, if I remember rightly, with their entwined initials engraved upon it—and when she showed it to Pompey she held his hand and stroked his cheek. He beamed and kissed her on her forehead. Cicero regarded the happy couple with the fixed smile of a dinner guest who has just swallowed something very unpleasant but does not want to reveal the fact to his hosts.

"You must come and see us again soon," said Julia. "I wish to know you better. My father says you are the cleverest man in Rome."

"He's very gracious, but alas I must yield that prize to him."

Pompey insisted on showing Cicero to the door himself. "Isn't she delightful?"

"Very."

"I tell you frankly, Cicero, I am happier with her than with any woman I have ever known. She makes me feel quite twenty years younger. Or even thirty."

"At this rate you will soon be in your infancy," joked Cicero. "Congratulations again." We had reached the atrium—to which, I noticed, the cloak of Alexander the Great and the pearl-encrusted head of Pompey had now been banished. "And I assume relations with your new father-in-law are equally close?"

"Oh, Caesar's not such a bad fellow once you know how to handle him."

"You are entirely reconciled?"

"We were never estranged."

"And what about me?" blurted out Cicero, unable to conceal his true feelings any longer. He sounded like a discarded lover. "What am I supposed to do about this monster Clodius you two have created to torment me?"

"My dear friend, don't worry about him for an instant! He talks a lot but it doesn't mean anything. If ever it really did come to a serious fight he would have to step over my dead body to get at you."

"Really?"

"Absolutely."

"Is that a firm commitment?"

Pompey looked hurt. "Have I ever let you down?"

• • •

Soon afterward the marriage bore its first fruit. Pompey rose in the Senate and read out a motion: that in view of the grievous loss, etc., etc., of Metellus Celer, the province he had been allotted before his death—Further Gaul—should be transferred to Julius Caesar, who had already been granted Nearer Gaul by a vote of the people; that this unified command would henceforth make it easier to crush any future rebellions; and that in view of the unsettled nature of the region, Caesar should be given an additional legion, bringing the total strength at his disposal to five.

Caesar, who was in the chair, asked if there were any objections. He swiveled his head left and right a couple of times, checking if anyone wished to speak, and was just about to move on to "any other business" when Lucullus got to his feet. The old patrician general was nearing sixty by this time—disdainful, feline, but still magnificent in his way.

"Forgive me, Caesar," he said, "but will you also retain the province of Bithynia?"

"I will."

"So you will now have three provinces?"

"I will."

"But Bithynia is a thousand miles from Gaul!" Lucullus gave a mocking laugh and looked around the chamber for others to share his amusement. Nobody joined in.

Caesar said quietly, "We all know our geography, Lucullus, thank you. Now does anyone else wish to speak?"

But Lucullus refused to stop. "And your term of office," he persisted, "will it still be for five years?"

"It will. The people have decreed it. Why? Do you wish to oppose the will of the people?"

"But this is absurd!" cried Lucullus. "Gentlemen, we cannot allow a single individual, however able, to control twenty-two thousand men on the very borders of Italy for *five years.* What if he were to move against Rome?"

Cicero was one of a number of senators who shifted uncomfortably on their hard wooden bench. But not one of them—not even Cato—wanted to pick a fight on this issue, for there was not a chance of winning. Lucullus, plainly surprised by the lack of support, sat down grumpily and folded his arms.

Pompey said, "I fear our friend Lucullus has spent too long with his fish. Things have changed in Rome of late."

"Clearly," muttered Lucullus, loud enough for all to hear, *"and not for the better."*

At that Caesar rose. His expression was fixed and cold: almost inhuman, like a Thracian mask. "I think Lucius Lucullus has forgotten that he commanded more legions than I in his time, and for longer than five years, and yet still the job of defeating Mithridates had to be finished off by my gallant son-in-law." The supporters of the Beast with Three Heads gave a loud roar of approval. "I think Lucius Lucullus's period as commander in chief might well bear investigation, perhaps by a special court. I think Lucius Lucullus's finances would certainly bear scrutiny—the people would be interested to know where he obtained his great wealth. And I think in the meantime that Lucius Lucullus should apologize to this house for his insulting insinuation."

Lucullus glanced around. No one returned his gaze. To be hauled before a special court at his age, and with so much to explain, would be unbearable. Swallowing hard, he stood. "If my words have offended you, Caesar—" he began.

"On his knees!" bellowed Caesar.

Lucullus looked suddenly very old and baffled. "What?" he asked.

"He should apologize *on his knees*!" repeated Caesar.

I could not bear to watch, and yet at the same time it was impossible to tear one's eyes away, for the ending of a great career is an awesome thing to behold, like the felling of a mighty tree. For a moment or two longer Lucullus remained upright. Then, very creakily, with joints stiff from years of military campaigning, he got down first on one knee and then on the other, and bowed his head to Caesar while the Senate looked on in silence.

A few days later Cicero had to dip into his purse again to buy another wedding present, this time for Caesar.

Everyone had assumed that if Caesar remarried it would be to Servilia, who had been his mistress for several years, and whose husband, the former consul Junius Silanus, had recently died. Indeed, around this time, such a marriage was rumored actually to have taken place when Servilia attended a dinner wearing a pearl which she announced the consul had given her and which was worth sixty thousand gold pieces. But no: the very next week, Caesar took as his bride the daughter of Lucius Calpurnius Piso—a long, thin, plain girl of twenty, of whom no one had ever heard. After some deliberation, Cicero decided not to send his wedding gift to Caesar by courier but to hand it to him personally. Again it was a dish of silver with engraved initials; again it was in a sandalwood box; and again I was charged with looking after it. I duly waited with it outside the Senate until the session was over, and when Caesar and Cicero strolled out together I took it over to them.

"This is just a small gift from Terentia and me to you and Calpurnia," said Cicero, taking it out of my hands and giving it to Caesar, "to wish you both a long and happy marriage."

"Thank you," said Caesar, "that is thoughtful of you," and without looking at it he passed the box to one of his attendants. "Perhaps," he added, "while you're in this generous mood, you could also give us your vote."

"My vote?"

"Yes, my wife's father is standing for the consulship."

"Ah," said Cicero, a look of comprehension spreading across his face, "now it all makes sense. Frankly, I had wondered why you were marrying Calpurnia."

"Rather than Servilia?" Caesar smiled and shrugged. "That's politics."

"And how is Servilia?"

"She understands." Caesar seemed about to move on, then checked himself, as if he had just remembered something. "Incidentally, what are you planning to do about our mutual friend Clodius?"

"I never give him a moment's thought," replied Cicero. (This was a lie, of course: in truth he thought of little else.)

"That's wise," nodded Caesar. "He isn't worth the waste of one's mental processes. Still, I wonder what he will do when he becomes tribune."

"I expect he will bring a prosecution against me."

"That shouldn't worry you. You could beat him in any court in Rome."

"He must know that, too. Therefore I expect he will choose ground more favorable to him. A special court of some kind—one that ensures I am judged by the whole of the Roman people on the Field of Mars."

"That would be harder for you."

"I have armed myself with the facts and stand ready to defend myself.

Besides, I seem to remember I beat you on the Field of Mars when you brought a charge against Rabirius."

"Don't bring that up! I still bear the scars!" Caesar's sharp and mirthless laughter stopped as abruptly as it had started. "Listen, Cicero, if he does become a threat, never forget that I would stand ready to help you."

Obviously taken aback by the offer, Cicero inquired, "Really? How?"

"With this combined command I shall be heavily involved in military campaigning. I'll need a legate to handle civil administration in Gaul. You would fill the post ideally. You wouldn't actually have to spend much time there—you could come back to Rome as often as you liked. But if I put you on my staff it would give you immunity from prosecution. Think about it. Now, if you will excuse me?" And with a polite nod he moved off to deal with the dozen or so other senators who were clamoring for a word with him.

Cicero watched him go with amazement. "That's a handsome offer," he said, "very handsome indeed. We must send him a letter saying we'll bear it in mind, just so we have it on the record."

That was what we did. And when Caesar replied the same day confirming the legateship was Cicero's if he wanted it, Cicero for the first time began to feel more confident.

That year's elections were held later than usual, thanks to Bibulus's repeated intercessions that the auguries were unfavorable. But the evil day could not be postponed forever, and in October Clodius achieved his heart's ambition and topped the poll for tribune of the plebs. Cicero spared himself the torment of going down to the Field of Mars to listen to the result. In any case he did not need to: we could hear the roars of excitement without leaving the house.

On the tenth day of December Clodius was sworn in as tribune. Again Cicero kept to his library. But the cheers were such that we could not escape them even with the doors closed and the windows shuttered, and presently word came up from the Forum that Clodius had already posted details of his proposed legislation on the walls of the Temple of Saturn. "He's not wasting his time," said Cicero with a grim expression. "Very well, Tiro. Go down and find out what fate Little Miss Beauty has in mind for us."

My state of mind as I descended the steps to the Forum was, as you can imagine, one of great trepidation. The meeting was over, but small groups of people stood around discussing what they had just heard. There was an excited atmosphere, as if they had all witnessed some spectacular event and needed to share their impressions with one another. I went over to the Temple of Saturn and had to shoulder my way through the crowds to see what all the fuss was about. Four bills had been pinned up. I took out my stylus and wax tablet. One was designed to stop any consul in the future from behaving like Bibulus, by restricting the ancient right to proclaim unfavorable auguries. The second reduced the censors' powers to remove senators. The third allowed neighborhood clubs to resume meeting (such associations had been banned by the Senate six years previously for rowdy behavior). And the fourth—the one which obviously had got everyone talking—entitled every citizen, for the first time in Rome's history, to a free monthly dole of bread.

I copied down the gist of each bill and hurried home to Cicero to report on their contents. He had his secret consular history unrolled on the table in front of him and was ready to begin work on his defense. When I told him what Clodius was proposing he sat back in his chair, thoroughly mystified. "So, no word about me at all?"

"None."

"Don't tell me he's planning to leave me alone after all his threatening talk."

"Perhaps he's not as confident as he pretends."

"Read me those bills again." I did as he asked and he listened with his eyes half closed, concentrating on every word. "This is all very popular stuff," he observed when I had finished. "Free bread for life. A party on every street corner. No wonder it has gone down well." He thought for a while. "Do you know what he expects me to do, Tiro?"

"No."

"He expects me to oppose these laws, merely because he is the one who has put them forward. He wants me to, in fact. Then he can turn around and say, 'Look at Cicero, the friend of the rich! He thinks it is fine for senators to eat well and make merry, but woe betide the poor if they ask for a bit of bread and a chance to relax after their hard day's work!' You see? He plans to lure me into opposing him, then drag me before the plebs on the Field of Mars and accuse me of acting like a king. Well damn him! I shan't give him the satisfaction. I'll show him I can play a cleverer game than that."

I am still not sure, if Cicero had set his mind to it, how much of Clodius's legislation he could have stopped. He had a tame tribune, Ninnius Quadratus, ready to use a veto on his behalf, and plenty of respectable citizens in the Senate and among the equestrians would have come to his aid. These were the men who believed that free bread would make the poor dependent on the state and rot their morals. It would cost the Treasury one hundred million sesterces a year and make the state itself dependent on revenues from abroad. They also thought that neighborhood clubs fostered immoral pursuits, and that the organizing of communal activities was best left to the official religious cults. In all this they may well have been right. But Cicero was more flexible. He recognized that times had changed. "Pompey has flooded this republic with easy money," he told me, "that's what they forget. A hundred million is nothing to him. Either the poor will have their share or they will have our heads—and in Clodius they have found a leader."

Cicero therefore decided not to raise his voice against Clodius's bills, and for one last brief moment—like the final flare of a guttering candle—he enjoyed something of his old popularity. He told Quadratus to do nothing, refused himself to condemn Clodius's plans, and was cheered in the street when he announced he would not challenge the proposed laws. On the first day of January, when the Senate met under the new consuls, he was awarded third place in the order of speaking after Pompey and Crassus—a signal honor. And when the presiding consul, Caesar's father-in-law, Calpurnius Piso, called on him to give his opinions, he used the occasion to make one of his great appeals for unity and reconciliation. "I shall not oppose, or obstruct, or seek to frustrate," he said, "the laws that have been placed before us by our colleague Clodius, and I pray that out of difficult times, a new concord between Senate and people may be forged."

These words were met with a great ovation, and when the time came for Clodius to respond he made an equally fulsome reply. "It is not so long ago that Marcus Cicero and I enjoyed the friendliest of relations," he said with tears of sincere emotion in his eyes. "I believe that mischief was made between us by a certain person close to him"—this was generally taken as a reference to Terentia's rumored jealousy of Clodia—"and I applaud his statesmanlike attitude to the people's just demands."

Two days later, when Clodius's bills became law, the hills and valleys of Rome echoed with excitement as the neighborhood clubs met to cele-

brate their restoration. It was not a spontaneous demonstration but carefully organized by Clodius's man of affairs, a scribe named Cloelius. Poor
men, freedmen, and slaves alike chased pigs through the streets and sacrificed them without any priests to supervise the rites and roasted the meat
on the street corners. They did not stop their revels as night fell but lit
torches and braziers and continued to sing and dance. (It was unseasonably warm, and that always swells a crowd.) They drank until they vomited. They fornicated in the alleyways. They formed gangs and fought one
another till blood ran in the gutters. In the smarter neighborhoods, especially on the Palatine, the well-to-do cowered in their houses and waited
for these Dionysian convulsions to pass. Cicero watched from his terrace,
and I could see he was already wondering if he had made a mistake. But
when Quadratus came to him and asked if he should gather some of the
other magistrates from around the city and try to disperse the crowds, he
replied that it was too late—the water was well and truly boiling now and
the lid would no longer fit back on the cooking pot.

Around midnight the racket began to subside. The streets became
quiet, apart from some loud snoring in odd parts of the Forum which
rose from the darkness like the noise of bullfrogs in a swamp. I went
gratefully to my bed. But an hour or two later something woke me. The
sound was very distant and in the daytime one would never have paid it
any attention: it was only the hour and the surrounding silence that made
it ominous. It was the noise of hammers being swung against brick.

I took a lamp and climbed the steps to the ground floor, unlocked the
back door, and went out onto the terrace. The city was still very dark,
the air mild. I could see nothing. But the noise, which was coming from
the eastern end of the Forum, was more distinct outside, and when I
listened hard I could pick out individual hammers being wielded—
sometimes isolated, more often falling in a kind of peal, metal on stone,
that rang out across the sleeping city. It was so continuous I reckoned there
must be at least a dozen teams laboring away. Occasionally there were
shouts, and suddenly the sound of rubble being tipped. That was when I
realized this was not building work I was hearing; it was demolition.

Cicero rose soon after dawn, as was his habit, and as usual I went to
him in his library to see if he needed anything. "Did you hear that hammering noise in the night?" he asked me. I replied that I had. He cocked
his head, listening. "Yet now it's silent. I wonder what mischief has been
happening. Let's go down and see what the rogues have been up to."

It was too early even for Cicero's clients to have begun assembling, and the street was empty. We went down to the Forum accompanied by one of his burly attendants, and at first all seemed normal, apart from the heaps of rubbish left after the previous night's carousing and the odd body sprawled in a drunken stupor. But as we approached the Temple of Castor, Cicero stopped and cried out in horror. It had been quite hideously disfigured. The steps leading up to the pillared facade had been taken down so that anyone wishing to enter the building was now confronted by a ragged wall, twice the height of a man. The rubble had been formed into a parapet, and the only access to the temple was via a couple of ladders, each of which was guarded by men with sledgehammers. The newly exposed red brickwork was ugly and raw and naked, like an amputation. Various large placards were nailed to it. One read: "P. CLODIUS PROMISES THE PEOPLE FREE BREAD." A second proclaimed: "DEATH TO THE ENEMIES OF THE ROMAN PEOPLE." A third said: "BREAD & LIBERTY." There were other, more detailed notices posted lower down at eye level that looked from a distance to be draft bills, and three or four dozen citizens were milling around reading them. Up above their heads on the podium of the temple was a line of men, motionless, like figures in a frieze. As we came closer I recognized various of Clodius's lieutenants— Cloelius, Patina, Scato, Pola Servius: a lot of the rogues who had run with Catilina back in the old times. Farther along I glimpsed Mark Antony and Caelius Rufus, and then Clodius himself.

"This is a monstrosity," said Cicero, shaking with anger, "a sacrilege, an outrage—"

Suddenly I realized that if we could see the men who had done this, they most assuredly could see us. I touched Cicero on the arm. "Why don't you wait here, Senator," I suggested, "and let me go and see what those bills say? It might be unwise for you to stray too close. They are a rough-looking lot."

I made my way quickly across to the wall, beneath the gaze of Clodius and his associates. On either side men with heavily tattooed arms and close-cropped heads leaned on their sledgehammers and stared at me belligerently. I quickly scanned the notices on the wall. As I had guessed, they were new bills, a pair of them in fact. One was concerned with the allocation of consular provinces for the following year and awarded Macedonia to Calpurnius Piso, and Syria (I think it was) to Aulus Gabinius. The other bill was very short, no more than a line: "It shall be a capital offense to offer fire and water to any person who has put Roman citizens to death without a trial."

I stared at it stupidly, not grasping its significance at first. That it was directed against Cicero was obvious enough. But it did not name him. It seemed more designed to frighten and harass his supporters than to threaten him directly. But then, like a great turning inside-out of my heart, I saw the devilish cunning in it, and felt the gorge rise into my mouth, so that I had to swallow the bitter taste to stop myself from vomiting. I stepped back from that wall as if the jaws of Hades had opened before me, and I kept stumbling backward, unable to take my eyes from the words, increasing the distance and willing them to disappear. When I glanced up I saw Clodius very plainly looking down at me, a smile on his face, enjoying every moment, and then I turned and hurried back to Cicero.

He saw at once in my expression that it was bad. "Well?" he said anxiously. "What is it?"

"Clodius has published a bill about Catilina."

"Aimed at me?"

"Yes."

"It cannot surely be as bad as your face suggests! What in the name of heaven does it say about me?"

"It doesn't even mention you."

"Then what kind of bill is it?"

"It makes it a capital offense to offer fire or water to anyone who has put Roman citizens to death without a trial."

His mouth dropped open. He was always much quicker on the uptake than I. He understood the implications at once. "And that is *all*? One line?"

"That is all." I bowed my head. "I am very sorry."

Cicero grabbed my arm. "So the actual crime will be to help keep me alive? They won't even give me a *trial*?"

Suddenly his gaze flickered past me, over my shoulder to the disfigured temple. I turned and saw Clodius waving at him—a slow and mocking gesture, as if he were waving goodbye to someone on a ship, leaving for a long journey. At the same time some of the tribune's henchmen started to climb down the ladders. "I think we should get out of here," I said. Cicero did not react. His mouth was working but only a faint croak was emerging. It was as if he were being strangled. I looked back at the temple again. The men were on the ground now and moving toward us. "Senator," I said firmly, "we really must get you out of here." I gestured to his bodyguard to take his other arm, and together we propelled him out of the Forum and back up the steps toward the Palatine. The gang of ruffians pursued us, and pieces of rubble from the temple started to fly past our ears. A sharp piece of brick caught Cicero on the back of his head and he gave a cry. The cascade of missiles did not stop until we were halfway up the hill.

When we reached the safety of the house we found it full of his morning callers. Not knowing what had happened, they moved at once toward Cicero as they always did, with their wretched letters and their petitions and their humble beseeching faces. Cicero gazed at them, blank with shock, and bleakly told me to send them away—"all away"—then stumbled upstairs to his bedroom.

Once the clients had been thrown out I gave orders for the front entrance to be locked and barred, and then I prowled around the empty public rooms, wondering what I should do. I kept waiting for Cicero to come down and give me orders, but the hours passed and there was no sign of him. Eventually Terentia sought me out. She was twisting a handkerchief between her hands, winding it tightly around her ringless bony fingers. She demanded to know what was going on. I replied that I was not entirely sure.

"Don't lie to me, slave! Why is your master collapsed on his bed and refusing to move?"

I quailed before her rage. "He has—he has—made an error," I stammered.

"An error? What manner of error?"

I hesitated. I did not know where to begin. There were so many errors: they stretched back like islands behind us, an archipelago of folly. Or perhaps "errors" was the wrong word. Perhaps it was more accurate to call them consequences: the ineluctable consequences of a deed done by a great man for honorable motives—is that not, after all, how the Greeks define tragedy?

I said, "He has allowed his enemies to take control of the center of Rome."

"And they are doing what, exactly?"

"They are preparing legislation which will make him an outlaw."

"Well then, he must pull himself together and fight them!"

"It is very dangerous for him to venture out of the house."

Even as I spoke I could hear the mob in the street outside chanting "Death to the tyrant!" Terentia heard them, too. As she listened I could see the fear tauten her face. "So what are we to do?"

"We could perhaps wait for nightfall and leave Rome," I suggested. She stared at me and, frightened though she was, just for a moment I saw in her dark eyes a glint of that ancestor of hers—the one who had commanded a cohort against Hannibal. "At the very least," I went on hurriedly, "we should restore all the precautions we took while Catilina was alive."

"Send out messages to his colleagues," she ordered. "Ask Hortensius, Lucullus—any you can think—to come immediately. Fetch Atticus. Arrange everything else necessary to secure our safety. And summon his doctors."

I did as she ordered. The shutters were fastened. The Sextus brothers hurried over. I even summoned the guard dog, Sargon, from his retirement on a farm just outside the city. By early afternoon the house had begun to fill with friendly faces, although most arrived shaken by the experience of passing through the chanting crowd. Only the doctors refused to come: they had heard about Clodius's bill and they claimed to fear prosecution.

Atticus went up to see Cicero and came down tearful. "He has his face turned to the wall," he told me. "He refuses to speak."

"They have robbed him of his voice," I replied, "and what is Cicero without his voice?"

A meeting was convened in the library to discuss what could be done: Terentia, Atticus, Hortensius, Lucullus, Cato. I forget who else was present. I sat there silent, stunned, in the room in which I had spent so many hours with Cicero. I listened to the others and wondered how they could hold a conversation about his future without his presence. It was as if he were already dead. The whole animating spark of that household—the wit, the quick intelligence, the guiding ambition—seemed to have fled out of the door, as it does when someone passes from the earth. Terentia had the coolest head present. "Is there any chance that this law won't pass?" she asked Hortensius at one point.

"Very little," he said. "Clodius has copied Caesar's tactics to perfection, and clearly means to use the mob to control the popular assembly."

"What about the Senate?"

"We can adopt a resolution in his support. I'm sure we shall—I'll propose it myself—but Clodius will take no notice. Now if Pompey or Caesar were to come out against the bill, of course, that *would* make a difference. Caesar has an army less than a mile from the Forum. Pompey's influence is immense."

"And if it passes," said Terentia, "where will that leave me?"

"His property will all be seized—this house, its contents, everything. If you try to assist him in any way, you'll be arrested. I fear his only chance is to leave Rome at once, as soon as he is well, and get clear of Italy before the bill becomes law."

"Could he stay at my house in Epirus?" asked Atticus.

"Then you would be liable to prosecution in Rome. It will be a brave man who gives him shelter. He will have to travel anonymously, and keep moving from place to place before his identity is discovered."

"So that rules out any of my houses, I'm afraid," said Lucullus. "The mob would love to prosecute me." He rolled his eyes like a frightened horse. He had never recovered from his humiliation in the Senate.

"May I speak?" I asked.

Atticus said, "Of course, Tiro."

"There is another option." I glanced toward the ceiling. I was not sure whether Cicero would want me to reveal it to the others or not. "In the summer Caesar offered to appoint the master his legate in Gaul, which would give him immunity."

Cato looked horrified. "But that would put Cicero in his debt and make Caesar even more powerful than he is already! In the interests of the state, I very much hope Cicero would turn that down."

"In the interests of friendship," said Atticus, "I hope he takes it. What do you say, Terentia?"

"My husband will decide," she said simply.

After the others had gone, promising to return the following day, she went up to see Cicero again, then came down and called me to her. "He is refusing to eat," she said. Her eyes were watery, but she jabbed her narrow chin toward me as she spoke. "Well, he may give in to despair if he must but I have to safeguard the interests of this family, and we do not have much time. I want you to arrange to have all the contents of the house packed up and removed. Some we can store in our old home—there is plenty of room, as Quintus is away—and the rest Lucullus is willing to look after for us. This place is being watched, so it needs to be done piece by piece, to avoid arousing suspicion, the most valuable items first."

And that was what we did, beginning that very evening, and continuing over the days and nights that followed. It was a relief to have something to do while Cicero stayed in his room and refused to see anyone. We hid jewelry and coins in amphorae of wine and olive oil and carted them across the city. We concealed gold and silver dishes beneath our clothes and walked as normally as we could to the house on the Esquiline and divested ourselves with a clatter. Antique busts were swaddled in shawls and carried out cradled in the arms of slave girls as if they were babies. Some of the larger pieces of furniture were dismantled and wheeled away like firewood. Rugs and tapestries were wrapped in sheets and trundled off in the direction of the laundry and then secretly diverted to their hiding place in Lucullus's mansion, which was beyond the Fontinalian Gate, just north of the city.

I took sole charge of emptying Cicero's library, filling sacks with his most private documents and carrying them myself to the cellar of our old house. On these journeys I always took care to skirt Clodius's headquarters in the Temple of Castor, where gangs of his men loitered ready to chase down Cicero if he dared to show his face. Once I stood at the back of a crowd and listened to Clodius himself denounce Cicero from the tribunes' platform. His domination of the city was absolute. Caesar was with his army on the Field of Mars, preparing to march to Gaul. Pompey had withdrawn from the city and was living in connubial bliss with Julia out in his mansion in the Alban Hills. The consuls were beholden to Clodius for their provinces. Clodius had learned how to stimulate the mob as a gigolo might caress his lover. He had them chanting in ecstasy. I could not bear to watch for long.

We saved the transfer of the most valuable of Cicero's possessions until almost the very end. This was a citrus wood table which he had been given by a client and which was said to be worth half a million sesterces. We could not dismantle it, so we decided to take it under cover of darkness to Lucullus's house, where it would easily fit in with all the other opulent furniture. We put it on the back of an oxcart and covered it in bales of straw and set off on the journey of two miles or so. Lucullus's overseer met us at the door carrying a short whip and told us a slave girl would show us where to put it. It took four of us to lift that table down, and then the slave led us through the huge, echoing rooms of the house until she pointed to a spot and told us to set it down. My heart was beating fast, and not just from the weight of our burden, but because I had recognized her by then. How could I not? Most nights I had gone to sleep with her face in my mind. Of course I wanted to ask her a hundred questions, but I feared drawing attention to her in front of the overseer. We followed her back the way we had come, retracing our steps to the grand entrance hall, and I could not help noticing how underfed she seemed, the exhausted stoop of her shoulders, and the gray hairs that had appeared among the dark. She was clearly enduring a harsher existence than she had been used to in Misenum—a capricious life, the life of a slave, determined not so much by the status itself as by the character of the master: Lucullus would not even have noticed she existed. The front door was open. The others passed through it. Just before I followed I whispered "Agathe!" and she turned around wearily and peered at me in surprise that anyone knew her name, but there was no trace of recognition in those lifeless eyes.

XIX

THE FOLLOWING MORNING I was talking to Cicero's steward when I glimpsed Cicero cautiously coming downstairs for the first time in two weeks. I caught my breath. It was like seeing a specter. He had dispensed with his customary toga and was wearing an old black tunic to show he was in mourning. His gaunt cheeks, straggled hair, and growth of white beard made him look like an old tramp. When he reached the ground floor he stopped. By this time the house had been almost entirely emptied of its contents. He squinted in bewilderment at the bare walls and floors of the atrium. He shuffled into his library. I followed him and watched from the doorway as he inspected the empty cabinets. He had been left with only a chair and a small table. Without looking around he said in a voice all the more awful for being so quiet, "Who has done this?"

"The mistress thought it a sensible precaution," I replied.

" 'A sensible precaution'?" He ran his hand over the empty wooden shelving. It was all made of rosewood, beautifully carpentered to his own design. "A stab in the back more like!" He inspected the dust on his fingertips. "She never did care for this place." And then, still without looking at me, he said, "Have a carriage made ready."

"Of course." I hesitated. "May I know the destination, so I can tell the driver where he is to go?"

"Never mind the destination. Just get me the damned carriage."

I went and told the ostler to bring the carriage around to the front door; then I found Terentia and warned her that the master was planning to go out. She stared at me in alarm and hurried downstairs into the library. Most of the household had heard that Cicero had gotten out of bed at last, and they were standing around in the atrium, fascinated and fearful, not even pretending to work. I did not blame them: their fates, like mine, were all tied up with his. We heard the sound of raised voices and soon afterward Terentia ran out of the library with tears pouring down her cheeks. She said to me, "Go with him," and fled upstairs. Cicero emerged moments later scowling, but at least looking much more his old self, as if having a heated argument with his wife had acted as a kind of tonic. He walked toward the front door and ordered the porter to open it. The porter looked at me, as if seeking my approval. I nodded quickly.

As usual there were demonstrators in the street, but far fewer than when the bill forbidding Cicero fire and water had first been promulgated. Most of the mob, like a cat at a mousehole, had grown weary of waiting for their victim to appear. Still, what the remainder lacked in numbers they made up for in venom, and they set up a great racket of "Tyrant!" and "Murderer!" and "Death!" and as Cicero appeared they surged forward. He stepped straight into the carriage and I followed. A bodyguard was sitting up on the roof with the driver, and he leaned down to me to ask where we were to go. I looked at Cicero.

"To Pompey's house," he said.

"But Pompey's not in Rome," I protested. By this time fists were pounding against the side of the carriage.

"Where is he, then?"

"At his place in the Alban Hills."

"All the better," replied Cicero. "He will not be expecting me."

I shouted up to the driver that we should head for the Capena Gate, and with a crack of his whip and a final flurry of shouts and thumps on the wooden panels, we lurched forward.

The journey must have taken us at least two hours, and in the whole of that time Cicero did not utter a word but sat hunched in the corner of the carriage, his legs turned away from me, as if he wished to compress himself into the smallest space possible. Only when we turned off the highway onto Pompey's long graveled drive did he uncoil his body and peer out of the window at the opulent grounds, with their topiary and statuary. "I shall shame him into protecting me," he said, "and if he still refuses I shall kill myself at his feet and he will be cursed by history for his cowardice forever. You think I don't mean it? I am perfectly serious." He put his hand in the pocket of his tunic and showed me a small knife, its blade no wider than his hand. He grinned at me. He seemed to have gone quite mad.

We pulled up in front of the great country villa, and Pompey's household steward sprang forward to open the carriage door. Cicero had been here countless times. The slave knew him very well. But his smile of greeting shriveled as he saw Cicero's unkempt face and black tunic, and he took a step backward in shock. "Do you smell that, Tiro?" asked Cicero, offering me the back of his hand. He raised it to his own nostrils and sniffed. "That's the smell of death." He gave an odd laugh and climbed down from the carriage and strode toward the house, saying to the steward over his shoulder, "Tell your master I'm here. I know where to go."

I hastened after him and we went into a long salon, filled with antique furniture, tapestries, and carpets. Souvenirs of Pompey's many campaigns were on display in cabinets—red-glazed pottery from Spain, ebony carvings from Africa, chased silverware from the East. Cicero sat on a high-backed couch covered in ivory silk while I stood apart, near to one of the doors, which opened onto a terrace lined with busts of great men from antiquity. Beyond the terrace a gardener pushed a wheelbarrow piled with dead leaves. I could smell the fragrance of a bonfire somewhere, out of sight. It was a scene of such settled order and civilization—such an oasis in the wilderness of all our terrors—that I have never forgotten it. Presently there was a little patter of footsteps and Pompey's wife appeared, accompanied by her maids, all of whom were older than her. She looked like a doll in her dark ringlets and simple green dress. She had a scarf around her neck. Cicero stood and kissed her hand.

"I am very sorry," said Julia, "but my husband has been called away." She blushed and glanced at the door. She was obviously not accustomed to lying.

Cicero's face sagged slightly, but then he rallied. "That does not matter," he said. "I shall wait."

Julia looked anxiously at the door again, and I had a sudden instinct that Pompey was just beyond it, signaling to her what she should do. She said, "I am not sure how long he is going to be."

"I am confident he will come," said Cicero loudly, for the benefit of any eavesdroppers. "Pompey the Great cannot be seen to go back on his word." He sat, and after some hesitation, she did the same, folding her small white hands neatly in her lap.

Eventually she said, "Was your journey comfortable?"

"Very pleasant, thank you."

There was another long silence. Cicero put his hand in the pocket of his tunic, where his little knife was. I could see that he was turning it around in his fingers.

Julia said, "Have you seen my father recently?"

"No. I have not been well."

"Oh? I am sorry to hear that. I have not seen him for a while, either.

He will be leaving for Gaul any day. Then I really don't know when I shall see him again. I am lucky I won't be left on my own. It was horrid when he was in Spain."

"And is married life suiting you?"

"Oh, it is wonderful!" she exclaimed with genuine delight. "We stay here all the time. We never go anywhere. It is a world of our own."

"That must be pleasant. How charming that is. A carefree existence. I envy you." There was a slight crack in Cicero's voice. He withdrew his hand from his pocket and raised it to his forehead. He looked down at the carpet. His body began to shake slightly, and I realized to my horror that he was weeping. Julia stood up quickly. "It's nothing," he said. "Really. This damned illness—"

Julia hesitated, then reached over and touched his shoulder. She said softly, "I shall tell him again that you are here."

She left the room with her maids. After she had gone, Cicero sighed, wiped his nose on his sleeve, and stared ahead. The aromatic smoke of the bonfire drifted over the terrace. Time passed. The light began to fade and Cicero's face, emaciated by his long period of fasting, filled with shadows. Eventually I whispered in his ear that if we did not leave soon, we would never reach Rome by nightfall. He nodded and I helped him to his feet.

As we drove away from the villa I glanced back, and to this day I am sure I saw the pale full moon of Pompey's face staring down at us from an upper window.

Once news of Pompey's betrayal became known, Cicero was seen to be finished, and I discreetly started packing in anticipation of a rapid exit from Rome. That is not to say that everyone shunned him. Hundreds donned mourning to show their solidarity, and the Senate voted narrowly to dress in black to show their sympathy. A great demonstration of knights from all over Italy was organized on the Capitol by Aelius Lamia, and a delegation led by Hortensius went to call on the consuls to urge them to defend Cicero. But Piso and Gabinius both refused. They knew that Clodius had it in his power to determine which, if any, province they would receive and they were anxious to show him their support. They actually forbade the Senate to put on mourning and expelled the gallant Lamia from the city on the grounds that he threatened civic peace.

Whenever Cicero tried to venture out he swiftly found himself sur-

rounded by a jeering mob, and despite the protection organized by Atticus and the Sextus brothers the experience was unpleasant and dangerous.
Clodius's followers threw stones and excrement at him, forcing him to
retreat indoors to shake the filth out of his hair and tunic. He sought out
the consul Piso and eventually found him in a tavern, where he pleaded
with him to intercede, to no avail. After that he stayed at home. But even
here there was little respite. During the day demonstrators would gather
in the Forum and chant slogans at the house calling Cicero a murderer.
Our nights were endlessly disturbed by the echo of running feet in the
street, shouted insults, and the rattle of missiles on the roof. At a huge
public meeting called by the tribunes outside the city, Caesar was asked
his opinion of Clodius's bill. He declared that while he had opposed the
execution of the conspirators, he also disapproved of retrospective legislation. It was an answer of great political dexterity: Cicero, when told of it,
could only nod in rueful admiration. From that point on he knew he had
no hope, and although he did not actually retire to his bed again, a great
lethargy took hold of him and often he refused to see his visitors.

There was one important exception, however. On the day before
Clodius's bill was due to become law Crassus came to call, and to my
surprise Cicero agreed to receive him. I suppose he was in such a hopeless
state by then, he was willing to take help from whatever quarter it was
offered. The villain came in full of concerned words. Yet all the time he
spoke of his shock at what had happened and of his disgust at Pompey's
disloyalty his eyes were flickering around the bare walls and checking
what fixtures were left. "If there is anything I can do," he said, "anything
at all—"

"I don't think there is much, thank you," said Cicero, who plainly regretted ever letting his old enemy through the door. "We both know how
politics is played. Sooner or later failure comes to us all. At least," he
added, "*my* conscience is clear. Really, don't let me detain you any longer."

"What about money? A poor substitute, I know, for the loss of all one
holds dear in life, but money would be useful in exile, and I would be
willing to advance you a considerable sum."

"That is very thoughtful of you."

"I could give you, say, two million. Would that be of any help?"

"Naturally it would. But if I am in exile, what hope would I have of
ever paying you back?"

Crassus looked around as if searching for a solution. "You could give me the deeds to this house, I suppose."

Cicero stared at him in disbelief. "You want this house for which I paid you three and a half million?"

"And a great bargain it was. You can't dispute that."

"Well then, all the more reason for me not to sell it back to you for two million."

"I fear property is worth only what someone is willing to pay for it, and this house will be valueless the day after tomorrow."

"Why do you say that?"

"Because Clodius intends to burn it down and build a shrine to the goddess Liberty, and neither you nor anyone else will be able to lift a finger to stop him."

Cicero paused, and then said quietly, "Who told you that?"

"I make it my business to know these things."

"And why would you want to pay two million sesterces for a patch of scorched earth containing a shrine to Liberty?"

"That is the kind of risk one has to take in business."

"Goodbye, Crassus."

"Think it over, Cicero. Don't be a stubborn fool. It's two million or nothing."

"I said goodbye, Crassus."

"All right, two and a half million?" Cicero did not respond. Crassus shook his head. "That," he said, rising to his feet, "is exactly the sort of arrogant folly which has brought you to this pass. I shall warm my hands at your fire."

On the next day a meeting of Cicero's principal supporters was called to decide what he should do. It was to be held in the library, and I had to scour the house for chairs so that everyone should have a place to sit. I put out twenty. Atticus arrived first, then Cato, followed by Lucullus and, after a long interval, Hortensius. They all had to endure a hard passage through the mob which had occupied the neighboring streets, especially Hortensius, who was roughed up quite badly, his face scratched, his toga splattered with shit. It was unnerving to see a man normally immaculate in his appearance so shaken and despoiled. We waited to see if anyone else would come, but nobody did. Tullia had already left Rome with her husband for the safety of the country, after an emotional scene with Cicero, so the only member of the family present was Terentia. I took notes.

If Cicero was dismayed that the vast crowds he had once commanded had dwindled to this small band, he did not show it. "On this bitter day," he said, "I wish to thank all of you who have so bravely struggled to support my cause. Adversity is a part of life—not one I necessarily recommend, you understand"—my notes record laughter—"but still: at least it shows us men's true natures, and just as I have shown my weakness, so I have seen your strength." He stopped and cleared his throat. I thought he was going to break down again. But this time he carried on. "So the law will take effect at midnight? There is no doubt of that, I take it?" He glanced around. All four shook their head.

"No," said Hortensius, "none whatever."

"Then what options are open to me?"

"It seems to me you have three," said Hortensius. "You can ignore the law and remain in Rome and hope your friends will continue to support you, although from tomorrow that will be even more dangerous than it is now. You can leave the city tonight, while it is still legal for people to help you, and hope to get out of Italy unmolested. Or you could go to Caesar and ask if his offer of a legateship still stands, and claim immunity."

Cato said, "He does have a fourth option, of course."

"Yes?"

"He could kill himself."

There was a profound silence, and then Cicero said, "What would be the benefit of that?"

"From the Stoic point of view, suicide has always been considered a logical act of defiance for a wise man. It is also your natural right to put an end to your anguish. And frankly it would set an example of resistance to tyranny that would stand for all time."

"Do you have a particular method in mind?"

"I do. In my opinion you should brick yourself into this house and starve yourself to death."

"I disagree," said Lucullus. "If it's martyrdom you seek, Cicero, why bother to do the deed yourself? Why not stay in the city and dare your enemies to do their worst? You have a chance of surviving. And if you don't, at least the opprobrium of murder falls on them."

"Being murdered requires no courage," retorted Cato with contempt, "whereas suicide is a manly, conscious act."

"And what is your own advice, Hortensius?" asked Cicero.

"Leave the city," he replied at once. "Keep yourself alive." He touched his fingertips briefly to his forehead and felt along the rusty line of dried blood. "I went to see Piso today. Privately he has some sympathy for the way you have been treated. Allow us the time to work for the repeal of Clodius's law while you are in voluntary exile. I am certain you will come back in triumph one day."

"Atticus?"

"You know my view," said Atticus. "You would have saved yourself a lot of trouble if you had accepted Caesar's offer in the first place."

"And Terentia? What do you say, my dear?"

She had put on mourning like her husband, and in her black weeds, with her deathly pale face, she had become our Electra. She spoke with great force. "Our present existence is intolerable. Voluntary exile smacks to me of cowardice. And try explaining suicide to your six-year-old son. You have no choice. Go to Caesar."

It was late afternoon—a red sun dipping behind the bare trees, a warm spring breeze carrying the incongruous chant of "Death to the tyrant" from the Forum. The other senators with their attendants left by the front door, serving as decoys to draw the attention of the mob, while Cicero and I crept out through the back. Cicero had a tattered old brown blanket draped over his head and looked exactly like a beggar. We hurried down the Caci Steps to the Etruscan Road, and then joined the crowds heading out of the city through the river gate. Nobody molested us, or even gave us a second glance.

I had sent a slave ahead with a message for Caesar that Cicero wished to see him, and one of his officers in a red-plumed helmet was waiting for us at the gate. He was very much taken aback by Cicero's appearance but managed to recover sufficiently to give him a kind of half salute, and then escorted us out to the Field of Mars. Here a huge tented city had been pitched to accommodate Caesar's newly mustered Gallic legions, and as we passed through it I noticed everywhere signs that the army was striking camp and preparing to depart: waste pits were being filled in, earth ramparts leveled, wagons loaded with supplies. The officer told Cicero that their orders were to begin marching north before dawn the next day. He led us to a tent much larger than the others and set apart on slightly higher ground, with a legionary eagle planted beside it. The soldier asked us to wait, and then lifted the flap and went inside, leaving Cicero, bearded and in his old tunic with his blanket draped around his shoulders, to gaze around the camp.

"This is how it always seems to be with Caesar," I remarked, trying to lighten the silence. "He likes to keep his visitors waiting."

"We had better get used to it," replied Cicero in a grim voice. "Look at that," he said, nodding beyond the camp toward the river. Rising from the plain in the dusty light was a great rickety edifice of scaffolding. "That must be the Pharaoh's theater." He contemplated it for a long time, chewing the inside of his lip.

Eventually the flap parted again and we were shown into the tent. The interior was Spartan. A thin straw mattress lay on the ground, with a blanket thrown across it; near to it was a wooden chest on which stood a mirror, a set of hairbrushes, a jug of water, and a basin, together with a miniature portrait of a woman in a gold frame (I am almost certain it was Servilia, but I was not close enough to be sure). At a folding table piled with documents sat Caesar. He was signing something. Two secretaries stood motionless behind him. He finished what he was doing, looked up, rose, and advanced toward Cicero with his hand outstretched. It was the first time I had seen him in military uniform. It fitted him as naturally as his skin, and I realized that in all the years I had observed him I had never actually seen him in the arena for which he was best suited. That was a sobering thought.

"My dear Cicero," he said, examining his visitor's appearance, "it truly grieves me to see you reduced to this condition." With Pompey there was always hugging and backslapping, but Caesar did not go in for that kind of thing. After the briefest of handshakes he gestured to Cicero to sit. "How can I help?"

"I have come to accept the position of your legate," replied Cicero, perching himself on the edge of the chair, "if the offer still stands."

"Have you, indeed!" Caesar's mouth turned down. "I must say you have left it very late!"

"I admit I would have preferred not to have come to you in these circumstances."

"Clodius's law takes effect at midnight?"

"It does."

"So in the end the choice has come down to me, or death, or exile?"

Cicero looked uncomfortable. "You could put it like that."

"Well, that's hardly very flattering!" Caesar gave one of his sharp laughs and lolled back in his chair. He studied Cicero. "When I made the offer to you in the summer, your position was infinitely stronger than it is now."

"You said that if Clodius ever became a threat to my safety, I could come to you. He is a threat. Here I am."

"Six months ago he was a threat. Now he is your master."

"Caesar, if you are asking me to beg—"

"I am not asking you to beg. Of course I am not asking you to beg. I would merely like to hear from your own lips what benefit you think you can bring to me by serving as my legate."

Cicero swallowed hard. I could barely imagine how painful this was for him. "Well, if you ask me to spell it out, I would say that while you obviously enjoy huge support among the people you have far less in the Senate, whereas my position is the opposite: weak at present with the people but still strong among our colleagues."

"So you would guard my interests in the Senate?"

"I would represent your views to them, yes, and perhaps occasionally I could relay their views back to you."

"But your loyalty would be exclusively to me?"

I could almost hear Cicero grinding his teeth. "I hope that my loyalty, as it has always been, would be to my country, which I would serve by reconciling your interests with those of the Senate."

"But I don't care about the interests of the Senate!" exclaimed Caesar. He suddenly pitched forward on his chair and in one fluid motion sprang to his feet. "I'll tell you something, Cicero. Let me explain myself to you. The other year, when I was on my way to Spain, I had to cross the mountains, and I went on ahead with a group of my staff to scout the way, and we came to this very small village. It was raining and it was the most miserable-looking place you can possibly imagine. Hardly anyone lived there. Really, you had to laugh at such a dump. And one of my officers said to me, as a joke, 'Yet, you know, even here there are probably men pushing themselves forward to gain office, and there will be fierce competition and jealous rivalries over who will win first place.' And do you know what I replied?"

"No."

"I said, 'As far as I am concerned, I would rather be the first man here than the second in Rome.' And I meant it, Cicero—I really did. Do you understand what I am trying to say?"

"I believe I do," said Cicero, nodding slowly.

"That is a true story. That is who I am."

Cicero said, "Until this conversation you have always been a puzzle to me, Caesar, but now perhaps I begin to understand you for the first time, and I thank you at least for your honesty." He started to laugh. "It really is quite funny."

"What is?"

"That I should be the one being driven from Rome for seeking to be a king!"

Caesar scowled at him for an instant, and then he grinned. "You are right," he said. "It is amusing!"

"Well," said Cicero, getting to his feet, "there is little point in carrying on with this interview. You have a country to conquer and I have other matters to attend to."

"Don't say that!" cried Caesar. "I was only setting out the facts. We need to know where we both stand. You can have the damned legateship—it's yours. And you can discharge it in whatever fashion you like. It would amuse me to see more of you, Cicero—really." He held out his hand. "Come. Most men in public life are so dull. We who are not must stick together."

"I thank you for your consideration," replied Cicero, "but it would never work."

"Why not?"

"Because in this village of yours I too would aspire to be the first man, but failing that I would at least aspire to be a free man, and what is wicked about you, Caesar—worse than Pompey, worse than Clodius, worse even than Catilina—is that you won't rest until we are all obliged to go down on our knees to you."

It was dark by the time we reentered the city. Cicero did not even bother to put the blanket over his head. The light was too gloomy for him to be recognized and, besides, people were hurrying home with more important things to worry about than the fate of an ex-consul—their dinner, for example, and their leaking roof, and the thieves who were plaguing Rome more and more each day.

In the atrium Terentia was waiting with Atticus, and when Cicero told her he had rejected Caesar's offer she let out a great howl of pain and sank to the floor, squatting on her haunches with her hands covering her head. Cicero knelt next to her and put his arm around her shoulder. "My dear, you must leave now," he said, "and take Marcus with you, and spend the night at Atticus's house." He glanced up at Atticus and his old friend nodded. "It's too dangerous to stay here beyond midnight."

She pulled away. "And you?" she said. "What will you do? Will you kill yourself?"

"If that is what you want—if that will make it easier."

"Of course it is not what I want!" she shouted at him. "I want my life returned to me!"

"That, I fear, is what I cannot give you."

Once again Cicero reached out to her, but she pushed him away and got to her feet. "Why?" she demanded, glaring down at him, her hands on her hips. "Why are you putting your wife and children through this torment when you could end it tomorrow by allying yourself with Caesar?"

"Because if I did I would cease to exist."

"What do you mean, you would 'cease to exist'? What piece of stupid clever nonsense of yours is that?"

"My body would exist but I, Cicero, I—whatever I am—would be dead."

Terentia turned her back on him in despair and looked at Atticus for support. Atticus said, "With respect, Marcus, you are starting to sound as inflexible as Cato. What's wrong with making a temporary alliance with Caesar?"

"There would be nothing temporary about it! Does no one in this city understand? That man won't stop until he is master of the world—he more or less just told me exactly that—and I would either have to go along with him as his junior accomplice or break with him at some later stage, and then I would be absolutely finished."

Terentia said coldly, "You are absolutely finished now."

• • •

"So, Tiro," said Cicero after she had gone to fetch Marcus from the nursery to say goodbye, "as my last act in this city I would like to give you
your freedom. I really should have done it years ago—at the very least
when I left the consulship—and the fact that I didn't was not because
I set no value on your services, but on the contrary because I valued
them too much, and could not bear to lose you. But now, as I am losing everything else, it's only fair that I should say goodbye to you as
well. Congratulations, my friend," he said, shaking my hands, "you have
earned it."

For years I had waited for this moment—I had yearned for it and
dreamed of it and planned what I would do—and now it had arrived,
almost casually it seemed, out of all this ruin and disaster. I was too overwhelmed with emotion to speak. Cicero smiled at me and then embraced
me as I wept, patting my back as if I were a child who needed comforting,
and then Atticus, who was standing watching, took my hand and shook
it warmly.

I managed to say a few words of thanks, and added that of course my
first act as a free man would be to dedicate myself to his service, and that
I would stay at his side to share his ordeal whatever happened.

"I am afraid that is impossible," Cicero responded sadly. "Slaves can
be my only company from now on. If a freedman were to help me, he
would be guilty under Clodius's law of aiding a murderer. You must stay
well clear of me, Tiro, or they will crucify you. Now go and collect your
belongings. You should leave with Terentia and Atticus."

The intensity of my joy was replaced by an equally sharp stab of grief.
"But how will you cope without me?"

"Oh, I have other slaves," he replied, making a feeble effort to sound
unconcerned. "They can accompany me out of the city."

"Where will you go?"

"South. To the coast. Brundisium perhaps, and find a boat. After
that—the winds and currents will decide my fate. Now fetch your things."

I went down to my room and gathered together my few possessions
into a small bag, and then I pulled out the two loose bricks behind which
I had hollowed out a safe. This was where I kept my savings sewn into a
money belt. I had exactly two hundred and twenty-seven gold pieces,
which it had taken me more than a decade to acquire. I put on the belt

and went upstairs to the atrium, where Cicero was now saying goodbye to Marcus, watched by Atticus and a raw-eyed Terentia. He loved that boy—his only son, his joy, his hope for the future—and with immense self-discipline he somehow managed to keep their parting casual, so that the lad would not be too upset. He held him in his arms and swung him around, and Marcus begged him to do it again, which he did, and when Marcus begged for a third time, he said no and told him to go to his mother. Then he embraced Terentia and said, "I am sorry that marriage to me has brought you to such a sad state."

"Marriage to you has been the only purpose of my life," she replied, and with a nod in my direction she walked firmly from the room.

Cicero next embraced Atticus and entrusted his wife and son to his care, and then moved to say farewell to me, but I told him there was no need, that I had made my decision, and that I would remain at his side at the cost of my freedom and if necessary of my life. Naturally he expressed his gratitude, but he did not seem surprised, and I realized he had never thought seriously for a moment that I would accept his offer. I took off my money belt and gave it to Atticus.

"I wonder if I might ask you do something for me," I said.

"Of course," he replied. "You want me to look after this for you?"

"No," I said. "There is a slave of Lucullus, a young woman named Agathe, who has come to mean a lot to me, and I wonder if you would ask Lucullus, as a favor to you, to free her. I am sure there is more than enough money here to buy her liberty and to provide for her thereafter."

Atticus looked surprised but said that of course he would do as I asked.

"Well, you certainly kept that secret," said Cicero, studying me closely. "Perhaps I don't know you as well as I think I do."

After the others had gone Cicero and I were left alone in the house, together with his guards and a few members of his household. We could no longer hear any chanting; the whole city seemed to have gone very quiet. He went upstairs to rest and put on some stout shoes, and when he came down he took a candelabrum and moved from room to room—through the empty dining hall with its gilded roof, through the great hall with its marble statues that were too heavy to move, and into the bare library—as if committing the place to memory. He lingered so long I began to wonder if he had decided not to leave after all, but then the watchman in the

Forum called midnight and he blew out the candles and said that we should go.

The night was moonless and as we reached the top of the steps we could see beneath us at least a dozen torches slowly ascending the hill. Someone in the distance let out a peculiar bird cry, and it was answered by a similar shriek from a spot very close behind us. I felt my heart begin to pound. "They are on their way," said Cicero softly. "He does not mean to miss a moment." We hurried down the steps and at the foot of the Palatine turned left into a narrow alley. Keeping close to the walls, we made a careful loop past shuttered shops and slumbering houses until we came out into the main street just by the Capena Gate. The porter was bribed to open up the pedestrian door and waited impatiently as we exchanged whispered farewells with our protectors. Then Cicero stepped through the narrow portal, followed by me and by three other young slaves who carried his luggage.

We did not speak or rest until we had walked for at least two hours and had gotten clear of the monumental tombs that line that stretch of road—in those days, notorious hiding places for robbers. Then Cicero decided it was safe to stop and he sat down on a milestone and looked back at Rome. A faint red glow, too early for the dawn, crimson at its center and dissolving into bands of pink, suffused the sky, outlining the low black humps of the city's hills. It was amazing to think that the burning of just one house could create such an immense celestial effect. Had I not known better I would have said it was an omen. At the same time, on the still night air, came a curious sound, harsh and intermittent, pitched somewhere between a howl and a wail. I could not place it at first but then Cicero said it must be trumpets on the Field of Mars, and that it was Caesar's army preparing to move off to Gaul. I could not make out his face in the darkness as he said this, which perhaps was just as well, but after a moment or two he stood and brushed the dust off his old tunic and resumed his journey, in the opposite direction to Caesar's.

GLOSSARY

aedile an elected official, of whom four were chosen annually to serve a one-year term, responsible for the running of the city of Rome: law and order, public buildings, business regulations, etc.

auspices supernatural signs, especially flights of birds and lightning flashes, interpreted by the **augurs**; if ruled unfavorable no public business could be transacted

Carcer Rome's prison, situated on the boundary of the Forum and the Capitol, between the Temple of Concordia and the Senate House

carnifex the state executioner and torturer

century the unit in which the Roman people cast their votes on the Field of Mars at election time for consul and praetor; the system was weighted to favor the wealthier classes of society

chief priest see **pontifex maximus**

consul the senior magistrate of the Roman republic, two of whom were elected annually, usually in July, to assume office the following January, taking turns presiding over the Senate each month

comitium the circular area in the Forum, approximately three hundred feet across, bounded by the Senate House and the rostra, traditionally the place where laws were voted on by the people and where many of the courts had their tribunals

curia in its original form, the main assembly of the Roman tribes (of which, prior to 387 B.C., there were thirty), consisting of a senior member of each

curule chair a backless chair with low arms, often made of ivory, possessed by a magistrate with imperium, particularly consuls and praetors

dictator a magistrate given absolute power by the Senate over civil and military affairs, usually in a time of national emergency

equestrian order the second most senior order in Roman society after the Senate, the "Order of Knights" had its own officials and privileges and was entitled to one-third of the places on a jury; often its members were richer than members of the Senate but declined to pursue a public career

Gaul divided into two provinces: **Nearer Gaul**, extending from the river Rubicon in northern Italy to the Alps, and **Further Gaul**, the lands beyond the Alps roughly corresponding to the modern French regions of Provence and Languedoc

haruspices the religious officials who inspected the entrails after a sacrifice in order to determine whether the omens were good or bad

imperator the title granted to a military commander on active service by his soldiers after a victory; it was necessary to be hailed imperator in order to qualify for a triumph

imperium the power to command, granted by the state to an individual, usually a consul, praetor, or provincial governor

legate a deputy or delegate

lictor an attendant who carried the fasces—a bundle of birch rods tied together with a strip of red leather—that symbolized a magistrate's imperium; consuls were accompanied by twelve lictors, who served as their bodyguards, praetors by six; the senior lictor, who stood closest to the magistrate, was known as the proximate lictor

manumission the emancipation of a slave

Order of Knights see **equestrian order**

pontifex maximus the chief priest of the Roman state religion, the head of the fifteen-member College of Priests, entitled to an official residence on the Via Sacra

praetor the second most senior magistrate in the Roman republic, eight of whom were elected annually, usually in July, to take office the following January, and who drew lots to determine which of the various courts—treason, embezzlement, corruption, serious crime, etc.—they would preside over; see also **urban praetor**

prosecutions as there was no public prosecution system in the Roman republic, all criminal charges, from embezzlement to treason and murder, had to be brought by private individuals

public assemblies the supreme authority and legislature of the Roman people was the people themselves, whether constituted by **tribe** (the comitia tributa, which voted on laws, declared war and peace, and elected the tribunes) or by **century** (the comitia centuriata, which elected the senior magistrates)

quaestor a junior magistrate, twenty of whom were elected each year, and who thereby gained the right of entry to the Senate; it was necessary for a candidate for the quaestorship to be over thirty and to show wealth of at least one million sesterces

rostra a long, curved platform in the Forum, about twelve feet high, surmounted by heroic statues, from which the Roman people were addressed by magistrates and advocates; its name derived from the beaks (rostra) of captured enemy warships set into its sides

senaculum an open space in front of the Senate House where it was traditional for senators to assemble before the start of a session

Senate *not* the legislative assembly of the Roman republic—laws could be passed only by the people in a tribal assembly—but something closer to its executive, with six hundred members who could raise matters of state and order the consul to take action or to draft laws to be placed before the people; once elected via the quaestorship (see **quaestor**) a man would normally remain a senator for life, unless removed by the censors for immorality or bankruptcy, hence the average age was high ("senate" derived from "senex," meaning old)

tribes the Roman people were divided into thirty-five tribes for the purposes of voting on legislation and to elect the tribunes; unlike the system of voting by **century**, the votes of rich and poor when cast in a tribe had equal weight

tribune a representative of the ordinary citizens—the plebeians—ten of whom were elected annually each summer and took office in December, with the power to propose and veto legislation and to summon assemblies of the people; it was forbidden for anyone other than a plebeian to hold the office

triumph an elaborate public celebration of homecoming, granted by the Senate to honor a victorious general, to qualify for which it was necessary for him to retain his military imperium—and as it was forbidden to enter Rome while still possessing military authority, generals wishing to triumph had to wait outside the city until the Senate granted them a triumph

urban praetor the head of the justice system, senior of all the praetors, third in rank in the republic after the two consuls

DRAMATIS PERSONAE

AFRANIUS, LUCIUS ally of Pompey's from his home region of Picenum; legate in the war against Mithridates; later, Pompey's nominee for the consulship

ARRIUS, QUINTUS former praetor and military commander, closely allied to Crassus

ATTICUS, TITUS POMPONIUS Cicero's closest friend; brother-in-law to Quintus Cicero, who is married to his sister, Pomponia

AURELIA mother of Julius Caesar

BIBULUS, MARCUS CALPURNIUS Caesar's colleague as consul, and his staunch opponent

CAESAR, GAIUS JULIUS effectively the leader of the populist faction in Rome; six years Cicero's junior; married to Pompeia, with whom he lives along with his mother, Aurelia, and daughter, Julia

CATILINA, LUCIUS SERGIUS former governor of Africa, beaten by Cicero for the consulship

CATO, MARCUS PORCIUS half-brother of Servilia, great-grandson of Cato the Censor; a stern upholder of the traditions of the republic

CATULUS, QUINTUS LUTATIUS former consul, member of the College of Priests, one of the most experienced men in the Senate, leader of the patrician faction

CELER, QUINTUS CAECILIUS METELLUS brother-in-law of Pompey (who married his sister), husband of Clodia, brother of Nepos; member of the College of Augurs; praetor; head of the most extensive and powerful family in Rome; a war hero with a powerful military reputation

CETHEGUS, GAIUS CORNELIUS patrician senator, one of Catilina's coconspirators

CICERO, QUINTUS TULLIUS Cicero's younger brother; senator and soldier; married to Pomponia, the sister of Atticus

CLODIA daughter of one of the most distinguished families in Rome, the patrician Appii Claudii; sister of Clodius; wife of Metellus Celer

CLODIUS PULCHER, PUBLIUS scion of the leading patrician dynasty, the Appii Claudii; former brother-in-law of Lucullus; brother of Clodia, with whom he is alleged to have had an incestuous affair; lieutenant of Murena, the governor of Further Gaul

CRASSUS, MARCUS LICINIUS former consul; brutal suppressor of the slave revolt led by Spartacus; the richest man in Rome; bitter rival of Pompey

GABINIUS, AULUS former tribune from Pompey's home region of Picenum; promulgated the laws that gave Pompey his extended command in the East; rewarded by Pompey with a legateship in the war against Mithridates

HORTENSIUS HORTALUS, QUINTUS former consul, for many years the leading advocate at the Roman bar until displaced by Cicero; brother-in-law of Catulus; a leader of the patrician faction; immensely wealthy; like Cicero, a civilian politician and not a soldier

HYBRIDA, GAIUS ANTONIUS Cicero's colleague as consul, descendant of one of the most illustrious families in Rome, but nevertheless once expelled from the Senate for corruption and bankruptcy

ISAURICUS, PUBLIUS SERVILIUS VATIA one of the grand old men of the Senate—seventy years old at the time Cicero becomes consul—a tough and highly decorated soldier, having triumphed twice; a former consul and a member of the College of Priests

LABIENUS, TITUS a soldier from Pompey's home region of Picenum; a tribune in Caesar's and Pompey's interests

LUCULLUS, LUCIUS LICINIUS former consul and commander of the Roman army fighting in the East against Mithridates until supplanted by Pompey; haughty, aristocratic, and vastly rich, his enemies in the Senate have contrived for several years to deny him a triumph and keep him waiting outside Rome; bitterly divorced from one of the sisters of Clodius and Clodia

NEPOS, QUINTUS CAECILIUS METELLUS brother of Celer and brother-in-law of Pompey, who sends him back from his legateship in the East to stand for the tribuneship and guard his interests in Rome

PIUS, QUINTUS CAECILIUS METELLUS pontifex maximus; sixty-six years old and ailing; adoptive father of Scipio

POMPEY, GNAEUS born in the same year as Cicero; the most powerful man in the Roman world; a former consul and victorious general who has already triumphed twice, he has been away from Rome fighting in the East—first against the pirates and then against Mithridates—for four years; married to Mucia, the sister of Celer and Nepos

RUFUS, MARCUS CEALIUS Cicero's former pupil, the son of one of his political supporters in the provinces

SERVILIA ambitious and politically shrewd wife of Junius Silanus, a candidate for the consulship; half-sister of Cato; long-term mistress of Caesar; mother of three daughters and a son, Brutus, by her first husband

SERVIUS SULPICIUS RUFUS contemporary and old friend of Cicero; former praetor, famed as one of the greatest legal experts in Rome; a candidate for the consulship; married to Postumia, a mistress of Caesar

SILANUS, DECIMUS JUNIUS married to Servilia, the long-term mistress of Caesar; member of the College of Priests; defeated once for the consulship and now planning to stand again

SURA, PUBLIUS CORNELIUS LENTULUS former consul, once expelled from the Senate for immorality; married to the widow of Hybrida's brother, stepfather to the youthful Mark Antony; making a political comeback as urban praetor, closely allied to Catilina

TERENTIA wife of Cicero; ten years younger than her husband, richer and of nobler birth; devotedly religious, poorly educated, with conservative political views; mother of Cicero's two children, Tullia and Marcus

TIRO Cicero's devoted private secretary, a family slave, three years younger than his master, the inventor of a system of shorthand

TULLIA Cicero's thirteen-year-old daughter

VATINIUS, PUBLIUS junior senator, famed for his ugliness; subsequently a tribune and a close ally of Caesar

ABOUT THE AUTHOR

ROBERT HARRIS is the author of *Fatherland, Enigma, Archangel, Pompeii, Imperium,* and *The Ghost,* all of which were international bestsellers. His work has been translated into thirty-seven languages. After graduating with a degree in English from the University of Cambridge, he worked as a reporter for the BBC's *Panorama* and *Newsnight* programs before becoming a political editor of *The Observer* and subsequently a columnist on *The Sunday Times* and *The Daily Telegraph.* He is married to Gill Hornby and they live with their four children in a village near Hungerford, England.

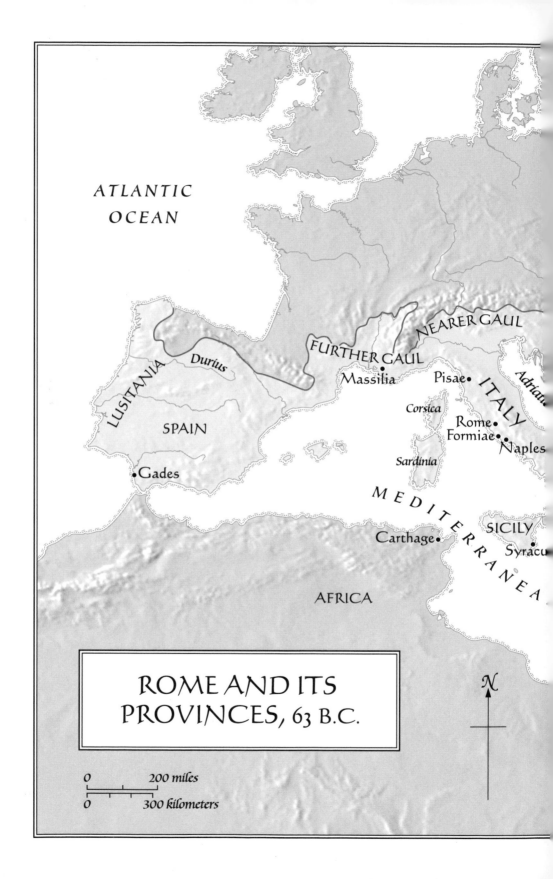

ATLANTIC
OCEAN

NEARER GAUL

FURTHER GAUL

Massilia

Pisae

Adrian

ITALY

LUSITANIA   Durius

Corsica

Rome
Formiae
Naples

SPAIN

Sardinia

Gades

MEDITERRANEA

SICILY

Carthage

Syracu

AFRICA

ROME AND ITS
PROVINCES, 63 B.C.

N

0   200 miles

0   300 kilometers